P9-CKY-154

GRAVEYARD SHIFT

Other Books by Kelly Lange

DEAD FILE
THE REPORTER
GOSSIP
TROPHY WIFE

GRAVEYARD SHIFT

KELLY LANGE

May 17, 2005 -

To Jenny -
You are such an
angel! I love you.

Kelly Lange

NEW YORK   BOSTON

This book is a work of fiction. Names, characters, places, and incidents are the product of the author's imagination or are used fictitiously. Any resemblance to actual events, locales, or persons, living or dead, is coincidental.

Mysterious Press
Warner Books

Time Warner Book Group
1271 Avenue of the Americas, New York, NY 10020
Visit our Web site at www.twbookmark.com.

The Mysterious Press name and logo are registered trademarks of Warner Books.

Printed in the United States of America

First Printing: May 2005

10 9 8 7 6 5 4 3 2 1

Library of Congress Cataloging-in-Publication Data

Lange, Kelly.
    Graveyard shift / Kelly Lange. — 1st ed.
        p. cm.
    Summary: "Los Angeles television reporter Maxi Poole must help her next-door neighbors' housekeeper locate her missing young son, Robert Ochoa"—Provided by the publisher.
    ISBN 0-89296-757-9
    1. Poole, Maxi (Fictitious character)—Fiction. 2. Women television journalists—Fiction. 3. Los Angeles (Calif.)—Fiction. 4. Missing children—Fiction. 5. Housekeepers—Fiction. I. Title.
    PS3562.A48495G73 2005
    813'.54—dc22   2004026462

for **SARA ANN FREED**

my beloved friend, editor, mentor

You left us much too soon.
I will love you always.

1

I don't get it," Maxi said, scowling at her boss.

"What part of 'you're working graveyard starting next week' don't you get?" the man asked, scowling right back at her.

The graveyard shift, also known as the nightside, the overnight, or dregs duty, is usually assigned to the lowest of the low in television news. The disgruntled two were Maxi Poole: thirty-two, popular news anchor-reporter, hardworking, reasonable, tall, trim, blond, dedicated; and her boss Pete Capra: pushing fifty, station managing editor, crack journalist, irascible hothead, decent enough guy, grouch. The two sat in his glassed-in office in the newsroom at Channel Six, the Los Angeles flagship station for UGN, the United Global Network.

"I haven't worked the graveyard since I was a cub reporter, that's what I don't get, Pete. And you've got a dozen reporters junior to me, that's what I don't get. And Kittridge has been working graveyard for the last year, and he's actually weird enough to like it."

"Yeah," Capra mused, leaning forward, dropping both elbows on his desk, resting his chin between his fists. "Kittridge does seem to like it. Never bitches. Think he's dealing drugs at night?"

"Probably. So why mess with a good situation for him, a good situation for you because he doesn't complain, and a good situation for me because I have a life?"

"You don't have a life, Maxi."

"*Excuse* me?"

"You're not married, you have no kids, you don't even date anyone. What life?"

"Well . . . I have a dog," Maxi said indignantly. "And I happen to anchor your multi-award-winning Six O'clock News, remember?"

"And you'll keep that show, at least for now. You'll come in at four, recut anything you shoot overnight that's any good, which will usually be nothing, as we know, anchor the Six, take off for dinner till nine, then go out on the street."

"For how long?"

"The graveyard is nine to six. You know that. You're done after you edit your stuff for the Morning News. If you're needed on the set, you'll stay a little longer, get some face time. Then you'll go home and have your life."

"You mean then I'll limp home and feed Yukon . . ." Yukon was her big, beautiful, five-year-old Alaskan malamute.

"Whatever."

She was mentally doing the math. ". . . and then I'll go out and do my run, come home, shower, fall into bed for a few hours in broad daylight, try to sleep till two in the afternoon, get up, get dressed, and come back in to work by four."

"That's right," Pete said, smiling benevolently.

"And that's going to be my *life?*"

Ignoring the question, Pete said, "So you're reassigned. To the graveyard. Starting Monday. Got it?"

Maxi considered the alternative. On-air talent in any television news market make up a very small club. If she refused the assignment she would have to bring in AFTRA, the television and radio artists' union, to engage in a fight with the company on her behalf. And thereafter she'd be branded a troublemaker among broadcasters. These nasty industry brawls become juicy gossip topics for everyone in the business, including the execs at other stations whom she just might need to hire her one day. Most general managers won't hire a "troublemaker"—they'll just put somebody else on their air, thank you very much. So in the television news business, refusing an assignment is called "eating a death cookie."

"Hey, I'm gonna let you keep your weekends off," Capra said then. The graveyard shift traditionally ran from Sunday night through Thursday night, with the reporter filing stories for the Monday through Friday Morning News. "Kittridge will pull the Sunday shift and cover the Monday morning show," he explained. "You'll do a package for the Saturday show."

"And I'm supposed to be grateful for that?"

"Damn straight. I've never done that for the graveyard grunt before."

"Graveyard grunt?"

"S'cuse me, Ms. Politically Correct. I have never done that for the overnight reporter before." Giving her exasperated.

"Oh, thanks. So you're not going to screw with my Saturdays, or make me anchor the 'march of death'?"

Staffers called the Sunday afternoon newscast the "march of death," because it accordioned to fill the time from the end of whatever national sports event the network was carrying until six o'clock, which meant it would often plod on for two hours or more, dredging up every drug bust, cheap heist, and drive-by shooting that happened during the past week.

"Not unless something big goes down. Earthquake, floods, wildfires, Streisand turns Republican. Or Streisand does a nude scene, even better." That thought, Streisand nude, caused him to make a face that suggested he'd just inadvertently eaten something sour.

Capra's attempt at humor was lost on Maxi. She looked hard at him. "Did you give up smoking again, and you want to punish somebody?"

"No, no—but I should," he said thoughtfully, and so saying,

he reached into his upper shirt pocket and pulled out a half-empty soft pack of Marlboros.

"You should give up smoking again?"

"And punish somebody," he finished, fishing a beat-up plastic lighter out of his middle desk drawer and lighting up.

Closing his eyes, Pete took a long drag. Leaning back comfortably in his ancient wooden desk chair with the scarred leather seat, he slowly let out a stream of smoke. Then he opened his eyes and looked at Maxi like a big, contented pussycat. "Mind if I smoke?" he asked.

With a you're-pathetic shake of her head, Maxi got up and walked out of his office.

Out in the teeming Channel Six newsroom she dropped into a chair next to Wendy Harris's computer terminal, muttering, "Damn. I am *not* freaking believing this."

Wendy was thirty, two years younger than Maxi, four foot eleven and rail thin, with an out-of-control mane of curly red hair and tortoiseshell glasses balanced on her freckled nose. She was Maxi's longtime closest friend at the station, and the producer of the Six O'clock News.

"What?" she asked Maxi, not taking her eyes off the screen or her flying fingers off the keyboard.

"Pete just assigned me to the graveyard shift."

Wendy stopped typing and turned squarely to Maxi, her brow wrinkled in disbelief. "You're kidding, right?"

"Wrong."

"What about the Six? Is he pulling you off my show? Am I gonna lose my anchor?"

"He says no. Says I can still do it."

"Whew! That's good."

"That's good if I can survive working fourteen hours a day."

"For how long?"

"Indefinitely."

"You can't. Nobody can."

"I know that. And he knows that, Wendy. I'm guessing at some point he'll yank me off the Six."

"But . . . *why?*"

"I have no clue."

"Didn't you *ask* him?" Incredulously.

"Of course I asked him. When does Pete ever explain what he does?"

"Good point. You piss him off lately?"

"Who knows? Everything pisses him off."

"True. But can he do that? What does your contract say?"

"It doesn't say he can't reassign me. I never addressed that possibility when I was doing my deal because it never occurred to me that he would demote me to the bottom rung. I mean, I've been at Channel Six News for nine years."

"So now you know. For next time."

"Oh, great. I'll be sure to include a clause that says the company can't bust me back to the 4 A.M. farm report in my next contract. That'll be only three years and five months from now. If I don't kill myself first."

"Suicide's not you."

"Well, I won't have to commit suicide. Some crazy, drugged-out, sleazebag rapist will nail me one night at three in the morning down on lower Third Street."

"Or South Central."

"You know, if I actually did get murdered, Pete would be rubbing his hands together congratulating himself on a boffo lead for the early block. Can't you hear the tease lines? 'TV news anchor killed in skid row bludgeoning—details at eleven.' Over a shot of me chatting on the set with a big goony smile. Even better if it happened during sweeps."

The three all-important "sweepstakes" months in the television news business, February, May, and November, generate the ratings on which stations base their commercial rates to advertisers. That's when all the stations run the most titillating, most explosive news stories and mini-docs they can come up with. "Lesbian Nun's Secret Baby!" That kind of thing.

"Yeah. Pete doesn't give a damn how he treats people," Wendy spat.

"A world-class sonofabitch."

"You could take this to Ryan, you know," Wendy said. "Ryan would be all over Pete's sorry ass in a minute."

Ed Ryan was the news director, Pete Capra's half-his-age boss, and no fan of Capra's. The two men were polarized on the philosophy of television journalism: Ed Ryan cared only about the ratings; Pete Capra cared only about the news. So even though his troops saw Capra as a heartless curmudgeon who ran his newsroom with a sledgehammer, they respected him as one of the last of a dying breed of news purists.

"Turn him in to Ryan? Jeez, Wen, I wouldn't do that to Pete," Maxi said.

"I know," Wendy agreed. "Pete's an asshole, but he's *our* asshole."

2

Tom McCartney hefted his bulging black canvas backpack up the steps to the back door of the Channel Six newsroom and leaned on the bell that was marked VISITORS, then reached into his pocket, fished out a handful of pills, and washed them down with a swig from a bottle of Evian. His lanky frame was clad in worn jeans, a blue work shirt, a faded khaki safari jacket that looked like it had been through wars because it had, and expensive Mephisto Barracuda walking shoes. His dark hair curled over his collar, not because it was a style choice, but because he tended to go too long between haircuts.

Since it had been his experience that only rarely did anyone answer the bell at the seldom-used back entrance to the local newsroom, he pounded on the glass door with the side of his fist.

McCartney didn't have security clearance at Channel Six, or at any other station. That's because he was a member of that most oddball of tribes—McCartney was a stringer. A newsie who works for no company, belongs to no unions or guilds, is a member of no professional groups or clubs, and has no loyalty to any news outlet, radio, television, or print. In short, a stringer, for the most part, is a journalist who can't get a job.

Since stringers don't have the benefit of a big company's

equipment, they tote their own or rented camera gear around town, looking for news to happen. They might have informers on the street who, for a ten or a twenty, will turn them on to something that's about to go down, or give them names of potential contacts who know the territory and the players. If they make a fair living they might have a laptop or even a radio scanner in the car.

And they almost always work at night. All night. On the graveyard shift. Stringers can't compete on dayside stories because broadcast stations and print media have their own reporting staffs out in the trenches all day. No sense shooting a wildfire in daylight when the stations have crews all over it—they certainly don't need to buy stringer tape of the story. But come the dark of night, media outlets usually have just one reporter—read one poor sucker—out there on the graveyard shift, who cannot possibly cover every sordid middle-of-the-night act of skulduggery, large and small, let alone even find them all. So out from the lowdown sludge of the City of Angels emerges this aberrant army of stringers, to prowl the nightside and ply their trade.

Like all TV journalists, stringers forage about, sniffing for a good story, and when they find it, they shoot it. But unlike affiliated reporters who file with their companies, stringers have to peddle their tape from station to station and show to show. If they land a taker, or more than one if the story is hot, it was a worthwhile exercise. If they don't, it was a losing investment of time and money. Sometimes you eat the bear, and sometimes the bear eats you.

Also unlike affiliated journalists, stringers never get the glory. Any glory. They could track down or stumble upon the second coming of Christ, but when they sell their tape of the story, even should it include a kick-ass interview with J.C. Himself, all clues to the stringer's identity will be obliterated—no pictures of him in the frames, and no voice, no name, no credit, no awards, no thank-yous, no go-to-hell. In the wide world of television newscasts the stringer does not exist. His story would be grandly teased all day on the station that bought it: "Exclusive interview with Jesus Christ outlining His plans for the world, on the news at four, five, and six!" Then on the shows, the anchors would lead with, "Good evening. Our top story tonight, in a stunning interview with Jesus Christ, here's what He has to say about . . ." The stringer's voice will have been edited out. Instead, you would hear the station's anchor voicing questions that the stringer had asked Jesus, over the footage that the stringer shot. Such is the lot of one of these disenfranchised night-shooters. All he would get would be his thirty pieces of silver.

In general, stringers are regarded in the television news business as a notch below pond scum. However, Tom McCartney was much more highly regarded in the industry because he had a history in legitimate news and a reputation for delivering the goods. Tom McCartney was regarded as a notch *above* pond scum.

McCartney used to have jobs. Good jobs. His last one was his best. He was a highly esteemed international correspondent for CNN. As such, he covered hot spots around the world, and he did it with distinction. Early on, armed with a broadcast journalism degree from Syracuse and a master's in business and international politics from NYU, McCartney blazed his way through the industry on hard work, a keen mind, and a fierce dedication to getting the story. Honing his skills, he'd moved up through the ranks of news markets from Atlanta to Philadelphia to Chicago to L.A., until he became one of the rising young stars for CNN on the West Coast.

But McCartney also had a jones, an ongoing love affair with pills and booze. It started during the Gulf war. While rolling tape, he was bucked off the skids of a chopper that was hovering over a land skirmish in Kuwait. When he hit the ground, his heavy camera crashing down on top of him, he'd ripped a shoulder out of its socket, broken what seemed to be most of his bones, and his face looked like he'd gone twelve rounds in the ring with Mike Tyson.

His doctors told him he was lucky to be alive. His accommodating nurses, responding to his charm, his rugged good looks, his quirky sense of humor, and maybe even to his multiple, severe injuries, gave their favorite patient plenty of extra attention, along with unlimited doses of Vicodin to ease his pain. And during months of recuperation at home, he took to washing down the oblong white pills with sizable swigs out of a vodka bottle.

He eventually got back to work, but he never got off the pills. Or the juice. After one too many somewhat slurred on-air deliveries, CNN dumped him, and nobody else would hire him. And now he was forty-two years old and prowling for news in the seamy underbelly of L.A. after midnight, like a vagrant digging for day-old bread in back-alley Dumpsters.

Everyone in the business knew Tom McCartney. Some vilified him for the loser he was, some held him up as an example of what they never wanted to become, and some, mostly seasoned journalists, admired him for the great reporter he had been. That group silently rooted for him, and were pleased when he nailed a significant story, saw it make air, and made himself some bucks into the bargain. And the thing with Tom McCartney that his colleagues had to admire, even if grudgingly, was that he absolutely would not back down. Would not give up. Ever. On a story, or on anything else. That double-dyed perseverance trait was tightly woven into the fabric of his makeup. Psychobabblers, civilian and professional, might call it extreme obsessive compulsion.

Maybe that was why he had never given up the booze and the pills, even now.

And why he stood pounding on the back door to the Channel Six newsroom for a good ten minutes until a newswriter, rushing by with a script in hand, happened to hear his beating on the glass and let him in.

He could have avoided all that hassle if he'd just made a call in advance for a drive-on, or announced himself at the guard desk down in the lobby. Not his style. McCartney always parked on the side street east of the sprawling United Global Network complex, hoofed it onto the midway, and came in through the back loading docks opposite Studio Nine, where they shot a long-running daily soap. From there he would eschew the bank of elevators and take the stairs two at a time up to the back entrance of the newsroom, then wait for someone to heed his banging. It was probably because he was never entirely sure that his calling card would get him in the front door. Anywhere.

"Hi, Tom," the young writer said. "Got something good?"

"Yup. Capra around?"

"He's in his office," the writer said.

McCartney took long strides down the back hall and out into the open newsroom, nodding to a few acquaintances as he passed their computer terminals. McCartney didn't really have any colleagues that he could call friends. He didn't cultivate friends. Didn't drink with newsies. He could have. They'd have welcomed his company; McCartney was nothing if not interesting. But he was a dedicated loner.

He tapped on the glass of Pete Capra's office door, and walked inside at the managing editor's bidding.

"What?" Capra blurted from behind his desk, not inviting him to sit.

"The PriceCo fire," McCartney said.

PriceCo was a giant discount store in South El Monte, an industrial city east of Los Angeles, where a fire of mysterious origin had broken out during the night. Tom McCartney had once again gone far beyond the norm to get the story.

"We were all over it on the morning show," Capra said. "We're recutting it for the Noon, and we'll have a reporter out there live for the early block."

"Do you have the new top?"

"What new top?"

"They're calling it arson."

"Last I checked that was the speculation. We reported that."

"They have a suspect. I've got him on tape."

This got Capra's full attention. "The wires didn't say anything about a suspect."

"I know." McCartney rummaged in his backpack. "That's why this one's expensive." He pulled out a small cassette.

"You had it transferred?"

"Just for you," McCartney said with his crooked grin.

Channel Six was the only L.A. news operation that used the M-2 system, a process that was new and expensive, was installed throughout the building, and was full of bugs, which made staff members crazy trying to make faulty tapes airworthy. Capra groused loud and often that somebody upstairs hadda get big kick-backs when they bought that pig, and he threatened at least ten times a week to take an ax to the machinery.

"You want to see it?" McCartney asked.

"Talk to me first."

"I rolled on this guy at the scene because he looked squirrelly. Nervous, but enjoying himself. Having way too good a time."

Capra got out of his chair. "Show me."

McCartney popped the M-2 into Capra's playback machine and the two stood back to watch. Establishing wide shots showed flames shooting through the roof of the low, sprawling warehouse, firefighters on the scene dragging hoses and hoisting ladders, and the usual looky-loos hanging around the action, the latter a sparse bunch because it was well after midnight. McCartney fast-forwarded to a zoom-in on one of the bystanders: a white male, fortyish, medium build, pale thinning hair, wearing a lightweight tan suit and wire-rimmed glasses. He was standing alone, a little apart, watching the flames.

"What time was this?" Capra asked, not taking his eyes off the figure on the screen.

"Three in the morning, around there. Guy looks like he went to a bar right from work, and went to the fire scene right from last call."

"Doesn't mean he set it. Coulda stopped on his way home to have a look."

"Guys in suits don't stop, park, get out of their cars, hike over to the fire lines, and slouch around watching a fire at 3 A.M."

The picture cut to a close-up of the man's face. Sweat beaded his high, bony forehead, his eyes shone in the firelight, and the beginnings of a smile flickered at the corners of his thin, gray mouth.

"A computer programmer for Dinex, a small software company in West Covina. Been there eleven years. Nerd type," McCartney said. "Name's Bernard Peltz."

The footage cut to McCartney voicing a series of man-on-the-street interviews, the standard news MOS technique. Maneuvering a handheld microphone, his camera lens moving from one person to the next in the scant gathering, he fired questions: "Your name, sir? You live around here? Do you work at the store? Ever shop here? Did you notice anything unusual tonight?"

Until he'd worked his way over to his target.

The man gave his name, where he was employed and for how long, said he just happened to be driving by, and no, he didn't see anything unusual. "Probably an electrical fire. That's usually what happens with a fire that breaks out when nobody's around," the man offered.

"El Monte Fire was on this guy too," McCartney said.

Capra narrowed his eyes. "How much?"

"Three thousand."

"You're insane, McCartney."

"I've been called worse," the reporter said with a humorless chuckle.

"You *are* worse. Fifteen hundred. Tops."

"Twenty-five, bottom."

"Two thousand. And I must be nuts."

"Twenty-five," McCartney reiterated, rewinding the tape. He punched the EJECT button, snatched it out of the machine, walked over to the chair where he'd set his backpack, and tossed the cassette into it.

"Okay, okay, twenty-five. But for Chrissake don't tell anybody—they'll commit me. And needless to say, I've got an exclusive on it. I'm not shucking out two-and-a-half large for you to peddle this tape all over town."

"Needless to say," the stringer echoed dryly.

"So, McCartney," Capra said then, "what's going on with the Nodori arrest?"

Gino Nodori was a second-tier actor in a weekly television cop drama who'd been arrested after midnight on a lewd-conduct charge in a public park the week before.

"What's going on with him? You know what's going on with him, Pete—it's on the wires. How come you didn't air my tape?"

"Nodori didn't make my lineup."

"You paid for it. Everyone else aired it. Two, Five, and Nine bought it from me. Seven had Caulley on it." Steven Caulley was the graveyard reporter for Channel Seven.

"Like I said, Nodori didn't make the cut."

"It was a helluva lot better story than six or eight others you aired last Tuesday," McCartney observed. "Talk radio was all over it."

"Doing any follow-ups?"

"Why would you want a follow-up when you didn't even air the bust?"

"Just asking."

"Nodori's out on bail. You can cover the court procedures on dayside with your regular staff," McCartney tossed out with a you-know-that-as-well-as-I-do look.

Capra's eyes skittered over to the wall for a beat, then back to McCartney. "I'm thinking follow-ups at the scene," he said.

"Huh? It's a gay hangout in MacArthur Park. What goes down in the men's john is the same ol' same ol'. With an occasional police rout, which nobody gives a damn about, and a one-in-a-million celebrity grab like Nodori."

"How about shooting some tape out there for me? A couple of cassettes every night for a while."

McCartney gave him a puzzled look. "What did I shoot at the Nodori bust that I don't know I shot?"

"So how about it?" Capra asked, ignoring the question. "Five hundred a night for no story, just some long-lens CUs of the dirt-bags who hang in that area of the park."

"Lemme get this straight, Pete. You want two tapes a night shot in MacArthur Park near the men's can. Weekend nights too?" Stringers rarely gave themselves the luxury of weekends off.

"Yeah," Capra said. "Weekend nights too. Shoot each tape at different times every night. And get faces."

"A thousand a night."

"Get outta town," Capra snapped back. "Five hundred, take it or leave it. I could get fucking *Rosie* to do this for me."

Harvey Rosenberg had the reputation of being the least competent stringer in the business, an eager, bumbling, two-hundred-and-forty-pound, Harley-driving television news wannabe, with top-of-the-line equipment paid for by his indulgent parents, talent yet to be proven in the business, and a predilection for tent-sized T-shirts and knee-length, baggy white shorts printed with gaudy orange flames—the joke went that Rosie must have bought a dozen pairs of those eyesores on sale somewhere.

"I'll take it," McCartney said.

His news nose told him that Pete Capra had to be looking for something big in MacArthur Park for that kind of sustained video surveillance. He lifted a hand to give him five on the deal.

"Oh, and in return for the easy bucks, I need you to do another job for me," Capra said, smacking McCartney's upraised hand.

"That pays money?"

"No."

"Why does that not surprise me?" McCartney took the arson tape out of his backpack and laid it on Capra's desk. "You want me to brief your writer on this?"

"Of course. The other job is to watch Maxi Poole."

"Nice job," McCartney said with a droll expression. "I already do."

"I mean on the street. She's working the graveyard starting Monday."

McCartney raised his eyebrows. "No kidding. She on your shit list, Pete?"

"Just show her the ropes on the overnight," Capra said.

"You've got Kittridge for that."

"I'm bringing Kittridge in on dayside."

"Good. One less reporter for me to ace on the shift."

"What, you think Maxi's no competition?"

"We'll see. The graveyard's a whole different scum-pit."

Capra was writing out a check. Another quirk with McCartney—he wouldn't wait for UGN payroll to cut him a check and put it in the mail like they did for the rest of the stringers. Tom McCartney ran a strictly COD operation.

Holding up the check, waving it back and forth as if to dry the ink even though he'd used a ballpoint, Capra said, "So you'll help Maxi get her bearings?"

"Sure," McCartney said, reaching out and snatching the check. He folded it in two and tucked it into the upper flap pocket of his jacket. "But, Maxi Poole on the graveyard? I don't get it."

"You don't have to get it," Capra said. "What I want you to do is take her into the park with you when you shoot my tape. Hover over her for a couple of weeks. Teach her the nightside. Agreed?"

"Orienting her on the shift is one thing, but what makes you think she'll put up with hovering?"

"You'll figure it out. And don't say anything to Kittridge; he doesn't know yet."

McCartney shrugged and turned to leave. Pete Capra knew he didn't have to tell the guy twice to keep his mouth zipped. Competition was fierce in television news, and for stringers, business could dry up at any given station with a misplaced word or move. And Tom McCartney could be counted on to be particularly discreet. Fact was, the man rarely talked to anyone, about anything.

"One more thing," Capra said before McCartney got out the door. "Don't tell Maxi I asked you to help her."

"Oh, *this* is gonna be easy—I'll just use my dazzling charm to get her into Mac*Murder* Park with me at two in the morning."

"Perfect. She'll never mistake your brand of charm for help. I'm serious," he added after a beat, "I want you to watch her back."

"Fun duty," McCartney said.

Capra rolled his eyes. "I'll see you in the morning with my MacArthur Park tapes."

"You want me to start out there tonight?"

"Jesus, *yeah*, McCartney, I want you to start out there tonight. It's money for nothing."

Tom McCartney smiled. He knew that Pete Capra never paid money for nothing.

3

oole!" Looming large in the doorway to his office, Pete Capra yelled across the newsroom at Maxi, who was still perched next to Wendy's computer station in medium-high dudgeon.

"Pete hasn't grasped the concept of our paging system," Maxi groused as she got up out of her chair.

"He's probably gonna tell you he was kidding about the overnight," Wendy said.

"Ten bucks?"

"Nope." Wendy knew better.

Maxi walked over to Capra's office. He handed her McCartney's M-2. "Cut this for the Noon," he said. "Check with El Monte Arson, or whoever's handling the PriceCo fire. Guy on this tape could be the suspect they're looking at. He's the last MOS on the reel. Tom McCartney's the shooter—he'll come looking for you in editing and brief you. He's probably back grabbing a cup of coffee."

With that, Capra turned away, went into his office, sat down at his desk, and proceeded to click on his computer keyboard. Maxi was still standing in his doorway. "Is that it?" she asked.

Capra glanced up as if he was surprised to see her still there. "Yeah, that's it." Exasperation in his look and tone.

Maxi wheeled around and headed for the edit rooms, feeling as if she'd been jerked out of the known universe and slam-dunked into the rabbit hole. Not that Pete Capra's brusqueness was in any way out of the ordinary. She just couldn't believe that he had nothing more to say about blithely assigning her to the punitive graveyard shift. Starting Monday.

On reflection, probably not so blithely. Pete had to have a reason for doing this, and she needed to know what it was. The one way she *wouldn't* find out, she knew, was by asking him again.

From across the newsroom, reporter Paul Kittridge caught Maxi's eye, gave her a wait-up gesture, and headed her way. Intercepting her, he steered her over to a far wall out of earshot of the morning shift.

"Got a minute?" he asked.

"Barely, Paul—I have to cut a tape." She gestured with Mc-Cartney's M-2.

"Aah. Well, it looks like I'm handing you the nightside baton on Monday."

"Capra told you?"

"No, but the whole newsroom knows."

The Channel Six grapevine was the healthiest plant in the building. Maxi didn't bother to ask how everybody knew before Capra even posted it. They just always did. But no one would mention it to her, since she was apparently the goat in this scenario. Or to Wendy either, knowing the two women were joined at the proverbial hip.

"How do you feel about it?" she asked Kittridge.

"Thrilled to be getting off graveyard before I grow fur and a set of fangs. I'll still be working it on weekends, though, with the rest of the week on dayside general assignment."

"Pete thinks you like the graveyard. He says you never complain."

"What sane person likes working all night and sleeping all

day? But you know Pete—if you bitch, he'll keep you on the shift longer just to fuck with you. But how do *you* feel about it, Maxi? I swear, this move takes me by complete surprise."

"Surprise? I've been blindsided. Is the grapevine also broadcasting *why* he's doing this?"

"No. Everyone's buzzing about it, but they're clueless why Pete's making the switch. I'm the junior reporter here so I know why *I* drew graveyard—but nobody can figure out why *you're* being shunted into the night."

"Speculation abounds, I suppose."

"Always."

Both of them were thinking, but neither one said, that in television news, a move to the graveyard usually prefaced a firing, the party line being it was last chance for the reporter to hone his skills and polish his act. The cynical logic being maybe the reporter would quit in disgust, which would save the company from doling out severance pay and unemployment benefits.

"Well, thanks for talking to me about it," Maxi said.

"Sure. Is there anything I can help you with?"

"Got any contacts I can use?"

"Tons. I'll print out a list of names and numbers for you. With a brief description of what degeneracy they're into, and what they can do for you."

"Thanks. And is there anybody I should stay away from?"

"That's a longer list. I'll give you that one too."

Maxi was viewing the PriceCo fire tape and making notes when Tom McCartney appeared in the open doorway of the edit room. She was always amazed at what the resourceful freelancer managed to come in with. Tom McCartney was known for nailing great stories before anyone else even knew about them, and for finding angles and nuances that nobody else saw. No other stringer shooting a nightside structure fire would bother to notice and roll on a possible arson suspect at the scene.

"Nice get," she said, looking up at him.

"Thanks. Any questions?"

"No—it's all clear. I'll call the arson investigators and see what I can find out. Did you notice if any fire brass talked to this guy at the scene?"

"No, but they were rolling tape, and I watched their shooter spending some time aimed in our guy's direction."

He was probably just following McCartney's lead, Maxi thought. Cops, sheriff's deputies, firefighters, and politicos recognized reporter Tom McCartney's solid gold instincts. "I wonder if they got his name."

"I don't know, but *you've* got his name. Maybe you can drop an ID on them."

"And maybe they'll return the favor with whatever they've got. Thanks, Tom."

"I'm just a giver," McCartney said with a silly smile. *Cute* silly smile, Maxi couldn't help noticing.

"By the way, you got much better stuff than Kittridge," she said. "How'd you get there so fast?"

"Trade secret." Another grin. A newsie rarely shows his hand. "And Maxi, here's my phone number."

McCartney laid a business card down on the edit desk in front of her. Maxi quickly scanned his name, phone number, and e-mail address on it, then looked back up at him with raised eyebrows.

"For your files," McCartney said by way of no explanation at all, and he turned to leave.

He knows, Maxi flashed mentally. *He knows I'm bounced to the graveyard.*

She slipped his card into her jacket pocket. Either Pete had mentioned it to him, or he'd picked it up among the rank and file. Damn, this nightmare was looking real.

Back in her office, Maxi was writing a track for the PriceCo arson piece when Felicia James opened the door and poked her head inside. A slim, attractive black reporter, Felicia was a five-year veteran at the station. "Hi, Maxi—can I come in?" she asked.

"Okay," Maxi said. "I'm jamming on this piece, but I have a minute."

Felicia pushed some papers and files aside on the small, worn sofa in front of Maxi's desk and cleared herself a seat.

"I can't believe Pete's putting you on the graveyard," she began.

"That makes two of us."

"I just want you to know that the newsroom is prowling with cats who are thrilled about it because they want your anchor job."

"Of course they want my anchor job," Maxi said evenly. "Why wouldn't they? They'd be fools if they didn't want to advance. I don't blame any of them for that, Felicia. Isn't that what you want too?"

"I'm happy with what I'm doing," the reporter said.

Funny, Maxi thought, she believed her. Felicia James was married to a successful Beverly Hills orthopedic surgeon, with two children in elementary school. The couple had an active social life, and Felicia was heavily involved with school events and several charities. She was probably the one reporter on staff who *didn't* want more.

"Well, thanks, Felicia," Maxi said. "Now, I've got to write this track, okay?" She didn't want to encourage or even listen to any gossip about her situation.

"Okay—I just thought you should know what the babble is out there," Felicia said, with a wide arm gesture toward the newsroom beyond Maxi's office door.

"It doesn't surprise me," Maxi said.

"Well, maybe this will surprise you—Christine Williams is actively lobbying for your anchor slot on the Six. Telling people she wants it and deserves it. She's coming on like a candidate running for office."

"That doesn't surprise me either. Christine is a hard worker, she's good, and she's the logical next-in-line for my show if it's up for grabs. Now, I really have to get to work here," Maxi said, giving her visitor a dismissive smile.

Felicia James got up, gave a little two-finger wave, and left. Maxi watched the retreating reporter, wondering how many more visits she'd have as her colleagues weighed in on her apparent demotion. It was a rule of hers never to get involved with newsroom politics. A maxim she'd learned early in this cutthroat business: *Keep your nose clean and your head above the fray.*

She turned her attention back to the PriceCo script on her computer screen.

4

Climbing the outside staircase to his thirties-era apartment in West Los Angeles, keys in hand, camera on his shoulder, backpack bulging with tapes and gear, Tom McCartney scoured his surroundings through dark mirrored Ray-Bans, checking that nothing seemed amiss. A habit he'd developed early in his news career when he'd shot a crack house, got two of the perps on tape, and came home after his story aired on several stations to find his apartment ransacked and his video equipment smashed. He'd moved out immediately, rented a post office box in the nearby business district, and never again used his home address on any document at all.

Keeping the bulky camera upright, he sidestepped the morning papers lying on his doormat and unlocked the door to his unit. Pushed it open. Stood still for a beat and did another sweeping surveillance scan inside. Then he went in, set the video camera down on the floor, closed and locked the door, and quickly checked out all five rooms.

His living room looked undisturbed. Spotless beige wall-to-wall carpeting. A vintage limestone fireplace in the middle of the back wall, a throwback to a time when L.A. apartment buildings were built with spacious rooms, high ceilings, and grace touches, as opposed to today's concrete efficiency boxes. Prewar they called them in New York; in Los Angeles they just called them old. Which was ironic, since nothing in La-La Land was very old, even going back to the time when eleven families had journeyed from the interior of Mexico and founded El Pueblo de Los Angeles, sweeping the resident Indians into the dustbin of history.

On the mantelpiece was a framed picture of his parents, along with a pair of Emmys, the latter being trophies from his CNN days. When he'd first moved in, his mother had taken it upon herself to help him get organized, and had fished the golden statues out of a box of his assorted junk and set them atop the fireplace. He'd left them there to please her. Still, every time he glanced at them it hurt a little. Not that he really wanted that job back—it just rankled that he couldn't have it.

He looked around the rest of the room. Comfortable cream-colored wide-wale corduroy couch facing the fireplace, flanked by two big matching club chairs. A six-foot-square teakwood coffee table in the middle of the grouping, its smoky glass top stacked with current issues of *Time, Newsweek, U.S. News, Vanity Fair, People,* and a few other publications. Tools of the trade. Built into the wall to the left of the fireplace, an entertainment center with top-of-the-line music system and an oversized Fujitsu plasma flat-screen TV. The wall to the right solidly lined with floor-to-ceiling bookshelves crammed with classic literature, history, political science, geography, philosophy, psychology, biographies, reference books, and some current novels.

He moved into the kitchen, which was old but clean, its appliances dating back to a '70s remodel before his time there. Breakfast nook on its far side. Then into the small formal dining room off the kitchen, which held nothing but gym equipment. McCartney didn't entertain.

Across the center hall was a large master bedroom suite with an updated bath and walk-in closet. The windows of the bedroom were hung with blackout shades to accommodate his off-kilter sleeping schedule—McCartney slept in the daytime. Next to the master was a second bedroom that he'd outfitted as an office, with computers, printer, scanner, fax machine, phones, editing and dubbing equipment, and walls lined with shelves holding videotapes archived by dates and story slugs.

He dropped his backpack onto a chair in the corner, went back into the living room, and knelt in front of his extensive music collection. McCartney had rock 'n' roll in his soul. He pulled up *Strange Animal* by Styx, popped it in the CD player, and Lawrence Gowan's classic "A Criminal Mind" blared through the apartment: *I stand accused before you, I have no tears to cry* . . . McCartney smiled. Better than drugs. He needed music like he needed the air he breathed.

Satisfied with his vigilance routine, he stepped back to the entryway and picked up his newspapers, then closed and bolted the front door. The place was neat, tasteful enough, no frills—a completely serviceable space. No pets, no plants, no problems.

He could afford better, but this was all he needed. And all he had ever wanted. The joys of having a house, a wife, children, totally eluded him, even though he came from a big family with loving parents. His brothers and sisters fit that happy-home picture, all of them. But not him. The family kidded that Tom, the youngest of five, must have been off hovering over some ancient war zone when the domestic gene was passed around. He'd never tried to analyze it; he just knew that they were right—the American dream had never been part of his plan. But he was a great uncle; his nieces and nephews adored him. Their parents, his siblings, would cringe when he would laughingly explain his successful MO with the kids: fill them full of sugar, give them cash, let them watch horror flicks, and send them home. It worked for him.

And he had women. None he would bring back to his apartment, and none he would bring around to the infrequent family dinners he felt duty-bound to attend then actually enjoyed when he got there. And none he would ever give his phone number to, even when they expressed interest. *Especially* when they expressed interest. Not that they weren't for the most part perfectly nice women, usually working in some area of the news business. He just wasn't in the market for a relationship, or anything that even remotely resembled one. For about a million reasons.

Picking up the heavy video camera by the front door, he carried it into the office while Gowan rocked on about how a person had to be made of cold stone to survive in this twisted world.

Back in the kitchen, he reached into a cabinet and got out a bag of his favorite coffee, a French roast blend of decaffeinated Colombian santos arabica beans. The coffee ritual gave him satisfaction: putting the rich beans through the proper grind, savoring the full-bodied aroma that filled the room, dropping a filter into the brew basket and spooning out the rounded scoops of coffee, filling the container with refrigerated bottled water, then watching the decanter slowly fill with the dark, steaming liquid. McCartney was precise about his coffee.

And about everything else he chose to include in his life. Like the daily workout regimen he would do next, a half hour of cardio on the tread, a half hour of weights, and a half hour of yoga. After that he would take a shower, turn off the ringer on his bedroom phone, and go down for an uninterrupted six hours of sleep.

But first, a task he wanted to take care of. Striding back into his office carrying a mug of the fresh-brewed, he sat down at his desk, flipped on his Gateway laptop, and logged onto the Internet. He intended to do some cursory digging into the background of one Peter Capra, television news managing editor at Channel Six, the UGN-owned station in Los Angeles. Maybe the research would glean a clue to the reason behind the odd assignment the man had handed him this morning, to randomly tape the perverts who hung out near the public restrooms in MacArthur Park.

5

Thursday night, ten to eight. Maxi was on her way home from work. Steering her aging black Corvette up Beverly Glen canyon, she gripped the wheel, bucking fast-rising headwinds that rocked the small car from side to side. It occurred to her that the Southern California devil winds were making a fitting pronouncement on this day from hell. Her PriceCo arson story on the early block went fine; the Six O'clock News she anchored went fine. It was just her life that sucked.

The graveyard shift, starting Monday.

That bleak thought consuming her, she didn't notice the person standing in the shadows of the leafy blue eucalyptus tree in front of her house until she pulled into her driveway and a woman ran toward her car, waving her arms and calling out, "Mrs. Poole! Mrs. Maxi Poole!"

Hitting the brakes and the door lock at the same time, Maxi raised her eyebrows quizzically and mouthed, "Yes?" through the window glass.

The woman stopped at the passenger side of the low-slung sports car and stooped to Maxi's line of sight. "Please, you help me, Mrs. Poole," she wailed.

Maxi saw red, swollen eyes in a blotchy face with no makeup.

A kindly face that seemed to register great distress. But she couldn't rule out that this could be a ruse, gang-bangers using a distraught-acting woman as a front. They could be behind the trees, ready to pounce, rob, carjack, kidnap—anything, she knew. This was Los Angeles.

"Who are you?" she asked through the glass.

"I am Carla Ochoa. They took my boy. My Roberto. He's two. *Usted ayudeme, Maxi Poole.*" You help me.

"*¿Cómo supo donde vivía?*" How did you know where I live?

"I have seen you coming from this house with *su perro grande,*" the woman said. Yukon. With a broad gesture southward, she added, "I work for Mrs. Lightner."

Mrs. Conrad Lightner, wife of Los Angeles city councilman Conrad Lightner, obstreperous archconservative on the still liberal L.A. council. Gladys Lightner, "Gladdy" in social circles, and in a certain segment of Westside ladies who lunch, she ruled. And she paid. But rumor had it that Gladys Lightner would stab your hand with a salad fork if you disagreed with her about tomorrow's weather forecast.

The Lightners lived five doors down from Maxi on the same side of the street. Maxi had interviewed Councilman Lightner on several occasions at city hall, but had only run into Gladys Lightner once. Run up *against* her, to be precise, and after that she had gone out of her way to avoid the woman. Mrs. L. had stopped Maxi on the street one morning when she was walking Yukon, and had angrily complained that the boy had been doing his business in the meticulously manicured rock gardens on either side of the gates to the Lightner estate.

Her perfect Yukon? "Not possible," Maxi had responded, smiling, trying to palliate the woman's ire. "I walk him every day myself; otherwise he's at home. I'm sure Yukon has never been in your rock gardens—if you're finding poop, it's some other dog's poop."

At that, Gladys Lightner had actually reached out and grabbed a handful of Maxi's sweatshirt, pulling her close, startling her, which caused Yukon to let out a series of sharp barks. Maxi swatted at her hand and the woman let loose, but she was shaking uncontrollably, her face contorted in rage. "You are *rude*, young woman," she'd sputtered, then wheeled around and marched toward her own front gates.

I'm rude? You're insane! Maxi had thought, kneeling and holding her trembling dog as they both watched Mrs. Lightner's stormtrooper retreat.

Gladys Lightner had not introduced herself at that time. Evidently she hadn't seen the need, figured everybody knew her, after all. And in fact Maxi did recognize her from having seen her picture several times in the society section of the *Westside Register*— the tall, reed-thin body and the spiky dyed-black hair belying her sixty-something years. Now here was the woman's housekeeper in tears on Maxi's doorstep.

"Wait here, Mrs. Ochoa," she said.

Scooting her car into the garage, she zapped the rolling door down behind her, went inside, came through the house, and opened the front door.

"Come in," she beckoned, and the Ochoa woman trudged heavily up the entry steps and followed Maxi into the kitchen.

"I'll make tea," Maxi told her, steering her unexpected guest to a chair at her kitchen table. "Then we'll talk."

She filled the kettle, set it to boil, and busied herself putting out the tea things. And observing Mrs. Ochoa. Hispanic, looked to be in her middle thirties, tending toward plump, with a pretty face and dark, wavy hair tied up with a large-sized pink plastic klippie. She wore loose-fitting jeans, a faded blue sweatshirt that bore the logo of the Los Angeles Dodgers, and a pair of well-worn sneakers. She had no purse, only a crumpled-up wad of tissues in her hand.

Setting two mugs of hot tea on the table, Maxi sat down opposite her and passed the sugar bowl and a carton of milk. "Now," she said, looking into two misty brown eyes, "tell me."

"My boy is in the house today. It's windy—terrible winds—so

I keep him inside. He was playing with his truck in our room. I had work to do. When I went back in the room, he's gone." She started quietly weeping.

"Gone? How long ago?"

"*Una hora,* maybe." One hour.

"You called the police, didn't you?"

"No. *No policía.*" No police, said almost fiercely. That signaled to Maxi that Carla Ochoa was probably in the country illegally.

"We *have* to report this to the police." Hoping the "we" would make the woman feel more comfortable about notifying the authorities.

"No," she pleaded. "Please, no."

"Where's Mr. Ochoa?" Maxi asked.

The woman looked up, as if the question took her by surprise. "He is gone."

"Gone where?"

"Gone since Roberto was baby. In Texas."

"Does he see his son? Does he send money?"

"No. He called Roberto once; I put my baby on the phone. But Roberto can't talk much yet—he just listened."

"And now you live with the Lightners?"

"*Sí,* very nice room. I work for the family."

"You looked all over the house for Roberto?"

"He is not allowed in the rest of the house."

"But you looked, didn't you?"

"*Sí,* missus."

"And in the yard?"

"Everywhere. Roberto is not home."

Maxi stretched her hand across the table, around the mug of tea that the woman hadn't touched, and took Mrs. Ochoa's hand. "I'll call a friend of mine," she said. "A friend with the police department who will know what to do about Roberto. And who won't hurt you, I promise."

This was tricky terrain. She couldn't confront the woman's legality status, because if she knew for sure that this was an undocumented worker, the law dictated that she would have to report her to the CIS, the U.S. Citizenship and Immigration Services. And for Maxi, breaking the law would put her job in jeopardy.

Well, getting *caught* breaking the law would put her job in jeopardy.

Her "friend" was Marcus Jorgan, Detective Two, with the LAPD's Robbery-Homicide Division. She'd worked with Marc on several stories.

"Do Mr. and Mrs. Lightner know?" Maxi asked.

"Missus knows. She say don't call nobody—we will find him. But Roberto doesn't come home. He's just small boy."

"How long were you waiting outside my house?"

"A while, yes. I don't know what to do."

It was after eight o'clock at night, January dark and low-fifties cold. Evening rush-hour traffic was back to normal now on busy Beverly Glen as neighbors in this residential area in the hills on the west side of the city tended to dinner, homework, and settling in with before-bedtime rituals. Maxi felt her stomach tighten. Where was this youngster?

"Come on," she said to Carla Ochoa, getting up from the table and grabbing her purse. "You and I are going down to talk to the Lightners, then we'll do what we need to do to find Roberto."

6

Councilman Conrad Lightner sat in his downtown city hall office after hours, putting together a position paper on the proposed restructuring of the Los Angeles Police Commission that he would expound on tomorrow in council chambers. An aide was racking up overtime pay typing and retyping his revisions into the computer. Lightner had no idea what to do with a computer, and had no intention of learning—he had enough "little" people around him to deal with the incomprehensible monsters.

In the outer office, his aide was hard at work. Young, slender, with a rosebud mouth and small, oval, gold-framed glasses over huge brown eyes. And a thick mass of chestnut corkscrews tied in an unruly clump at the nape of her neck with what looked like a couple of shoelaces. Amy-something. Working part-time while she studied public administration at USC. Brainy. Adorable. Untouchable.

Lightner sighed. They were all untouchable, all the cute, young, fuckable ones who toiled and learned in L.A.'s downtown center of government. Untouchable for him, anyway. They would never be able to pin the "sexist pig" sobriquet on him. For one thing, if he dared make a pass at any of them they would never take him seriously—he was everybody's old uncle around here.

And for another more significant reason: If by some miracle he ever did get one of these baby dolls in a compromising position, so to speak, and he got caught, it would be all over for him. Period. Yes, he'd be publicly humiliated, he would probably be ousted from the council, and he might even go to prison, but all of that paled by comparison to what would be the real peril in such a situation: Gladdy would kill him. The formidable Gladys Parsable Lightner would find out, and she would probably kill him. He had too often borne the brunt of her wrath for even the smallest of perceived offenses. One time she went totally ballistic and whacked him about the head and ears with her hair dryer because of a wet washcloth left on the floor.

When he got back in from dinner an hour ago, he'd had a message on his Audix from Gladdy. The boy was gone, she'd said. The housekeeper's kid. Gone—that's all she'd said. Not gone for now, or gone for good, or gone the Lord knew where or why. Lightner never liked the kid. The little runt shuffling in and out of the maid's room dragging his scruffy blanket everywhere, fingers in his mouth, head down, never saying a word—barely two and the kid was creepy.

Besides, Con Lightner had had more than enough of kids. His own. Two sons, both grown. He and Gladdy had replaced themselves on the earth, but unfortunately, those two blessed events did not make the world a better place, as it turned out. The older one, Jerrold, was married to a trailer-trash bimbo who dressed in spandex capris, four-inch heels, fishnet stockings, and pink fake fur. Jerry was a "businessman," which in his case was a euphemism for small-time hustler. He'd already pleaded out one con job, and seemed to be involved in yet another at the moment—some kind of scheme for funneling prescription drugs out of Canada that hadn't exploded yet. But it would. "Con's con," the old man privately called his number one son. Some joke.

His younger son, James, was a drug addict. Gladdy adored James; Con didn't even know where he lived. He was sure his wife knew but he never pressed it, didn't much want to know—he'd personally opted out of that loop after James had been nailed in one too many drug busts that hit the press and caused him a shit-load of public embarrassment. James seemed to be the only person in her orbit who did not rouse the terrifying Gladys Lightner choler, ever. Gladdy insisted that her Jamie had a good heart, that this was just a "phase that he'll grow out of." Lightner figured at thirty years old, you were who you were gonna be. James Lightner had been married to Aly, a schoolteacher, the smart one. So smart, she left him.

Councilman Lightner would have liked to flee as far as he could get from ferocious Gladdy and their dysfunctional offspring, but he couldn't. It was Parsable money, not his modest govern-ment salary, that kept him in their six-million-dollar villa on Bev-erly Glen. Even more important, if anyone could get him elected mayor of Los Angeles, then maybe even governor of California, Gladys Parsable Lightner could. And Gladdy's boys—he subtly disclaimed paternity when he could—came as a package deal. So he put up with the lot of them, and tried to operate below the radar within their respective orbits. Jerrold and James had thus far presented the two with no grandchildren, and as far as Lightner was concerned, that was a blessing.

With a little knock on the open door, Amy walked into his of-fice and handed him her latest printout. Riffling through the pages, barely scanning the text, Lightner nodded. He knew that he would facilely dance around the words on the pages to get his meaning across to his colleagues on the chamber floor in the morning.

"This is fine," he said to her. "Let's go home."

He stood in the doorway to the outer office and watched from under lowered lids as Amy scampered like a gangly colt to the coatrack in a corner. Nimbly, she lifted a funky gray knitted cloche off a hook and pulled it down over her wooly curls, then shuffled into a coarse navy peacoat. Buttoned it over her reddish-orange simulated eelskin miniskirt, topped with a purple cotton jersey blouse with a low scoop neck. A cheap silver heart medallion on a chain. Black leather shoes with two inches of rubber soles. She carried a large fake leopardskin tote that doubled as a purse. Gladdy would figuratively hold her nose at this outfit. At all of these kids today.

Kids. You couldn't call them kids. Couldn't even call them girls. Lightner was from that generation of men who thought "girls" was a more complimentary cognomen than "women." He'd found out the hard way over recent years that you don't call them girls.

He shook his head as he watched Amy skitter out the door without so much as a good night. These eight-dollar-and-sixty-two-cents-an-hour, self-important little chicklets in their mismatched rags, complaining loudly if you didn't call them women. That's what the world had come to.

Councilman Lightner sighed again, picked up his briefcase, turned out the lights in his office, and took the elevator down to the parking structure. He maneuvered his late-model gold Lexus sedan through downtown city streets and onto the Hollywood Freeway northbound, toward Beverly Glen and home.

Gliding along in medium traffic, his heavy car buffeted by the strong Santa Ana winds, he started to feel the itch. Tried to will it to go away. Bypassed his exit, the off-ramp onto Sunset Boulevard that would take him to the Westside, and continued on the freeway for another half a mile, then found himself exiting at Hollywood Boulevard and driving west toward Vine Street.

The damn itch. He had to scratch it.

7

Maxi fairly marched down the grade toward the Lightners' garish manse, Mrs. Ochoa firmly in tow. The strengthening Santa Ana winds, originally called Santana winds after a Spanish variant of "Satan," rasped at their faces as if to urge them back, impede their mission. These seasonal winds roared out of the arid desert to the east and squeezed through the coastal mountain passes, where they compressed to gale-force velocities and lashed the Los Angeles Basin, sucking moisture from every wisp of vegetation and every stick of wood, causing or exacerbating the deadly Southern California wildfires that Maxi reported on the news. Hence, the rattling devil winds invariably inculcated Maxi with a sense of foreboding. The great Los Angeles noir writer Raymond Chandler called them Red Winds "that come down through the mountain passes and curl your hair and make your nerves jump and your skin itch."

The Lightners' sandstone Georgian colossus, built out almost to the street in the narrow canyon and completely lit up by harsh spots around its perimeter, was an eye-jolting misfit among the quietly understated neighboring homes in rustic Beverly Glen. Mrs. Ochoa led Maxi to a pedestrian door cut into the imposing iron gates in front of the estate, and with trembling hands she fished her house key out of her pocket and let them onto the property. As the two women made their way over the interlocking concrete pavement blocks to the elaborate stone entry, the massive, carved cherrywood front doors parted and the imposing form of the lady of the house materialized in the arched doorway. The redoubtable Mrs. Gladys Lightner, arms crossed sternly over her chest. Maxi could feel Carla Ochoa visibly shrink into herself. With a small nudge, she urged the woman forward.

"Roberto is home, *por favor?*" she asked Mrs. Lightner tentatively.

"No, Roberto is not home, *por favor,*" the woman mocked in singsong, her face contorted with contempt. "And you're no help, Carla, disappearing like that. Where the hell have you been?"

She leveled her gaze squarely at Mrs. Ochoa and spoke as if Maxi wasn't standing next to her. Though it had been three or four years ago, Maxi figured that the woman surely remembered the incident with her dog.

"I ask . . . I ask Mrs. Poole to help me," Carla stammered.

"Ms. Poole," Maxi corrected. "Maxi." She extended a hand to Gladys Lightner.

Ignoring her, Mrs. Lightner said to her housekeeper, "Come in, Carla."

"I'd like to help," Maxi offered, as the woman turned abruptly to enter her house.

"There's nothing you can do," Mrs. Lightner retorted with a sideways look, tossing the words crisply over her shoulder.

Gladys Lightner went into her foyer with Carla Ochoa following behind, and Maxi closing the door after them. Mrs. Lightner glanced behind her, saw that both women were inside, and let out an exaggerated sigh of annoyance. The three continued on through the house and into a huge, brightly lit stainless steel kitchen that dazzled. Mrs. Lightner led the way through the kitchen into a spacious family room and seated herself on a flowered couch. Carla sat opposite her, and, uninvited, Maxi sat too.

"Ms. Poole," Gladys Lightner began, "let me say right at the outset, no police."

"That's not possible, Mrs. Lightner. It's been over an hour now, and—"

"No police," Gladys Lightner interrupted, pointing a long, bony, red-tipped index finger directly at the spot between Maxi's eyes.

"Perhaps you don't understand, Mrs. Lightner," Maxi responded evenly, suppressing an urge to grab the woman's finger and give it a hardy twist. "A child is missing, and that takes priority over any other consideration. I'm amazed, and appalled in fact, that you haven't called the authorities yet."

"Do you mind telling me what business this is of yours?"

"Not at all. It's my business as a concerned citizen. Don't you care that this little boy is missing, Mrs. Lightner?"

"We're not calling in the police," she reiterated. "We're going to wait until my husband, Councilman Lightner, comes home. He'll know what to do."

Maxi gave the woman an I-don't-believe-this shake of the head and pulled her cell phone out of her purse. Flipping it open, she punched in a digit that speed-dialed the number for Detective Marcus Jorgan.

"LAPD—Jorgan," he answered. Big stroke of luck, he actually happened to be in the squad room.

"Hi, Marc, it's Maxi. We have a missing child here—a two-year-old boy." She went on to give him the sketchy details she had.

She listened to him for a beat, then looked up at Mrs. Lightner. "He needs your address," she said. When the woman offered nothing, she asked her again. "What number is this on Beverly Glen, Mrs. Lightner?"

Gladys Lightner's response was to get up from the couch and angrily huff over to a black granite-topped bar at the far side of the room. She went behind the counter, stooped to open a small refrigerator, pulled out a bottle of water, uncapped it, took a long sip, and slammed it down on the stone top.

"Mrs. Lightner isn't cooperating, Marc, for whatever reason," Maxi said into her phone.

She was pretty sure she knew the reason. If and when the press got hold of this, and if Carla Ochoa was in fact in the country illegally, L.A. city councilman Conrad Lightner would find himself in a firestorm of bad publicity. Rumor had it that he was going to make a run for mayor. Employing undocumented help at home would nip that aspiration before it got off the glide path.

"Marc, you know my house on Beverly Glen. The Lightners are five doors south on the same side of the street. I'm there now. What? Oh, of course Lightner's address would be in the public record. Anyway," she couldn't resist saying out loud so the abusive Gladys Lightner could hear, "when you get to the Glen you can't miss it—it's the only house on the street that looks like a stone fortress from a Harry Potter movie, and it's lit up like a night shoot."

The detective asked Maxi if she would still be in the house when he and his partner got there.

"I'd like to be," she said, "but I'm not popular here, if you get my drift. I'll probably be on the street out front. Bye, Marc."

As Maxi dropped the phone into her jacket pocket, Gladys Lightner pronounced icily, "So, do you have your story now, Ms. News Vulture?"

"No, ma'am," Maxi said. "I'll get it when my camera crew arrives."

"Get out of my house," the fuming Lightner threw back, her cheeks blossoming into two bright red welts. "And Carla, you're fired. I want you out of here by morning."

The already distraught Carla Ochoa let out a wrenching sob. Maxi's heart was breaking for the woman, this mother whose child was missing, and who was being thrown out on the street. She could guess what Gladys Lightner was thinking—threatened with exposure of her housekeeper's legality status, the woman figured that it would go better for her and her husband if Mrs. Ochoa were an *ex*-employee. She could make up something later about what she knew and when she knew it.

"You can come and stay with me until you get yourself settled somewhere," she heard herself saying to the Ochoa woman, who looked at her in disbelief.

"Don't worry, Carla," she said. "I have a small guest room. You're welcome to it until you find another job. Roberto too, of course, when he comes home."

Maxi took one of her cards out of her purse, scribbled her home number on it, handed it to Mrs. Ochoa, then headed for the entrance foyer.

"Bitch!" Lightner muttered, loud enough to be heard as Maxi was easing herself out of the hand-carved front doors.

That stopped her. With a hand on the polished brass door handle, Maxi turned to face Gladys Lightner. "You'd better let Detective Jorgan in when he gets here, Mrs. Lightner," she said. "I wouldn't force him to swear out a warrant if I were you. That would *really* reflect badly on your husband. And you can bet that I'll put *that* on the news."

With a parting look at the stricken housekeeper, she said, "Call me, Carla," and let herself out the door.

Grateful that the pedestrian door opened from the inside and allowed her to get off the property without further confrontation, Maxi took out her cell phone again and punched in the direct-dial number for the Channel Six desk.

"Riley," she said when the nightside assignment editor answered. "It's Maxi. I need a crew ASAP."

She told him why, and, glancing up at the number carved into one of the stone stanchions astride the iron gates, she gave him the Lightners' street address.

"Marc Jorgan from Robbery-Homicide should be here within thirty minutes—I'm not sure who he'll be partnered with, but they're coming from Parker Center. Can you bust a crew out here by then?"

A short pause, then, "Good, I'll be here."

She snapped her phone shut and waited at the curb, the devil winds whipping her clothes around her and howling past, helter-skelter, on their angry flight over the Mulholland ridge and down into the L.A. Basin.

8

Councilman Conrad Lightner turned into the now familiar narrow alley off Vine Street south of Hollywood Boulevard. He'd called in advance on his cell phone, asked if he could schedule a "haircut." "Sure," said Marilyn, or Monroe, one of the two sisters who ran the "salon." Sisters? Maybe, maybe not, but either one was fine with him. Two delectable young black women with big, streaked-blond hair who didn't talk a lot, didn't take long, and didn't charge that much. Considering.

Bypassing the back side of a scarred, dirty, faded pink stucco building with the two "client parking spaces," as the girls called them, each marked M&M in bold hot pink spray paint on the cracked, grimy asphalt, he was pleased to see that the girls had no other clients at the moment. Unless other johns eschewed the obvious parking spaces just as he did—there was always that possibility. He drove farther down the alley and pulled his Lexus up flush against a filthy, reeking Dumpster behind a dry cleaner's, which was closed now. Good that he was in his personal car; he would never bring his city vehicle here. Getting out of the Lexus, he was hit with the acrid smell of dust mixed with rotting food and soured urine, so strong it couldn't be obliterated by the thirsty Santa Ana winds.

A police officer he knew, in relating a hilarious incident involving a very dumb perp, had described these two working girls who were part of the story and where they operated—off an alley in the flats of old Hollywood, in a dump with a back door and the spray-painted parking spots. Con Lightner had long forgotten what the cop's story was about, but he couldn't stop fantasizing about Marilyn and Monroe. Until one day he decided to go see for himself.

Lightner walked, slunk really, head down, coat collar up against the wind, back to the pink building. He opened the battered metal rear door, walked up the creaky flight of stairs, and made his way down the dank corridor to the front entrance of the sisters' apartment. The actor Hugh Grant was nailed with a hooker just three blocks from here, he was thinking. Hugh Grant went on *The Tonight Show* and joked about it, then became an even bigger star than he was before; Con Lightner knew that if *he* were caught it would finish him. He was acutely aware that he was putting himself in great danger of being exposed in this seedy place, performing illegal acts. Coming here terrified him every time. A shrink would tell him that was part of the excitement, the risk of discovery. Lightner didn't think so—he just wanted to get laid.

In answer to his knock, one of the sisters looked through the peephole and he gave a little wave. Opening the door with a flourish, she fairly sang, "Well, hello-o-o, Councilman," flashing a gleaming, toothy smile that showed a wide strip of dark pink gums. He wished these two wouldn't call him "Councilman," even when there was nobody else around.

"Monroe?" he ventured. Last time he'd guessed Marilyn, and he was wrong. Not that they looked that much alike—he just never remembered which one was which.

"I'm Marilyn," she said, and giggled. "Monroe is busy." With a jerk of her voluminous, springy curls, she indicated a closed door on the left, which he remembered from previous occasions to be Monroe's room.

She took his hand and ushered him through the other door off what was the tiny apartment's living room, the M&M "reception area," they called it. Into Marilyn's room. One of these days, he always promised himself, he was going to take them up on their offer of a twofer at their economy price. He always promised himself that before sex; after sex, he always no longer gave a damn.

As usual, he left his clothes on. Also as usual, he unfastened his belt, lowered his zipper, and dropped down into the stained, flower-printed chintz-covered chair in the corner of the room. As usual, it was quick. No foreplay. And again, as usual, he got up, zipped up, and laid three twenties on the rickety dresser while Marilyn opened the door to make sure the coast was clear for him, and he scooted out of there.

Damn, this is stupid, he thought, his usual self-recrimination after the fact. He was risking all, and for what? It wasn't even that good. Lately he'd taken to dusting off an old fantasy, having to do with him bounding off the football field at Washington High in Lancaster out in Southern California's high desert country where he grew up, having just scored the winning touchdown, and having one of the hot, popular cheerleaders—he couldn't remember their names either—put her arm around him and go off with him. To a motel near campus.

Not that that had ever happened in real life. Oh, he was on the varsity squad, all right, but he hardly ever got in the game, he never scored the winning touchdown, and he never, ever got the girl. That's why it was a fantasy, even back then.

Car keys in hand, he lumbered down the back staircase and up the alley to his car, zapped it open, and quickly wedged himself under the wheel. Glancing nervously behind him, he fired up the big Lexus and carefully maneuvered out of the narrow alleyway. Took a left on Morningside Court, then a right on Sunset, and headed west toward Beverly Glen, listening to the unsettling devil winds whistling across the windshield.

*   *   *

Maxi was staked out on the sidewalk in front of the Lightner estate. Most of the time in television news, when you think you've got an exclusive, you don't. Most of the time your hungry competitors get wind of what you've uncovered, from police scanners, from a disgruntled or disloyal tipster at your own station, from the news gods, from wherever. But damned if they didn't always show up, Maxi lamented, as she watched the big red Channel Seven live truck careen around the corner onto Beverly Glen, followed a few minutes later by Channel Four's white news van, then more vehicles—television, radio, print, even stringer Rosie Rosenberg on his garish flame-decorated silver Harley. And Tom McCartney in his black Humvee, acknowledged star of the nightside. No tabloids, at least—this missing two-year-old wasn't national news. Yet.

Maxi's own crew had arrived first. Now she stood in front of the Lightners' gates with microphone in hand and her shooter standing next to her, camera hoisted on his shoulder. They'd already shot exteriors, and were set to grab shots of Detective Marcus Jorgan and his partner as they approached the house and entered the property. Those might be all the visuals she'd get, Maxi knew, over which she would voice the story for the Eleven O'clock News.

Her cameraman was called Jersey—not because he came from New Jersey, though most people assumed he did. His name was James Jersey. Newsies on the street started calling him "Jersey Jim" years ago, and somewhere between then and now it got shortened to Jersey. He was a veteran shooter, in his middle forties, tall and angular, and he was quiet, efficient, and fast. An added bonus, he also happened to be a nice guy. Jersey was among the small coterie of camerapersons that Maxi was always grateful to draw.

An unmarked black Ford Crown Victoria, recognizable as a police vehicle by most seasoned journalists, pulled up on the opposite side of the street a few houses down. Jersey rolled tape as Detective Jorgan emerged from the driver's side, his partner from the passenger side, and together the detectives crossed the street and headed toward the Lightners' front gates. As they brushed past the Channel Six camera, Maxi said into her microphone, "Detective Jorgan, what do you know about the missing child?" then popped the mike under Marc Jorgan's chin.

She already knew what Jorgan knew because she was the one who'd told him. But to dress up the on-air story she needed some "sound"—otherwise the piece would have to air with only Maxi's voice-over.

"Not very much, Maxi," Jorgan said into the mike. "Only that a child is missing—a child who lives in this house."

"City Councilman Conrad Lightner's house."

"Yes, this is Councilman Lightner's house," Jorgan said. "We'll know more after we talk to the residents inside."

With that, the detective turned away from Maxi and punched a knuckle into a high-tech doorbell mounted on the ornate stone post to the left of the gates. Neither he nor his partner spoke to any of the other reporters who were shouting questions at them, which Maxi considered her due since she had called in the missing person report to him. She'd worked with Marc Jorgan several times before on cases, and this was a professional quid pro quo. She couldn't stop the rest of her colleagues from pouncing on her story, but she might have the only sound, unless the detectives gave a briefing when they came out.

Or unless Conrad Lightner came home.

And he did.

Councilman Lightner's gleaming Lexus pulled up through the crowd of media at his gates, and he made the mistake of rolling down his window to ask the mob that was trampling all over his begonias what the hell was going on. Lights came on, cameras rolled, flashbulbs popped, and reporters staged a food frenzy yelling questions at the man.

"Whose child is missing?" "What do you think happened here, Councilman?" "How could someone get through these gates and into your house without being detected?" "Doesn't this have to be an inside job?"

Then Rosie, the overweight stringer in the baggy white shorts with the orange flames all over them, his camera rolling and squared directly on Conrad Lightner's face, shouted, "Where were you tonight, Councilman? There was no answer at your office a while ago."

When Lightner just looked at him, blinking in the bright lights, Rosie pressed. Almost as if trying to help him. That was Rosie. "Did you go out to dinner?" he asked. Still rolling. And in the two-second lull, the stringer gamboled right on up to the driver's side door of Lightner's car, wielding his state-of-the-art Panasonic DVCpro minicam and a handheld microphone, stuck the mike in the councilman's face through the open window, and said again, innocently enough, "Did you just come from dinner somewhere, sir?"

The rest of the newsies just watched, and rolled, and marveled. They were first of all amazed at Rosie's newfound cojones, thrusting himself into the forefront like that, then doubly intrigued by Councilman Lightner's reaction. Mute. Giving them deer-in-the-headlights.

Lightner had apparently punched a zapper in his car, because the big gates started slowly parting outward, causing a few of the newsies to skitter backwards out of harm's way, and the councilman's sedan cruised inside the gates and on into the four-car garage. At almost the same time the pedestrian door buzzed and the detectives walked onto the property. On all of them, cameras were rolling.

Maxi had led the Eleven with her live shot from in front of the Lightners' house. She'd gone for two minutes fourteen, rolling in sound on tape from Detective Marc Jorgan going onto the property, then tape of the seemingly dazed councilman arriving at the estate, not in his comped city ride but in an expensive gold luxury car, then more words from the detective when he and his partner had come out of the house. The partner's name, supplied by Riley on the newsroom desk, who'd done the legwork, was Detective Remo Sanchez. A new partner for Jorgan since his last partner had moved to Vice. Again, Jorgan had not said much, but again, he'd said it to Maxi Poole. Understandable to the rest of them—Detective Marcus Jorgan was a source whom Maxi had cultivated.

"We're calling in the FBI on this case," he'd commented briefly into her microphone. And nothing more was seen nor heard from the family inside. But Maxi broke the story, she owned it, and she'd had the lead on the Eleven.

That should have made her feel good, but it didn't. She was worried about the little boy and heartsick for his mother. After leaving the station earlier, off for the night, she'd come home to this breaking news story that had literally turned up in her own front yard. A child gone missing, but at this point the councilman was the story as much as the boy. Everyone was on top of this one, or would be, and unless little Roberto Ochoa was found very soon and his disappearance explained, it was going to expand and intensify. That's what news stories did, and by the time it was over, there was no telling who'd be left standing.

The detectives were gone; the newsies had all fed in and were pulling out.

"Jump in the van, Maxi," Jersey said. "I'll pack up, and run you home."

"Thanks, Jersey—I'm just up the street; I can walk."

"No. Get in. I'm going to drop you, and I'll wait until you get inside and lock your door," her cameraman insisted. Looking out for her. Someone had evidently gotten inside this neighboring house earlier tonight and snatched a child.

While Jersey finished cramming gear into the rear compartment of the live truck, Maxi sat in the front passenger seat and waited. Looking idly out at the Lightner estate, feeling mildly depressed, unsettled, her mood exacerbated by the roaring winds. A movement from a downstairs window caught her eye. Squinting, she could make out the blue Dodgers sweatshirt. Carla Ochoa. She was watching Maxi.

Lowering the window, Maxi stuck her head out of the van, waved to the woman, and made a gesture like she was dialing a telephone then holding it to her ear. "Call me," she mouthed. Reinforcing her invitation to take her in, at least for now. She needed to do something to ease this woman's pain.

Jersey jumped into the driver's seat and slammed the door shut, buckled up, fired up the engine, made a screeching U-turn on Beverly Glen, and rolled up the hill toward Maxi's house. She was feeling better.

When she walked through her front door Yukon came bounding to greet her, and she heard her phone ringing. Pausing for just a beat to ruffle the big dog's silky neck, she hustled into the kitchen with Yuke on her heels, switched on the overhead light, and grabbed the phone. It was Mrs. Ochoa, crying.

"Yes, Carla, of course I meant the invitation to stay with me," Maxi said. "The police are looking for Roberto. Get some sleep. In the morning, pack up all your things. I'll pick you up, and we'll bring everything up here. Early, because I have to get to work, okay? I'll be out in front of the Lightners' house at seven o'clock."

"Mrs. Lightner is very angry with me, because—"

"Shame on her, Carla," Maxi interrupted. "She should be hugging you and helping you. Go in your room, close the door, say some prayers for Roberto, and try to sleep. Never mind Mrs. Lightner. You'll be out of there tomorrow."

She said good-bye and hung up, and almost immediately, the phone rang again. "Yes?" she said, figuring Mrs. Ochoa had forgotten to ask her something.

"Hi there," a familiar voice responded, and Maxi felt her heart lurch. She carried the phone over to the built-in kitchen desk, pulled out the chair, and dropped into it.

"Richard!"

Richard Winningham was the station's senior correspondent,

currently on assignment in Iraq. In television news, the title of senior correspondent has nothing to do with how long a reporter has been on staff; in fact, Winningham had been at the station for only a few months. But he'd earned high marks at the UGN-owned station in New York as their crime reporter, and Pete Capra had hired him away with a hefty raise and the new title and had him transferred to Southern California. When terrorist tensions continued to mount, Capra assigned him to cover the Middle East for Channel Six.

"It's nice to get you instead of your voice mail," Richard said, a smile in his voice. Between the time difference and their mutually crammed schedules, it was rare when the two connected voice-to-voice.

Maxi had been pretty much romantically unencumbered, as she liked to put it, since the end of her marriage more than a year ago. She and Winningham had become close when he saved her life while she was covering the murder of a well-known Hollywood actor. The actor just happened to be Maxi's ex-husband, which prompted her to get much more deeply involved in the investigation than was journalistically ethical. Or healthy, as it turned out. While a deranged woman held her hostage at knife-point, Richard and Pete Capra had managed to find her with no time to spare and get her to safety. Since then, Maxi had considered Richard Winningham to be her very good friend. And maybe her long-distance semi-significant other, since there had been major chemistry between the two of them from the get-go. But they both knew that in this business an office romance almost always turns out to be a very bad idea. That and the fact that the man was two continents away.

"How are you, Richard?" she asked, hearing a bit of tremolo in her own voice. Her dog must have heard it too; from where he'd settled on the floor at her feet, Yukon stood up and let out a sharp bark, which Richard heard.

"Hey, tell Yuke I said hello," he said. "And that I miss him."

"We both miss you," Maxi returned.

"Me too you, kiddo."

Exchanging those kinds of mild endearments was pretty much the heaviest it got between them.

Well, except once. On the day after Christmas last year. Actually, the night after Christmas. The night before Richard was leaving for Israel on assignment.

Oh yes, Maxi remembered that last night she saw him. Every detail. In fact, she had mentally replayed the whole scenario many times. She wondered if he ever did, or if that was just a girl thing. It started with a candlelit dinner at a romantic restaurant on Beverly Boulevard. At a table tucked in a corner of its heated outside patio lined with ficus trees studded with tiny white lights. Over a heady bottle of French Merlot. She didn't have a story for the Eleven that night, and he had a flight out to Tel Aviv in the morning. Those few hours were stolen, and all theirs to enjoy each other.

And they did. It was explosive, which hugely surprised them both.

Or not. Thinking back on it even now gave Maxi stirrings in all the usual places.

"Tell me you've got some time off and I'll be seeing you. Or that Capra is reassigning you home," she said to him.

"In my dreams, Maxi."

In mine too, she thought.

Richard broke the spell. Seems one of them always did. "So what's this about the graveyard shift?"

"You heard?"

"Kriegel e-mailed me." Doug Kriegel was the business editor at Channel Six, and a friend to both.

"I still can't believe it," she told him.

"Tell me everything."

She did. And finished her abbreviated highlight reel with, "So my life is over."

"It better not be," Richard said. "I haven't had nearly enough of it yet."

"Enough of *my* life?"

"Yeah, enough of your life."

"Well . . . so . . . when am I going to see you?"

"Nothing's scheduled right now, but you know I'll get there."

"Sooner or later . . ."

"Sometime. We need to drink another bottle of that excellent Merlot. What year was that?"

Code for "we need to have sex again"? Maxi wondered. She hoped so. She wanted a lot more than wine with Richard Winningham. But she knew her quirky self well enough to realize that it could be just because, for several reasons, the man was unavailable.

9

Friday morning, twenty to seven. Tom McCartney had just gotten home from work. He'd shot an overdose outside the Anaconda, a trendy club on the Sunset Strip that featured booming metal, watered-down drinks, and teenagers with phony IDs passing around illegal street drugs made up of who-knew-what components. Tipped by a bartender he knew at a nearby club who'd told him some kid was in convulsions on the sidewalk in front of the Anaconda, he'd sped to the scene and caught most of the action. A young guy sprawled out on the pavement, surrounded by his teen posse and a growing crowd of onlookers. The paramedics skidding to the curb, loading the patient into the LAFD van, slamming the back doors, and screeching off. McCartney got it all on tape. In follow-up phone calls he'd found out that the boy, just seventeen, was DOA at Cedars.

Drugs. The senseless killer. Kids who hadn't even started their lives yet, giving it all up in the quest for a high that was kickier than yesterday's. Urban youngsters pushing, pushing, pushing the edge, and some of them going over. McCartney saw it happen all the time, from the wealthy Westside to East L.A. and down to the South Central ghetto. He hated and feared it, but he profoundly understood it.

Because he could not have gotten through last night without the pills.

He'd been clean for a couple of weeks, but fell off last Wednesday when they pulled a headless floater out of Ballona Creek just before midnight and the sight and the stench and the degradation of the scene he shot gave him a searing migraine headache. So he took four Vikes when he got home in the morning just to get to sleep. Then six more when he woke up at around five o'clock. When he went out into the field that night he took his stash with him, and by midnight he was semi-zonked. And he'd pretty much stayed that way until last night.

But at least this time he'd kept his hands off the vodka bottle. What the hell, one out of two's not bad, right?

This episode had turned out to be manageable. Didn't miss any work. Didn't wake up in Singapore with a four-day growth of beard. And maybe one of these days he would kick the tabs for good. He knew he shouldn't keep them in the apartment, but he'd tried flushing them a few times and had severe episodes of cluster migraines that would send him up the walls, waiting through the night for a pharmacy to open.

Back then he didn't dare use the all-night drugstores—they were more apt to spot something suspicious about his own scribbled handwriting on the sheet from the prescription pads he'd managed to steal. And to lessen the risk of a pharmacist trying to put a call through to the fictitious doctor whose name he'd faked, he never used the same drugstore twice, and he never wrote script for more than thirty tablets at a time.

That was what he did until he found his contact. Smithie. A huge black 'banger with a massive shaved head, one gleaming gold tooth in front, a preference for loose sweatpants and billowing yellow Lakers shirts, and prominent black-rimmed glasses with thick, rose-tinted lenses. Smithie got him as much Vicodin as he wanted, and nothing changed hands except Benjamins.

The problem, as McCartney saw it, was that he was prone to these violent, searing headaches, and Vicodin was the only painkiller he'd found that was able to knock them out. But unlike occasional users, for him it took increasingly more and more of the chunky white pills to do the job. Then by the time the pain was gone, he'd find himself just liking the pills again. Loving the pills. Needing them.

He made a promise to himself—he wouldn't take any at all today. It was fairly certain that once he'd made up his mind, made that commitment to himself and said it out loud about ten times over, he would be able to summon the discipline to stick to it. For a while, at least. A decapitation knocked him off the wagon, and a drug OD reeled him back in. Scared him straight. He'd be fine. This time.

McCartney's home dubbing equipment had capacity to run off just one tape at a time, so when he needed quantity, which was the case for most of the stories he shot, a home copy job took too long. Time was king in television news. He'd had the "Anaconda Club OD" cassette duplicated to six copies at a twenty-four-hour dubbing house on Highland Avenue that had rows and rows of machines going simultaneously, and Two, Four, Five, and Thirteen had bought his exclusive for their morning news.

He knew that Pete Capra wouldn't buy it; he hadn't even offered it to him. Capra wouldn't exploit an underaged kid on television news, a rarity among editors. The story wasn't particularly unusual in La-La Land, but the pictures were dramatic. That's all most of the stations wanted these days—screaming visuals. He knew most of them would go ape over a youngster dying on the sidewalk on the teeming, glitzy Sunset Strip. Capra was different. The majority of news outlets in the L.A. market were run by carny barkers now. Capra was a throwback. He was a journalist. Even rarer, he was a journalist with ethics.

McCartney didn't share Capra's compunction. Nor did he feel any real sadness for this teenager. He was just glad that it wasn't him, and pleased that he'd gotten some marketable footage. After making the rounds with the story, he'd driven over the hill to

Channel Six in Burbank and dropped off Pete Capra's two cassettes from MacArthur Park. In all, a profitable shift.

He planned to do his morning workout, shower, then grab some sleep. When he woke up in late afternoon he'd get dressed, have "breakfast," then scoot over to his bank branch, deposit his checks, do some errands. Come home, freshen up, go back out to work. His usual daily ritual. McCartney was a man of habits, and his habits were largely spartan—if you didn't count the times when he lapsed and got into a baggie of pills, like this week, or fell into a bottle of Smirnoff. Or both. He told himself, again, that this little episode of Vike was just to blunt the pain of the migraines he'd had for three days and to prevent more of them from coming on. And it was over now.

In his office, the red light on his phone was blinking. He dropped his backpack on the floor next to his computer setup and sat down in his desk chair to retrieve his messages. Just two of them—it was still early. One from a newswriter at Channel Thirteen who was working on his Anaconda OD story, asking for a couple of identifiers for subjects on his tape. He returned that call first. Checked his notes, supplied the names of the two paramedics at the scene, and apologized for not listing them on his shot sheet.

The other was a return call from Phil Strykker, longtime news producer at KBAY-TV, an independent station in San Francisco. When McCartney had Googled Pete Capra yesterday morning he'd learned that before coming to Southern California thirteen years ago Capra had been a reporter up at KBAY. Not being network-owned, KBAY contracted with CNN for its world news coverage, so McCartney had fed reports from time to time to the station's news division. He'd gotten to know Phil Strykker, who had taken in most of his feeds, and with whom he'd worked a few times while covering stories for CNN up in the Bay Area, and he'd put in a call to him yesterday. McCartney punched in the number that Strykker had left. Evidently the producer still worked the morning shift—he picked up.

The two did a little catching up, then McCartney asked Strykker what he remembered about a reporter who'd worked there named Peter Capra. There was a pause, and McCartney could picture the newsman sitting at his cluttered desk in a crisp white shirt and tie, running a hand through his neatly clipped salt-and-pepper beard.

Strykker told him that Capra had been a terrific reporter, but as he remembered it, he'd been asked to leave KBAY because he seemed to be obsessed with a story he'd been covering about an alleged serial killer who hung out in Golden Gate Park who'd had the Bay Area terrified for a time, a man who killed with cyanide. They never caught the killer, but Capra wouldn't leave it alone, Strykker said—he would not move on to other stories, or didn't seem able to. Rumor had it that the news director had finally told Capra he needed to get some therapy for this unhealthy preoccupation, and Pete and the station came to a mutual parting of the ways. Strykker said the last he'd heard, Capra had packed up his family and moved south.

Tom McCartney made a mental note to look into the San Francisco serial killer story that had seemingly run Pete Capra and his family out of the Bay Area.

10

Friday morning, seven o'clock, at the Lightner house on Beverly Glen. When Carla Ochoa opened the front door, Maxi was taken aback to see her looking ashen, dazed, red-eyed, and even more distraught than she had been the night before.

"Carla! What's *wrong?*" she asked.

The woman said nothing, just looked at Maxi as if she couldn't figure out who she was.

Maxi silently answered her own question: *Everything* was wrong. Carla Ochoa's little boy was still missing. There had been no further news. Updates on the child's disappearance had peppered the wires since she'd broken the story on the Eleven O'clock News last night, but by this morning the police still had nothing concrete to go on, or so stated their advisories.

As they'd planned, Maxi had come to take Mrs. Ochoa up the street to her own house. More important, she was taking the woman from this hostile environment to a safe haven so she could focus on the search for her son. The toddler had been missing for twelve hours now, all through a cold and blustery January night, as wintry as it gets in Southern California when the eerie Santa Ana winds make the ubiquitous urban coyotes emit quavering howls, suggesting primitive danger.

Maxi had parked her beat-up Chevy Blazer at the curb in front of the Lightners' gate, the fifteen-year-old heap that was her second car, backup wheels to get her to work whenever her nearly-as-old Corvette wouldn't start, and roomier than the 'Vette when hauling was required. Giving Carla a hug as she went inside, she asked, "Did you get any sleep?"

"I . . . I don't know." The housekeeper's faint, shaky reply.

The little Ochoa family's personal belongings were stacked in piles on a bench and in a few boxes on the floor of the Georgian villa's marble entry foyer. The meager accumulation of neat and clean items told Maxi that Carla Ochoa took good care of her things. That suggested that the woman took good care of her son.

"Come on, Carla," Maxi said, "let's get your stuff out of here."

The two made several trips down the walkway through the gilded wrought iron gates and out to the dented Blazer, carrying clothes, boxes, and a small collection of toys and piling them into the rear of the truck.

As they walked, Maxi went over the ground rules with Carla: The woman was welcome to stay in her guest room, but she would not be working for her. Maxi didn't need household help, she explained. Her house was small, there was just herself and Yukon, and there was not much upkeep required. She took her clothes to the dry cleaner, she said, and tossed her laundry as needed into the stacked washer/dryer combo on the small service porch out back. And she had a professional cleaning crew come in for a few hours twice a month to do the heavy work.

Mrs. Ochoa didn't respond. Her brown eyes looked glazed. Maxi realized that the woman hadn't heard a word she'd said. Putting a hand on her shoulder, she felt tremors deep within her body. Her left eye had developed a tic.

"Carla?" she said.

"I will help you." In a voice weak and scratchy.

"No, that's not necessary, Carla. I can't pay you. Don't worry about that."

Maxi didn't broach the question of the woman's legality.

There was no reason for her to know Mrs. Ochoa's status. She didn't want to know.

"I'll help you," the housekeeper repeated.

Maxi feared that Carla might be in shock. But taking her to emergency at UCLA Medical Center, the nearest hospital, would bring in another layer of bureaucracy and could heighten her despair. Talking to her might help, she thought. She asked about Roberto. What he'd been wearing yesterday. Carla mumbled that he didn't have any of his toys with him, or his favorite picture books. Not even his little blankie, she said—he always kept his blankie with him. "He will be so frightened, and maybe hungry, and very cold," the mother lamented, and tears spilled over her cheeks.

Maxi kept talking as they worked, kept trying to ease her anxiety. Carla said that the phone in the Lightner house had rung several times the night before, and that Mrs. Lightner had become very angry each time it did. It would have been the detectives, the LAPD's latent-print technicians, a gang of reporters, many diverse people and agencies with an interest in the case, Maxi knew. It was Mr. Lightner who'd answered all the calls from the kitchen phone, Carla said, and she'd come out of her room and stood nearby each time she heard the phone ring, hoping it would be news of Roberto. There had been none. But the calls had kept coming.

She kept reiterating that Mrs. Lightner had been very furious with her. Odd behavior, Gladys Lightner's, even given her attempts to squelch any ensuing negative publicity, Maxi thought but didn't say. When the two finished packing up the Blazer, Carla said she needed to leave a note for Mr. Lightner to let him know where she'd be if there was news about Roberto.

"Mr. Lightner? Not *Mrs.* Lightner?" Maxi queried.

"*El Sr. Lightner está a cargo,*" she said. Mr. Lightner is in charge. That was a surprise to Maxi.

And the Lightners owed her a week's pay, Carla said. "Plus

severance pay?" Maxi asked. The woman shrugged, and wept some more.

It was going on eight o'clock. They could hear morning sounds coming from upstairs. That was Mr. Lightner, Carla said—he would be getting ready to go to work downtown.

Carla sat at the kitchen table with a writing tablet and a pen, laboriously printing out a note in English to Councilman Lightner. Her hand was trembling. Maxi helped by writing in her own address up the street on Beverly Glen, along with her home phone number. That's when they heard the howl. A man's throaty wail. Maxi bolted out of the chair, across the kitchen, and up the center stairs, with Carla Ochoa behind her.

"What is it?" Maxi yelled, fearing the worst. Fearing for Roberto.

From the landing at the head of the stairs she heard low cries now, and she traced the sounds to one of the bedrooms.

"Is Mrs. Lightner's room." Carla was panting.

"The Lightners have separate bedrooms?" Maxi threw behind her, still running.

"Sí. Two bedrooms," huffed Mrs. Ochoa.

Bounding through the open door of the master suite where the cries were coming from, Maxi stopped short just inside. Gladys Lightner, in a colorful purple silk dressing gown, purple high-heeled feathered slippers, and with a gaping wound in her chest, lay on the floor in front of an antique writing desk in a pool of blood. Councilman Conrad Lightner stood over her, his white dress shirt stained, and his two hands, held out to his sides, smeared with blood.

11

Pete Capra, back in his office after the morning meeting, was doing the usual—fielding phone calls, assigning reporters, checking rundowns, putting out fires—but his mind was on one of the field tapes from MacArthur Park that Tom McCartney had dropped off at the station that morning. He'd run it half a dozen times, each time freezing the frame on the face that looked so familiar to him—the same face he thought he'd seen in the stringer's tape shot outside the grungy park restroom when they'd busted that television actor last week.

This latest tape seemed to confirm to Capra that he was right. Maybe. At the very least, the face he'd iso'd sure looked like the suspect in question. More precisely, it looked like the man would probably look after having aged thirteen years.

Back when he was a general assignment reporter for an independent station in San Francisco, before the television news business generated big bucks for stations and networks, back when they let you take weeks, even months, to investigate a story, he covered an elusive serial murderer whom the press had dubbed the "walk-in killer" because he invaded homes all over the Bay Area seemingly with little difficulty. He walked through back doors and sliders, crawled into windows and louvers, over transoms, even through pet doors—if there was a way, he got himself in. Once inside, he sometimes ransacked, sometimes raped, and always murdered. With cyanide. A grade-A sicko.

And Capra had seen his face. Once.

At least he thought he had.

He was in San Francisco's Mission district interviewing one of the perp's near-victims who had escaped the killer—a private duty nurse who had just gotten home from work when the intruder hoisted himself through a side window of her ground-floor apartment. He was loping down the hallway toward her, in black jeans and a black T-shirt, his metal murder kit in hand, when she'd caught a glimpse of him—this before quickly ducking into her bedroom and throwing the deadbolt. Locked inside, she picked up the phone and called 911.

The guy took off. But she was one of only two intended victims who had seen him clearly and lived to tell about it. Jeannine See. Late twenties, red-haired, gutsy, and terrified. She'd helped the SFPD detectives every way she could, including talking down a description of the would-be assailant to a department sketch artist for a composite drawing. But to this day, and after five more murders ascribed to him over the following year, they never did catch up with the man, a killer whose bizarre murder weapon was cyanide.

Peter Capra was at Jeannine See's apartment one afternoon, doing an interview with her after the composite sketch had hit the airwaves and the newspapers. The two were sipping coffee and talking at a game table in See's living room in front of a big bay window that looked out on Portola Street. No camera that day—this was a fact-finding interview to see if she had recalled anything new about the suspect that would warrant requesting a crew for a follow-up story.

He'd tossed out a question, and she'd turned to the window as if to gather her thoughts. And gasped. And got up so fast that she knocked her chair over backwards and scurried away from the window.

"What?" Capra had asked, startled, still seated across the table.

"It's him," she'd breathed, "the man who was in here. He's standing out there."

Capra turned and looked out the window. There on the sidewalk stood a man who resembled the composite drawing his station had carried on the news, down to the shaggy red mustache. Damn, he'd thought at the time, why didn't he have a camera crew with him? When the man spotted the reporter looking out at him, he did something that stunned Pete Capra—he waved! Actually waved to him before backing off down the street. Capra had replayed that one gesture in his mind at least a thousand times.

Jeannine See had turned white. She stood leaning against the inside wall out of the window's line of sight, bent over, clutching both arms around her stomach and cowering. Capra could see her chin trembling in profile. She was absolutely sure it was the same man, she'd said, the man who had probably murdered four women and had come very close to killing her. He was even dressed in the same clothes. Black jeans, a black T-shirt with the left short sleeve rolled up over what looked to be a pack of cigarettes, dirty gray-and-white running shoes, she had no idea what brand. But she'd identified a tattoo on his upper left arm this time. Said she was able to see a corner of it from the window. She'd first caught such a fleeting glimpse of the tat—a dark ink-blue anchor with a green-and-red snake wound around it—when the man was "this close" in her own hallway, swinging his arms, that in her agitated state she'd forgotten about it when she'd talked to the forensic sketch artist. When she saw the man that second time, she saw part of the tattoo again, and it brought to mind the whole emblem. Yes, it was him, she'd said, there was no question. Obviously back at her apartment to try again. And she moved out that afternoon.

The SFPD sketch artist added the anchor/snake tattoo to the man's composite drawing, and the new top was the lead on the news all over the Bay Area that night. "Walk-in killer tries to get at nurse again—would-be victim identifies tattoo!" Still, they'd never nailed him.

But they had come close. Citizens had reported a man of the suspect's description three different times, complete with the anchor/snake tattoo on his left arm just beneath the rolled-up sleeve of his black T-shirt. Each time in sprawling Golden Gate Park, once inside the men's restroom and twice nearby. Two of the witnesses had said that the man attracted their attention because he wasn't doing anything, wasn't going anywhere, was just standing around, hanging out. All three sightings were in the daytime, since most law-abiding citizens tended to avoid the park after dark. And in each instance, by the time the police had arrived the man was gone.

After studying the murders, the victims, and the crime scenes, police profilers had determined that the suspect was almost certainly not gay, that he was heterosexual, but he probably loitered in that area of the world-famous park for a sense of community, a feeling of some kind of attachment to others who might be like him. This man was very smart, they'd proffered, probably having a near-genius IQ. He knew that he was "different," and he suffered intense feelings of inadequacy because of it. He'd learned that by being around other societal misfits, even striking up friendships of sorts with some of them, he wouldn't feel so feckless; he would feel a likeness, a kinship with these men, a sense of belonging. This man needed society, they'd said, and in fact he had probably held high-level jobs at one time before his psychopathic personality had completely degenerated to that of a perverted killer. The SFPD had set up night-and-day surveillance in the area of the park near the restrooms where he'd been sighted, but the suspect was never seen again, probably warned off by the ongoing, comprehensive broadcast and print news coverage of the story and the stakeouts, and the department finally ran out of patience and resources for the operation.

Capra had seen him. For no more than an instant and through glass, but he'd seen him. And that face gave him a stunning jolt of shock, pain, and terror, the residue of which he had never gotten over. Nor had he gotten over the curious sensation that the suspect knew, and cared, that he, Pete Capra, was inside that house. He would never forget the image of the man blatantly waving at him from the street. Now, after thirteen years and in a different city, he thought he might be looking at that face again. Twice on cassettes shot after midnight in the vicinity of the same seedy restroom in *this* city's most prominent park.

His thoughts were interrupted by the sharp jangle of his red phone, the one reserved for emergencies.

12

Boss, I need a crew right now, on Beverly Glen, just down from my house," Maxi blurted before Pete Capra had a chance to say hello. She was talking on her cell phone while running down the steps from Gladys Lightner's bedroom suite, tugging Carla Ochoa behind her.

"What's up?" Capra said, sounding as if he was doing something else when he said it, and he probably was, Maxi knew.

Making an effort to keep her voice even during her frantic race down the staircase, she told Capra that she'd just found L.A. city councilman Conrad Lightner's wife—her neighbor—lying dead on her bedroom floor, and the councilman standing over her body, dripping with blood.

"When?"

"Two minutes ago. I called 911 right away. Nobody has this yet, I'm sure, but they'll be picking it up on the scanner any second." She gave Capra the Lightners' address and hung up.

Dropping her cell phone into her jacket pocket, Maxi quickly steered Carla to the bottom of the stairs, through the entry foyer, out of the mansion's front door, and into the passenger seat of her Blazer. She'd made a point of leaving the Lightners' front door and gates open behind them to accommodate the police response she'd summoned. Fumbling in her purse, she found her keys, hoisted herself up into the driver's seat, started her truck, negotiated a fast U-turn, and sped up Beverly Glen.

"We'll wait here," she said, screeching to a stop at the curb outside her own front door.

"Wait for . . . ?" Carla squeaked, looking panicked.

"Wait for the police to arrive. And a camera crew from my station—I have to report this. We're safe here, and we'll be able to see them when they pull up."

"Mrs. Lightner . . . was she—?"

"I don't know," Maxi interrupted. She figured that the sight of the bloodied body on the floor had Carla Ochoa terrified for her young son.

The hot devil winds wracked the SUV, causing it to rattle and sway. Maxi let her head drop back onto the headrest and closed her eyes. She couldn't blot out the image of Gladys Lightner's body. Or of her husband, the councilman, smeared with blood. He hadn't said a word, just stood in the upstairs bedroom looking down at the lifeless body of his wife on the floor, holding both arms and bloody hands out to either side as if to protect his clothes from being bloodstained.

Which they already were. He hadn't yet put on his suit coat, and the front of his white shirt was bloody, as were his blue-flecked tie and his navy trousers. Blood clinging to the front of his woven black leather belt had begun to congeal, and there were blood spatters on his highly polished black shoes. Spatters, Maxi had noticed, not blotches or smears. A significant blood transfer pattern—spatters. Which meant that he could have been there when it happened. And that it could have happened after he got dressed this morning.

Gladys Lightner's bed was unmade—she had apparently slept in it. And got up this morning, applied some makeup, slipped into a fancy dressing gown, and put on a pair of frilly, high-heeled slippers. So it had to have happened this morning. And there seemed to have been nobody else in the house this morning besides the councilman, Carla Ochoa, and Maxi. And the deceased.

For the ninety seconds that Maxi was in the room, Lightner had stood there without moving. "Councilman, the police are coming," Maxi had said, as if he had neither seen nor heard her make the call from her cell phone three feet in front of him.

Maybe he hadn't. He'd seemed to be in shock. Who wouldn't be? she'd realized, whether he'd killed his wife or not. That's when she'd bolted out of the room, pulling Carla Ochoa with her.

Carla was crying softly now, crouched down in the front seat next to her. Maxi's instinct was to get her safely inside her own house, but she couldn't take the chance that she might miss the police. She made some ineffectual noises in an attempt to calm the woman, and waited.

Within minutes the police arrived, two uniforms in a marked squad car from LAPD's West Los Angeles Division. Maxi jumped out of her truck into the middle of the street and ran down to meet the officers as they bounded out of their cruiser. While she trotted along beside them, identifying herself and quickly filling them in on what she'd seen inside the Lightners' house, the Channel Six live truck rumbled to a stop at the curb behind the black-and-white. Her cameraman was Jersey again. He blasted out of the truck rolling, and handed Maxi a microphone, as the police, guns drawn, ran through the Lightners' open gates.

So, Con Lightner did it?" Capra said to Maxi. It wasn't really a question.

"What makes you say that?"

"It's always the husband." Pete shrugged dismissively.

With a shake of her head, Maxi shot him an I-don't-believe-you! look, but she knew that was Pete. Sexist, cynical, and usually right. She didn't bite. But they both knew that this was going to be a huge story. And that Los Angeles city councilman Conrad

Lightner, representative from West Los Angeles, district number five, was in very deep trouble.

They were sitting in Capra's office behind his closed door discussing the coverage. Besides exteriors, which the rest of the press corps who'd come after her also got, Jersey was able to shoot inside Mrs. Lightner's bedroom while the councilman was being questioned downstairs by Detectives Marcus Jorgan and Remo Sanchez, who'd arrived from Robbery-Homicide. The pair had been assigned to the murder of Gladys Lightner because of the link to the Ochoa boy's kidnapping from the same house the night before. During much of Lightner's questioning Maxi had hovered out of sight behind a door, listening. If Jorgan had seen her, he didn't say anything; he knew that Maxi would not use any information she wasn't entitled to.

Channel Six News had not been thrown off the property, and had not been restrained from airing Maxi's footage. At least not yet. Maxi and Jersey figured that the councilman had not rallied sufficiently yet to think about that. Most likely they would be enjoined from showing any video that had not been shot from the public street in front of the house by the time the later shows went on the air and the lawyers got into it.

Meantime, the station broke into the network morning show with a special report, showing a wide shot of the Lightner master bedroom suite taken from the far side of the bed, at an angle that concealed the body on the floor. It showed forensic personnel working the crime scene, close-ups of blood staining the plush white carpeting, and Mrs. Lightner's little honey- and cream-colored Lhasa Apso with a pink bow in her hair padding about the room whimpering. But no gory pictures of the dead body. Such shots would be deemed offensive, against UGN policy to air.

But Jersey did videotape Gladys Lightner's body. That footage had been immediately locked up in the dead file, the row of cabinets along the back wall of the tape library where all footage that could not be aired was stored for safekeeping in the event it was needed later for possible legal reasons. This had all the makings of a high-profile news story that reeked of lawsuits waiting to happen. Taking full advantage of their unusual access, Jersey also shot every square inch of the master suite, in case anything in it turned out to be relevant as the story unfolded.

Ironic, Maxi had thought—the reason they had not been tossed off the property was because the person who surely would have run them off was dead.

"So, boss," she ventured to Capra now. "You want me on this story, right?"

"Wrong," he said. "I want you on the graveyard."

"But . . . I *broke* this story," she stammered. "It's *mine!*"

"Read your contract. No story is yours. It's the intellectual property of Channel Six News."

She knew that, of course. "Ya, but—" she began in frustration.

"Graveyard, Maxi. Starting Monday."

"How *could* you—"

"Go cut Lightner for the Noon, but write it around the interior footage—we'll probably be restrained from showing it by then," he said, turning his attention back to the pile of work on his desk.

Maxi clamped her lips together and looked away from him. Her eyes lit on his supersized black umbrella standing in a corner—if she could have whacked him with it without getting fired, arrested, or sued, she would have. Instead, she stomped out the door into the newsroom, willing herself to calm down.

Never let them see you squirm.

13

Pete Capra sat at his desk, fingering Tom McCartney's cassette. First time out, the stringer had earned his five hundred bucks. Capra got up and shoved the thing into his office tape player again, and fast-forwarded to the face that had been haunting him for thirteen years. At least it could be the face.

And again, he froze the frame on the dark visage and studied it. Was it the man? Or had he just become so obsessed with his indelible mind-graven image of the suspected killer over the years that he'd finally flipped out behind it?

He sat down again, and with a grunt, he reached behind his chair to his suit jacket hanging on a vintage wooden coat tree and pulled his worn leather wallet from the inside pocket. Carefully, he extracted a yellowed newspaper clipping that had frayed and split along its creases. And as he had done hundreds of times over more than a decade, he studied the grainy composite drawing on the newsprint. Then he looked at the face projected on his television monitor. Back and forth.

No mustache now. Older, certainly. Same broad, straight nose, same hooded eyes, though more heavily lined now. But most identifying of all, the same dark mole high on the outside of the man's right cheek. Though prominent on his twenty-five-inch television screen, the mark was barely visible in the small newspaper drawing, but Capra remembered that mole. It had been described by his eyewitness back then, Jeannine See, to the San Francisco police sketch artist.

Assuming it was the man, Tom McCartney had no idea whom he'd caught on tape, twice now, but Capra knew that this shooter was not one to miss the scent of a story. Fine with him; McCartney was a top journalist. He'd been tempted to hire the stringer more than once, but was always stopped by the tales of addiction that clung to him. Too much liability. Twenty years ago, yes, a station, a newspaper, would go with enterprising reporters who were known to get the goods, even if they did booze up, use drugs, whatever. Back then it didn't matter—what mattered was aggressively digging up the news. But in today's politically correct climate, and today's economy, you couldn't take that risk—you had to answer to the suits. Pete Capra missed the old days.

It wouldn't surprise him, though, if McCartney figured it out, put the story together. Or parts of it. He wouldn't give the stringer any help, couldn't. Couldn't associate himself with the story, or the "face"—there was too much at stake for him personally. But if McCartney cracked it he'd buy the story from him, demand an exclusive, pay him big bucks, and run with it. And he'd have Maxi Poole wrap it around, give her the face time on it. He owed her that. And maybe this time he would help get the suspected killer off the streets for good.

He thought about Maxi. Call him sexist, but he'd never before assigned a woman to the graveyard shift. Most of his colleagues didn't do it either. Now he'd put his own star reporter out there, in jeopardy on the overnight, but he'd told her nothing. Prepared her for nothing. He did not want her on this story, but he did want her hovering around its periphery. Tricky at best, dangerous at worst, but he had his reasons. Looking up at the image frozen on the screen, he asked himself the question again: How big a risk was he taking by putting Maxi Poole in proximity to this man, if indeed he was the Bay Area "walk-in killer"?

Capra had always protected his staff, always felt strongly about his responsibility in that area. Two months ago he'd hauled ass down to Parker Center at two-thirty in the morning to bail out one of his reporters who'd been pulled in on a DUI. The same morning, after a few hours' sleep, he was back downtown making a deal for his employee with the ADA, then he'd slammed the guy into rehab to the tune of forty thousand bucks out of his news budget. Another time he'd nailed a stalker right outside the building who'd written mash notes to his new and very young weekend weatherwoman. Turns out the stalker was carrying a tricked-out .45 automatic, which he'd pointed foursquare at Capra's chest. While staring down the blue steel barrel, Capra had calmly reached into his shirt pocket, fished out his cell phone, and called the Burbank PD. Big risk. It ended okay—nobody got shot and the perp was locked up. A deranged fan who'd become obsessed with a pretty young image on the screen. But Capra had been there for her. For both of them. For all of them. Even for Maxi Poole last year when she'd gotten herself trapped inside the home of a psychopathic killer on what she'd thought was going to be a routine interview. He'd slammed into the house with his reporter Richard Winningham and they'd gotten her out of there.

But now he was putting Maxi at bodily risk, and he couldn't tell her why. Yes, he'd agonized over doing it. Even felt bad about yanking her from the Lightner story. Pulling her off what could be an award-winning investigative story, one that she had single-handedly broken. But he had to do it. Maxi Poole was blond, the most visible blonde on the news, at the top-rated television station in Los Angeles. More to the point, she was "Pete Capra's blonde." She worked for him. A fact that would not escape this killer, if it was him. And if it was him, it was a fact that Capra was almost certain would smoke him out.

He rationalized that Maxi was smart, she was no easy mark. And he'd given McCartney a money gig, shooting tape for him in MacArthur Park. In return he'd asked the stringer to watch Maxi's back. Still, if Capra were being completely honest with himself, he would acknowledge that he was using his own reporter as bait.

It might have been coincidence, but the long-ago serial killer who had haunted him for more than a decade, the possible possessor of the face he was staring at now on his big-screen monitor, had murdered only blondes.

After feeding her story on the brutal murder of Gladys Lightner for a live cut-in on the UGN network's morning news show, which ran daily from seven to nine after the early local news, Maxi had driven Carla Ochoa to her own house up the street, helped rush her things inside, given the woman her spare key, and told her to make herself at home in the guest room off the kitchen. That took five minutes. Then, still in the run-down Blazer, she'd sped down Beverly Glen and eastbound across the Valley to the station to cut, write, and voice her story on the murder for the News at Noon, leaving a weepy Carla Ochoa behind in her kitchen.

Now she had a couple of hours to spare between intro'ing the story live on the Noon and recutting it for the Four. No point doing it this early, because in the universe of news, a volatile breaking story could change substantially within the next couple of hours. Or within the next couple of minutes. She would wait until close to four o'clock to rewrite it, adding a new top if there was one, and including any new information that might surface between now and then. This story had all the earmarks of a lead—therefore, barring earthquake, plane crash, or some such, this one would need to be ready to air at the top of the hour.

The latest update on the wires indicated that Conrad Lightner had not been arrested, but that since his at-home interrogation by RHD detectives Jorgan and Sanchez, he had retained a lawyer, Martin Hodel, known to be one of the best and most powerful criminal defense attorneys in the city.

Maxi opted to use the spare time she had now to pull some file footage out of the tape library on Los Angeles city councilman Conrad Lightner, to use in the story where needed for background. With an editor, she compiled a reel of possible inserts, dropped the cassette slugged "Lightner Backgrounder" on her desk for editing into her piece for the Four, then left the office to make a quick run home—she needed to check on Carla Ochoa, see how she was doing, and if she needed anything. There was still nothing new on the woman's missing son.

Driving the rattly Blazer too fast up Beverly Glen from the Valley floor toward Mulholland now, Maxi was trying to make some sense out of the events of the last two days. Where was Roberto Ochoa? Who killed Gladys Lightner? How were the two events connected, if they were? Did any of it hang on the councilman? But what possible motive could he have for killing his own wife? And possibly ruining his own life?

She concentrated on these questions to keep her mind off the fact that she was seething at her boss. She couldn't believe that Pete Capra was yanking her off this one. The sequence of events surrounding the Lightners would be seeping out over the weeks and months to come in a major ongoing story, and she was the reporter who had broken it live. But the man was sticking with his plan to put her on the overnight. Damn him and his graveyard shift. Beginning Monday. Drunks, car thefts, cheap little drug busts, midnight second-story heists. She might as well be out of the news business.

She could rage, but of far more importance than being booted off the story, or her deflated career, she needed to help find that little boy. To help bring Roberto Ochoa home to his terrified, heartsick mother.

Pulling up to the front of her own small house in the Glen, she could see several news trucks and official vehicles down the street, congested around the Lightners' mansion. She decided not to leave her truck parked at the curb. In this business, safety was an ingrained priority with her. Or was it paranoia? Whatever, she jammed the button on the remote that opened her garage, gunned the vehicle inside, zapped the door down behind her, got out of the Blazer, and went through the connecting door that led into her kitchen.

Carla Ochoa was sitting at the kitchen table, red-eyed, the ever-present tissues wadded in one hand, looking desolate.

"Nothing?" Maxi asked.

"No. *Nada.*" Then the tears came again.

"They'll find him," Maxi said, stretching an arm around the woman's gently quivering shoulders. "They'll find Roberto, Carla," she said again, softly. Trying to be comforting. Impossible, of course, to comfort a mother who'd lost her child.

Yes, they would find him, Maxi knew. What she didn't know was whether they would find him alive or dead, and Carla Ochoa knew that too.

14

Friday night, just after midnight. Tom McCartney had two things on his mind: how to get himself a piece of the Lightner murder story, and finding out what or whom Pete Capra was looking for in MacArthur Park. When his sisters would ask about the exciting stories he covered, he'd shrug it off, telling them it was just a living. But he didn't really feel that way. It wasn't just a living; it was what he lived for. Given his present somewhat sorry circumstance in the field of television news, his passion for breaking a story was even stronger now than ever because the big ones, the jewels, were so much harder for him to hook onto.

The murder of City Councilman Lightner's wife and the kidnapping of their housekeeper's son—those related stories were definitely the main event on the L.A. news card at the moment. Most top stories were ephemeral, very quickly dropping in status to the proverbial "yesterday's news," but all of his news instincts told him that this one was going to mushroom. But for him to get in on it from his lowly vantage as a nightside stringer, an outsider, he needed to find an angle that nobody else had.

And now he thought he might have one. He'd been out on the Lightner lawn with the rest of the newsies the night the Ochoa boy was kidnapped, and he'd seen the look on the councilman's face when Rosie asked him where he'd been. Surprise. Embarrassment. Fear. Guilt. McCartney was pretty sure that Conrad Lightner had something to hide. After the Lightner murder story broke today, he'd canvassed his sources on the street to see if he could turn up anything at all on the councilman.

Besides the Vikes he scored from Smithie, he also made regular purchases of crack and smack, which he kept on hand to pay informants when they were helpful. Some of them wanted cash, but most preferred drugs—it saved them from having to deal with the middleman. They liked doing business with Tom McCartney. And McCartney liked doing business with them, because in their territory nothing much of interest involving the dealers, the suckers, and the players escaped their notice.

Tonight, he might have struck pay dirt concerning a pair of hookers whom Conrad Lightner allegedly frequented. Word on the street was that L.A. city councilman Conrad Lightner had been seen several times going in and out of a seedy apartment building on the flats of Hollywood that was the place of business for two well-established local working girls. McCartney intended to check it out.

As for what was up with Pete Capra's fixation on the crowd that hung out around a public men's john, he had no clue, but he intended to find that out too. Nice thing was, he was out here shooting sleazebags in MacArthur Park on Capra's nickel. Not that Capra paid for it, the UGN network did. But like any good executive, Capra was known to be as tight with his news budget as he would be with his own money. And this moonlight operation was costing Channel Six three-thousand-five a week. Not cheap. No question there was something here, and it had to be big.

By Los Angeles standards, MacArthur Park, on thirty-two acres west of downtown, is old. Built in the late nineteenth century and located in what was then one of the city's most fashionable residential districts, it was first named Westlake Park, and nicknamed the "Champs-Élysées of Los Angeles." The area remained home to largely upper-class families through the mid-1940s. After World War II the park was renamed for General Douglas MacArthur, and the neighborhood had already begun changing for the worse. Over the past three decades, MacArthur Park, in the LAPD's Rampart Division, had become the habitat of transients, drunks, drug dealers, heroin addicts, and street gangs that fought over the turf, the most vicious battles being those of the crack cocaine wars of the 1980s. For years, one gang had held the northwest corner, another the southwest, while the northeast belonged to purveyors of phony immigration papers and other documents, and the southeast served as an open-air drug bazaar. It was not uncommon for bloated bodies to be fished out of the park's still scenic lake, and the restrooms were the domain of both male and female prostitutes as well as johns, addicts, and perverts of every stripe.

McCartney had been taping creeps from behind a clump of dense foliage outside the men's restroom for the better part of an hour, stopping and starting, zooming in on faces either entering or emerging from the rectangle of dusty yellow light in the open doorway. Hidden by the growth, his camera on his shoulder, leaning up against the thick trunk of a coral tree, he was trying not to inhale the odors of sour filth, sweat, and excrement emanating in almost palpable waves from the grubby concrete structure, so strong they made him want to gag from twenty feet away.

When he'd first walked toward the place tonight, a long-limbed buck in shiny black leather pants and scuffed leather vest, with steel stud cuffs on both wrists, inky, slicked-back hair, and a slew of dark purple tats on his beefy arms, had tried to engage him in conversation. "Hey, dude," the guy had tossed out. *Original,* was McCartney's silent take. "Hey, dude, come on over and have some fun. Or are you just down here taking pictures?" When McCartney didn't respond, the man shrugged and went inside.

Nice life. And he'd thought *his* life was grim. Not by half. He'd chuckled to himself. It always did him good to see how *both* the other halves lived, because he saw himself belonging to neither. He saw himself caught somewhere in the middle between the successful well-to-do and the bottom-feeder scumbags, and for him, in between was comfortable.

After the party boy in black leather had confronted him, he'd slipped back into the brush. He'd been shooting these lowlifes for two nights now. Last night he'd figured it didn't matter if they saw him—his tape was not going on the air, and these creeps would just think he was one of them, a pervert who liked to video other perverts, hopefully doing perverted things. His camera bore no station logo—it could pass for sophisticated home video equipment. A lot of these deviates got off being on camera, and most of them were so stoned that they couldn't put two thoughts together anyway.

Capra had told him to get faces. Tonight, getting more of a feel for this sinkhole, McCartney realized that the guy Capra was looking for, whatever his story, most likely would not want to be photographed. So he stood in the cover of heavy foliage now, getting close-up shots of dirty, depressed, and desperate-looking faces. Capra was looking for some weirdo for some reason. Thinking it through further, McCartney assumed that if Channel Six's top journalist was after some guy, there were probably other people after him too.

Pete Capra stood behind a tree, watching Tom McCartney lean against another tree. *What kind of fucking kid's game am I playing?* he chided himself. Hide-and-seek? He'd told Kris that he had to work past the Eleven tonight, running down a lead on the Lightner murder. His beautiful Kris—he had no idea why she put up with him. Funny, neither did anyone else, as so many of their friends were overly fond of pointing out to him. Well, mostly his friends in the news business, but they were the ones who knew him best.

He and Kris had been married for twenty-six years, their kids grown and gone now and doing well. But Kris had been there back when he'd lost twenty pounds and many nights' sleep obsessing over the San Francisco serial cyanide killer. And he always suspected that she knew why, though they'd never talked about it. He couldn't talk about it, and that had probably been the reason why she wouldn't. Kris knew him like nobody else did, and always, she quietly supported him. No way in hell was he about to let her know that this sonofabitch was back in their lives.

Maybe.

Part of him fiercely wanted it to be the guy, and part of him prayed that it was not.

So he crouched in the shadows, watching stringer Tom McCartney watching the putrid, insect-infested doorway to the restroom. Good buffer, these trees. He couldn't let the stringer see him. And he certainly couldn't let his longtime nemesis see him, if he surfaced tonight.

Maxi had to finally admit to herself that the prospect of getting to sleep was looking grim. She glanced over yet again at the illuminated face of the clock radio on her bedside table. The digital readout said 2:38 A.M.

Carla Ochoa was settled in the downstairs guest bedroom, probably not sleeping either, she knew. Young Roberto was on both their minds. And Gladys Lightner. And the dead woman's husband, the councilman, smeared with blood when they saw him this morning in the big house down the street. The house that had been Carla and Roberto's home until this morning. It was more than twenty-four hours now since the little boy had vanished.

The odd part was that there had been absolutely nothing to hang this on. No clues at all, at least none that she knew about. No forced entry. No fingerprints that weren't expected to be on the doors or windows or inside the house. None of the neighbors had heard a noise, or witnessed a scuffle, or seen anyone they thought might be unusual around the Lightner house. Forensics had swept up hairs and fibers—it was still too early to tell if there were any that couldn't be accounted for, all of this according to Marc Jorgan. Both times that Maxi had phoned the detective, he'd taken her call but had rushed her off the phone. She knew he had no time to spare. This was a child missing. The FBI would be coming into it—it was looking like a kidnapping.

She heard Yukon give a little moan. Guess her pooch couldn't sleep either. Probably because her big furry Alaskan malamute knew that his mistress couldn't sleep. And because there was a stranger in the house.

"C'mere, Yuke," she said, and dropped an arm over the side of the bed.

Without opening her eyes, she heard Yukon pad across the carpet, then sit himself down with a hundred-pound *whoomp* beside her bed. Then she felt his sweet, wet nose nestling into the palm of her hand. Idly, she stroked his silky head. Last year he was almost killed when an insane woman brandishing a knife broke into their home and slashed him. Yukon had saved her life then, but almost lost his own. She would never forget his fight to recover, and her intense fear that she was going to lose him. Now he was fine, he was here, and the two of them took care of each other.

Quietly petting her sweet wooly boy brought on a wave of calm, and she felt herself starting to drift. But her dreams were a phalanx of scenes through a green night-vision scope—dark, chaotic, and frustrating.

Until she was jolted awake by a scream.

15

Maxi leaped out of bed and Yukon sprang to his feet, the big dog letting out a low growl while she checked her clock radio for the time, scooped up her cell phone from the bedside table, grabbed a white cotton robe off a chair, and was tying it around her as she bolted out of the bedroom door and down the stairs toward the source of the scream. It was 6:43 on Saturday morning.

She was about to yell for Carla Ochoa, then realized that might not be prudent.

Slowing down, skulking in bare feet with Yukon at her heels, she first peered around the corner of the hallway into the living room, then walked through it and into the small adjoining dining room, cell phone in hand. Wishing it were a knife, or a baseball bat. Or a gun. Not that she knew how to use a gun. Next, she approached her kitchen and looked inside. All of which took little more than a minute from the time the scream had shocked her awake.

Mrs. Ochoa stood by the back door off the kitchen, in rumpled gray sweats that looked like she'd slept in them. She was holding a sheet of paper. A photograph, Maxi could see.

"What is it?" she demanded.

Carla held out the photo. "It was in the envelope," she said, pointing a trembling finger at a large manila envelope on the kitchen counter that had MRS. OCHOA printed in block letters on its face.

Maxi backed away, giving her two palms up to ward her off. "Carla, put the picture down on the table so I can see it, but don't put any more fingerprints on it," she said, sounding more terse than she'd meant to.

It was an eight-by-ten computer printout of a color photo on flat white paper. A little boy with full cheeks, dark wavy hair, brown skin, sitting on a straight-backed wooden chair, looking up at the camera, probably coerced to do so, his face corkscrewed into a wail, his nose running, tears visible under his eyes. He was dressed in blue jeans and a dirty yellow T-shirt, white socks and sneakers, and both his feet were tethered to the chair legs with what looked to be gray duct tape; both hands were pulled behind the chair back, most likely also restrained. The chair was set against a cracked, grubby-looking Sheetrock wall painted a drab industrial green. There was nothing else in the picture.

"Roberto?" Maxi asked, knowing the answer. She was already punching in the speed-dial number for Detective Marc Jorgan on her cell.

"Yes. Roberto." Carla Ochoa affirmed it with a nod, whimpering softly now.

"Where was it?" Maxi asked, then turned her attention to the phone. She left an urgent message on voice mail for Jorgan after being told by a female desk officer that the detective hadn't come in yet.

"*Aquí*. On the floor." Carla pointed to a spot.

"Slipped under the door?"

"I think so, *sí*."

"Nothing else?"

"No. Nothing else."

Maxi pulled open the back door without going outside. The hot Santa Ana winds had died down, leaving behind their characteristic morning window of warm air that would cool back to January chill by afternoon. She looked around at the shrubbery, the grass, the steps, the walkway. She'd been meaning to have that warped threshold repaired so that water, bugs, and spurious missives could not seep or be jammed under her door. Maybe the messenger had tried the front door and couldn't force the envelope under it—that entry had been fitted with a watertight rubber threshold. And maybe he or she had bypassed the mailbox for the shock value of depositing it directly inside the house. Or to get it noticed first thing in the morning rather than later when the mail was gathered. One thing Maxi knew for sure: It was not there on the kitchen floor when she'd turned out the lights six hours ago.

"Don't go outside this door," she said to Carla. "There might be footprints, or fingerprints." Or clues in the bushes, or fresh tire tracks, or even, she thought, some weirdo lying in wait.

Her cell phone rang in her hands. Jorgan. He'd picked up her message and was on his way.

Councilman Conrad Lightner sat in his den, in his favorite camel-colored mottled leather chair, the heavy green Varanasi drapes drawn, Gladys's usually yappy little dog lying listlessly on the rug beside him, and the television tuned to a cable channel that had been blaring wall-to-wall coverage of the murder of his wife and the kidnapping of his former housekeeper's kid.

They were running endless footage of himself and Gladdy "in happier times," most of it familiar stuff: the couple arriving at some gala, him making a campaign speech or accepting an award. An army of reporters were weighing in on every possible angle of the story, including his last election campaign, when there had been some allegations of illegal contributions. He picked up the remote from the end table beside his chair and zapped the MUTE button.

It was early Saturday morning. The sun was barely filtering through the windows of the elegant Georgian manse, vacant now except for him. He'd been slouched in this chair since the cops left yesterday. He'd dozed off a few times, he knew, fitfully. In the chair. With the TV on, his legs up on the ottoman, one of Gladdy's ugly crocheted afghans over his knees, this one in a dizzying pattern of green, brown, and orange, and a brandy snifter of Southern Comfort in his hand.

And the dog beside him. Janie. He hardly even knew Janie; she'd always avoided him. Now she was cowering on the floor next to him, wouldn't leave his side. He hadn't even known where her food was. When she kept whining and nuzzling his leg last night, he'd found a giant bag of kibble under the kitchen sink. He'd just poured some of the dry stuff into her bowl on the kitchen floor, then as an afterthought, he'd filled the matching bowl next to it with water. Screw Janie. She was just another pain in the ass.

Much as Janie had always downright adored Gladdy, his wife had never lifted a finger for the little mutt. Carla Ochoa, the housekeeper, had always tended to her care and feeding. But Carla wasn't here. He'd seen a note she'd left on the kitchen table yesterday saying she was staying at that newscaster Maxi Poole's house up the street and to please send her check there. And please let her know right away if he heard anything about Roberto. So either the woman had quit, or she'd been fired by his wife. He didn't know which. Either dumping the help or having them bolt was a semi-regular occurrence in the Lightner household.

Not that he gave a damn about which it had been this time. His wife's blood was smeared all over the upstairs bedroom, mixed with the cops' black fingerprint powder, his future in politics was almost certainly in the shitter, and his whole world was spinning out of control.

The detectives thought he did it. The two smartasses from LAPD's Robbery-Homicide Division. The murder, and probably the kidnapping too. He knew that's what they thought from the way they'd interrogated him for half the day yesterday. Their leading questions, their arrogant tones of voice, the smug, knowing looks they'd shot from one to the other. Talk to them, they'd said, or he could be talking to the FBI. Maybe looking at a federal rap if they linked the murder to the kidnap case. They'd hinted that he shouldn't think about leaving town. Where the hell was he going to go? he'd tossed back at them. He was an elected holder of public office, in case they didn't know it. He would be going back to work.

Work. Would he even still have a job? He had to get out of this chair. Do something. Make some phone calls, get those two bloodhounds off his back. But who could he call? Over the years he'd always been there for other guys who'd gotten their nuts caught in a wringer—who'd gotten nailed soliciting prostitutes, or knocking up women not their wives. Whatever. He was the good old boy who'd called in favors to help his cronies out of various jams. Now what about him? Was there anybody he could call on for help? What would they be thinking about this, all his buddies, L.A.'s power brokers? He knew the answers to his questions. Sex was one thing; murder was a whole different can of crap. And with the news streaming out of his television set, the whole fucking city knew before breakfast about his wife's murder yesterday.

His stomach was in knots. He was half in the bag; his head was pounding; his hands were unsteady. They hadn't read him his Miranda rights, hadn't arrested him, but he'd gone ahead and lawyered up. Was that a good idea, or did it make him look guilty? Who the hell knew?

16

The world gets to sleep in on Saturdays, but not Tom McCartney. His Saturdays were business as usual: after prowling for news all night, he'd made the rounds in the early hours peddling the tape he'd shot to the usual stations, just not to the usual people at the usual desks. On Saturdays and Sundays, the news industry's weekend middle managers were in place at the respective helms.

Last night's shift was productive. He had searched out Conrad Lightner's pair of blowsy prostitutes, who had coyly suggested, after he'd promised them anonymity and cash, that maybe they *did* know the councilman after all. He had set up an interview with the two of them that he would shoot in silhouette, which always lent high drama to a news piece; that story would be a lead for a bunch of stations, he figured, and lucrative for him. He'd had to laugh—the ladies had chosen next Thursday for the shoot because they said Thursday was usually their slowest night, being just before the weekend. And for a sizable deposit up front, they'd promised not to tell any other news outlet about their connection to Councilman Conrad Lightner. These two were businesswomen.

Meantime, he had scored three sales this morning with a late-night drug bust in Little Tokyo. And he had shot two more MacArthur Park cassettes that he would deliver to Pete Capra at Channel Six on Monday morning. Friday night must be degenerates' night out; an army of creeps were on parade last night while he was in the park.

And so was Pete Capra.

After being confronted by the overly friendly joe in leather, McCartney had ducked for cover into the woodsy area on the south side of the men's room, and he had become immediately aware that there was somebody else nearby. Lurking. Though minimal, he'd sensed movement. Some slight crackling in the underbrush. Then shallow breaths. At first he'd assumed it was one of the pervert night crawlers, doing whatever the hell they did out there by moonlight in the heart of the downtown L.A. park.

He'd slapped a mirror attachment over his viewfinder, and damned if he didn't get a glimpse of Peter Capra behind him, in his usual newsroom uniform of rumpled suit, conservative rep tie over blue oxford button-down shirt, and scuffed-up brown loafers, peering out from the cover of the broad trunk of an ancient live oak. McCartney was floored. In a million years he wouldn't have expected that of Capra. All of his dealings with the news exec were as up front and straightforward as it gets.

What the hell was the guy thinking, stalking him like that? Or stalking whoever he was looking for, more likely. But it made McCartney understand just how important finding his mystery man had to be to the Channel Six managing editor.

It also made him realize that for some reason, Pete Capra was about to involve Maxi Poole in this. And that Capra'd had a much thornier agenda in mind than just general orientation when he'd enlisted McCartney to look out for his reporter on the graveyard shift. He wondered if Maxi was in on the secret. He guessed that she was not.

McCartney had pretended he didn't see Capra, because Capra obviously didn't want to be seen. After about twenty minutes of the one-sided cat-and-mouse game, McCartney had to work at stifling an urge to jump out of the bushes and yell, *"Boo!"* But Capra was more than half past forty, a smoker and a drinker—a scare like that could give him a heart attack, and Pete Capra was one of the few station guys McCartney actually respected. Liked, even.

Besides, this caper provided a little bit of steady income. That, and it was way too intriguing to pull the wheels off it.

Detective Marc Jorgan bagged and tagged the computer printout picture of Roberto Ochoa, while his partner Remo Sanchez secured Maxi Poole's backyard with yellow crime-scene tape, this as the two waited for the mobile crime lab to arrive at the reporter's house in Beverly Glen. The kidnapper who had the little boy might have been here, he knew, and if so, there was a good chance that he would have left his signature somewhere at the scene. They almost always did.

Jorgan had felt physically sick when he saw the picture of the boy tied to a chair, thinking about what the toddler must be going through. There had been a rash of child snatchings all over the country lately, and it was a fact of low-life that when sensational cases made the news, the stories invariably gave other scumbags ideas.

And he didn't like that Maxi Poole was hip-deep in it. The kidnappers obviously knew that the boy's mother was staying here. They were probably aware of whose house this was, and still they'd brazenly come here to the home of a prominent television newscaster. Or they'd sent some other goon. It told him that these people were reckless, stoned out, or just dumb. Or all of the above. That's what most of the L.A. street punks were, and all too often it made for a combination that turned lethal.

It was probably about money; kidnapping usually was. If so, the mark certainly wouldn't be Mrs. Ochoa. Both Jorgan and his partner had felt certain that the targets were the councilman and his wealthy wife, but now Mrs. Lightner was dead. So why would the kidnappers want to terrify the boy's mother by delivering that staged, threatening picture of her son to Maxi Poole's house? It had to mean that they wanted to get the story out, that their intent was to put their target on alert.

If not money, it was passion. Someone wanted the kid, or someone wanted to hurt somebody else by using the kid. Was the abduction connected to the murder of Lightner's wife? If so, there was an extremely dangerous game being played here. What did the player or players hope to gain? And who were the losers? Mrs. Lightner, certainly. And her husband—seemingly affable, avuncular, well-known conservative Los Angeles city councilman Conrad Lightner.

Or was he part of this?

So far, Marc Jorgan had a mess of questions and no answers.

Jorgan had known Maxi Poole since she was a young reporter just out of college and eager to learn. He'd met her when she was covering one of his crime scenes back then, and from that time on she'd inundated him with calls, peppering him with questions, about police procedure, departmental protocol, or about specific cases, begging to roll with him on homicide calls, phoning him with tips of her own. He'd been struck from the beginning by how smart she was, how much she wanted to learn, and how hard she was willing to work. In his experience with the press, there were two kinds of television reporters—the ones who cared about spraying their hair, and the ones who cared about reporting the news. When he'd first laid eyes on Maxi Poole, a young blond beauty, he'd figured her for the former, but soon learned that she was among the latter—and that group was the minority, at least in his decade and a half of dealing with the media.

Now she was in danger of *making* news, and he didn't like it.

His partner had questioned the mother at length in Spanish. She spoke better than passable English, but Jorgan found that people were usually able to think better in their first language.

He'd pinpointed the location of the father, a possible suspect. Trinidad Ochoa, thirty-seven years old, lived in Texas, was remarried, had fathered a child since Roberto and had another one on the way, got spotty work in construction, and when Jorgan had reached him by phone last night the man didn't seem to much care that his firstborn was missing. But you never knew what motivated people. A check with the El Paso PD and the Texas DMV told him that Ochoa lived in a big house in a tony part of town, and drove a late-model Mercedes SL500 Roadster and a new Lincoln Navigator SUV. Not consistent with the paydays from random construction jobs.

Now this photo confirmed what the mother—what every mother—fears most. The boy had definitely been kidnapped and was being held somewhere. What they didn't know was where and why. He would phone the father with this new information. If he got any kind of vibe at all from the guy that he might be involved, he would take a trip to Texas and check him out in person. Other than that, there wasn't a lot more that he and his partner could do but wait for the kidnappers' next move, which the photo told him there most certainly would be. Some kind of demand. His first priority was to find the boy, his second was to find the bad guys, and time was crucial. The more time that went by, the more volatile this situation would get.

The doorbell rang.

Maxi came out of her study and moved toward the front door, her dog, Yukon, at her heels. Holding up a hand to stop her, Jorgan went to the door himself, his right hand gripping his Beretta nine.

Peering out from the front living room window, he recognized one of the two men at Maxi Poole's door. Special Agent William McFarland from the L.A. office of the FBI, with another guy—African American, younger, shorter, stocky—standing behind him down on the second step. McFarland's partner, he figured. Both men were dressed in the Fibby uniform: dark suits, crisp shirts, conservative ties, sunglasses. His lieutenant had told him that they'd be calling in the Bureau. That meant all of Jorgan's case files would have been copied over to the FBI team. He hated that.

And he hated his apparent luck of the draw on this case. Everyone knew FBI agent Bill McFarland to be an arrogant asshole who would shoot first and try to figure it out later.

Before Detective Jorgan had arrived and taken the computer photo of Roberto Ochoa into evidence, Maxi had made copies of it. Wearing gloves and handling it gingerly, she'd slipped it into a plastic sleeve and run it through her copier. Twice. One print for the station to use on the news, and one for her files, to hold on to and study.

She'd thought about keeping the picture under wraps until Monday. It would be a great "get" for her first damn shift on the damn graveyard, and she was fairly certain that Jorgan and Sanchez would not put the photo out in the press until they'd run it through forensic testing, if at all.

That idea took less than a minute of consideration before she gave it up, because airing the picture could possibly smoke out somebody with information on Roberto, and she had no moral right to squelch it. Besides, holding it back for thirty-six hours was just bad journalism, exclusive or not. So she told Marc Jorgan that she had made copies, and that the station would have the photo on the news tonight. Jorgan had let her know he didn't like it, but there was nothing he could do about it. He'd asked her not to release the photo, but he hadn't objected strongly. He knew it was her job, and in this case it was her right, since the picture had been hand-delivered to her home. She'd gotten it first. Now she was gunning her old Corvette down the hill on her way to the station to put the kidnap photo story together, write her lead-in and tag, and shoot her stand-ups. So much for her Saturday off. That was the nature of the beast.

The nocturnal messenger had to know that Carla Ochoa was staying at a house up the street from the Lightners on Beverly

Glen, and probably would have connected newscaster Maxi Poole to that house. Which told her he would have been pretty sure that the reporter would put the photo on the news. So the kidnapper had something to gain from getting the picture of Roberto out to the public. There would be reaction after it aired on the early block tonight, and maybe she would learn something.

She had studied the picture with a magnifying glass. It was a color digital photo printed off a computer. The chair Roberto was tethered to was pushed up against a dingy green wall, exposing no clues to his whereabouts that she could discern. The chair was rough-hewn, with traces of mottled paint, royal blue mixed with light green. Colorful, cheap, handmade, Mexican. And the scared little boy with tears streaming down a face that broke your heart. She would have a cameraperson shoot the picture on tape at the station, then enlarge the taped image on a monitor and see if it told her anything else.

Ethnic Mexican furniture. The father? In Texas, living near the Mexican border? Or professional kidnappers, in it for ransom? Carla Ochoa had confirmed that the clothes her son wore in the picture were the clothes he'd worn on Thursday. Two days ago now. The terrifying question—was Roberto Ochoa still alive?

17

Sunday morning. Usually Maxi's favorite time of the week. Sleep in, lounge over an omelette and her special fresh-squeezed watermelon and grapefruit juice, peruse the Sunday papers, throw in a load of laundry, do her run, take Yukon to the dog park, wash her hair, get into a good book, a movie, a project, friends—a complete R&R day to get body and soul refreshed and ready for the week to come.

Not this morning.

Her mind was on a tear. Yesterday the criminalists had found shoeprints leading from the front of her house around to the back, then up the back stairs to her kitchen door, and back down again and around to the street. They had lifted the prints with foil and photography, and Jorgan told her the crime lab was testing them for brand, size, design on the sole, degree of wear, and random marks and scratches. She had since been totally spooked by the phantom who was wearing those shoes. A line from Gordon Lightfoot's "Sundown" played over and over in her head and she couldn't turn it off. *Sundown, ya better take care, if I find you been creepin' 'round my back stairs.*

Checking yet again, the digital clock radio on the nightstand beside her bed glowed 6:23 A.M. She couldn't be sure that she'd really slept at all, just turned and churned, and maybe dozed off for increments of minutes, during which time she was beaten up in her dreams, to a twangy, annoying "Sundown" soundtrack, by armies of small mutants in huge shoes whose objective was to frustrate and terrify her and generally startle her awake every time. Easily done.

No point staying in bed, on the battlefield. She got up, brushed her teeth, tied a robe over her sleep shirt, and quietly padded down to the kitchen followed by Yukon, both of them careful not to wake Carla Ochoa in the downstairs guest room. The woman needed whatever sleep she could manage.

And she saw it. Another standard nine-by-eleven manila envelope on her kitchen floor, evidently again having been slid under her kitchen door.

Yukon headed right for the envelope. Her initial instinct was to snatch it up from under his nose and rip it open, but instead she said, "No, Yuke!" The boy backed off—her dog knew when she meant business. Leaving the envelope where it lay, she picked up the phone on the kitchen counter and punched in the speed-dial number for Marc Jorgan's cell phone.

"Yeah?" he managed, his voice raspy with sleep.

"It's Maxi. I just found another envelope shoved under my kitchen door, Marc."

"Don't touch it."

"I didn't. But before you get here, I have to tell you that I'll need two copies of whatever's in the envelope when you retrieve it."

"What for?"

"You know what for."

"I don't want you to put another one on the news," Jorgan said. He was more alert now. Waking up.

"I know you don't. But I have to."

"Or what?" he asked.

"Or . . . or my dog might eat it before you get here."

Jorgan sighed. Yesterday's photo on the Saturday night news

had brought out more than two hundred calls and e-mails from the public, and he and Sanchez had worked into the night trying to cull the potential leads from the nuts. So far no leads, plenty of nuts.

"I'll be there in fifteen," he said, and hung up.

Pete Capra was starting to worry about himself. Worse, Kris was worrying about him too. He'd always made it a point to not bring newsroom problems home with him, because there were always newsroom problems, and if he allowed them to, they would seep insidiously into his home life and make it hell. This time, though, he'd failed badly. Even lost his appetite. Shouldn't complain, he told himself—he could stand to lose a few pounds. Twenty or thirty.

He was sitting in his office in the Channel Six newsroom at seven in the morning—on a Sunday. Another clue that he was off his feed, figuratively as well as literally. He and Kris had a pact that weekends were sacrosanct, barring massive fires, disastrous flooding, a major plane crash, a killer earthquake, dangerous riot-ing—any of the cataclysmic phenomena known to bring the City of Angels and surroundings to its knees with some regularity. There were none of those in evidence this weekend, but here he was at work. Not working. Thinking. Thinking about the face he thought he'd seen on the Nodori tape, and on one of McCartney's new tapes. He wished he had Friday night's and last night's tapes in hand to look at them, but McCartney wouldn't know that he would be here on the weekend, and he *would* know not to deliver them to anybody else at the station.

Maxi was going out on the graveyard tomorrow. He'd told her to team up with Tom McCartney for a while when she could, learn some pointers from the savvy stringer on the vagaries of the overnight. She'd looked at him stonily, didn't respond. She wasn't talking to him much these days anyway. But she heard him. And he'd told McCartney to take Maxi with him for a few nights on his MacArthur Park runs to give her the benefit of his experience on the shift, without telling her that he was working these shoots for her boss. All systems were go, Capra thought. If his hunch was right, Maxi's presence in the park could smoke out the San Francisco killer suspect. If this guy *was* the San Francisco killer suspect.

Was he playing God here? Was he doing something he might regret for the rest of his life? Whatever the answers, he knew that he was committed to the plan. And that Tom McCartney would be there with Maxi should there be trouble. Maxi was sunshine, smiles, L.A.'s anchorwoman, Sugarloaf's "Green-Eyed Lady." McCartney was dark, dangerous, he knew the nightside terrain, and he knew the world of deviates. He would be her shadow out there. And he would be especially vigilant in the park late at night, knowing that something had to be going on, that something of great interest to Channel Six News was potentially going down there.

And if the face on the tapes belonged to the man he thought it did, he *would* show up in the park again, Capra knew—the man who haunted him would not change his habits. Like a lizard poking its head above the slime, he would continue to surface in the obvious places.

Maxi and Detective Marc Jorgan, both wearing gloves, stood at Maxi's kitchen table staring at the second computer-generated photo of Roberto Ochoa delivered in as many days. This one looked to have been taken in the same room as the first one, with the same stained green walls for background. No chair in the shot this time. Roberto, still in the dirty yellow T-shirt and jeans, was standing, untethered, head thrown back, elbows up, both fists balled up and digging into his eyes, tears streaming over his cheeks. The two-year-old looked cold, miserable, and terrified, his face scrunched up in pain and fright.

Maxi's first thought: Could they spare Carla Ochoa this heart-searing picture of her son?

"No," Jorgan told her. "We need to show it to her. She might see something we don't."

"What do they want?" Maxi asked.

"We'll find out."

"What can we do?"

"You can keep it off the news, Maxi."

"But airing it might help."

"It might make them angry."

"Marc, they want this photo out there. Why else would they go to the trouble of staging and shooting it, and delivering it here? They saw that I put the other picture on the air last night."

"Can you wait?"

She hesitated, knowing that the police always hold things back for good reason. Elements of the crime that only perpetrators would know. "There's nothing I'd rather do, Marc," she said, thinking also about saving this exclusive for her first shift on the graveyard. "But no, I can't."

She looked back at the picture, then drew it closer with a gloved hand.

"What?" from Jorgan.

"What's that?" she asked the detective, pointing at the photo. On the left side of the printout, on the floor, was the corner of something a dark fire-engine red.

"Looks like a toolbox," Jorgan said, peering closely.

"Doesn't mean much, does it?"

"Not really. Everybody's got a red toolbox."

True, Maxi thought. She had one herself, in her garage. Still, she shuddered to think what might have come out of that toolbox to torment little Roberto Ochoa.

18

Maxi's first story on the graveyard was a behemoth, literally, on a family in Westwood that kept a tiger in their house as a pet, which tonight had mauled their child. When would they learn? This was not the first time some seemingly normal citizens had somehow acquired a baby tiger cub, delighting in how cute it was, how innocent it played, never believing that the animal's killer instincts were bound to kick in at some point. Why did these people so often have to find that out the hard way, Maxi wondered, and usually at the expense of an innocent? In this case their twelve-year-old daughter, who'd lived her young life in the belief that her parents would never put her in harm's way. As most children did. Now the youngster could lose her arm.

The Channel Six assignment editor had picked up the story on the police scanner and tipped Maxi to it. With a few investigative phone calls she'd found out that the little girl had gotten up in the night and was padding her way along an upstairs hallway to the bathroom when the animal had attacked. For whatever reason. Didn't matter. That's eventually what growing tigers did, wasn't it?

The child was being loaded into an ambulance when Maxi and her shooter got there. They'd caught a woman on tape in what looked like a nightgown with a tan raincoat thrown over it being hustled out of the house and into a police car. Hadn't that mother had the common sense to demand that this now hundred-and-fifty-pound cat be sent off to an animal sanctuary or a zoo? And there were two other children in that home, one of them a very upset young teenaged girl who was standing helplessly on the porch wrapped in a chenille bathrobe, hugging herself in distress.

And the neighbors? Why hadn't they complained long ago? Maxi had talked to two of them on camera, an elderly couple who had been awakened by the sirens, the paramedics, the police cars, the commotion next door. Did they know there was a tiger living in that house? Maxi had asked. Yes, they knew. Well, weren't they concerned? Certainly, but it wasn't their business.

More misguided adults. Of course it was their business. Now a child had to pay the price.

Maxi broke into the station's late-night rerun of a '70s cop movie with the tiger mauling story, which included shots of the tranquilized animal being hoisted up onto a police flatbed vehicle and hauled away. And a reaction shot of the man of the house looking wistfully after the animal before climbing into the back of the police car with his wife. Then the cruiser peeling out, following the ambulance. To UCLA Medical Center, Maxi learned, the hospital closest to the tiger house.

Maxi felt bad for everyone involved. The young girl who was maimed for life. The parents, who had to be devastated. Who had to know now how foolish they'd been. The other children in the family, siblings who were bound to be sad, frightened, confused. Even the tiger, who was just being a tiger, after all.

Shooting right beside her on the lawn in front of the house was Tom McCartney, all over the action, his face buried in his viewfinder. The three network-owned stations had their overnight staff reporters on the scene, but none of the independents did, which promised McCartney a few lucrative sales if he could get his cassettes to them before the rest of the stringer army weighed in with their versions of the story.

When the last of the crowd had left the scene—the paramedics with the injured child, the girl's family, the cops, the neighbors, the looky-loos—and the working press were packing up, McCartney looked over at Maxi. "Want to come with me on a quick shoot later?" Meaning after he had his tiger tape dubbed off to cassettes to pitch to the independents in the morning.

"Uh . . ." Maxi responded.

"I'll be at MacArthur Park on the Wilshire side at two-fifteen," he tossed at her while stuffing tapes and gear into his backpack, then loping toward his Hummer parked at the curb. Before she could answer, he jumped into his SUV and sped away.

There it is, Maxi thought. Capra's dictum. Get together with McCartney for a while and learn the shift. Obviously he'd asked McCartney to baby-sit her, and the stringer was complying. Well, Capra was still her boss, and she was going to do everything he ordered so he wouldn't have some reason to fire her that the union would have to accept. For a while, at least. She hated kissing up like that, but she knew that this was an elite, brutal, closed business. She would have to do it to save her career, let alone her job.

And she had no reason not to join McCartney—she'd already gone live with her tiger mauling story. Now she had plenty of time before she had to go in to the station to write and edit the piece for the morning show.

Twenty past four in the morning on Tuesday at Cantor's Delicatessen, a popular all-night spot in the Fairfax district. As he sat over a bowl of oatmeal, reading the bulldog edition of the *L.A. Times*, McCartney had been surprised to see Maxi Poole come into the restaurant, surprised that she'd shown up for coffee after all. Earlier, she had parked her car behind his SUV at the curb outside MacArthur Park and they'd walked onto the grounds together, McCartney hauling his camera gear. The park looked forbidding after dark and he did some running patter, as if the sounds of normalcy and fun might ease her jitters. And in fact they did.

"This place is the scene of one of the dumbest songs of the sixties," he'd said, and proceeded to sing the lyrics from songwriter Jimmy Webb's anthem "MacArthur Park."

"*MacArthur Park is melting in the dark, all the sweet green icing flowing down . . .*"

McCartney warbled on about someone leaving the cake out in the rain and he couldn't take it because it took so long to bake it and now he'd lost the recipe, and it was like pressing a pair of striped pants with love's hot iron.

Maxi had broken up. "That is *not* how the song goes," she'd said.

"That is *exactly* how the song goes," he'd responded, eyebrows raised.

"But it was a huge hit in the sixties—"

"And everybody was stoned in the sixties, so what did they know?"

"So how come you know all the words?"

"'Cuz I was stoned too. What most people don't realize is that the legendary sixties decade actually ran from 1967 to 1977. By the mid-seventies I was a card-carrying teenager."

"And you were *stoned?*"

"Actually, I was high on rock 'n' roll. Good songs, bad songs, I knew them all. Now, in my dotage, I forget what stories I covered yesterday but I still remember the words to all those songs."

And now he was literally stoned, he'd thought but didn't say. Last night he'd picked up a police call on the rape and murder of an eighty-four-year-old woman in Venice. He'd shot the story, and it had made him sick. Sick at heart, enough to make him stop at an all-night drugstore on his way home from selling his tapes and pick up a fifth of vodka. He drank half of it before he fell into bed this morning, no workout, no shower, just oblivion. Then tonight, before he'd come out to work, he drank the other half. That's why he needed the oatmeal, to settle his queasy stomach. And the coffee, to sober him up the rest of the way. What bothered him most was that he'd only been clean for five days this time, and he *was* counting. His between-times had been getting shorter, and that was not good. But that innocent, elderly woman should be alive, and all the evil, useless dirtbags on the planet should be dead.

He'd forced himself not to think about that because it infuriated him. Instead, he launched into more of "MacArthur Park," making Maxi laugh again at the incongruous lyrics.

He had steered her over to the vicinity of the restrooms. Lowering his voice, he'd talked about his work on the nightside, what it entailed, and how Pete Capra had asked him to give her any help he could. He'd told her to ask him if she had any questions at all. When he'd hoisted his camera on his shoulder and started rolling tape, she'd asked him what he was shooting.

"Can't tell you," he'd said with a preoccupied smile.

"Sure you can," she'd said. "My crew's gone back to the station. I'm not going to burn your story."

"Well, I could tell you," he'd responded, "but then I'd have to kill you." They'd both chuckled at that. She didn't ask him again. Protecting an exclusive was any reporter's prerogative.

When he'd finished shooting, he'd asked her if she wanted to join him for a bite at the popular all-night deli. Now she was on her third infusion of caffeine, trying to stay awake, she complained. Not that she ever slept much, she said, but this was way past her bedtime. Way past any normal person's bedtime. But she had to hang in there, had to cut her tiger story and intro it on set on the Morning News.

"So how're you liking your first night on the graveyard?" McCartney asked her between spoonfuls of cereal, which was dinner for him, he'd mentioned.

"Not," she said.

"Oh c'mon, that was a kick-ass story."

"I'm asleep," Maxi retorted. And yawned.

"You'll get used to it."

"I fervently hope I won't have to."

"Hey, you might like it."

"Not in *this* lifetime." Turning serious, she added, "Besides, I might lose my anchor slot. Which I've worked long and hard for."

"What makes you think you'll lose it?"

"First of all, if you're not a rookie at Channel Six the graveyard is a stepping-stone to getting fired, everybody knows that," she explained. "Second, even if Capra doesn't want to fire me, he knows that I can't pull these hours for long. Four in the afternoon till six in the morning. Unless the graveyard shift is temporary, he'll yank me off the Six."

Again, McCartney was surprised. He wouldn't have expected that she'd confide in him, at least on this subject. Still, as a nighttime independent stringer he was far removed from Channel Six office politics, so he was probably as good a sounding board for her as any.

"Who would get your anchor job?"

"Probably Christine Williams. She's next in line for it and she's very good."

"Does she want it?"

Maxi gave him a look that said *get serious!* "I'm sure she's already buying the jackets."

"So you wouldn't be an anchor anymore, you'd be a general assignment reporter, and the lowest reporter in the pecking order at that."

"Exactly." He could see hurt and resignation in her expression.

"Would you have to take a pay cut?"

"No. I have a contract. But I certainly wouldn't be offered anything near comparable the next time around." She thought for a minute, then added, "But it's not about money, Tom. I live modestly; I don't need a lot of money. It's about this nightmare being a career-ender."

"I certainly know about that," he offered.

"Maybe it won't come to that."

He could see that she was becoming uncomfortable with this

conversation, so he changed his tack. "Well . . . why *are* you out here anyway, do you know?"

"Don't have a clue." And he could tell that she didn't.

But McCartney thought he did. Should he level with her? Tell her what he knew about Capra's quest to find some murder suspect who possibly hung with the all-night creeps in MacArthur Park? McCartney was pretty sure that it had something, or everything, to do with Pete assigning Maxi Poole to the graveyard shift. And now he was even more sure that if he was right, Maxi knew nothing about it.

He decided not to go there. He didn't know her that well, and he didn't want to jeopardize his leg up on Capra's story, whatever it was. Over the weekend he had researched the San Francisco serial killer case that had apparently caused Capra to bolt out of the Bay Area. He had called in a favor from one of his old CNN colleagues, who'd located archived tape of the so-called San Francisco "walk-in killer" story in the then fledgling all-news network's tape library, and had copied and overnighted a cassette to him. Third- or fourth-generation footage, but still readable resolution. There were two cut pieces on the cassette, both showing a police sketch, a composite drawing of the alleged serial killer. McCartney had mounted the CNN tape on one of his home screens and cued it up to the composite drawing. Then he'd put his own tape of the Nodori bust in MacArthur Park on a monitor right beside it and forwarded through it, looking for a match.

Though it wasn't conclusive, he did find a face that could be the face in the San Francisco police artist's sketch, albeit more than a decade older. What especially made it a possible match in McCartney's opinion was the small, dark birthmark on the suspect's upper right cheek in the composite. He'd enhanced the clearest frame of the face on his own tape, enlarged it digitally, and saw the mole. In the same place. And he saw what he thought Pete Capra saw: that the two images could be of the same man. The alleged cyanide serial killer who had murdered at least nine times in the Bay Area before vanishing into the San Francisco fog.

"Want more coffee?" he asked Maxi now.

"I'd float out of here. But thanks, Tom."

"You looked good going live with the tiger."

"To the half dozen people who were up and actually watching Channel Six at three in the morning."

"Well, this story has legs. No pun intended," McCartney added with a somewhat sheepish grin. "It'll probably go all day."

Maxi agreed, grudgingly.

"I've got to get in to the station and cut it for the Morning News," she said, stifling another yawn. "God, I hate this shift. Hate everything about it."

She gathered up her purse and made moves to leave the booth.

"See you tomorrow night?" he said.

" 'Fraid so," she grumbled, but flashed him a smile.

And she was gone.

Interesting woman, McCartney mused, and went back to sipping his coffee and reading the *Times*.

19

Tuesday morning, just after eight o'clock. Sitting at her desk in the Channel Six newsroom, producer Wendy Harris was puzzled. She was still thinking about the morning meeting in the pit, the open conference area where the staff met several times each day to set the news budgets. The "early" meeting, as it was referred to, got under way at 7:10 A.M. after the Morning News went off the air. It was the day's first assemblage for the dayside executive producers and line producers to select the stories to be covered, review what tape they had in the house and what tape they would be efforting, argue over story assignments, and map out a tentative rundown for each upcoming show, tentative because news was a dynamic entity, ever-changing hour by hour, this being L.A. where anything could happen and almost always did. Managing Editor Pete Capra routinely presided.

This morning's top story was a breaker: the early-morning murder of a prostitute in Hollywood, and the ME's preliminary examination strongly suggesting that she was killed using an odd MO, an injection with some kind of fast-acting poison. Stringer Tom McCartney had shot the crime scene and brought in the tape. Ordinarily this story would be relegated to the middle of the virtual inverted triangle of space and importance that formed the shape of any day's news, but McCartney had uncovered a potentially explosive angle—City Councilman Conrad Lightner's name was listed in the dead prostitute's black book. That, and because poison was such an unusual murder weapon, and because it was the second murder of a prostitute in Los Angeles within three weeks, knocked Maxi's tiger mauling story down to second lead behind it.

The first victim was a young, blond prostitute who'd been seen after midnight working a downtown high-rise hotel lounge, and was found the next morning in a Dumpster off Flower Street, stabbed to death. Today it was a black hooker, her body found in an alley behind a seedy apartment building on Selma Avenue near Vine Street, a woman so far identified only as "Marilyn," according to some pink printed business cards found in her purse.

Capra had assigned today's murder to all the dayside shows—the Noon, the Four, the Five, and the Six. Story assignments at the morning meeting often did not hold up through the day, but at this hour the prostitute poison murder led all. The problem, as Wendy saw it, was that apart from assigning reporter Christine Williams to shoot the victim's apartment and report the story from that vantage, Capra had seemed to completely ignore the serial killer angle and to downplay the cyanide angle, instead focusing solely on the Conrad Lightner connection. Several producers had tried to talk to him about it but he had pointedly shut them down.

Wendy thought that this one called for team coverage, and she'd said so. Check out the apartment, yes, but also revisit the principals in the earlier prostitute murder—talk to the witness who knew her, and interview the original detectives who were on that case before both prostitute murders had been turned over to the LAPD's Robbery-Homicide Division this morning. And, Wendy had argued, they should do some canvassing around the downtown hotel where the first victim had worked the night before she was killed, find other witnesses who'd known her or known of her, check out any similarities between the two murders, look for friends, associates, even customers of both victims, the whole nine yards. The Lightner connection made a good lead, but if this was a serial killing, then the councilman more than likely had nothing to do with the murder. For all they knew, the number for Lightner's office could have been in the woman's address book because she had something to say to her city councilman—she lived in his district, after all, and prostitutes vote too. To Wendy, the serial killer angle was the most compelling aspect, and should lead the story.

"No," the boss had said. Just no, with no explanation.

What was Capra thinking? That these were only prostitutes? That would be totally uncharacteristic of Pete, she knew. He would never make that kind of distinction. Pete Capra was an egalitarian, murder was murder, and serial killers, if that was what they were dealing with, terrified a city. She couldn't imagine what was behind her managing editor's baffling response to this major breaking story.

20

Tuesday morning, eight-thirty. Maxi finally dragged her tired body over the threshold of her own kitchen door after her first night on the graveyard shift. Carla was sitting at the table, and Maxi dropped wearily into a chair across from her.

"How are you doing?" she asked the woman.

"Not so good."

"I know. No word yet."

"I call my friends. Is okay to use your phone?"

"Of course. I told you to, Carla."

It had been Maxi's idea that Mrs. Ochoa call people she knew, her friends in the Mexican-American community. Tell them where they could find her now, and listen for any insights they might have about what could possibly have happened to Roberto. Have Carla employ her own news instincts: be proactive, play the sleuth. Sure, it could be for naught, but you never know what you might come up with.

"My friend say Roberto's father is very rich man now. He lives in a big house. *Muy grande*. Maybe he take Roberto."

Maxi got the logic. That maybe Carla's ex-husband now had the money, the means, and the desire to abduct his son.

"What's your friend's name?" she asked.

"Alma Perez. She knows us when we are married. She know him."

"She lives in Texas?"

"She live here now. She saw you tell on the news that my Roberto is gone. She say she is very sorry to hear this. And she know Trini Ochoa's new wife. She say they are *personas muy ricas ahora*." Very rich people now.

"Did she say where Roberto's father got all this money?"

"*Sí. Drogas.*" Drugs.

A familiar story. Marketing illegal drugs from Mexico. A quick source of wealth for the hundreds of *payasos* operating on the Texas side of the Mexican border, men who were almost always cut down early by either imprisonment or death.

"We need to tell this to the police," Maxi said.

"You think he take my boy?"

"I don't know. But we need to report this. Mr. Ochoa's new wealth, I mean. And how you think he's making his money."

Before Carla could digest the possible consequences to her of making such a report to the authorities, Maxi fished her cell phone out of her pocket and punched in the speed-dial digit for Marc Jorgan.

Councilman Conrad Lightner was jarred awake by the obtrusive jangling of the desk phone in his den. Forcing heavy eyes open to half-mast, he looked around, and for half a beat he had no idea where he was.

Oh yeah, he thought, as his morning brain unclouded—a little bit at least, given the many shots of Southern Comfort he'd consumed the night before, his drug of choice. *Time I dragged my ass out of this chair anyway,* he told himself, pulling his two hundred and sixty pounds up to a standing position. Not easy. He grunted. And hobbled over to the clanging telephone.

"Councilman Lightner," he rasped into the receiver.

"Dad . . ."

Number one son, Jerrold Lightner, his firstborn. Jerry only called him when he wanted something, usually money. And usually he knew enough to call his mother for that. There was no love, no real affection, and in fact very little communication between father and son.

"Yeah," Lightner grunted.

"Sorry about Mom."

"Yeah," Lightner said again. Let *him* talk—it was his nickel.

"Is there a will?" his warm and feeling son asked now.

"I don't know. I haven't got there yet."

He *had* gotten there, of course. As soon as the detectives were through with him on Friday he'd made a call to Jonah Jacobs to ask about the will. Jacobs was the longtime Parsable family attorney, whom Lightner had acquired by marriage. The lawyer hadn't heard yet that Lightner's wife, heir to the Parsable millions, was dead. He'd asked what had happened to Gladys. He'd expressed sorrow. But no condolences to Lightner. Jonah Jacobs didn't like Conrad Lightner.

The lawyer had curtly dismissed him on the phone, saying he would have to look into the situation and get back to him. Jonah Jacobs had never shown any real respect for Conrad Lightner, just a sort of grudging civility, even after Lightner was elected to the Los Angeles City Council. In Jonah's eyes, Con Lightner had always been just an expensive hanger-on whom his wealthy wife had gotten elected to public office so he would more appropriately fit the role of husband to Parsable royalty.

The councilman was very much aware of what was clearly stated in the copy of his wife's will that had long rested in one of his file drawers. He was just hoping that Gladys had not instructed her attorneys, without his knowledge, to draft a new will over the years. Certainly she had threatened to do so often enough during any number of her famous screeching, pounding tirades.

"There's gonna be a memorial," he told his son now.

"I'll be there. When is it?"

"I haven't got there yet either. I'll let you and James know."

"Do you have Jamie's number?"

"No, but unless he's living under a rock, he'll hear about his mother's death on the news and call."

James Parsable Lightner, number two son, the crack addict. Killing himself on street drugs.

"He probably *is* living under a rock," his older son replied dryly.

"Whatever," Lightner said. He didn't really care anymore.

Obviously, neither did his brother. "If he's even still alive," was Jerrold's arch retort.

"I'll have Jonah call you," Lightner said.

"Elaine wants to come too."

Elaine, Jerry's bimbo wife. Lightner was sure that Ms. Fishnet Stockings was also profoundly interested in her husband's mother's will.

"You'll get a call," he said, and he hung up.

"*Useless sonofabitch,*" Lightner muttered, padding back over to his leather chair and dropping back into it.

He and Gladdy had never commingled their funds. Mainly because when they married, Con Lightner didn't *have* any funds—his job clerking for the mayor didn't provide for much more than the rent on his tiny studio apartment in Van Nuys and the upkeep on his used Toyota Corolla. But he was a tall, good-looking kid way back then, and he showed up in place of the mayor at many a Westside charity bash, often being called up onstage to present a scrolled city commendation or a letter of good wishes on behalf of His Honor. That's how he'd met the young and rich Gladys Parsable. And charmed her. He took her to movies, and roller-skating in Venice, and to baseball games where they would sit in the cheap seats eating Dodger dogs and yelling their hearts out. When he proposed to her and she actually said yes, young Conrad Lightner knew that he had fallen into a velvet-lined gold mine.

Her will, of which Gladys had given him a copy years before when the world was young and happier, left their residence to him and divided everything else three ways, between himself and their two sons. Which meant that when the dust settled, he would get his share of the Parsable millions.

Nearly forty years with the woman—he had goddamn earned it.

21

Tuesday night, quarter to eight, dinnertime for normal people. Not for Tom McCartney; he had just finished breakfast an hour ago. He couldn't even imagine living like normal people. Sitting in his H2 in West Los Angeles, parked on Olympic near the corner of Veteran where he knew the signal would be good, he was idly working the scanner, switching frequencies. From station assignment desks, to police, to city fire, county fire, to the sheriff's helicopter, and back again to the news outlets—ABC, NBC, CBS, CNN, Fox, the network-owned stations, the independents—surfing for news.

One of his small band of informants had just called his cell with something that had potential. Chinatown. The Three Dragons restaurant. Penlight in hand, glasses on his nose, McCartney checked his Thomas Guide for the location while the scanner squawked and he half-listened. *"This is KMJ-572 to minicam 14, do you read?"* The local ABC station's assignment editor. *"This is 14, go ahead."* An ABC-7 shooter. *"Fourteen, meet John Marshall at McDonald's fast food in Boyle Heights, First and Soto, possible robbery in progress, police responding . . . what's your ETA?"* John Marshall was one of the Channel Seven reporters—he would be headed to the scene in his personal car. *"Six or eight minutes. Over."* The crew. *"Ten-four, 14 . . . keep me posted. Out."* The desk jockey. Minimum chat on the radio frequency, but it was all there. Routine story assignments would be given out on the frequency; for anything hot, major breaking, or exclusive, the desk editor would try to use cell phones or land lines so he wouldn't be overheard.

McCartney jammed the Hummer into gear and headed for Chinatown. Reaching into his music rack in the console, he pulled out a favorite vintage Stones CD and pushed it into the player. He had it all going on now. The frequent ring of his cell phone, the drone of KNX all-news radio, the caterwaul of the scanner, Mick rolling it out, Keith screaming on his F-hole guitar, all of it over blaring street noise and the roar of the powerful Humvee engine. McCartney's ears heard and his brain compartmentalized. Business as usual.

Jagger powered into "Midnight Rambler" and McCartney could relate. *Wrapped up in a black cat cloak, he don't go in the light of the morning.* Oh yeah, the midnight rambler.

Under the Stones, the scanner crackled. Donnie Flax on the Channel Six desk—McCartney knew the kid's voice. He grabbed a pen and jotted an address. Maybe he'd have time to follow up on Flax's shoot after he wrapped at the Three Dragons.

Wednesday, one-forty in the morning. After anchoring the Six, Maxi had gone home to spend her dinner hour with Carla Ochoa. Since the weekend, which had come and gone with no breakthrough, the woman had given in to a kind of quiet desperation. Six days now. Almost a week, and nothing further had been heard from Roberto's kidnappers. No demands, no more photos, no news at all.

Maxi had brought home a big container of fish, zucchini, and mushrooms from H. Salt, Esquire in the San Fernando Valley— nobody cooked up a mess of fish like H. Salt. She wanted to get Carla to eat. She had found the woman sitting disconsolately at the kitchen table, as usual. Kleenex wadded up in her hand, as usual.

Maxi had popped the fish and vegetables in the oven to reheat and recrisp, while she scrubbed lettuce leaves, tomatoes, celery, cukes, and an avocado, chopped them up for a salad, crumbled macadamia nuts over the top, and whisked up an olive oil and balsamic vinegar dressing. All of which pursuits extended to just about the outer limits of her culinary skills. She was trying hard to pick up Carla Ochoa's spirits just a little.

Carla didn't move. Seemed not to have the energy to move.

Setting silverware, plates, and napkins on the table and the food between them, Maxi had taken a seat opposite her and helped herself to dinner. And looked up at Mrs. Ochoa, who was somewhere in her own head, staring off into the middle distance.

"You have to eat, please, Carla," she'd said, extending the platter of fish and veggies toward her.

"*No tengo hambre, missus,*" Carla had murmured, waving off the dish. I'm not hungry, missus.

"Maxi. Please call me Maxi, Carla. You must be hungry. You haven't eaten in days. Starving yourself is not going to help Roberto. You have to be healthy for him when he comes home. You have to stay strong, so you can help—"

The profoundly devastated look on the housekeeper's face had made Maxi stop. *Just listen to yourself,* she'd inwardly chided. She was sounding like a teacher lecturing an errant pupil.

Carla started to cry again. "I can do nothing," she'd said forlornly.

Maxi's heart was breaking for her. There seemed to be nothing on the horizon to cling to for hope that Roberto would be safely returned to his mother. She'd put the platter down on the table and reached for Carla's hand.

"Everything that can be done is being done, Carla. The police are on top of this. The FBI has come into the case. Maybe what you need to do is to get out of this house during the day. Try to get a new job." *Get your mind off Roberto*, she'd thought but didn't say. After all, how *could* this mother think about anything else?

"I don't know where to get a new job."

"Sure you do. You've gotten jobs before." *Careful how you advise this woman—she's probably illegal*, Maxi had warned herself. Although she would love to, she could not refer her to any of her friends.

Or could she? She could if the woman had papers. But she couldn't ask her directly. Then she'd know for sure. A thin line here.

"Carla, do you need help getting a green card?" she'd ventured.

"Maybe we'll go back to Salvador. *Solo deseo a mi Roberto.*" I just want my Roberto.

More tears.

Maxi had eaten hurriedly, cleared the table, and left Carla Ochoa where she'd found her, sitting at her kitchen table. She had to do more for the woman, she knew. She would start by dancing around her legality status with her, and helping her to make it right, if need be.

Planting a gentle kiss on the woman's forehead, she'd departed hastily to go back to the station to begin her second centuries-long shift on the graveyard. Once there she had scoured the wires, checked with the desk for any activity on the police scanners, called a few contacts from the lists Kittridge had provided, then rolled with her crew on a cat rescue up a tree in a West L.A. front yard.

A frigging cat rescue! The best story she could come up with. She'd have to romance it big time to get it slated on the morning show lineup. Maybe as the kicker. She could be in danger of becoming known as the cat woman—last night a tiger, tonight a pussycat. She sighed.

This cat's name was Dashiell Hammett. Maybe she'd pull some file footage from the classic movie *The Maltese Falcon*, sex up this lame story with a little Bogart. Jeez. This was her life, while the fascinating, critical panoply of world, national, and local news played out on the dayside. Without her.

This blockbuster, which she was sure was going to crack this town wide open, was going down in the postage-stamp front yard of a little house on San Vicente. Well, hopefully, the cat was going down. At the moment the furry Himalayan, lush gold with sable points on his ears, nose, and tail tip, stood proud and defiant up high in the profuse flowering of a lacy California pepper tree. He'd been there since early morning. The little girl of the house, five-year-old Katie, had refused to go to bed until Dash came down. After doing everything they could, round about midnight her parents, in desperation, had called the fire department. The call went out on the scanner, and there she was. Lured by a couple of elements. A distraught five-year-old and a cat named Dashiell Hammett.

She and her crew were the only newsies there. No kidding. Donnie Flax, a painfully thin young black man who wore sideways baseball caps and baggy T-shirts that reached down past his knees, was filling in for Riley on the assignment desk tonight. Donnie had told her that Kittridge used to spend many a night hanging in the newsroom if nothing decent broke.

"Doing what?" she'd asked him.

"Dunno," he'd said. "Writing his novel, I think."

Not Maxi the Assiduous, product of way too much Catholic school discipline. She would file a story on every damn shift, whether she needed to or not. And they could use it or not. "Dashiell Hammett" would be shot, written, edited, dressed up with glitzy graphics and some Bogey, bookended with an intro and a tag that reeked of sincerity and pathos, and presented on the Morning News. Maybe when the harried morning producer saw the "Dashiell Hammett" slug he wouldn't realize that it was about a cat till the damn piece went to air.

Her shooter was Darryl Dawson, nicknamed Delirious because he always seemed so spacy. Fact is, he wasn't. He did just fine with her house shots, her tree shots, her little-girl shots, mom-and-dad shots, cat shots. Come to think of it, she mused, it would be very hard to screw this one up. She was just finishing her stand-up when Tom McCartney's black H2 screeched to a stop at the curb.

McCartney zapped down the driver's side window and called out, "Yo, Poole!"

Maxi felt her face redden. Caught using the powerful resources of the mighty UGN network to chronicle the saga of a cat up a tree.

She wasn't about to let him see her blush. "You covering this?" she called, dead serious, as if there'd be no reason on earth why he wouldn't.

This elicited a hearty laugh from McCartney. "Right," he said, easing out of his Hummer, slamming the door shut, and glancing over at the brawny city fire guys packing up. "Maybe I could do a sort of your-tax-dollars-at-work piece."

"A human interest story," she threw back defensively, gesturing toward little Katie cradling Dashiell Hammett in her arms. Even Delirious rolled his eyes, she noticed.

"So, are you done here?" McCartney asked.

"Why?"

"Uh-oh. We're a little testy." He walked over to where she'd done her stand-up, picked up her purse from the base of the camera tripod, and handed it to her.

"Well, what the hell did *you* shoot tonight that's better?" she demanded to know, beyond humiliated at being caught by a colleague doing Dashiell up a tree.

"Um . . . a gangland-style shooting. Two brothers."

"You're lying. Where?"

"Chinatown. In the back room of a restaurant. Ancient rivalry between them and another family."

"Anybody dead?"

"Ah . . . one guy." Reticent.

"Why didn't I know about that?"

"Mr. Tom has wide-ranging and expansive Oriental tipsters on the overnight," he deadpanned.

"So Mr. Tom knew there'd be a shooting?"

"No. Mr. Tom knew there'd be a confrontation. Mr. Tom knew four Chinese-American men very, very angry. Mr. Tom knew these men carry concealed. Mocking nonsensical city laws—"

"Okay, okay, I get it."

"White girl should come with Mr. Tom through bowels of the city late at night—"

"Oh sure, that's a great idea. I'll cover all your stories, then Channel Six will be one less customer for Mr. Tom. What's in it for you?"

"I already have enough business from Capra," McCartney said thoughtfully.

"What's that supposed to mean?"

He ignored the question. "Look, I'm already dubbed and ready to rock 'n' roll," he said, patting his backpack. Meaning his cassettes on the Chinatown shooting were ready for sale in the morning when the various station news directors and managing editors came in to work. "You've got plenty of time to cut your, uh, cat thing."

Maxi couldn't help laughing. He was trying hard now to make her less uncomfortable, which she found gallant under the circumstances.

"Dashiell Hammett," she said.

"Huh?"

"That's the cat's name."

"Dashiell Hammett?"

"Yeah. That guy." She pointed to Katie still holding her cat, as her mother and dad thanked the firefighters who'd rescued him. "And yes, I have plenty of time to cut Dashiell Hammett before the morning show."

"Yes. Um . . . so what I was trying to say, want coffee?"

"How did you find me here, anyway?"

"Mr. Tom rules the night. Knows everything."

She chuckled again. "Okay. Cantor's again?"

"Cantor's again. But first we go to the park."

The park again. On another one of McCartney's mysterious night shoots. Intriguing. Maybe she'd find out what they were all about. Or maybe she'd find out what Tom McCartney was all about. Also intriguing.

She got into her car and followed his Hummer to MacArthur Park.

22

Aren't you going to eat?" Tom McCartney asked Maxi. They were sitting in Cantor's Deli, in the same scarred-up red leatherette booth they'd been in the night before. It occurred to Maxi that McCartney must be a regular.

"Do they always save this booth for you?"

"When they can. How about a sandwich? Their chopped liver on rye is a house specialty."

Maxi's stomach gave an involuntary lurch. "Just coffee," she said. "I had dinner."

"What time was that?"

"Around seven, at my house."

"Hours ago—"

"Who can eat at four in the morning?"

"I can. Everybody on the nightside can. This is like . . . our lunch hour. Or maybe early dinner. But I'm gonna have breakfast."

Maxi shuddered. She wasn't hungry. Just trying valiantly to stay awake. And it was only her second night on the graveyard.

"Poached eggs soft on whole wheat, no butter, side of bacon crisp, small OJ, coffee," Tom McCartney was telling the cheerful, forty-something waitress who'd just materialized at their table.

"You got it, Edward," she said, favoring him with a wide, toothy smile and giving her full head of auburn curls a flirty little toss. She turned her attention to Maxi. "And for the lady?"

"Just coffee, please," Maxi said.

"Suit yourself. Coffee right away, Edward?"

"That'd be great, Jan," Tom said, and he gave her a big smile right back.

The waitress picked up their menus and bustled off.

"Why does she call you Edward?" from Maxi.

"Edward R. Murrow. Her little joke."

She has no idea who I am, though, Maxi thought. On the day-side shifts, most of Los Angeles recognized her. But not the night people. The night people weren't watching television news during the day. They were doing other things. Like sleeping.

Night people. And now she was one of them.

And Tom McCartney was the undisputed king of the night people—he was shooting gunfights while she was shooting cats. If she had to be out here on the graveyard shift, Capra was right, she could learn a lot from him.

"So, what do you know—anything you can share?" she asked.

"Well, I just lost a jewel. That prostitute who was murdered in Hollywood yesterday—I had an exclusive interview set up with her for tomorrow night. Did you know that Conrad Lightner's name was in her black book?"

"Of course. I saw your story on our air yesterday. And she was actually going to talk to you?"

"She and her partner, another hooker. In silhouette, and for a big payday."

It was called checkbook journalism—stringers, being independent operators, could pay for interviews if they had the means and the inclination. For most of the stations' news divisions, however, money for information was strictly against policy.

"Well, you did a great job on the story. How did you get onto it, and where the hell was I?"

"It was after we left here yesterday morning. You went to the station to cut your tiger mauling story, and when I went out to my car I picked up the prostitute murder on the police scanner. It's five minutes from here over to Vine Street. It just worked out."

"Big sale, huh?"

"Five stations. But not as big as the interview would have been with the two prostitutes actually fingering Lightner."

"How did you find out that Lightner's name was in her book?"

"One of my street sources told me the councilman frequented her apartment. I told the detectives at the crime scene, and in return they told me they'd found his name in her book. They have no love for Lightner. But there wasn't any solid substantiation that he was one of her johns. The ladies were going to give that up on tape tomorrow."

"Can you use the information?"

"No. No proof now. Lightner would sue my ass."

"Maybe the victim's partner will talk down the line."

"That's what I'm hoping—they were both doing Lightner. So just in case the partner does come around for me, you can't use this, okay?"

"Don't worry. I just do cats."

"Maxi," McCartney said, looking at her squarely now, "I told you I have some business from Pete Capra . . ."

"Yes, you did. But you didn't explain."

"Your boss has me shooting that tape for him in MacArthur Park. Every night."

She looked astonished. "Why? What are you shooting in the park? He's got me out here and I'm on his payroll, and Kittridge before me—why would he pay you for night shoots?"

"I'm not sure why. But I want to talk to you about it."

She paused for a moment, processing what he was telling her. Then, "Are you sure you're supposed to tell me? I mean, if *Pete* didn't fill me in on this . . ."

"I'm sure I'm *not* supposed to tell you. But I want to. I've thought about it, and I think we could work on this together. Up to you, Maxi—do you want to hear what I've been doing for your boss?"

Maxi flashed on Capra holding back on the station's coverage of the prostitute murders. Not like him. Wendy couldn't believe it. Was their boss having trouble at home? Or was something else clouding his judgment? Or maybe McCartney's information would provide a clue as to why the hell Capra had put her out here on the graveyard.

"Okay, Tom," she said. "But in strict confidence. You can't let him know you told me. And obviously I won't either. Deal?"

"Deal."

McCartney took a quick look around the restaurant to assure that nobody was tuned in to their conversation. And he saw Rosie—fellow nightside stringer Harvey Rosenberg—leaning against a thick oak divider rail a few feet away and looking toward the two of them.

"Hi, Rosie," McCartney said to him. "C'mon over and join us."

Maxi knew Rosie, but not well. She did know that he was the butt of jokes in the Channel Six newsroom.

"He's deep down a good guy," Tom said quietly to Maxi, as Rosenberg lumbered toward them with a big, happy grin on his face. "He kinda hangs out here around this time of morning. When I'm here, I always invite him to sit with me. Nobody else ever does." A pause, then, "You don't mind, do you?"

"Of course not," Maxi said.

But she did mind. Now she wouldn't hear what McCartney had to say about shooting tape for Pete Capra. Also, she had to admit, she was liking being alone with Tom McCartney. An admission that surprised her. *What's* that *about?* she asked herself. And she answered herself with all the candor she could muster: *Because he's interesting. Because he knows the nightside. Okay, and because he's sexy.*

"Hi, Tom. Hi, Maxi," Rosie said, as McCartney moved over to make room for him on his side of the booth.

"Rosie. What's happening?" Tom asked, and Maxi said hello.

"I got an interview with Councilman Lightner tonight." Big smile again.

"You *whaaaaat?*" McCartney, giving Rosie his full attention at that. And Maxi was amazed. Every newsie in L.A. had been trying for days to get an interview with Conrad Lightner.

"At his house. He talked to me on camera," Rosie said.

"Did you dub it off? Are you all set to bring your tapes around to the stations first thing and sell it?" McCartney asked.

Looking out for him, Maxi thought. She liked that.

"Yup," Rosie said. "I had a dozen cassettes made, and I've left messages with all the stations, as well as Fox, CNN, *Hard Copy,* and even *ET.* Told the desk jockeys to put it in the log for the morning people."

"Good," McCartney said, and held up a hand. "I'm proud of you, Rosie. How'd you get him to talk?"

Rosenberg lit up, obviously pleased with the compliment, and gave McCartney a high five. "Kept pestering him," he said.

"What did he say?" Maxi asked Rosie.

"He said he didn't do it. Didn't kill his wife."

"That's what they all say," McCartney offered between bites of eggs and bacon.

"But he said he knows who did."

"Yeah, they always know who did it, too. O.J. said we should look in the world of Faye Resnick. So did Lightner tell you who did it?"

"He said it was professional kidnappers, and that his attorney has an investigator chasing it."

"Whatever, Rosie, you've got a winner," McCartney said. "How much you gonna charge for the story?"

"That's what I wanted to ask you," Rosenberg said. "How much do you think I should ask for, Tom?"

"Two thousand flat on a nonexclusive basis," McCartney told him. "Hold out for it. If a couple of stations share, like they do, no problem, it's still an excellent payday for you, Rosie."

"Thanks, man. Where should I start?"

"I'll make you a route," McCartney said.

He took a black felt pen out of his inside jacket pocket and started jotting down the names of stations on the back of a white oblong napkin. Handing it to Rosenberg, he said, "Here's how you do it. When you leave here, go up Fairfax, then hang a right on Sunset. Two and Five are close together down that end of Sunset on opposite sides of the street. Be there before the suits get in at seven. Then double back west to CNN—their news director, Fred Finley, comes in an hour later. Next, go to Nine and Thirteen, then out to the Valley to Four, Six, Seven, and *Hard Copy*. And while you're at Four, be sure to go upstairs to the third floor, to the *Today* show bureau—they've got separate budgets. The bureau chief is Heather—terrific lady. Also while you're in the neighborhood, it couldn't hurt to pay a call on *True Crime*, that new WB show—they've been covering the Lightner murder and kidnapping. I put that address on the list in case you don't know where they are."

Rosenberg studied the napkin. "Thanks, Tom. This is a big help."

"And Rosie, call each of the dayside execs personally on your cell phone as soon as they get in and tell them what you have. Tell them you're coming around with it within the hour. Tease them on the phone with Lightner telling you on tape that he knows who killed his wife. And tell them it'll cost them two grand; get them used to that idea before you get there. Some of them will make their deals with other stations they do business with, split up the cost. Others will bargain with you. You have to live with that."

"Okay . . ." Rosenberg looked a little overwhelmed. This was his first important exclusive.

"How the hell did you get Lightner to talk, anyway?" McCartney asked again.

"I've been calling him every day since that night I taped him in his car." Referring to six nights before when the Ochoa boy went missing, and the councilman had come home to find the media gang-bang camped out at his gates. "I think he's starting to like me."

"No, Rosie, Lightner doesn't like you," McCartney said. "He wants to use you for something. And that could be a good thing. So let's talk about your strategy with him now."

23

Early Wednesday morning in a small, overly cluttered, dingy third-floor apartment on Devonshire in the city of Chatsworth, deep in the San Fernando Valley on the western fringe. Jerrold Lightner woke up, squinted for a minute, and sat up, pleased to greet the day for a change.

His wife slumbered deeply beside him, snoring lightly, last night's makeup caked in the lines around her eyes and mouth, one false eyelash strip half off and askew, glue clinging to its edges, the thing fluttering up and down with her breathing, looking like some flighty caterpillar in a mini windstorm. Dyed platinum hair streaked with clumps of garish purple and fuchsia sprouting from black roots, all gummed up stiff and dry with half a can of hairspray. Jerrold always told her that between the cigarettes and the hairspray, he wouldn't want to see her lungs.

"Worry about your own damn lungs," she'd tell him.

Elaine. Laynie, she liked to be called. Laynie Lightner. She was a cocktail waitress at the trendy club Roxy on the Sunset Strip. The passion had long since gone out of their marital union, but for now it was convenient. Jerrold liked her weekly paychecks and nightly tips, which kept him in cigarettes and booze, and she liked the quarterly checks that came in from his mother, which paid the rent. He did have her signature on an airtight prenup. No way would she ever get her hands on any serious family money.

Jerrold couldn't wait to get his own hands on the money. The Parsable fortune that he'd been promised by his mother years ago. Millions, and millions, and millions. Yes!

He wondered if his father really didn't know that he was getting nothing. Zero. Living privileges in the flashy house on Beverly Glen that he'd shared with his wife, his expenses to be paid by the Parsable estate, which would be in the hands of the two Lightner sons. Sons the father had no use for, and had let them know it in ways large and small for all of their lives. Jerrold wished he could be there to see the old man's face when he got the news. Zip for Daddy, if his mother had kept her promise to him.

He would have to find his brother. Preferably dead. If James were out of the equation, he would get *all* of his mother's money. Yowsah!

At least that's what his mother had always told him. "If anything ever happens to your brother, Jerrold, and he doesn't have heirs, you'll be responsible for the entire estate. And if your father is still living, you'll set up a generous allowance for him—Jonah and the partners will work out an appropriate amount through the years according to the cost-of-living indices at the time."

And finally, finally, finally, she died. Murdered. Couldn't happen to a finer old broad, he mused. She was probably screaming tirades at Saint Peter right now because he wouldn't let her inside the pearly gates. Jerrold had been waiting to cash in for about twenty years now, and in his opinion, it was way past about time. But he had to tread lightly as the Parsable family legal team wound its way through probate. Very lightly.

And he had to find James. He would start by calling Jamie's ex-wife. A smart cookie and a real looker. She'd probably wish that she'd hung in, now that his junkie brother was gonna be rich.

Or not. Aly Lightner had found out the hard way that Jamie was impossible to live with. He remembered that Aly had wanted a family. You can't have children with a drug addict. You can't have any kind of a life with a drug addict. Maybe she'd remarried; Jerrold had no idea. But she had always seemed to be a good-hearted woman, he'd give her that. He knew that Aly had helped James, had taken him in when he hit the gutter again and again, even after they were divorced. Maybe she still loved him.

And maybe she knew where he was.

Their mother had known where he was. Gladys Lightner had made a stab at tough love. Her son would have to straighten up before she'd help him substantially again, she'd said, meaning she wasn't going to dish up the big bucks for rehab programs anymore, which were invariably wasted on James. But she had never stopped sending his quarterly checks, even though she used to complain that her younger son would probably just snort the money up his nose. Jerrold knew that Jamie had broken their mother's heart. But she definitely had still loved him. And she had definitely known where he was, always.

But she was dead.

He picked up the phone and dialed the elementary school in Northridge where he was pretty sure that Mrs. Aly Lightner still taught third grade. He needed to get to his brother before the loser made some heirs.

24

Maxi asked herself again what the hell she was doing in shorts, a tank top, and bare feet in a seedy section of downtown Los Angeles at seven-forty in the morning struggling through Thai kickboxing motions at a sweaty dump called Fairstein's Gym, round-the-clock training headquarters for the city's gnarly boxing types, with a wiry, weathered, actually endearing old guy named Zeke.

Zeke the Beak, as he was introduced to her with a perfectly straight face by Tom McCartney this morning, which caused her to take note that the trainer's nose was way too big for his face. It was an anti–Bob Hope nose, curving downward, so that when he barked out the moves she was afraid he was going to take a bite out of it. Kick one, kick two, spin around, kick three.

It was McCartney's idea. "You have to be able to defend yourself out here with all the crazies on the night shift," he'd said at Cantor's Deli a few hours ago. "I mean, just look at you—a blond, green-eyed beauty with a drop-dead body. You're a magnet. An incandescent target. Might as well have a bull's-eye painted on your shirt." She liked that he'd noticed that her eyes were green.

"So I'm taking you down to Fairstein's," he'd said.

"Okay. Next week," she'd agreed, stifling a yawn.

"No—this morning. After you cut your cat in a hat."

"Cat in a tree. Then I need to go home and walk my dog, then fall into bed."

"This morning at seven. I'll meet you at Fairstein's Gym on Grand Street downtown—I'll give you the address."

He'd taken out his pen again, written the address on another napkin, and pushed it over to her side of the table. She'd picked it up, looked at it, and put it in her jacket pocket. In her present state of mind, having a minor crush on Tom McCartney and being desperately sleep-deprived, she probably would have acquiesced if he'd said he was taking her to the Vincent Thomas Bridge this morning, where they were going to jump into the deep waters of Los Angeles Harbor in full view of the crew and the sightseers aboard the legendary *Queen Mary*.

Men. She couldn't help falling for them, but she couldn't seem to go the distance with them. Couldn't live with them, couldn't live without them, and couldn't shoot them.

Oh, and that was another thing. Did she own a gun? McCartney had asked. Of course not.

"We have to get you a gun," he'd said.

"Come on, Tom, I'm not a cop. I'm a reporter," was her reply.

"You need a gun. You can't kill anyone with a microphone."

"Unless you factor in the boredom thing," she'd offered, cracking herself up with that one.

He ignored it. "We're going to get you a nice, efficient little gun, and you're going to learn how to shoot it."

"I hate guns."

"Doesn't matter. Once you know how to use it safely, we'll get you a license to carry concealed."

"Are you nuts? Concealed where, in my handbag? So I can go in there to fish for my keys and shoot my own foot through my Prada purse? Besides, you can't get a license from the county to carry a concealed weapon unless you're a peace officer or you can prove you're in grave danger."

"You can prove you're in grave danger."

"From whom?"

"From me, for one person," he'd said with that devastatingly sexy crooked grin. "Watch out, Maxi Poole."

That gave her heart a little rush. Fine. She'd get a gun. Or a thousand-pound alligator if that's what Tom McCartney decided she needed for protection. Why was she so her own woman in every single area that mattered in life, but mush when it came to a man she was attracted to? She made a mental note to work on that.

Kick one, kick two, spin around, kick three.

McCartney had left the gym as soon as she was duly ensconced in the capable hands of Zeke the Beak. He had things to do, he'd said. Like she had nothing better to do than knock herself out with a punching bag. Ughh.

"What's your last name, Zeke?" she managed now with as much breath as she could muster, to take her mind off the burn.

"The Beak," Zeke said, and cackled. One tooth was missing on the upper right side. Bicuspid. Probably knocked out of his mouth in the ring.

Kick one, kick two, spin around, kick three.

"Higher, Maxi," said the Beak. "Higher and harder."

She wanted to smack him. Her lungs were wheezing with pain, and she knew it was going to hurt just to walk tomorrow. Her dog had to be pissed that she wasn't home yet to take him out. Maybe she could ask Carla to walk Yukon in the mornings before she got home. Yuke definitely did not get why she was gone all night now, and at home sleeping half the day. And forget about his playtime. No early-morning Frisbee in the dog park anymore, at least till the weekend, if she didn't just sleep the whole weekend for forty-eight hours straight. So now she was neglecting her only child.

And here she was, kicking the air, punching a bag, running in place, breathing in dust mixed with sweat. With Zeke the Beak. A five-foot-four geezer who was strong as an antelope and had no last name. She would be doing this every Monday, Wednesday, and Friday morning now until Zeke was satisfied that she could kick down or punch out an attacker, according to the agreement Tom McCartney had made with him without consulting her. Unadulterated pain, and she would be writing checks for the privilege.

And tomorrow she and Tom were going shopping for a gun. Then every Tuesday and Thursday morning they would go out target shooting on the practice range. Until she could shoot to kill.

All of this so she could maybe keep some low-life nightcrawling pervert from killing her.

She wanted her old life back.

25

Zeke Fairstein lifted the towel from around his neck and wiped the sweat off his face. Seventy-something, diminutive, sinewy, and leather-skinned, he wasn't getting any younger and his bones let him know it. But whaddaya know, he thought, he had watched Maxi Poole on the news for years and she shows up in his gym this morning.

With Tom McCartney. He'd known McCartney since the reporter had come knocking on his door a few years back asking to do a profile on him and his all-night workout clients. He liked McCartney. McCartney was a no-bullshit guy, an endangered species here in "Hollywood adjacent." He remembered his first five minutes with him.

"I'm only a stringer," he'd said to Zeke. "Can't guarantee you this'll go on anybody's air."

"So why should I put up with you?" Zeke had asked him.

"Because maybe it'll get on, and maybe you'll get more business, and maybe I'll get paid," he'd said.

"That simple?" Zeke had asked.

"That simple," McCartney had shot back with that lopsided grin of his.

And sure as hell, the damn thing ran as a three-part series on

Channel Nine and made him some kinda hero. And got him even more movie stars coming through here, looking to get in shape for their next roles.

Maxi Poole wasn't a movie star, but she was a star—everybody in L.A. knew her from the news. And she was dogged. McCartney told him that she had worked all night, was tired, and from what she said, her regular exercise regimen was limited to a few runs per week, some lifting, and walking her dog. But she had the mojo. He watched her put everything she had into it. And in the process, she'd let loose with a few four-letter words that let him know she was feeling the pain. Oh, she wasn't going to get Linda-Hamilton-in-*Terminator* buff, which he'd been responsible for, but Zeke knew he could get Maxi Poole in good enough shape to defend herself if needed. Because she had the will, and that was half of it.

Maybe more than half of it. Back in the seventies Zeke had trained Oscar Ramirez, a skinny kid from East L.A. who had seven brothers and sisters and never got enough to eat, turned him into the middleweight champion of the world. When the youngster had first walked into the gym with his uncle, a movie extra whom Zeke had trained for years, he took one look at the scrawny boy and said, "You're joking, right?" Wrong, said the uncle—this kid was getting beat up every day at school. And at home, too, by his older brothers. "He's gonna get killed someday, Zeke, so you gotta make him strong."

And he did. Took him on, and made him the champ. That's because the kid had the will. He would never forget the day Ramirez won the title, an upset against a tightly wound mini-gorilla from Mozambique. After the bout was over, after the hoo-ha died down and the press took off, he and the kid sat alone in the locker room and Ramirez cried. Was embarrassed about it, swore Zeke to never tell anybody, but he cried. Hard and soft, Oscar Ramirez was.

And that's what he saw in Maxi Poole.

* * *

Twenty to nine on Wednesday morning. Maxi was driving northbound on the Harbor Freeway from Fairstein's Gym downtown, finally headed home after her first kickboxing workout. Which was beyond grueling. She was sweaty, exhausted, aching everywhere, and effectively out of the news business.

Dashiell Hammett up a tree—*give me a break*. It ran as the kicker on the morning show. There were some chuckles from the staff, and a raft of phone calls from cat lovers. Wendy Harris, who had three cats at home and fed five or six more of them out in the bush, raved to Maxi that she was going to submit the Dashiell Hammett piece for an Emmy Award in the feature category. "Get a grip," Maxi had told her with a laugh.

When she went past Capra's office and said, "Morning, boss," he deliberately wouldn't look at her. She shrugged it off. She didn't know what had soured their relationship, but she refused to take it personally. Whatever was going on in that brooding Sicilian head of his, she was determined in the belief that it was *his* problem, and that she was a professional journalist and a good employee.

Meantime, Christine Williams was on the prostitute poison murder, Kittridge was covering city hall now, Capra had sent Felicia James to Colorado for the rape trial of an NBA star—even pathetic stringer Harvey Rosenberg had an interview with City Councilman Conrad Lightner, which would probably lead the early block tonight.

And Maxi had sore muscles, an estranged dog, a distraught woman living with her, a boss who hated her, and a cat up a tree.

Cute cat, though, Dashiell Hammett. All she wanted was to get home and get to bed. That was another thing she would never get used to—trying to force her way into enough hours of healthful REM sleep in the middle of the day.

Her world was upside down. Even to being caught on the freeway in morning rush-hour traffic on her way *home* from work. Upside down.

She thought about what Tom McCartney had told her after Rosie left them at Cantor's to go peddle his Lightner tapes. McCartney said that Capra had assigned him to shoot tape every night in MacArthur Park, near the men's john, and to get faces. And that Capra had actually shown up in the park one night, hiding behind some bushes. "If Pete Capra is so hot to find some mystery guy, there's gotta be a big story there," McCartney had reasoned.

Seemed logical. Her first emotion had been a little bit of relief. Maybe she didn't have to be afraid for her job after all. Maybe Capra had put her on the overnight to see if she could break this story that he was onto, whatever it was.

But that made no sense. Why would her boss shove her out into the night without laying out for her whatever this big story was, like he always did? How could she break a story if she didn't even know what she was looking for? She was mystified. Just another puzzle in her current upside-down world. When she went out on shift tonight after anchoring the Six she was going to meet Tom McCartney at his apartment, and he was going to run copies of the tapes he'd shot so far for Capra. See if anyone on them looked familiar to her.

Traffic was slowed to a crawl leaving the downtown interchange now. Maxi turned up the volume on KLOS, bombarding her car with rock 'n' roll to keep her awake. Stevie Nicks singing "After the Glitter Fades." *Well, I never thought I'd make it here in Hollywood, I never thought I'd ever want to stay.* Maxi sang along, ad-libbing her own lyrics. *"Well, I never thought I'd have to learn to kickbox, I never thought I'd have to shoot a gun."*

Reporter Christine Williams hadn't logged in her tapes the night before, the footage that she and her crew had shot in and around the New Otani Hotel in downtown Los Angeles near where they'd found the body of the first murdered prostitute, a stabbing victim.

That in itself was not unusual. It was after midnight when they'd wrapped. John Gilroy, Christine's shooter last night, said he had labeled the tapes and given them to Christine, then gone on home to Orange County, which was in the opposite direction from the station in Burbank. And since Christine was shooting interviews for incorporation into a piece on both murders to run today on the early block, and not for air on last night's Eleven, it made sense for her to take the tapes home without driving all the way in to the station to log them in—she would just bring them in to edit this morning.

But Christine had not come in this morning. That *was* unusual. She had reserved an editor for eight o'clock, and it was now after ten. Her editor had been sitting in the bay for two hours, drinking coffee and reading the morning papers. You didn't waste editor time, or edit machine time—that was a cardinal sin in the newsroom.

Calls to her home had produced no answers. Just her voice mail. *"Hi, this is Christine—you can try me at work at UGN, or leave a message at the sound of the tone."*

First her editor called, then the dayside executive producer, and finally Pete Capra, trying both her home number and her cell phone. No answer. Maybe she had had car trouble. But Christine would call in. *Whatever* had happened, Christine would call in. Pete Capra didn't like it.

Capra didn't like the story either. He'd limited Channel Six's coverage from the get-go, assigning Christine to just the second prostitute murder. But Williams was a good reporter—she'd gotten the manager of the New Otani Hotel's permission to shoot inside the bar where the first prostitute had been spotted the night before she was found dead, and she'd gotten two of the hotel lounge regulars to agree to go on camera and tell what they knew about the victim.

When Christine, a dayside reporter, had asked for permission to record these witness statements on tape after hours, Capra couldn't turn her down. He was already hearing rumors that some disgruntled staffers thought he was shortchanging the prostitute murder stories. They were right. Yet he didn't explain it, nor did he change his station's coverage of it. But he couldn't go so far as to deny Christine Williams a crew after she'd efforted key elements of the story on her own time.

So Christine had taken John Gilroy, the shooter next up in the rotation, to downtown L.A. last night after the dinner hour, when the New Otani Hotel bar people routinely gathered in the lounge, some to have a nightcap, some to wind down after dinner and a pressurized business day, some to enjoy after-theater time with friends, and others to watch the action of the high-class call girls who frequented the bar, or to be part of it.

Williams and Gilroy had worked the lounge from about ten o'clock until after midnight, Christine doing interviews, bridges, and stand-ups, and the cameraman recording it all on tape and shooting B-roll—hotel exteriors and footage of the bar and environs, pictures to lay over sound.

It had been about a half hour since Capra had sent Gilroy and Ray Springer, one of his editors, over to Christine's Westside condo in a company truck to make sure she was okay. He hadn't heard back from them yet.

26

Mulholland Drive is a twenty-one-mile strip of woodsy roadway that hugs the top of the twisting ridge dividing the Los Angeles and Beverly Hills side of the Santa Monica Mountains from the flats of the sprawling San Fernando Valley. Parts of it are home to the very, very rich, while at the same time its shrouded precipices are a favored venue for murder, suicide, dumping bodies and stolen cars, and speed freaks losing control around its treacherous curves. Street gangs run regular drag races along Mulholland on Saturday nights. Some win, some lose, and some take the long, long plunge.

This was Mulholland Drive on Wednesday morning. At the top of an old fire cut on the Valley side near Split Rock Road, just west of the gated enclave of pricey homes called Beverly Park, where L.A. Lakers great Magic Johnson lives with his family in a sixteen-million-dollar villa, yellow crime-scene tape was strung from the largest in a stand of thorn trees to a weathered wood power pole, close to the mouth of the dirt turnoff. Two LAPD officers had responded to a tip from a jogger from Beverly Park who had been running with his Jack Russell terrier, a breed of the rich. The dog had led its master over to the fire road.

Just over the crest of the berm, partly hidden in the dense

brush and crumpled up against the trunk of one of the gnarled thorn trees, lay the body of a woman in a black gabardine business suit and high heels, her purse tossed off to the side—a body apparently thrown there. A woman killed and discarded. Los Angeles, city of 2.6 murders a day.

The uniform officers didn't touch the body. Or the purse. They steered clear of the terrain within the perimeter of the yellow tape. They had called in the find, and now they stood guarding the crime scene, waiting for the homicide detectives to arrive.

When Maxi got home from her kickboxing session, Carla Ochoa wasn't there, and Yukon was antsy. Still in shorts and running shoes, she threw on a windbreaker against the January morning cold, slipped Yukon's lead off its hook near the garage door, stroked him vigorously, and told him she appreciated that he hadn't peed in the house. This did not placate him. He gave her a long-faced frown. The boy was annoyed.

"Well, you should have had *my* night," she groused, and took him outside. He didn't let a full minute go by before he did his business on their own front lawn. Then he gazed up at her with a that'll-show-you look. What's a mother to do?

She wondered where Carla had gone. The woman didn't have a car, so she would have had to take a bus. Buses weren't easy from the top of Beverly Glen. She'd have had to walk all the way down to Sunset Boulevard to the south, or the other way, north, up and over the hill down to Ventura Boulevard on the Valley side. A couple of miles or more either way. Or maybe somebody had picked her up. Maxi looked around the kitchen for a note from Carla. Nothing.

Having gotten Yukon back home and fed, she had fallen into bed. No shower, even after the sweaty kickboxing. Too weary, could barely keep her eyes open. She'd clean up on the other side of her nap, before she went in to the station to anchor the Six.

It seemed as if she had just dropped off to sleep when the

phone beside her bed startled her awake again. Damn, meant to turn the ringer off, she scolded herself, and glanced over at the readout. It was the office. Wendy Harris's line.

"Yeah, Wen," she mumbled into the receiver.

"Max, are you awake?"

"I am now. What's up?"

"Christine is dead."

"What?"

"Christine Williams has just been found murdered."

A pause, while Maxi digested this. "Where? How?" she gasped.

"They just found her. Off Mulholland, west of Coldwater. Everybody's here. You'd better come in."

"I'll be there," Maxi said, and hung up the phone.

Pete Capra blamed himself for this.

Early reports were calling it another possible poison murder. The poison that had killed the prostitute in Hollywood had since tested out to be cyanide—that much had been revealed to the press. Now the MO in this murder looked the same. There was a presentation of redness and distended swelling around an injection site on the upper right arm, a face that looked to be contorted in pain, and a bitter-almond smell emanating from the body. The latter information had not been made available to the press by the LAPD; Capra had called a friend and longtime source of his in the Robbery-Homicide Division.

"Bain and Gittleson are on this one, Pete. I can't give you any information," the detective had said at first.

"Jesus Christ," Capra had erupted to his source, "she's my reporter!"

The deceased was Christine Williams. Capra mentally retraced her known activity on her last shift. She had gone out before noon and shot a story on an Indian gambling casino that ran on the early block. After the three shows, she had taken her own car and met up with a crew at the New Otani Hotel downtown. She had apparently been killed sometime after she'd left that shoot, and her body dumped into a culvert off Mulholland Drive above Beverly Hills. Her new silver Caddy CTS was still in valet parking at the downtown hotel. Did she get too close to the case? Did the killer want to send some kind of gruesome message? This murder resonated with anxiety and fear in the Channel Six newsroom, and Capra felt strongly that it was on his head. That if it weren't for him, Christine would be alive.

Christine Williams was blond.

Pete's locked himself in his office," Wendy Harris told Maxi, sotto voce.

It was almost noon. Maxi had quickly showered, dressed, and driven her Blazer to the station, and the two now sat in front of Wendy's computer terminal in the newsroom. Maxi glanced over at Capra's glassed-in office again. He sat crouched over his desk; hadn't moved since the last time she looked.

"Has he assigned anyone to the story?" she asked.

"Who knows? He hasn't come out of there since before it hit the wires. I'm sure he was alerted before any of us knew."

"We never figured out why he didn't want team coverage on the first cyanide murder, made a big point of ignoring the serial killer angle, and we all dissed him for it," Maxi said.

"I think Pete knows a helluva lot more about that story than he ever let on," Wendy said.

"And now this. Looking like cyanide again. What do you make of it?"

"Again, Pete knows something."

"And he's terrified of it," Maxi finished.

"Turns out with good reason," Wendy said dismally.

"Has anyone contacted Christine's family?"

"I did. I went down to Personnel. Christine's father is deceased; her mother lives in Palm Desert. And there's a brother in

Illinois, near Chicago, a computer programmer. I called them both; they're coming here."

"She was married twice. Should we call the husbands?"

"They'll hear about it," Wendy said. "And they'll do what they want. She'd divorced both of them, and she didn't have children."

"So sad," Maxi lamented. "So damned sad. What's the station going to do?"

"I don't know. We can't get to the man." Wendy looked toward Capra's office again. "It's too soon," she said. "Everyone's in shock."

"Wen—I know something," Maxi said then. "I *think* I know something. Let's go talk in the cone." A reference to what the two jokingly called "the cone of silence," a usually deserted cubicle with three pay phones on the ground floor where the two women would meet when they had something they needed to talk about and didn't want to be seen or heard. The newsroom was too public, and their glass-fronted offices were too visible.

"Okay. See you there."

Two minutes later they met downstairs, and Maxi started to bring Wendy up to speed on what Tom McCartney had told her the night before, about Capra paying him to look for someone in MacArthur Park. And even showing up himself in the park after midnight. "Obviously he doesn't want me to know about this," she said.

"Or anybody else. I haven't seen any tapes slugged 'MacArthur Park' logged in. Unless he labeled them something else. But I'd have noticed if any tapes came through the system that didn't correspond to stories we're covering. They'd have jumped out at me on the log. How come McCartney told you about this, by the way?"

"He wants in on the story. I'm sure he thinks I can get something more out of Capra."

"It'd still be Capra's story. Yours, really, if you broke it. Mc-

Cartney's a stringer—he doesn't get credit on the story no matter what happens."

"I'm guessing with McCartney it's not the credit, it's the money," Maxi said. "He's had some hefty paydays from Capra."

"I heard he's got a great apartment, with every high-tech toy that money can buy."

"Who said?"

"The 'odd couple.'"

The "odd couple" were a pair of married stringers, Joe and Jona Best, post-hippie types who prowled around the stations at all hours of the night with two bedraggled kids in tow. Wendy often dealt with them when she produced the Eleven O'clock News. And they were always the source of a wealth of gossip about the nightside, if anyone cared.

"Well," Maxi said, "I'll find out firsthand tonight."

"Because . . . ?"

"Because I'm going over to Tom McCartney's apartment, and he's going to show me copies of the tapes he's shot so far for Capra—the tapes that might have this mystery man on them."

"Get dubs," Wendy said. "Tell him to run off copies for you. If he does have all those toys, then he has dubbing equipment. Tell him you have some people you want to show them to without telling them what it's about, to see if you can get an identity."

"He says the guy might be an alleged serial killer who did at least nine murders in the San Francisco Bay Area before he vanished. Get this, Wendy—murders with cyanide."

"Jeez!" Wendy nearly exploded.

"Wait. There's more. This was thirteen years ago. And the reporter who covered the story for KBAY News up there was one Peter Capra."

27

Wednesday afternoon, just after four o'clock. Councilman Conrad Lightner was still sitting in his den, in his chair, in the same rumpled polyester jogging suit he'd been wearing for two days, watching the news. He hadn't been to work since Friday, the day his wife was found murdered. Anyone would understand that. He'd been grieving. And planning her memorial, to take place sometime after the police released her body. It would be huge—all the city bigwigs would be invited. A few short, moving eulogies from himself, the sons from hell, maybe the governor, whom he'd known back when the man chaired the L.A. board of supes, certainly the mayor, who he knew was weak and whose job he coveted. Then a reception at the house, he'd have Spago cater—

His doorbell rang, the *ding-dong* echoing through the high-ceilinged manse, pitching him out of his reverie and into a place of dread. He got up and walked warily to the door.

Shit, this is it, he sighed, peering out through a foyer window at the two men standing in front of his gate. Cops, no question—he knew the look. There was nothing he could do but let them in.

When he buzzed them through the gates and opened up his front door, the taller of the two said, "Councilman Lightner? Detective Marcus Jorgan, LAPD," holding up his badge displayed in a worn leather wallet as he proceeded up the walk toward the doorstep. "And this is my partner," indicating the other man. "Detective Remo Sanchez."

"Don't I know you?" Lightner asked, squinting against the lowering late-afternoon sun backlighting the two men.

"We were here the night the Ochoa boy disappeared," Jorgan said.

"Oh yeah, right, I have your cards somewhere—" For a minute Lightner thought that this might be just about the kid.

Wishful thinking.

"Councilman Lightner, I'm going to advise you of your rights," Jorgan said, wasting no time as he walked purposefully up the front steps, removing a card from his inside coat pocket as he moved. "You have the right to remain silent. Anything you say can and will be used against you in a court of law . . ."

Lightner felt beads of sweat forming and running down the back of his neck. "Wait, wait, wait," he said. "Come inside. We need to talk about this."

He swung the big front door open and stood aside to let the men through, then led them into the small parlor off the foyer. The "receiving" room, as Gladys had always grandly called it.

He invited them to sit. They declined. He offered them drinks. They declined. "Well then, what's this about?" he asked, shuffling uncomfortably on his feet opposite them.

"It's about murder," Jorgan said dryly, then continued reading from the card he was holding: "You have the right to consult with an attorney, and/or to have one present when questioned by the police; and if you cannot afford an attorney, one will be appointed to represent you—"

"Guys, you've got the wrong man," Lightner protested, smiling amiably, holding his hands palms-up in front of him in a gesture of earnest pleading. "Can we talk about this?"

"Sure we can. Downtown. Would you please put some shoes

on, Councilman," Jorgan said, looking down at the man's stockinged feet.

When Lightner started to protest again, this time giving them a friendly little chuckle, Sanchez interrupted him.

"Sir," he said, "let's go."

The newsroom was uncharacteristically subdued. None of the usual banter, camaraderie, curses, jokes, constant chatter, loud yelling across the fifty-something desks in the panoptic open space. The Channel Six family was feeling the loss of one of its own.

Maxi had known Christine Williams for as long as the reporter had been at the station, more than seven years. Christine could be difficult, hard-nosed, judgmental, even catty at times, but she was a solid reporter who could always be counted on to get the story. And Maxi had seen her vulnerable side, more than once. She'd liked Christine.

Pete Capra had finally come out of his office and assigned Paul Kittridge to put together an obit. The murder of Christine Williams led the early block. Maxi anchored the Six, all the while fighting to keep from shedding tears on air.

After the broadcast she went upstairs to the newsroom and dropped glumly into a seat beside Wendy's computer station. The network news was on now, and UGN *Tonight*'s second lead, after Iraq, was the bizarre murder by suspected cyanide poisoning of Los Angeles television news reporter Christine Williams. Maxi could see that Wendy had been crying.

"Are you going to dinner?" her producer asked, trying to cover up her tears.

"Who can eat?" Maxi said. "I'm going home, see if I can get an hour's sleep before I go over to McCartney's apartment. I didn't sleep at all last night, and right now I could doze off leaning against a wall. Besides, Carla Ochoa wasn't there when I got home this morning, and I want to make sure she's okay."

"Did you call her?"

"Yes. She doesn't answer my phone but we have a signal—I ring once, then hang up and call again, and she knows it's me. I've been getting no response, and she doesn't have a cell phone," Maxi said. "And she doesn't have a car, so she can't have gone far, I don't think."

"Poor woman. Right now I feel bad for the whole damn world," Wendy said, and this time a tear escaped her eyes and splashed over her cheek.

"I know what you mean," Maxi said, and gave her a hug.

Tom McCartney had iced down a bottle of Amberhill California Chardonnay, because Maxi Poole was coming over at eight. In case she wanted a glass of wine. Doubtful—she was working, and between last night's long shift and the workout he'd put her through with Zeke this morning she had to be exhausted.

He had made the decision to tell her about her boss's clandestine hunt for a mystery man, possibly an alleged serial killer he'd covered years ago, and his own involvement in it, because together they would have a better shot at breaking the story. In truth, McCartney knew he was never really going to "own" this story, no matter what he uncovered. Stringers never did. Channel Six would own the story. But he could get himself a rich piece of it, a great payday if he could crack it, and more money down the road if he came up with subsequent sidebars. And he had a much better chance of doing that if he had reporter Maxi Poole in the loop. Maxi had access to Capra, and Capra was the key.

Besides that, he liked Maxi. A lot. And he didn't like seeing her worry that for some reason she'd been demoted to the graveyard shift, that for some reason she was out of favor with her boss, that she was about to lose her anchor job, and perhaps be phased out of the station altogether. On-air talent were routinely shuffled through stations like revolving doors, and when they found themselves "on the beach," they rarely knew the reason why. But in this case, McCartney thought he knew the reason. It had to have everything to do with Capra's search for some "face" that he had inadvertently shot during the Nodori arrest in MacArthur Park, and Maxi ought to know about it.

He didn't have to tidy up his apartment; the place was always neat. Funny, that trait had not been passed down to him from his parents. His mother and dad, along with his four brothers and sisters, had always been a messy bunch. Maybe his own penchant for order was a reaction to his upbringing. Or, more likely, just part of his rigidly obsessive nature.

He wondered if Maxi would be hungry. He ate out most of the time and never kept much food in the place, but he'd brought in some gourmet takeout from upscale Bristol Farms in West L.A. that afternoon. Again, just in case. Fresh shrimp and spicy cocktail sauce with lemon slices; a container of carrot, raisin, and walnut salad; some prosciutto with thinly sliced melon wedges. And from a shelf in his pantry he'd pulled down the round tin of British almonds that his mother had sent for the holidays. He had to laugh at himself, behaving like a regular Martha Stewart.

What was all the fuss about? This was a reporter he worked with coming by to look at a couple of tapes. Still, it was nice to have something to offer her—he had never been much of a host.

Oh, who am I kidding? he scoffed at himself. This wasn't just a reporter. This was Maxi Poole.

The spacious second bedroom in Tom McCartney's West L.A. apartment was a combination office and edit bay. The room had a choice selection of every high-tech piece of equipment, gadget, and techno-toy on the market. Settled in the only chair in the room, a comfortable black leather desk chair, Maxi watched McCartney's tapes while he hovered over the monitor, freezing frames, pointing to faces, looking up to gauge her reaction, then forwarding the action again.

He was going over what he'd found out about Capra leaving

his job at KBAY in San Francisco thirteen years ago, probably because of an obsession he'd developed with an elusive serial killer he'd been covering. Then he ran the two cut pieces on Capra's so-called Bay Area "walk-in killer" that had aired on CNN, freezing the frame on the SFPD composite sketch. In his presentation, Maxi was finding Tom McCartney interesting, businesslike, efficient, solicitous, endearing, even charming.

And yes, sexy, in his worn cigarette jeans and oversized shirt, which was dark olive green, rumpled, and designer, she saw—the label on the pocket read KRIZIA. Upscale Italian. Evidently the stringer business was good to him. She had a feeling that any business he chose would be good to Tom McCartney. If he'd really wanted to be a rocket scientist, he seemed to be the kind of guy who would apply himself and make a go of it.

But he really wanted to be a journalist, that was obvious. It was easy to see that his heart and soul and all of his efforts were right there, in his work. And he was good, she knew. But it was widely acknowledged in the business that he had addiction demons, and that he continually fought them.

Didn't seem to hold him back at all on the job, though—a little bit of the Rush Limbaugh syndrome, maybe. But at one time it had, according to the stories about him, during his CNN years, under rigorous pressure. Now he was his own boss, accountable to no one. When he would disappear for a while from time to time, no one knew for sure if he was on a story, on vacation, or he was using.

In any case, he certainly was the shining star of the L.A. stringer world, and looking around at his upmarket digs, Maxi figured that Tom McCartney probably made even more money now than he had at CNN. And he'd made his mark as a news-gathering original, the lone cowboy of the nightside. Looking squarely at him now—narrow, black-rimmed glasses on his nose, squatting on bent knees over a pull-out drawer full of video-tapes—Maxi felt a definite stirring down to her toes.

She reflected on that. Her relationship with colleague

Richard Winningham was a sometime thing, long absences punctuated by short visits replete with romance, fireworks, and secrets—as exciting as it gets. But totally impractical. In another time, under different circumstances, she felt that she might fall in love with him, but Richard was continents away, on indefinite assignment in the Middle East, and they had no commitment to each other. But Tom McCartney was here. And, she thought with irony, her Irish hormones did tend to kick in when least expected.

He caught her looking at him. Reflectively, almost sadly. Because the sadness of the day permeated her mood. She'd found Carla Ochoa at home, crying again. There was still no word about her missing boy. A friend had recommended her for a job, she said, and had come by for her this morning and taken her for an interview; that's why Maxi hadn't found her at home. Was it a good job? Maxi had asked. The woman had responded with a shrug. Maxi was profoundly sad for Carla. And the horrendous specter of Christine Williams's murder last night hung over everything.

"What can I get you, Maxi?" McCartney asked. Kindly. She got the feeling that he understood. They'd talked about Christine's murder when she first got there. And Mrs. Ochoa and her kidnapped son.

"Nothing, Tom. I'm fine."

"Tea. I think you need a lovely cup of hot herbal tea."

His enthusiasm and concern were so engaging that it made her smile. "Tea would be nice," she said.

"Okay. Maxi, you know Pete Capra very well. Why don't you go through these tapes again while I make tea, see if you spot anything resembling a clue to what your boss could be looking for in the park."

He pressed the PLAY button on one of the machines again and strode out of the room. She sat back and studied his tape of the Nodori arrest in MacArthur Park—not the raw footage, but a cut piece from his raw that had aired on L.A.'s Channel Two. One of the faces, shown fleetingly two or three times, sparked a hint of recognition in her. She got up, went over and stood in front of the machine, rewound the tape, and watched the piece again. This time she pressed the PAUSE button midway through, freezing the frame on the man who had caught her attention. The longer she stared at the screen, the more she felt that she'd seen that face before. An imperfect oval; the man looking to be about fifty; short, rust-tinged graying hair; intense brown eyes set wide apart; reddish, shaggy eyebrows; a mole high on his right cheekbone; a long, straight, patrician nose; slightly cleft chin. Prominent mouth.

The mouth. That's what looked especially familiar to her. Full, almost pouty lips, but set in a kind of straight-lined purse. She'd seen it before. Who was it?

Maybe she was dreaming.

McCartney came back into his office carrying a large bamboo tray, which he set down on a side table next to Maxi's chair.

"Tea for us," he said. "And munchies. I'll bet you haven't had dinner."

She hadn't had dinner. In fact she hadn't taken the time to eat all day, and the array of canapés that Tom had spread out looked delicious. This man made her feel comfortable, even on this most uncomfortable of days.

The frame was still frozen on his playback machine. "Check out that face," she said, indicating the static picture on the screen. "Do you know who he is?"

McCartney looked over at the image. "Hey, I flagged that same guy," he said.

"Why? Is he some kind of celebrity?"

"I'll show you why."

He walked over to the adjacent machine that was still loaded with the CNN "walk-in killer" tape, fast-forwarded to the composite sketch of the suspect, and pressed PAUSE. Then he stood back and again compared the same two video pictures he'd studied over the weekend, looking first at one, then the other. Maxi came over beside him and did the same.

"Notice anything?" he asked.

"You're thinking it could be the same person?"

"But thirteen years older."

"So this could be Capra's long-lost nemesis, the one he's looking for in the park?"

"Or he could be a man Capra *thinks* is the serial killer who got away. Does the drawing look like our guy on the Nodori tape to you?"

Maxi could see some similarities. The reddish hair, the angular bone structure, the mole on his cheek. But one image was just a sketch drawn from a witness's description more than a decade ago, and the other was a grainy shot of the face of an onlooker behind the principal action, actor Gino Nodori being escorted by two police officers, shot in the dark of night in an overgrown public park.

"Maybe," she said dubiously. "What would Pete's Northern California killer be doing down here in MacArthur Park?"

"Don't know. We'll have to find out."

Maxi continued to peruse both pictures. Besides the tenuous comparison, there was something else that she couldn't put her finger on.

McCartney was excited. "I think we might have made a connection here, independently. Memorize the face, Maxi, and let's look for this guy in the park."

She agreed, they would keep an eye out for that face on future park prowls.

Sitting down in Tom's chair again, she picked up her steaming mug of tea. Thoughtful. Because what she saw in the face of the man on the Nodori tape was something entirely different from what McCartney saw. Something familiar that still eluded her, but she knew that it had nothing to do with the composite drawing of the alleged San Francisco cyanide killer.

28

So the old man is in the slam! Jerrold Lightner pondered that with enormous satisfaction. It was Wednesday night, a little after nine. He sat in the dark on the skimpy concrete balcony off the living room of his Chatsworth apartment on a dirty, scuffed-up white plastic chair, still in his pretend-designer suit from Marshall's Discount Clothing on lower Ventura Boulevard, a longneck Bud in one hand, a cigarette in the other. His wife had left for her job at the Roxy in their old Ford Explorer. They didn't even have two cars. A crap life, he lamented, and he deserved much better.

Late in the business day, his mother's attorney, Jonah Jacobs, had finally returned his call. When Jerrold asked about his mother's will the lawyer ignored the question, and instead let him know that his father had been arrested that afternoon. Later, of course, he saw it on the news. Plastered all over the news, in fact. Eclipsed only by the murder of the good-looking chick reporter from Channel Six.

How could he help? he'd asked the family barrister, feigning sincerity. Knowing that he couldn't help. Wouldn't, even if he could. But happy to put up the pretense. He knew that Jacobs had no use for his father either, and was most likely deep-down delighted that the authorities were holding Gladys Parsable Lightner's widower in custody for her murder. The longtime Parsable family counselor was probably convinced that his father had killed his mother. That worked for Jerrold.

But the sonofabitch had refused to confirm his expectations about the will, the disposition of his mother's millions. Wouldn't tell him anything. "There's to be a reading," Jacobs had said somberly. "You've already been notified by mail."

"When is—" Jerrold started, but Jacobs had hung up.

Oh well, he hadn't wanted to appear eager. He was supposed to be in mourning. What a joke. One dead, the other behind bars. Perfect.

He'd grabbed his keys and gone immediately downstairs to the bank of faux brass-plated mailboxes in the apartment building foyer and opened the box labeled LIGHTNER. Sorting through the stack of mail as he walked back up the stairs, he found it, in a weighty parchment-colored envelope bearing the formal letterhead of his family's law firm.

In his haste to get at the thing, he'd ripped the back right off the envelope. Pulled out the single sheet of letter paper. Tomorrow! Sonofabitch could have told him on the phone. But no, he had to do things the old-fashioned way. Probably billed his mother's estate for yet another exorbitant hour by posting the notification in a letter. The reading was to be tomorrow at three-thirty in the afternoon. Well, thanks a lot for no notice at all.

Of course, with Elaine and him, the damn letter could have sat in their mailbox for days—they weren't exactly diligent about picking up the mail. It was usually catalogs and assorted junk. And bills.

He wouldn't have to worry about the damn bills anymore, Jerrold mused with a satisfied smile. Maybe he would hire someone just to write his damn checks. A business manager. To manage his business. He couldn't wait.

Now he had to find James. Aly had told him that the last time they'd connected, about a year ago, his brother was living in a rusted-out recreational vehicle on a chicken farm in Topanga Canyon. He had no phone at the time. Nor did she have an address for him. It was somewhere in state parkland off Entrada Road, she said. And she had no idea if he was still living there.

Or if he is even alive, Jerrold thought.

He was not thrilled at the prospect of spinning his wheels cavorting in the wilds of old Topanga looking for an ancient RV, but he had no other leads. There were tons of squatters in Topanga, last refuge of the drugged-out, time-warped hippie crowd. Only one person would have known for sure where James was. Their mother. She had always made it a priority to take care of Jamie, no matter what, and Jerrold felt that his brother surely would have kept in touch with her, if for no other reason than to stay on the receiving end of her quarterly doles. Although Jamie always did maintain that, rages and all, he loved their mother. Understood her, he'd always said. Go figure.

James Parsable Lightner, the younger of Gladys Lightner's two sons, was taller, smarter, better-looking, wittier, more creative, more charming, more everything, dammit, than he was. He even had better teeth and all his hair, God knew how with the way he abused his body. James had always been his mother's favorite, no question. His brother was more like her, while everybody said that Jerrold favored the old man, although he couldn't see it. And Jerrold always got the feeling that his mother disapproved of him. Which galled the hell out of him, because she never expressed any disapproval whatsoever of James, the golden child. Just concern. And a firm conviction that he was going to be just fine, as soon as he "found" himself. Christ on a frigging crutch.

It would be nice if *he* could find James before the damn will reading. He'd give it a shot first thing in the morning, in the light. Tonight he had other fish to fry.

Councilman Conrad Lightner sat on a metal folding chair pushed back against a wall in a small, dingy interrogation room on the third floor of LAPD headquarters at Parker Center, his hands cuffed in front of him. No table, nothing to even lean his elbows on. Still dressed in the maroon polyester sweatsuit, rumpled togs that looked like they'd been slept in, and they had. A three-day growth of beard. He'd wanted to shower and shave and change into a suit, put on a mantle of dignity, but they wouldn't let him.

They had left him alone for hours, manacled, stewing in his own sweat, sitting in this damn chair in this damn room trying not to wet his pants. They hadn't even let him put on his watch back home—told him it would be taken away from him during the booking process anyway—so he had no idea what time it was. Finally this pissant detective shows up and lets him call his lawyer. But he doesn't let him pee. Later, he says. Standard torture lite, and he would make the asshole pay for this.

Detective Marc Jorgan sat in another folding chair at a scarred-up metal table in the middle of the room, facing him, a file open on the table in front of him. The other idiot, Sanchez, was probably behind the one-way glass wall, Lightner figured, glancing up at the mirrored surface. Sanchez and who the hell knew who else. He had claimed his rights, refused to talk until Hodel got there.

But Jorgan was talking. Telling him he would be formally charged with the murder of his wife. That the crime lab techs had gathered culpable physical evidence at his home. That it would go down a lot easier for him if he would own up to what happened. That at this early juncture in the case, Jorgan could probably arrange a deal with the prosecutors for the councilman, a deal that would preclude the death penalty.

At that, Lightner exploded. "The *death* penalty! Are you out of your fucking mind?"

"No, sir," Jorgan said, referring to his notes and documents, maintaining his deadpan, maddeningly low-key tone. "Under California law, a conviction of first-degree murder could result in a death sentence if the court finds that one or more special circumstances apply."

"*What* special circumstances?" Lightner demanded.

"Multiple murder. We have information linking you to the murder of the prostitute in Hollywood."

The prostitute, not *a* prostitute, like Lightner would know exactly which prostitute the dick was talking about.

And of course he did.

Where the hell was Marty Hodel?

"We figure," Jorgan droned on, "that you killed your wealthy wife to make sure that she never found out about your extracurricular activities and cut you off, and also so you could have any damn hookers you wanted anytime you wanted them, and your wife's millions to pay for them. And that this prostitute had damaging information on you and was blackmailing you with it, so you got rid of her. The second one's always easier."

"Oh, sure. And I did it all with cyanide," Lightner sneered.

Martin Hodel had just been escorted into the room by a uniformed officer, and he heard that. "Con, do not say another word," he barked at his client.

Jerrold Lightner had to use his motorcycle, his vintage banana- and cream-colored Harley-Davidson four-speed rat bike, which he didn't particularly like to do after dark, but he had no choice— Elaine had their SUV parked somewhere down on the Strip. He'd changed into jeans and a sweater, and he planned to use his driving gloves inside.

Inside his parents' house.

He had a set of keys that his mother had given him long ago, and he knew the alarm code. The house would be empty—his mother was dead, his father was in lockup, and the housekeeper and her kid were gone. There would be nobody intruding on his intrusion. Only Janie would be at the house, and he was betting that she could use some food and water right about now, and maybe a walk around the grounds. Then he would take her home with him. Janie, in fact, happened to be his favorite member of the family.

He didn't for a minute believe that his father did not know his mother's disposition of her estate. Telling his son that he wasn't aware was Con, the pol, doing his usual posturing, he was sure. Jerrold's objective was to see if there was a copy of his mother's will in the house, and see if it was the same as the copy his mother had shown him some years ago that totally cut his father out. While he loathed his father, he couldn't count on his mother; you never knew who she was more incensed with at any given moment, himself or the old man. He needed to see if the wills were the same and, if not, check the dates on his father's copy. That would tell him which one had precedence, and exactly where he stood. In case he had to do something about it.

Getting into the house had been no problem. And there were enough lights left on, inside and out, to make it easy for him to get the job done. He'd wheeled his bike onto the property, zapped the big iron gates shut behind him, then opened the front door and headed for his father's den. And almost immediately heard the *tap-tap-tap* of Janie's paws on the wood parquet floor.

"Hold on, little girl," he said as she approached him now. "First me, then you, okay? Don't worry, I'm not going to leave you here alone."

He gave her a little rub, and she settled herself down on the hundred-and-fifty-year-old Kermanshah rug and watched while Jerrold rummaged through his father's old oak file cabinet. In leather gloves. That made him chuckle—maybe he'd seen too many thriller flicks. He wasn't there to steal anything, after all; he just wanted to get a gander at his father's copy of his mother's will, if he had one.

Well, maybe he'd just steal the little original Modigliani on his father's study wall, which he had always admired, mainly because his dad had always bragged that the damn thing was worth a bundle. With any luck, his father would never be back here to even notice that it was gone.

On the other hand, what was the bloody rush? he thought. If his copy of the will was valid, and if James was out of the picture, it was just a matter of time before this whole house and everything in it would belong to him. Bye-bye Chatsworth. Bye-bye third-floor walk-up dump. Hello mansion, and hello Rolls!

And bye-bye Elaine. A rich guy like him could afford a classy, long-legged, beautiful trophy wife. *After* he had himself a couple of years of outrageous fun.

He found what he was looking for filed under "W" for will. How hard was *that!* Jerrold took out the folder, which was marked JACOBS, SAMUELSON & JOHNS, and brought it over to his father's desk. He pulled the chain on the antique Case desk lamp, opened the folder under its circle of light, and cut through the legalese and the charity bequests to the proverbial chase.

I, Gladys Parsable Lightner, being of sound mind and with full intention aforethought, bequeath etc., etc. . . . *the rest of my worldly possessions, including* blah, blah, blah, *to be divided equally between my husband, Conrad James Lightner, and my two sons, the elder being Jerrold Henry Lightner, and the younger* yada, yada, yada . . .

Three ways, not two!

Jerrold quickly went back to the top to check the date. And there it was. This will pre-dated the draft his mother had shown him by more than five years. So the one he'd seen was the valid one. Just as his mother had promised him. The new draft read that his mother's millions were to be divided up just two ways, the bulk of the estate to be split half-and-half between himself and James. Nothing for his father except the right to live in this mausoleum till his death.

Way to go, Ma.

And the old man thinks he's in the money. That thought made Jerrold smile.

He scooped up the shivering dog, who, in her excitement, immediately peed all over his expensive new black cashmere sweater. "Shit," he yelped, and dropped her to the floor. Jerrold Lightner scowled, wiping his hands on his jeans, trying to brush the sopping urine off his sweater, while the little pup looked up at him balefully and yapped at the affront.

"Oh, you go to hell too," he snapped at her. "What do I need with another mouth to feed anyway?"

Leaving her looking up at him with big, hurt eyes, he slammed out the door and locked up the house behind him, wheeled his bike out through the automatic gates, climbed on his Harley, and revved up for home. All the while thinking about the will.

Aside from the fact that he smelled like a piss-soaked diaper, he was a happy man.

29

Thursday, ten past one in the morning. Maxi was behind the wheel, flying on the Santa Ana Freeway heading north toward MacArthur Park. On her way in to the station to write the fire story she'd just shot she intended to stop outside the park, on the Alvarado Street side near the restrooms, and take a look down the broad roadway that by day teemed with kids and nannies, seniors feeding the pigeons, hot dog vendors, the usual park population.

She had no intention of actually going into the park alone at this hour. Although McCartney was there at different times every night, he'd told her. She wondered if he was there now, on his assignment for her boss, trying to catch on tape the mystery man they had earmarked earlier tonight.

She wanted to just sit and watch the scene for a while, see if she could spot any movement from the street, any night people. Maybe someone resembling the man she'd seen on McCartney's Nodori piece, with the pursed lips and the mole on his cheek. The man she felt looked somehow familiar for some reason that she couldn't nail down in her mind. Not that she really expected the man on the tape to be conveniently lurking about out there, but since it was sort of on her way, and since she had plenty of time before the dayside editors came in at four, she would take the opportunity to scout the nightside park terrain.

And if she did see that mystery man ambling along the park's main thoroughfare, then what? How about, *Excuse me, sir—I recognize your face. I don't know your name, but I suspect that you could be the man who killed a bunch of women up in Northern California, and are maybe killing more of them down here now. Why do I suspect you? Oh, because you remind me of somebody but I can't place who, and my friend thinks you look like a thirteen-year-old sketch. And I'd like your exclusive story in order to redeem myself on the graveyard shift, so please just wait right here while I call the station for a crew so I can interview you.*

Yup, *that* was gonna happen.

She wasn't surprised at how much traffic there was, even after midnight. At no time of the day or night was there a shortage of denizens of the Southland rolling on the L.A. freeways. Los Angeles was a sprawl of a legion of suburbs in search of a city, home to a mobile civilization that had risen to its early cohesive whole *after* the invention of the automobile, not before, so it had not been forced to thrust itself upward into skyscrapers. It needed only to keep pushing farther and farther outward as it grew, because it had wheels to get itself anywhere, Maxi thought idly, as she motored along with the pack. Her gaze swept slowly from one side to the other and back, at the profusion of neon-lit fast-food joints, car dealerships, and industrial parks, all set in lush, bucolic landscaping. That was another fact of Southern California life: Anything and everything will grow here.

She had just covered a devastating structure fire on the south side of Anaheim, a time-honored Presbyterian church that had been built in the mid-forties—a beloved landmark in that community, she'd been told by onlookers. Her cameraman shot faces lit by the glow of the fire, some stricken, others just sad as they watched the red-orange flames breaking through the roof of the old wooden building, its rafters just so much dry and rotting tinder fueling the conflagration, while burning embers the size of pineapples rained down on the church grounds beneath. When Maxi and her crew had wrapped, packed up their gear, and left the scene, there was but one partial church wall still standing, smoking, its cracked and melting stained glass windows in jagged ruins, now telling just half the story of biblical times.

They would rebuild and move on, Maxi thought—that's what we human beings do.

Her thoughts drifted to Tom McCartney. He had given her tea and sympathy tonight, and a copy of his raw footage of the Gino Nodori bust in MacArthur Park, which had three different shots of the man they had isolated, the man McCartney thought somewhat resembled Pete Capra's suspected San Francisco serial killer composite sketch. McCartney had asked her not to take the cassette to the station, or tell anyone about it. She'd leveled with him that she needed to show it to Wendy Harris—that Wendy was her producer, a tough journalist, and a close friend. Wendy would be a tremendous help in their attempt to get to the bottom of this story, Maxi told him, and she was totally trustworthy. McCartney gave a worried look but acquiesced. A sign that he trusted her. In her Blazer after leaving his apartment, she'd called Wendy on her cell phone and left a message asking her to stop by her house in the morning on her way in to work—she wanted to show her McCartney's Nodori footage.

For Tom McCartney to share his tape and information on whatever was going on between himself and Pete Capra implied that she would reciprocate, share with him anything that she might learn about her boss's alleged serial killer—that was understood. And fair. But how would he benefit if they broke this story together? she'd asked him. Channel Six would own it then—the station wouldn't have to buy it from him.

Other stations would, he said. And he was right.

Funny, how energized she'd felt after leaving his apartment earlier, even though she'd had virtually no sleep for thirty hours. She'd felt like she could take on the world. Well, take on the night, anyway.

It was close to nine o'clock when her cell phone had chimed from inside her purse. Riley from the assignment desk, sending her to the church fire. McCartney was on his knees at the time, spreading port wine cheddar topped with caviar on tiny Asiago crackers and feeding them to her one by one. On his knees beside her because she was sitting in the only chair in his office, and he'd made it his mission to get some food into her. She'd jotted the address and directions to the Anaheim fire in her reporter's notebook, told Riley she was on her way, then looked up at Tom McCartney, who was still kneeling there. "I have to go," she'd told him, and he knew that. His face was about ten inches from hers.

She was not sure who kissed whom first, she just knew that it happened. And that it was one of the most sensual twelve seconds of her life.

Carla Ochoa was awakened by what sounded like a scraping or scuffling noise. She propped herself up on one elbow to listen— it seemed to be coming from outside, at the back of the house. Quietly, she slipped out of bed, tiptoed out of Maxi Poole's guest room, and moved down the hall to the door that led into the kitchen. Yukon padded out of Maxi's room and down the stairs, and stood at attention beside her. By the faint luminance of the alarm system's red motion lights she could see something actually being shoved under the kitchen door from the backyard.

Reaching down, she grabbed on to Yukon's collar to keep him from pouncing. With the dog in tow, she crept over to the window, staying low and out of sight. Moonlight diffused through the trees revealed a short, slender man in a dark leather bomber jacket on the back doorstep, crouched down and supporting himself on one knee.

Carla's heart lurched as she moved quickly away from the window. But she had seen him. Had recognized him. Raoul Montez. The rough, usually unkempt handyman who worked for the

Lightners, and who had regularly made unwanted sexual advances toward her, which she'd regularly resisted as nicely as she could. Sometimes not so nicely.

She didn't budge; barely breathed. In the stillness she heard him go down the back steps and shuffle around to the front of the house. After a minute or so, she heard an engine start up outside. His truck, she figured. She knew his beat-up red pickup. She heard it rattle off. Carla exhaled. Moving over to the door that led to the dining room, Yukon at her heels, she snapped on a wall light switch, then walked cautiously back into the kitchen.

On the floor by the back door was another manila envelope, in about the same spot as the first one had been. She stared at it for half a minute but didn't touch it, and Yukon knew this time not to touch it too. Trembling, she went over to the built-in desk in the kitchen where Maxi Poole had left a pad on which she'd written some important phone numbers. Her private number at the station, her cell phone number, numbers for Pete Capra and Wendy Harris in case of emergency, Maxi's mother and father in New York, the vet's office, and two numbers for the police detective, Marcus Jorgan.

She dialed the detective's number, as Maxi had instructed her to do if anything at all were to happen concerning Roberto.

Thursday morning, sometime between midnight and dawn. Not that he would be seeing the sun come up. Councilman Conrad Lightner couldn't believe he was in prison. They had transferred him to Men's Central on the eastern edge of Chinatown, the largest jail in the free world, currently home to about seven thousand other assholes.

Yes, he was an asshole, he berated himself, to have let it come to this. No matter what troubles or scrapes he and his brothers had gotten into as kids, his mother would always say to them, "And what part did *you* play in this problem, son?" And she would make them analyze the situation over and over until they came up with an answer, which sooner or later they would. Something like, "If I didn't hit him . . ." Or, "If I wouldn't have said nasty things to her . . ." "If I'd gotten my homework done on time . . ." Lightner had learned early on that most of life's woes invariably came right back to one's own doorstep. Not that it had ever kept him from fucking up.

And once again, a problem of his own making had come barreling back to roost, and this one was giant. He heaved his bulky body over from his left side to his right, trying yet again, and again in vain, to find some comfort on the narrow cot's foul, greasy, inch-thick mattress. What a shithole. A cracked sink with brown water coming from one rusted-out tap, and a metal toilet with no seat that was encrusted with slimy green mold at the water level. If you needed to take a crap, you did it in front of the guards patrolling the halls. They had let him have a toothbrush and toothpaste, a sliver of soap, and half a roll of coarse brown paper towels. No toilet paper. No phone, no newspapers, no magazines, no books, no radio, no TV—just plenty of time to think.

He'd had a perfect plan, he'd thought. That plan had gone amok, thanks to Raoul the retard. But he was in the clear. No reason for Marty Hodel to strike a deal. They couldn't pin anything on him. Not his wife. Not Marilyn. Not the kid's kidnapping. And when he was cleared, his constituents would be indignant about the way he'd been treated, incarcerated for no reason, and after a few dozen rousing speeches at strategic venues all over the city they would make him mayor when he stood for election.

Now he had to get the hell out of here. Marty had been able to schedule a bail hearing for Monday. Meantime, he was lucky they hadn't put him in a cell with hardened criminals and deviates. He didn't want to be somebody's wife.

That thought made him actually chuckle—at over two hundred and fifty pounds and in his sixties, he probably wasn't the type of wife these toughs courted.

For now, he just had to take a pass on the porridge and the

beans—he fucking did *not* want to have to sit down on that toilet.

Detective Marc Jorgan stood in Maxi Poole's kitchen, looking at the latest photo of the boy, Roberto Ochoa. Were these people jokesters? This one was a picture of the youngster sitting at a table, eating a bowl of soup, or cereal, or something, with a big smile on his face. Christ, Jorgan thought, maybe it was ice cream.

The boy was dressed in different clothes now. In the picture he was hidden from the waist down by the table, so Jorgan couldn't see the boy's pants or shoes, but Roberto was wearing what looked like a white cotton shirt, a little big for him but clean. Not the stained yellow T-shirt he'd had on in the first two photos, the shirt he was wearing when he was snatched, according to his mother, who stood by now, nervously hovering.

Jorgan studied the new photo carefully, looking for clues to Roberto's whereabouts. The walls were light-colored—not the dingy industrial green of the last two pictures. It could be just a different room, but he got the sense that it was a different place altogether. A different house or apartment. The texture was different. The light was different. The ambience was different.

So the boy had most likely been moved. And he actually looked like he was being well taken care of. He looked happy. You couldn't fake that with children. Kidnappers and terrorists could make adults act happy for photos, but you couldn't do that with kids. Even if you were able to coerce them to smile, you knew it when a child was upset, or scared, or both. In this picture, Jorgan could see that Roberto Ochoa's smile reached his eyes.

He'd located Maxi on her cell—parked at the edge of MacArthur Park, she'd said, at one-thirty in the morning. He didn't like that she was working this overnight shift. What was wrong with UGN? Didn't they have men to put on that duty? Maxi would probably say that he was being sexist if she knew he had those thoughts. Nor would he dare say that about the women officers whom the department put out on the night watch.

Maxi was on her way home now. He was not going to give her a copy of this photo. He didn't want this one on the news. She might give him a fight over it, but this one was his.

30

Early Thursday morning, one-thirty-five. Maxi closed her cell phone after talking to Marc Jorgan, and it rang again in her hand. Tom McCartney. Her heart did a little leap thing at the sound of his voice. Which annoyed her.

"Where are you?" she asked him.

"In the park. And you're outside."

"How did you know?" Stupid question to ask a reporter.

He ignored it. "What's up?" he asked.

"I'm on my way in to the station to cut my St. Albans Church fire. Anaheim. The church is a total loss."

"Arson?"

"No indication, at least not yet."

She didn't tell him about the latest photo of Roberto Ochoa being delivered to her house a while ago. This story was hers, and more than that, it was at her house. And she had to be careful about getting too cozy with McCartney. At least professionally.

Personally, may the good Lord help her, she couldn't wait.

With the phone to her ear, she started up the Blazer and headed north toward Wilshire Boulevard. Her ancient SUV was her designated graveyard-shift vehicle tonight—fifteen years old but it ran just fine, thank you. A few years ago she'd considered for a minute having it painted, but decided she liked it the way it was. Lived-in. If she ever wanted to sell the heap, she'd get about five dollars for it.

"Want coffee?" McCartney asked.

"I can't tonight, Tom." She didn't explain.

"No problem. Are we still going shopping in the morning?" For a gun. "Sure."

"Nine o'clock?"

"Works for me." Another day with little or no sleep. But she wanted to see him.

"Sierra Guns and Ammo in the Valley—I gave you the address."

"On Ventura Boulevard. I've got it."

"Great. I'll meet you there."

"Uh—Tom?"

"Yo?"

"On the coffee. Can I have a rain check?" Didn't want him to think the kiss had scared her off.

"You bet. See you at nine. If you can't make it, call my cell."

He clicked off. She was heading west on Wilshire now, toward Beverly Glen and home. Marc Jorgan was at her house with Carla. He'd told her that Carla saw and recognized the man who delivered the photo tonight. She had to hurry home and see what that was about, then rush in to the station to cut her fire story. At least she wouldn't have to stick around to intro it live on the morning show—the producer wanted a self-contained package, so she'd done a stand-up from the scene. That would give her time to meet with Wendy and show her the mystery man on the Nodori raw footage before she went over to the Valley to meet McCartney at the gun store.

Thursday morning, about quarter to three. LAPD Detective Marcus Jorgan, with Maxi Poole and a cameraman in tow, was about to roust one Raoul Montez out of bed.

When Carla Ochoa ID'd the man who'd shoved the latest photo of her son under Maxi's back door, he'd run a DMV trace on Montez. Since it was on the far side of normal business hours he'd had to wake up his friend Nelson Broderick in Sacramento, deputy director of the Licensing Operations Division of the California Department of Motor Vehicles.

Broderick was not happy about this, but he did go into his study and access his laptop, which was linked to his computer at the office. But not before he'd gotten Jorgan to agree to buy him dinner next week at Ruth's Chris, the pricey steakhouse on Beverly Drive. Broderick had business in L.A. on Wednesday, he said, and Wednesday night would be perfect for him.

Jorgan felt himself wince as he okayed the date. Prime steaks at Ruth's *started* at twenty-five bucks a pop, and that was before the drinks, the wine, the appetizers, side dishes, and dessert. If Jorgan had a wife, this is where he'd take her. Maybe it was a good thing he didn't have a wife.

It took Broderick less than five minutes to call him back with an address, and Jorgan had driven there from Maxi Poole's house, with Maxi following right behind him. There was no keeping her out of this loop. Besides the fact that she'd been in the thick of this case from the night the boy was taken, and that she was the one who'd tipped him to it, and the photos were delivered to her home, and the kidnapped boy's mother happened to be staying with her, it is, after all, a free country—you're allowed to drive anywhere you want to. Maxi had stayed glued to him while he made the call to Broderick, she'd heard him ask for the trace on Montez, and when he rolled out, she peeled out after him in her battered Chevy Blazer, with her big dog Yukon sitting tall in the passenger seat beside her.

The address Broderick had given him was in Valencia, twenty-two miles north of Los Angeles, off the 5 freeway near the Ventura County line. Before they left, Maxi had called her station for a crew. Her cameraman, whom she introduced as Jersey, had gotten there before them from UGN in Burbank, and he'd had time to case the environs. He and Maxi were in touch by cell phone, and he'd reported that the address was a trailer park in a wooded area south of Magic Mountain. Maxi called Jorgan on his cell and shared the information.

Jersey had waited for them about a quarter of a mile away from the location, parked on the deserted street that fronted the mobile home park. When Jorgan and Maxi rolled by in tandem, he'd pulled out in the big Channel Six live truck and fallen in behind them. The three vehicles reached the entrance to the drab trailer park and pulled up side by side in the dirt. The three drivers got out in unison and loudly slammed their doors. These people were going to need some waking up.

Maxi had left Yukon in her truck, which clearly ticked the boy off. She'd cracked the front windows about a third of the way down to make sure he got enough air, and as the three trudged up a long dirt driveway that led inside the park, they could hear him whining. Yukon was rightfully pissed to be left behind, Maxi told the other two, but she didn't want to put her pup in harm's way.

The three were approaching what looked to be a manager's shed now, Marc Jorgan with gun drawn, Maxi with wireless microphone in hand, and Jersey with camera hoisted on his shoulder and headlamp glaring, rolling tape. The crude shed was about the same size as the average trailer but built of wood shingles and standing on a concrete slab, with a hand-painted sign tacked to its siding that spelled out HAPPY TRAILS in glazed acorns glued to plywood. They couldn't see a doorbell, so Jorgan called out through a bullhorn. A sleepy-looking Hispanic man in boxer shorts and a tattered white undershirt opened the door. While scratching the bottom of his heavy belly, he looked grumpily at the raucous trio.

"Keep it down, you could wake up the dead. Whaddaya want?" he rasped.

Jorgan badged him. "What's your name, sir?"

Waking up some, the man identified himself as Manuel Aliva, manager of the trailer park.

"We're looking for Raoul Montez," Jorgan said.

Montez was in number eight, Aliva said. No wife, no kids, no pets, he lived alone, at least when he don't have some chickie in there, were Aliva's mumbled answers, in heavily accented English, to Jorgan's questions. And yes, he was probably home now; Aliva had seen the guy's truck in front of his trailer earlier tonight. But evidently he had not seen him leave after midnight to deliver a photograph to Maxi Poole's house.

"I don't want no trouble," Aliva said as the three set off down the path to number eight.

"Right," Jorgan said without looking back.

Raoul Montez's trailer was a run-down, dirty-yellow manufactured home up on concrete blocks, bolstered by corrugated aluminum with rusted edges set against the skirting. It had a built-on porch that housed an old metal stove, and a noisy air-conditioning unit protruding from a window in what was probably the sleeping area. Three overflowing trash cans and an assortment of boxes filled with fetid garbage littered the dry dirt out front, and parked near the door was a scraped and dented red Ford pickup.

Marc Jorgan's banging and a couple of barking dogs from neighboring trailers apparently startled Montez out of bed. The torn screen door to the trailer opened and a slight man of medium height peered out, rubbing his eyes, his face pinched, squinting against the harsh television light at these people who had invaded his castle at three in the morning. He couldn't have been sleeping for very long, they knew.

"Where's the Ochoa child?" Jorgan demanded.

"I don't know about the boy," Montez blurted.

"How do you know it's a boy?" Jorgan asked.

This evidently confused the man—he looked blank and said nothing.

"Are you Raoul Montez?"

That one he could handle. He nodded. And Jorgan read him his rights.

"Mr. Montez, do you understand what I've just read to you?" Jorgan asked him then.

"Sí," Montez replied, though he looked like he understood nothing.

"May we come in?" Jorgan asked.

"No. Usted no puede venir aquí." You can't come in here. Montez held firm to the metal pipe railing around the rickety porch, blocking entrance to his trailer.

"Don't make me wake up a judge, go all the way downtown to get a warrant, and come back out here," Jorgan barked.

Montez shrugged.

"You were identified by an eyewitness a couple of hours ago when you delivered a photo of Roberto Ochoa to this woman's house," Jorgan said, indicating Maxi, who held the microphone toward Montez's chin.

"I don't know nothing," Montez said, lifting up his palms, letting the screen door bang shut behind him.

"What do you mean, you don't know? You were there. The boy's mother saw you. She knows you. You work for the Lightners."

"I don't know what's inside the envelope," he said. "I'm delivering it for someone."

"Who?" Jorgan demanded.

"No puedo decir," Montez demurred. "If I say, this person will kill me."

"You're coming to police headquarters, Mr. Montez."

With that, Jorgan reached out and pulled the man's hands in front of him and snapped a pair of plastic handcuffs on his wrists. He locked him inside his Crown Vic while he did a search of the trailer. Roberto Ochoa was not inside.

31

Thursday morning, a little after six, at Maxi Poole's house on Beverly Glen. Carla Ochoa was still asleep in the guest room. Maxi had just gotten home after her long and bizarre night on the graveyard shift, and Wendy had been on her way in to the station to work the dayside.

"We're the proverbial ships," from Wendy.

They were in Maxi's study perched in front of her big-screen television monitor, screening Tom McCartney's raw Nodori tape. Maxi waited for the first shot of the mystery man to roll into view, then quickly punched the PAUSE button, freezing the image on the screen.

"That's him," she said.

Wendy scrutinized the image. "This is the guy Tom McCartney thinks could have been a serial killer in San Francisco?"

"Yes. Do you recognize him?"

"No. Should I?"

"I can't help feeling I've seen him before."

Maxi fast-forwarded to two more shots of the man on the tape. Wendy stared at each of the images. "Hmmm . . . he does look familiar. But they're not really good visuals. Got any better shots of him?"

"Tom McCartney might—he's been shooting tape at the same location every night for a week."

"And if this is that killer, what's his story?"

"Thirteen years ago the man was a suspect in at least nine murders up in the Bay Area, then suddenly he completely disappeared."

"Like the Zodiac killer." Wendy was from San Francisco.

"That's right. And as I said, Pete Capra was KBAY's reporter on the story." She told Wendy what McCartney had learned about their boss's seeming obsession with this alleged killer, and how he'd even lost his job over it.

"There's always the one story that haunts you," Wendy mused. "Are there any pictures of the suspect?"

"No. Only a sketch made from an eyewitness's description told to a police artist." She opened a folder on her desk and showed Wendy an Internet printout McCartney had made for her of a *San Francisco Chronicle* article on the alleged Bay Area "walk-in killer," complete with the composite drawing.

"And you think this is the same guy," Wendy said, looking from the composite up to the face frozen on Maxi's television monitor, just as she and McCartney had done the night before.

"Could be—he'd be thirteen years older. This mole shows up in the drawing," Maxi said, pointing to the birthmark on the man's right cheek.

"We need a close-up." Wendy was squinting at the screen now.

"That has to be why Capra assigned Tom to shoot tape in MacArthur Park. For some reason he must figure that the guy hangs out there. A regular."

"So the point is, *Capra* thinks it's the killer, right?"

"That's what we're guessing. Capra hasn't said a word about any of it. Tom just cobbled this scenario together from tapes and information off the Net and from a couple of his colleagues at CNN and KBAY."

"But why would Capra keep this a secret? Why wouldn't he

put his staff on it? Or at least you, Maxi, since you're out there at night. I mean, this must be why he put you on the graveyard, don't you think?"

"Good questions. I don't know what to think."

"Are you sure Pete hasn't brought the police into it?"

"I doubt it. You know the desk is aware of all stories that involve law enforcement. We'd know."

"Maybe he just confided it to one of his pals at Parker Center, kept it off the log," Wendy offered.

"I don't think so, Wen. It's way out of LAPD's jurisdiction—this case was never theirs."

"Okay—so where do we go from here?"

"If he's out there I'm gonna find this guy. Bring him to Capra with a big red ribbon tied around his neck. Maybe I'll take him to lunch in the commissary and invite Pete to join us. We'll have that hash thing they always make on Monday from last week's leftovers—that'll kill him."

"Not funny, Max. You're dealing with some whack-job who prowls around with the L.A. bottom-feeders after midnight. This is a dangerous game—he could be Christine's killer."

"And if he is, he could kill again. And probably will if he isn't stopped."

"It's not your job to stop him, Maxi."

"I'm not after the man. I'm after the story. And if the story helps nail the man, even better."

Wendy thought for a beat, then said, "I think we should confront Pete and demand that he tell us what the hell this is about. He's manipulating you."

"True, but you know Pete. He's got his reasons to stay mum, justified or not. Which means he'll only shut us down."

"Maybe that would be a *good* thing," Wendy countered, looking hard at Maxi.

"Not yet," Maxi said. "Let's not tip Capra that we know anything. He's trying to keep us all in the dark—let's pretend we are, and see what crawls out from the night slime."

Wendy gave a resigned shrug and picked up the "walk-in killer" file folder, which contained copies of the composite drawing of the suspect and several dated stories from San Francisco newspapers. While she looked through the material, Maxi mulled over the dizzying events of the night before. Marc Jorgan had phoned her from her own house—Carla Ochoa had called him there; another photo of Roberto had been shoved under her door. She'd dashed home to see the new computer-generated picture: little Roberto actually looking well and happy. Carla Ochoa identified the midnight mailman, Jorgan made the guy's address, and she did a ride-along to the man's happy home with a crew in tow. It was a wild scene, ending with one Raoul Montez being taken downtown. But they didn't find Roberto.

She'd agreed with Jorgan, even though she had it all on tape, to keep the trailer rout of Montez, along with the new photo of Roberto, off the morning news until the detective could question the man, this in the interest of the kidnapped boy's safety. Also, Jorgan didn't want the FBI team on the case alerted to this new development yet. He didn't trust the hotheaded lead agent, Bill McFarland. She'd asked him how he could get away with not bringing the Bureau up to speed immediately, and he had just winked. Jorgan had Montez in custody, and he wanted first crack at the man in the interrogation room. She'd agreed to keep the bust off the air, at least this morning.

Wendy finished going through the "walk-in killer" file and closed the folder. "So you're going to look for this creep in MacArthur Park," she said.

"I'll be fine," Maxi second-guessed her friend. "No need to worry, Wen—you'd be amazed at how many people are hanging in the park in the small hours."

"Sure—all perverts and crazos."

Maxi chuckled. "Hey, they're my people. The night people. They'd protect me if it came to that."

Wendy just rolled her eyes.

"Seriously, MacArthur Park is right around the corner from

the Rampart station. A 911 call from my cell phone would bring the police in minutes."

"What if you don't have minutes?"

"What if my pantyhose catch on fire? C'mon, Wen, lighten up."

From long experience, Wendy Harris knew she wasn't going to change her friend's mind about seeking out this alleged killer who could be in their area now, prowling the nightside. She looked at her watch. "I've got to get in for the morning meeting."

"Oh, and I'm going to buy a gun," Maxi said.

"What?"

"Tom McCartney's idea. He says I need it for self-defense on the graveyard, and I can get a county license to carry concealed." She grinned.

"This isn't funny, Max."

Maxi sighed. "Listen," she said, as she and Yukon walked her producer to the front door, "do you think you could get your hands on the tapes Pete's getting from MacArthur Park so we can scan for this guy?" She turned and indicated the image still up on the screen.

"Doesn't McCartney make duplicates?"

"Yes, but I don't want to ask him for them. Try to find Pete's tapes."

"Sure, easy," Wendy said, giving Yukon a quick neck rub. "Lend me your new gun and I'll just point it at Pete and say, 'Put up your hands and gimme all your tapes.'"

32

Thursday morning, five after nine, at Sierra Guns & Ammo on Ventura Boulevard in Sherman Oaks. Looking around the place, Maxi was overwhelmed, confused, and totally uncomfortable with the whole concept of purchasing a gun, let alone actually toting the thing in her purse along with her car keys, makeup kit, and reporter's notebook. But Tom McCartney had convinced her that she needed to be able to protect herself out on the graveyard. She'd asked him if *he* carried a gun at night, and he didn't answer the question, just gave her one of his *duhhh!* looks. A gun, and the kickboxing. Tomorrow morning she was due for another pounding session with Zeke. She felt her joints emitting a quick spurt of pain just from the sense memory of it. And she bemoaned the prospect of getting a half-decent night's sleep ever again.

Maybe Tom McCartney was right about her need to be able to defend herself if it ever came to that, considering what she was finding out about the Bay Area serial killer who used cyanide, who might now be doing his deadly work down here in Southern California, and given the man's longtime connection with her boss. Her boss who had assigned her to the overnight shift that would seem to put her directly into this man's orbit. McCartney had grasped the situation before she did. It had now been determined that both the Hollywood prostitute and Christine Williams who'd been covering the story had been murdered with cyanide.

But a gun? As standard equipment for a reporter? Nobody ever told her in journalism class that a gun after dark should be part of her gear. How about a dog after dark? Yukon went to the station with her whenever she did fill-in anchoring on the Eleven O'clock News. The troops who worked the late show adored him, called him "Newsdog." Her plan was to take him out with her every night on the graveyard, as soon as she knew her way around the nightscape a little better. Yuke looked significantly threatening sitting in the front seat of the car with her, but in truth, the boy was just a big old cuddly bear, her gentle giant. His job was to *look* scary, not actually *be* scary. She didn't expect or want him to fight anybody off, especially since last year's terrible slashing—in reality, *she* felt responsible now to be protective of *him*.

So she was going to buy a gun. Today.

The store owner obviously knew Tom McCartney. The two men were doing guy talk about Maxi as if she wasn't in the room, their dialogue ping-ponging from one to the other about what would be the most appropriate firearm for her. Just as well she was excluded, she figured, since she didn't have a clue what they were talking about anyway.

"She'll need to take a basic firearms safety class, of course," the owner, Arthur Brinker, was saying to McCartney.

"I think I'm going to put her with Chaz," McCartney said. "He's got that slick new place over in Glendale now, have you seen it? With a totally contained ten-lane shooting range. And with a bunch of certified instructors, he offers a comprehensive syllabus."

"Yeah, Chaz is one of the best with the basics—safety issues, use, storage, transportation, cleaning."

"And he brings in cops and lawyers to discuss the legal and practical issues related to using a firearm in self-defense."

"That's critical. The Sampson brothers are good, too, you know."

"Too far out for her. They're in Castaic."

"Oh, yeah. She probably works long hours. Well let's take a look at the inventory."

"Okay. I want something that feels comfortable in the hand. She's an absolute virgin, Art."

Virgin?

"Hmmmm." The owner took a look at Maxi. "Small hands."

"Strong, though. When she gets it, she'll get it."

Maxi scanned the wide array of stock on display in glass cases. She watched as McCartney and the gun dealer walked along the aisles, the owner removing gleaming weapons from cases one by one, and the two discussing the merits and drawbacks of each different offering. From where she stood she was able to pick up just pieces of their conversation. "How about this nifty Colt Python?" "The standard police-issue Beretta nine is still sexy . . ." "What's Smith and Wesson come out with lately?" "You like the SIG Sauer, Artie?"

She caught up with them and followed behind. Figured she should at least try to look interested, since this exercise was all about her. Then she heard the shop owner pronounce his opinion. "I'd go for the Glock 19, Tom." Art pointed to a gun in one of the cases.

"Because . . . ?"

"Because first of all, we know that self-loading pistols are the best for self-defense, and particularly for concealed carry." He lifted the gun out of the case and handed it to McCartney. "See, this baby is light, and it has a safe-action trigger system that will allow her to shoot fast and straight."

"Yeah, and it won't have a negligent discharge. Like a conventional SIG double-action self-loader I had once. It had such a long, hard trigger pull on the first shot that even with tons of practice I couldn't hit as fast with the first shot as I could with subsequent shots."

What language are they speaking? Maxi wondered.

"And you don't want the Colt for her," Art put in. "Requires way too much attention to operating the external safety lever. She might not always do it correctly, particularly under stress."

"I think you're right. The Glock has a relatively short, light trigger pull that she'd be able to manage." He examined the gun in his hand.

"Exactly. The trigger pull is the same on every shot, and whenever her finger is off the trigger, this pistol is drop-safe. And there are no external safety controls to manipulate."

"Or *forget* to manipulate," McCartney said, and they both laughed.

"And this one is just about the smallest and lightest self-loader there is in nine-millimeter, which is the size I think is right for her." He took the gun from McCartney and turned it over in his hands. "Besides, it's smooth and snag-free, a definite plus for concealed carry."

"And how about this low bore axis?" McCartney pointed out to the dealer some feature that completely eluded Maxi. "I mean, that makes recoil a lot easier to manage, doesn't it?"

"True," Art said. "And this one has relatively few parts. Makes it easy to disassemble and maintain."

"How much?" McCartney asked.

"Four hundred and twenty. Plus ammo, cleaning apparatus, and a holster if she needs one."

"Nah, no holster. Women carry in their purses. Oh, let me ask you something, Art. Can this grip shape and size be modified with aftermarket screw-on panels?"

"No, it can't. If the stock Glock grip feels good in her hand, great. If it doesn't, you need to buy her something else, that simple."

"But I heard that Hogue has come out with a rubber sock that slips over the Glock grip, which would give it a softer surface and a more rounded shape. You know about that?"

"Forget it," Art said. "That rubber grip tends to grab on cloth. Makes the gun less concealable."

"Good point."

"Look, man, I think this Glock 19 is overall the best self-loading pistol for her. The safe-action trigger system will give her the fastest, most accurate first shot on the market, and the first shot is the one that wins gunfights."

Great, Maxi thought. *Gunfights.*

Tom took the weapon of choice from Art and put it in her hand. "How does this one feel, Maxi?" he asked her.

"Fine," she said out loud. *Like I'd know*, she said to herself.

"We'll take it, Art," McCartney said, taking the Glock from her and handing it back to the proprietor. Maxi was glad to get the thing out of her hands. "Outfit her with whatever she needs," he continued, "and she'll be in business."

Oh dear God, I want my old life back, Maxi thought as she handed the gun dealer her credit card.

33

Thursday afternoon, one-fifteen. Detective Marc Jorgan was shifting in place, trying to settle into a coach seat built for Lilliputians on a Southwest Airlines Boeing 737 bound for El Paso. Historic El Paso del Río del Norte on the Tex-Mex border along the scenic Rio Grande, the oldest city in the state of Texas, home to legendary Spanish merchant Juan María Ponce de León, and home to Trinidad Ochoa, former husband of Carla Ochoa and father of Roberto.

This morning Jorgan had taken handyman Raoul Montez into custody, but the man was not talking. In this country, you couldn't force a prisoner to talk. It was obvious to the detective and his partner that Montez was afraid. Somebody had gotten to him. Someone who knew that Montez had access to the Lightner estate had hired him, coerced him, or otherwise put him up to becoming involved in the kidnapping of Roberto Ochoa, whether it was simply delivering the pictures to Roberto's mother at Maxi Poole's house, or pulling off the actual kidnapping, or something in between.

Since Raoul Montez had been spotted by Mrs. Ochoa dropping a third photo of the kidnapped boy at Maxi's home this morning, Jorgan's thoughts had gone to the boy's father, reportedly living in a pricey house in the Lone Star State. He'd decided to take a trip to Texas and have a look.

Needless to say, this was going to be a surprise visit to the Ochoa household by LAPD Detective Two Marcus Jorgan. He was carrying duplicate prints of the photos of Roberto that had been deposited under Maxi Poole's back door. He especially wanted to check out the dining table at Mr. Ochoa's house, see if it matched the table in the latest picture. And the cereal bowls—was there a set of dishes in a sunny yellow-and-orange plaid pattern in the house? And most important, did there happen to be a two-year-old in residence who resembled the young boy pictured in the three photos he had in his overnight bag?

Jorgan was considering these questions when the flight attendant came by again. MARIELA. That's what the nameplate pinned on her jaunty denim shirt spelled out, the crisp top worn with navy blue shorts, flat shoes, and an incredible pair of long, lean, golden legs. Which he tried not to notice. Shorts in January?

"More nuts, Detective Jorgan?" Mariela fairly beamed, flashing a smile that lit up the cabin.

Curly red hair. Lots of it. Extending a well-manicured hand that was holding two foil bags of honey roasted peanuts. A silver ring—on her thumb. He glanced at her left hand. Just a set of two small matching turquoise-and-silver rings on her pinkie. Jewelry with a romantic blend of Mexican and American culture. Like Mariela. Country singer Marty Robbins started singing in his head: *Out in the West Texas town of El Paso, I fell in love with a Mexican girl* . . . Mariela. Jorgan was a closet romantic. Deep closet—his cop colleagues could never know that about him or the teasing would be merciless and forever.

"Okay," he said to Mariela. Didn't really care about the peanuts, but he wanted to kind of prolong the moment.

Pathetic. I have to get a life, he thought, accepting the snacks. Still trying to arrange his six-foot-two frame in the middle seat of a middle row toward the back of the cabin—the only seat left when he'd bounded onto this first-come-first-serve no-frills flight just minutes before takeoff.

No frills if you didn't count the flight attendant. Mariela. Was she flirting with him? Or was she just doing her job? He looked up at her, still standing there with an amused look on her pretty face. She was saying something to him.

"Excuse me?" was his brilliant response.

"I said, would you like more cranberry juice, Detective?"

That was one of his problems. It had been so long since he'd had a date that he couldn't even tell anymore if women were flirting with him or not. He smiled up at Mariela, shook his head, handed her his empty plastic drink cup with the miniature napkin jammed inside, and looked at the peanuts on the wobbly plastic tray in front of him. What was he going to do with those?

Stuffing them in his jacket pocket, he closed his tray-table, as they call it in airline-speak, and turned his attention back to his newspaper. No telling when he was going to get the romance part of his life right. He had long had a crush on Maxi Poole, but so did half of Los Angeles, at least through the tube. But she went out with *him*, didn't she? That creative thought made him smile. She went out with him to murder scenes.

He had the home address of the Trinidad Ochoa family in his bag, courtesy of the El Paso PD, who had been watching Ochoa for a while, he was told. The man lived in a ritzy house in a fairly ritzy part of town, was married to a younger woman who stayed at home with their child, the couple owned two upmarket late-model cars, he favored European designer suits and Italian shoes. "Whoa, you really *are* watching," Jorgan had observed. "What kind of socks?" That remark had elicited a throaty Texas chuckle out of the EPPD lieutenant he had on the phone, who went on to say that the department had done a little off-and-on surveil when they'd learned from an informant that Mr. O. seemed to be having way too many visitors way too late at night.

Jorgan didn't get into it with him. His job was to find the boy.

*　　*　　*

Thursday afternoon, three-thirty-seven, in the conference room of the mahogany-paneled Century City offices of Jacobs, Samuelson & Johns, attorneys at law, specialists in estate planning. At the head of the table sat the venerable Jonah Jacobs, there to conduct the formal reading to the family of the last will and testament of their client, Gladys Parsable Lightner, deceased. To the left of Mr. Jacobs sat another of the firm's partners, attorney Tracy Philbin, who'd also worked on this matter. Beside her was a paralegal named Bradley St. Denis, and next in line at the table, an assistant introduced as Penny who was poised to take notes.

On the opposite side of the table sat the family, consisting in total of just one member—Jerrold Henry Lightner, older son of the deceased.

Jerrold had dressed for the occasion. Light blue summerweight suit, which was the only weight he owned since he maintained that there was no winter in Southern California. White shirt, black tiger's eye cuff links, and wide flower-print tie that even he realized might be just a bit too cheerful for this kind of event.

But what the hell.

When this was over, and they got the paperwork done, Jerrold figured he could buy a few dozen of those classy ties he'd seen in Bijan's window on Rodeo Drive for about three hundred bucks a pop. If he wanted to.

He glanced down at his own lime green, cerulean blue, and mustard yellow creation and couldn't help a tiny smile. He covered it up by putting an elbow on the glass-topped conference table and resting his chin on the back of his hand, raising a quizzical eyebrow at the somber-looking group opposite him, letting them know that he was way past ready to begin here.

He hadn't been able to find James. Considered that a good thing. He'd ridden his Harley up into Topanga Canyon this morning and banged on the doors of fifteen or twenty shacks, sheds, RVs, and trailers, asking about one James Lightner. Thirty years old, tall, dark hair, good-looking, probably stoned. Figured these canyon dwellers might recognize one of their own. And he presented a snapshot of his brother and him taken on a trip home during spring break of Jamie's senior year at Berkeley. The picture was seven years old, but James had never looked much different. Thinner, if anything.

People handled the photo, squinted at it, held it up to the light. Looked at Jerrold, then back at the photo. And handed it back to him, shaking their heads. Nobody had seen this guy. He wondered if any of them could have recognized Jamie even if they'd just had breakfast with him. Wondered if they could recognize their own kids.

It wasn't as if he'd had much time to do a proper search. But this bunch of legal zombies on the other side of the table obviously hadn't been able to find James either, he mused, or his brother would be here. It would be this firm's job to have sent James his checks from the trust over the years, but Jerrold was sure that they must have been going to some anonymous mail drop somewhere. Who knew if Jamie was even picking them up, or if it was some lowlife who'd done his brother in and had been living off the checks himself. Nothing would surprise Jerrold, given the desperate druggie circles his brother drifted in and out of. He wondered how much legal crap you had to go through to declare a person dead.

Jonah Jacobs poured himself a glass of water from the pitcher on the table, then loudly cleared his throat. "Anybody else?" he asked, holding the pitcher up.

Mumbled no's from his lackeys.

Could we just get the hell on with this? Jerrold wanted to scream. But didn't.

"Mr. Lightner," Jacobs began, not looking at him, adjusting his glasses, opening the thick brown binder in front of him. "We are gathered here to inform the family of Mrs. Gladys Parsable Lightner of her final wishes, as stated formally and notarized in this original document comprising her last will and testament . . ."

Jerrold mentally rolled his eyes.

". . . to wit, 'I bequeath the sum of five hundred thousand dollars to the Los Angeles Philharmonic Association under the musical direction of Esa-Pekka Salonen for the purposes of . . .'"

Yah, yah, yah, Jerrold thought, his mind wandering now as Jacobs jabbered through the list of charities. Until he came to his father. That got his full attention.

". . . to my husband, Conrad James Lightner . . ."

Nothing, Jerrold pleaded silently. *The old man gets no money, let's hear it.*

". . . only the right to reside in said Beverly Glen residence for as long as he wishes, or until his death, the expenses incurred in maintaining the property to be paid by the estate, the disposition of which to be overseen by the Century City law firm of Jacobs, Samuelson and Johns . . ."

Yes! No millions for Daddy! Now here comes the good part. Jerrold sat at attention, watching the old barrister's lips.

". . . and to the elder of my two sons, Jerrold Henry Lightner, I leave monies to pay off all of his outstanding debts, the total amount not to exceed two hundred thousand dollars. And to my younger son, James Parsable Lightner, the sum total of the rest of my earthly possessions, including liquid assets, real property, stocks, bonds, annuities—"

"Whaaaaaaat?" Jerrold yelled, scraping his chair backwards, jumping to his feet, and thrusting both fists down hard on the table.

The gang of four just looked at him.

"Read that again," Jerrold demanded. "The part about me and my brother . . ."

Jacobs obliged.

"That's not possible," Jerrold bellowed. "My mother showed me a copy of her will. She left half to me and half to James. She *promised* me she was leaving—"

"Well, she didn't," Jacobs said curtly, cutting him off, barely able to hide the hint of glee in his eyes despite his tenebrous visage. "This document was executed last October, and supersedes any other existing wills."

"This is *shit*," Jerrold barked. "I'll *contest* it!"

"That is your right, Mr. Lightner." From Jacobs. Then he added, "But I must inform you that your mother's estate will not be liable for legal fees arising from a will contest or any other such legal action on your part having to do with her bequests."

Jerrold felt like he was going to throw up.

"Do you have any questions, Mr. Lightner?" Jacobs asked him, as if he were a waiter who had just recited the night's specials.

Jerrold said nothing. He could feel his face burning with rage.

"Well, we have a question to ask you," Tracy Philbin said then, which was the first time she or any of the others had spoken.

Jerrold stared at her.

"Can you help us find your brother?" she asked.

Jerrold banged his fists on the table again, then wheeled around and headed for the conference room door. On his way out he turned, and in answer to Ms. Philbin's question, he shouted in the general direction of the four of them, *"Fuck you."*

34

Thursday night, in the Channel Six newsroom after the Six O'clock News. Wendy Harris sat at her computer terminal archiving the show. Maxi perched on a chair next to her, cell phone to her ear, engrossed in a conversation.

Finished, Maxi folded her cell and dropped it into her jacket pocket. "That was Marc Jorgan," she said.

"Oh?" Wendy's hands were flying on the keyboard.

"He's in El Paso. Just paid a surprise visit to the Ochoa boy's father."

"And . . . ?"

"And no sign of Roberto there. And the house doesn't match the third photo in any way. He says that Trinidad Ochoa doesn't seem to really know his two-year-old son. He has another son now, and a young wife who's pregnant again."

"Busy guy. Could be he's keeping the kid somewhere else till the heat's off," Wendy tried, still working her computer files.

"Anything's possible, but Marc says he doesn't see it. Ochoa and his wife haven't been in California since the year before last, on their way to Vegas, and that checks out. Roberto was only two months old when he and Carla split, he said, and Ochoa married the present wife soon after."

"And Carla moved here," Wendy said.

"Yes. Ochoa says he hasn't seen Roberto since he was an infant."

"Nice dad."

Maxi shrugged. That was an old story.

"What about all the wealth?" Wendy asked. "Didn't you say he's rich now?"

"Marc says the El Paso PD has been investigating a high-stakes trail of drug smuggling that Ochoa may be a part of. They brought in the DEA and the Texas narcs. That investigation is of no interest to the L.A. team on the kidnap case."

"Still, if the guy has money, he could have paid someone to come up here and snatch Roberto for him."

"Why would he do that?"

"Because he can."

"There's no evidence that would tie the man to the kidnapping, Wen. Marc says he's satisfied that Ochoa is clean on this one."

"What does Carla Ochoa think of her ex-husband?"

"She says she hardly knows the man. They were married for less than a year."

"So, a dead end in Texas. Poor little boy."

"And his poor mom."

"It's great of you to let her stay with you, Maxi. Are you going home on your break?"

"No. I'm having dinner with Tom McCartney."

Ten after seven at Kate Mantilini's on Wilshire at Doheny. Maxi and Tom had a booth by the windows looking out at the broad boulevard. Heavy traffic outside and a noisy crowd inside. They sat opposite each other, settled cozily in the privacy of the tall-backed wooden benches, perusing Kate's long, luscious menu.

Comfort food. Perfect. Exactly what Maxi needed, and to hell with the diet, she decided, which was basically a way of life for her. Not tonight. She was looking at a toasted turkey club sandwich, plenty of mayo, and a beer. And maybe a side order of Kate's famous onion rings.

She liked being with Tom McCartney.

He put the menu down, took off his black-rimmed glasses, dropped them into his top flap pocket, and looked over at her. And smiled.

The smile was actually the killer. When she thought about Tom McCartney, fantasized about him really, it was always with that sexy, crooked smile.

"What do you want to drink?" he asked, signaling their waiter.

"An ice-cold Amstel Light in one of their frozen glasses."

McCartney ordered her beer and an iced tea for himself. Maxi had heard that he was a recovering alcoholic.

"No booze?" she asked.

"No booze," he said, and grinned again. "If I had a beer, then it might be two, then three, and later maybe a couple of shots of vodka, then the rest of the bottle. And that would only be at dinner."

"Not good." Maxi smiled back at him.

"No. Been there."

"Does it bother you if I have a beer?"

"Not at all. I have to live in the world."

"Sounds like you've got a handle on it."

"Not completely," he admitted, and changed the subject. "By the way, Rosie wants to know if you're coming to Cantor's for coffee tonight."

"Why's that?"

"I think he wants to talk to you about Lightner. He's got this idea that you should interview him."

"Tom, every newsperson in the country, me included, has tried to get Councilman Lightner on tape. The only one he'll talk to is Rosie. Twice now."

"What a guy, huh?"

"Well, sure, it's great for Rosie. But what makes him think the man would talk to me? And for that matter, why would Rosenberg want to share his exclusive?"

McCartney laughed. "The second question's a mystery. I wouldn't give you one of my exclusives no matter how crazy I was about you," he said. "But Rosie roller-skates to a whole different flock of swans."

Crazy about you? Maxi echoed silently, and immediately felt warm all over. And hoped that he didn't notice her color up. *Damn*, she thought, *I am such a* girl.

"Anyway, he seems to think Lightner will talk to you."

"A jailhouse interview?"

"Don't wear stripes."

"I guess Councilman Lightner wants to tell the world he's innocent. Again."

"And he knows that with you, the UGN network will pick it up," McCartney said.

"Well, Capra bought both of Rosie's interviews with him and the UGN network *did* pick them up. I don't get it."

"So talk to Rosie."

"At Cantor's tonight?"

"Four, four-thirty. The usual time."

"If I'm not staking out the men's john in MacArthur Park."

"Or fishing a cat out of a tree," McCartney deadpanned.

Which prompted Maxi to swat him on the head with her menu. "Would you believe that I got more calls, faxes, and e-mails on Dashiell Hammett than on any five stories that I've done all year?"

"I do believe it," McCartney countered. "But that is not a commentary on the state of journalism today. It's a reflection on society today."

"Obviously on the segment of society that watches television news, which can't be a bad thing for us folks in the business."

Having said that, she wondered how long she was going to wax defensive about Dashiell Hammett and sweet little Katie. Which reminded her of little Roberto. Even younger, and lost.

"Did Rosie ask Lightner about the Ochoa boy?" she asked.

"I don't know. Ask him. Tonight, if you can be there."

"I will. I'll try to meet you at Cantor's. It all depends on what's going on out there."

"Want to come out with me on a good one tonight?"

"What good one?"

"I've got a South Korean kid who's gonna rat out his filthy-rich parents. At midnight. Down on Ardmore south of Olympic."

"Koreatown."

"Yeah, but you should see the house this kid lives in. A completely remodeled classic California bungalow worth at least half a million. He's fifteen and he lives all alone in it with a dog, two cats, and an aquarium full of Siamese fighter fish."

"No adults?"

"A housekeeper comes in five days a week."

"And on weekends?"

"Party time, I guess."

"So where are these filthy-rich parents?"

"In Seoul. Running their hugely successful international fur business."

"It's not even legal, letting a minor live alone. Maybe it is in Asian countries, I don't know, but here it's called child endangerment."

"Evidently the parents are getting around the California law by claiming this house as their primary residence. The kid says they get here three or four times a year. But they want him to get his education here. He's going to UCLA when he graduates from high school, he says."

"That is a good story, a sociological exposé. Why does this teenager want to talk about it?"

"I think because he doesn't have any adult role models in his life and he's picked me. I met him last year at a school science fair I covered, and he's smart. I've taken him to a few Dodgers games. Taught him the national pastime. And he's taught me a lot about his culture. I want to tell his story, and he's agreed to it."

"Won't he get in trouble with his parents?"

"He says they'll never know. Evidently there's such a huge disconnect there that they don't know his friends, they don't know what he's doing in school, they don't know if he's getting laid or doing drugs—they don't know their son."

"Is he?"

"Is he what?"

"Getting laid or doing drugs?"

"Probably. Because there's nobody there to stop him. Anything could happen with a kid in that situation, and the story I want to do is, he's not the only one. He knows other kids who have been dumped here alone by wealthy parents living abroad. They think all they have to do is throw money into the mix and everything's okay."

"That's awful."

"So do you want to come with me?"

"I thought you wouldn't give me one of your exclusives," she said. *No matter how crazy you might be about me*, she finished silently.

"No matter how crazy I might be about you," he said then, and laughed. "I'm not giving you this one. I'm just inviting you to come along with me."

"To hold your notebook?"

"To hold my hand." He reached across the table and took her hand. Playfully. She thought. It felt good. She left her hand there for a beat before pulling it away.

He was laughing again. At her? At her discomfort? Oh God, he was probably laughing just because he's a normal, happy guy. What did that say about her, analyzing his every word and move? Something she'd always done with men, come to think of it. *I need a remedial course in Relationships 101*, she lamented silently. She had flunked that one a few times.

"Maybe," she answered his question. "Let's see if I can find a story to file for the morning show first."

35

Half past midnight in the Channel Six newsroom. Almost all of the late-shift staffers had gone home. Only Wendy Harris remained, inputting on the next day's story budget, and Donnie Flax, working the overnight desk. The regular Eleven O'clock producer had asked Wendy to swap tonight; he had Hollywood Bowl tickets. That worked for her. She was hoping for a chance to nab what she thought might be the MacArthur Park tapes out of Pete Capra's office after the place emptied out. Risky business, but she had a plan.

Finally, Donnie stood up and stretched. "I'm going to the can, Wendy," he said. "Will you catch the phones for a few minutes?"

"Sure, Donnie." Wendy didn't look up.

As soon as the assignment editor disappeared around the corner and headed for the restroom, Wendy got up and walked over to Pete Capra's darkened office. As a sometime producer on the late shift, she had a master key that opened every door in the newsroom, in case she needed to get at something for the Eleven after all the managers had left for the day.

Right now she needed an illicit look at some tapes she'd noticed in Capra's office. Well, maybe not illicit exactly, but not strictly kosher, either.

She looked through the glass door of Capra's office and saw that it was still there, the small carton of tapes on the floor beside his desk that she'd been noticing for about a week now on her frequent meets with him on news business.

Wendy had a theory about that particular box of tapes. If they were news tapes that Capra was viewing, he would've put them back in the tape library each night before he went home. He was a stickler on his rule that all personnel must return tapes to the library when not using them, to make them available to others working on the same stories. He'd even had a sign hung in the tape library that warned: BOGART THE TAPES, PAY A FINE. And he made his famous periodic sweeps through the cubes like the tape police, levying fines on producers, reporters, writers, and editors who were holding tapes that they weren't using.

So why would *he* hold news tapes?

He wouldn't. So these tapes were not news tapes, Wendy reasoned.

She took a look behind her. No sign of Donnie. Using her master key, she opened the door to Pete's office, approached the carton on the floor, and nosed into it at the stash of cassettes. Quickly sorting through them, she saw, as she'd suspected, that the labels were all dated, numbered, slugged "MacArthur Park," and signed by Tom McCartney.

Phones jangled in the newsroom, as they constantly did. Wendy ignored them. Scooping up the carton, she bounded out of Capra's office, pulling the door locked behind her, zipped across the newsroom and down the back hall, and ducked into one of the now deserted edit bays.

It was against union rules to even touch editing equipment if you were not a NABET union editor. If she got caught, it could mean her job. But there was nobody around at this hour. She figured that the old "if a tree falls in the forest" rule applied. And quickly pulled out one of the tapes and popped it into a playback machine.

And there he was, cued up to the time code listed on the tape box—the same man Maxi had pointed out to her on Tom Mc-Cartney's Nodori tape.

Second cassette—same man again. And on through the carton of tapes, all shot in a park setting at night. Viewing went quickly, because each cassette was cued up to the image of the mystery man. With the black clothes, the fading red-gray hair, the mole on his cheek, he was easy to spot. Eight tapes shot on five different nights, the dates and times noted. After she had gone through all of them, Wendy picked up the phone in the edit bay and speed-dialed Maxi on her cell phone in the field.

"This is Maxi," was the response.

"What are you up to, Max?"

"Finishing a shoot at a gas station robbery. A teenager. He wasn't stealing money; he was stealing gas. Evidently he knew how to tamper with the automatic pump. But he set off a silent alarm, the cops happened to be around the corner, and they nailed him with the hose in his hands. We picked it up on the police scanner."

"When are you coming in with it?"

"Could do now. Why?"

"I've got some tapes I want you to see, and I've got to return them soon."

"Return them where? It's after one in the morning."

"Return them to where I stole them from. Hurry."

Wendy left the edit room carrying Capra's box of tapes—she didn't dare leave them in EJ, the editing department, even for a few minutes. Turning the corner into the newsroom, she saw the "odd couple" and their two young kids lounging in chairs around her desk. Joe and Jona Best and their twins, a boy and a girl, eight or nine years old. Because they were often seen up at all hours of the night, people in the news business wondered if these two kids ever went to school.

"Whatcha got?" Wendy asked, giving them major abrupt as she dropped into the chair in front of her computer terminal, her signal for no small talk please, she didn't have time for it, and anyway, these kids should be in bed. She wasn't up for listening to any of the OC's gleeful gossip; she wanted them out of the newsroom before Maxi arrived.

"An explosion," Joe said. "In Northridge. A gas heater in a garage."

"Anybody dead?" Wendy asked.

"Nope."

"Anybody hurt?"

"Nope."

"Damage to the house?"

"Just the gas heater."

"Can't use it, Joe. Thanks anyway." Wendy gave the couple a dismissive smile and turned to her computer screen.

"It's good filler," Joe said, still pitching.

Wendy turned to him. "Joe, we don't do filler. We do news. And we've got Maxi Poole on the graveyard. If you're gonna bring us stuff off the nightside it has to be good."

"You mean we have to compete with the dynamic duo?" Joe put out with a smirk.

"What does that mean?"

"Maxi Poole and Tom McCartney. They're the golden couple out there in the weird hours."

"What are you talking about, Joe?"

"Oh, you know," Jona joined her husband. "They're a couple. They're working together."

"On stories?" Wendy wondered if these two had picked up on the MacArthur Park mystery man shoots.

Joe and Jona exchanged smug glances. "Looks like they're working together on more than stories," Joe said.

Wendy caught their meaning. "You're wrong, guys," she said. "Now, you've gotta excuse me—I have work to do."

* * *

Maxi came into the newsroom, logged in her "Gasoline Theft" tape with Donnie at the desk, and dropped down beside Wendy at her computer terminal.

"Are we going to the movies?" she asked with a twinkle.

"Oh yeah. Stuff these tapes in your tote and meet me in Edit Room Nine. We can't let Donnie know we're using the machines. For his own good."

Maxi laughed. "So he won't have the problem of deciding whether he should report us or just hold it over our heads."

"You got it. I'll go by way of the ladies' room; you go out the door and come in the back way."

"Okay, Sherlock. Gimme the contraband."

Wendy kicked the box of tapes over to Maxi's tote bag on the floor under her desk. Maxi piled the tapes into her bag, shouldered it, stood up, said a loud good night, and left the newsroom.

Three minutes later she joined Wendy back in Edit Nine. The two viewed the tapes with the natural sound potted down, studying all of them several times over and comparing each one against the others. And quietly discussing what they saw.

"This one's on a road leading into the park from Wilshire Boulevard," Wendy said.

"And here we've got swings and a jungle gym in the background—see the outlines?"

"Yup—and a bunch of garbage cans over here. Know where this is?"

"I know exactly where it is," Maxi said. "It's by the lake, not far from the spot on the last two tapes."

"Okay, now look at this one," Wendy said. "Look at what he's wearing. You can really see his clothes in this shot."

"Black jeans, black T, no jacket, and it's cold out there. Some kind of running shoes."

"Is that an earring?"

"Think so. A little hoop."

"And look . . . he's got a bag." They could see what looked to be a leather waist pouch attached to the man's belt, about a foot wide and six or seven inches deep.

"I'm betting he lives close by," Maxi said. "And since we've seen him on the same path three times, probably north of the park on the downtown side. Maybe the Westlake district. Or he parks his car on that side, if he has one."

When they were finished, Wendy piled the tapes back into the carton. "You satisfied?" she asked Maxi.

"Perfectly. Where were those?" she asked, with a nod of her head toward the tapes.

"In Pete's office. I'll get them back in there. Getting caught returning stuff isn't as bad as getting caught stealing it, is it?"

"Just act like you know what you're doing."

Wendy grinned. That was one of their maxims, handed down from Maxi's mom. *Act like you know what you're doing, and they'll think you do.* "So," she said, "would you recognize him?"

"In a heartbeat."

"I still think it's a bad idea, Maxi. Dangerous."

"McCartney will be out there with me. He's looking for him too, and if this turns out to be a big story, he deserves a piece of it."

"Oh, about McCartney . . ."

"What about him?"

"What's up with you and him?"

"What do you mean?"

"The odd couple were in tonight. They implied that you and Tom McCartney were more than just colleagues. They said you two were a couple."

Maxi looked at her. "Tom is terrific," was all she said.

Just three words, but Wendy knew her friend well enough to read the subtext. "Oh God," she said. "Are you sleeping with him?"

"No."

"Good."

"But I'm thinking about it," Maxi said.

36

Cantor's Delicatessen on Fairfax, early Friday, 4:12 A.M. Maxi and Tom were in McCartney's regular booth near the middle of the restaurant, watching as Harvey Rosenberg pushed through the front door, tripped over a customer's foot, excused himself, looked around the place, then lit up when he saw them.

"Ya gotta love him," McCartney said to Maxi with a grin. He slid over to make room, and Rosenberg lumbered down the aisle and sat himself down in the booth with a whump.

"Hi, Rosie," Maxi said.

"Evening, Maxi, Tom—nice out tonight, isn't it?"

"Uh, Rosie," McCartney said, "what's up with those pants, anyway? I mean, it's winter. And those shorts—"

"Cool, aren't they?" Rosie beamed, glancing down at his flame-printed baggies.

"Where'd you get 'em?" McCartney asked.

"The 99 Cents store on Olympic. Only ninety-nine cents, can you believe it? I bought every pair they had."

"How many?" asked McCartney, with a frown.

"Nine pairs."

"Oh boy," from Maxi.

"They match my bike," Rosenberg said happily.

McCartney opened his mouth to say something, then apparently changed his mind. He leaned back and raised a hand toward Rosenberg. "Rosie, they're you. Gimme five."

Maxi could see that as a mentor to the younger stringer, McCartney was torn between trying to help Rosie dress better and not hurting his feelings. And he'd chosen the latter. Probably a wise choice, she thought, because maybe you couldn't change Rosie. She didn't think it was about money; she'd heard that Rosenberg's father was a successful contractor who built pricey houses on the Westside. More likely it was about taste, which you were not going to change in a guy in an hour over a plate of blintzes.

She studied the young man. About twenty-five years old, wispy corn-colored hair already thinning on top, round face, double chin, thin lips, patchy stubble, John Lennon glasses, and weighing close to two-fifty, she guessed. He sat opposite her with his bare, pudgy elbows on the table, seemingly intent on peeling the label off the catsup bottle. Change Rosie? You probably couldn't.

"Tell Maxi what you told me about Lightner," McCartney said to him.

Still diligently chipping away at the Heinz label, he glanced up at Maxi. "I don't think he did it," he said. "Kill his wife, I mean."

"Why is that?" Maxi asked.

"I don't know—he's just too . . . I don't think he could," Rosenberg said.

"Do you think he could have *had* it done?" she asked him.

"Yah—he's a delegating kinda guy. But I don't think he did."

"He sure had motive," McCartney said. "I hear the wife had maybe twenty, thirty million in family money and was plenty tight with it."

"Yup, that's what he told me. And I get from some things he's said about her that she was pretty much of a screaming crazy, besides."

"You think he's all broken up that she's dead, Rosie?" McCartney again.

"No, I don't think that. I just don't think he killed her."

"The world thinks he killed her," McCartney pressed. "And the DA certainly thinks he killed her. You've probably talked to him more than all of them, Rosie. So why don't you think he's good for it?"

"Just stuff he says. And the way he says it."

"What about the Ochoa boy?" Maxi asked. "Do you think he knows anything about who took him?"

"You know, I've asked Mr. Lightner about that in a dozen different ways. That one I'm just not sure about."

"Do you still have the raw of your one-on-ones with him?" Maxi asked. The full interviews shot before they were edited for the cut pieces.

"Sure," Rosie said. He had the catsup bottle stripped almost clean now.

"I'd love to view it," she said.

"Do you want to interview him, Maxi?" he asked, ignoring her remark that she'd like to view his raw tapes. Maybe McCartney was teaching him a few things after all.

"I've tried. He won't talk to me. He'll only talk to you, Rosie, you know that."

"Not anymore. They won't let me in Men's Central with my camera."

Maxi knew why. No credentials. "They don't let stringers in the jail," Rosenberg added. Honest guy.

"Look," Maxi leveled with him, "Lightner has been your exclusive, Rosie. Why would you want to give him to me?"

"Because Councilman Lightner wants to keep his story out there. I told him I thought the best way was to talk to you, Maxi. That you'd keep it on the network, keep the interest up."

"Do you like him, Rosie?"

"Not really. But it's not right to let him fry if he didn't kill anybody, is it?"

"You think you can get me an interview with him?"

"I'm gonna talk to him this morning."

Maxi watched as Rosenberg swept up the shriveled shavings of the catsup label in his two hands, dropped them into a paper napkin, and neatly folded the package over on itself.

"Too bad they don't have ashtrays anymore," he observed as he placed the wadded-up napkin over to the side of the table and picked up a menu.

Change Rosie? Maxi thought about that again. Why would anyone want to change Rosie?

37

Kick one, kick two, spin around, kick three," Zeke Fairstein chanted as Maxi slammed into the leaden bag with the burning flat of her foot. Fairstein's Gym was crowded with sweaty Friday morning regulars.

"Rear back further on the kicks; give yourself more momentum," Zeke called out. "I want to see much more intensity here, more force. C'mon, Maxi, don't wuss out on me. Higher! Harder!"

Maxi winced and kick-smashed the bag again. And again.

She had wanted to wear her Nikes this time so it wouldn't hurt so much, but Zeke said no shoes. "Gotta suck it up, girl—no pain, no gain."

So, plenty of pain. Not just in her feet, but all over. She commiserated with her fellow sufferers in the gym. Two guys a few feet away, one short and slight, lying on a bench and pressing enormous amounts of weight, grunting mightily with every lift, and the other one tall, hairy, and about a hundred pounds overweight, cranking a jump rope in place, sweat running in rivulets down his face and bare torso. Both of them apparently also on the physically-punished-by-Zeke program.

She had to admit, she was developing a fondness for Zeke the Beak Fairstein, who she'd since learned was this agony shop's founder, owner, and prime torturer. Relentlessly committed to her pain though he was, the guy had a great big streak of warm. When they'd first met, he'd asked her how Yukon was.

"How'd you know about Yukon?" she'd asked him.

"That story you did at the dog park up on Mulholland a couple years back. With a bunch of folks and their dogs, and you had Yukon with you."

"Oh, sure—that was the day they opened the park expansion to the public," Maxi said. She'd smiled thinking about that day, with a zillion pooches, large and small, running and playing and catching Frisbees and making new doggie pals. And getting into a few dogfights. Kids will be kids.

He told her that back then he'd had a lovable, gentle Doberman mix named Champ who'd lived for fourteen years. Champ went everywhere with him, he'd said wistfully. And today he pulled a treat for Yukon out of a crumpled brown paper bag. A giant plastic-wrapped chicken jerky rawhide bone.

"They like to chew on these," he said.

"Yukon will *love* this. And he'll be very touched that you remembered him." She tossed the bone into her gym bag and gave Zeke a hug.

Tom McCartney was sitting on the sidelines, backwards on an old wooden chair, arms folded across the top of it, watching. Seeming quite pleased with himself about the proceedings here, she noticed. The architect of her new excruciating schedule. Bad enough she was on the graveyard shift; now three mornings a week she was hurting bad in this downtown sweat tank, and on the other two she was shooting her new gun in Glendale, thank you Tom McCartney. But he sure looked sexy sitting on that chair in jeans and a muscle shirt.

What was in it for him, she wondered, that would prompt him to give her so much attention? He had admitted that accompanying her to these sessions (ordeals?) did cut into his daily routine, which was stringent, as he described it. And the man worked seven days a week.

"You don't have to baby-sit me," she'd told him. "I committed to this; I'm doing it."

"I'll come for a while," he'd said. "Till you're used to it. It'll get to be routine for you, you'll see."

She was beginning to see that McCartney was a man who thrived on routine, despite his anything *but* routine profession. When she'd mentioned this, he'd told her that he had to *make* habits to help him *break* habits. To help him stay away from the substances that were his nemesis. The two Vs, Vicodin and vodka, he'd confided, then seemed embarrassed that he had.

Did he have help with it? *It*, she'd called his addictions. Still an uncomfortable subject, for her at least, and evidently for him too. But she'd pressed. Rehab of some kind? AA support?

No, he'd told her, he was trying to do it cold. When she ventured that going it alone must take a lot of strength, he'd responded that everything took a lot of strength. Everything that counted. And he'd changed the subject. Surprised her by asking her out on a date.

"You mean . . . a *date* date?" she'd said, to make sure she knew exactly what he meant when he invited her out to dinner.

"Well, yeah. Is dinner on Saturday night a real date?"

"Don't you have to work?"

"I'll go to work after our date."

"So, dinner?"

"Um . . . and a movie. Isn't that how you do it?"

"I think it's how *they* do it," she'd said. It had been so long since she'd had a regulation date that she wasn't entirely sure either.

"Okay," he'd said, "pick a movie."

"What haven't you seen?"

"Nothing since *Mary Poppins* when I was seven."

"You don't like movies?"

"I don't know. We'll find out."

So they'd made a Saturday night date for dinner and a movie.

*   *   *

Rosie's coming on our date tomorrow night," McCartney told her when she'd finished her session and they were walking out of the gym. He'd just gotten off his cell phone. Presumably having had a conversation with stringer Harvey Rosenberg.

"Wait a minute. Then it's not a real date," she protested.

"Do you want to interview Lightner?"

"Is the bear Catholic?"

"Rosie set it up for us to get in to see him in Men's Central tomorrow before the dinner hour."

"Really? What time's their dinner hour?"

"Five-thirty. And they eat breakfast at six in the morning. I couldn't do time."

"Me either. They don't let you color your hair, do they?"

"Don't think so. Robert Blake went white."

"So what's the plan?"

"We're going in at five. You'll see how you get along with the councilman, and if he agrees, you'll set up an interview with him for next week."

"Works for me. Then after we meet with Lightner at Men's Central, we're going on our date?"

"Yes. With Rosie."

She groaned. "Dinner with Rosie? Then to the movie?"

"Dinner with Rosie," he said, "then to my place to watch Rosie's raw tapes with Lightner."

38

Friday morning, ten-twenty, at Men's Central Jail in downtown Los Angeles. Councilman Conrad Lightner was fuming. He had been advised by mail that in lieu of his enforced absence from the reading of his deceased wife's will, the minutes of which were recorded yesterday, herewith he would find a copy of Gladys Parsable Lightner's last will and testament as drafted and dated on October such-and-such, blah, blah, blah . . .

So stated the letter from the firm of Jacobs, Samuelson & Johns that had been hand-delivered to him in the inmate visitors room this morning by Somebody St. Denis from his late wife's law firm. And the document enclosed with it had slapped him across the face, knocked him on his ass. A brand-new will, negating all previous wills, evidently drawn up by Gladys three months ago without his knowledge and cutting him completely out of the money. He couldn't even sell the fucking house, according to the document. Should he vacate the Beverly Glen villa, whether by choice or by death, it was to be sold and the profits reverted to the Gladys Parsable Lightner estate, which was willed almost in its entirety to his younger son James, the drug addict. As to whose whereabouts nobody had a clue.

Would James surface and take care of his old man? he wondered. Kick a little chunk of the frigging millions his way? Hardly likely, given the state of their relationship, which was nowhere. Never had been. Even when the boys were kids, before James ever started up with drugs, Lightner never played ball with them, never helped them with their homework, never took them anywhere. He was too busy campaigning, working, doing the requisite social dinners, and the rest of it. Let's face it, he'd been a lousy father. Truth be told, he didn't really like kids. Maybe that's why his two were so screwed up to begin with. A little late to think that James might all of a sudden be struck with some kind of spirit of benevolence toward his old dad.

But what if they never found Jamie? What if he was dead? Would his father be considered his next of kin? He was sure that James wouldn't have bothered to draft a will—from the time he was a teenager, all that kid ever thought about was where his next fix was coming from. So if Jamie turned up dead, and his new estate went into probate, maybe Lightner would land in clover, come out with the big bucks after all. Meantime, as soon as he got out of this rathole on Monday, he would talk to a lawyer about grounds on which to contest this new goddamn will.

Maxi Poole was coming in tomorrow to meet and greet, and set up a television interview. If he agreed. Of course he would agree. In fact, he would pay her to put his story on the air if he had to. He needed to let L.A. see him all sincere, all broken up, all innocent as hell.

Maxi Poole, that cute babe from the news, and no more Gladys to stop him from lusting after and jumping on any of them, should circumstances permit. Even in prison, he felt free.

He'd be going back to work next week. They couldn't stop him. He'd been elected by the people, and he hadn't been convicted of anything. He couldn't wait. It was going to be a whole different life for him. Even if he couldn't pull off getting his hands on Gladdy's millions, he had a great home, according to the will her estate would pay the bills, he had a good job, a nice salary from the city, plenty of opportunities to make some don't-tell money on the side, and, best of all, he had his freedom. Freedom from Gladys after forty years. And there was no way they were going to nail him for her murder.

39

Saturday afternoon, twenty to four. Maxi was in her bedroom walk-in closet, shuffling clothes, trying them on, debating wardrobe choices. Deliberating over what to wear to go inside downtown's gritty Men's Central Jail, like it mattered. And it did, because Tom McCartney was picking her up at four. And after the meeting with Lightner, they were going to have their Saturday night date. Sort of. Rosie would be along.

She settled on jeans, a short white cashmere sweater, a fitted black leather jacket, and black boots. The jeans for jail, the clingy cashmere for McCartney, the designer blazer for a business look, and the boots for whatever sludge she'd have to walk through in the lockup.

They would be going to McCartney's apartment to look at Rosie's raw Lightner tapes after dinner. She fervently hoped that Rosie would know enough to split after they finished viewing.

Her doorbell rang. McCartney had never been to her house before. She was a little jittery. Letting Carla get the door, she spritzed her favorite fragrance into her hair, "Sunset Boulevard by Gale Hayman." Which made her smile. If she were to put out a signature perfume she'd have to call it "Boxing Gym by Maxi

Poole." Or "Maxi's Men's Central." Then there's "Parfum de Dark Park," or "Eau de Graveyard Shift." Glamorous, her life.

She did a fast final mirror check, then started downstairs. As first dates go, this one was beyond weird.

Councilman Conrad Lightner sat as straight as he could manage, his bulk hanging over the seat of the small folding chair at the dingy metal table in the interrogation room they'd assigned him to receive his journalist guests. Trying to look normal despite the frigging orange jumpsuit, the Jesus sandals with the dirty white socks, and the sweaty prison guard with a gun and a sour expression hovering in the doorway.

The two reporters sat across from him, both looking at him expectantly now: Maxi Poole, the foxy blonde from Channel Six, and Thomas McCartney, the independent journalist who looked like a taller, younger, hungrier Al Pacino. Harvey Rosenberg, the character he'd been using to get his side of the story out, had set up this meeting.

All of the media wanted his story, he knew, but he'd been spilling to Rosenberg because the kid seemed to be the least dangerous reporter he'd ever come up against in his career, and he'd come up against most of them over the years. This Rosie was easy. Rosie believed him. And Rosie didn't work for any one station, so all of them bought his stuff and aired it. Perfect situation for him, but now that he was in the county jail they wouldn't let Rosenberg inside with his gear. True, he would probably be getting out on bail the day after tomorrow, but he couldn't be entirely sure. Best to hedge his bets.

No cameras today—this was a pre-interview, a let's-see-if-we-all-get-along meet. Oh yeah, he could get along with Maxi Poole.

What a creep!" Maxi breathed when they were back out on the downtown street in the gathering January twilight.

"No kidding," McCartney responded, guiding her to the adjacent municipal parking structure. "But you knew that."

"Everybody knows that," she said. "Do you think he did it?"

"Killed his wife?"

"And maybe the prostitute."

"Yes. I think he did both of them. He had the means, the motive, and the opportunity."

"True. But I don't think he did it."

"Why not?"

"Something he said."

"Which was . . . ?"

Maxi thought for a beat. "He talked about a knife. He mentioned that they've never found the knife his wife was stabbed with."

"And . . . ?"

"And it wasn't a knife."

"I never heard that."

"The police didn't let that out." Jorgan had told her.

"Then what was it?"

"I don't know. I only know that Mrs. Lightner was stabbed to death, obviously with some kind of blade, but it wasn't a knife. But you can't use that, Tom, and you can't tell anyone. *At all*," she added, for emphasis.

She'd amazed herself, confiding that piece of information to McCartney. She didn't even want to *think* about what Marc Jorgan would say if he knew she'd disclosed it to anybody, even her boss. But she trusted Tom McCartney. Looking over at him now, thoughtful behind the wheel of his big, solid Hummer, she felt good with him; she felt safe with him. She was sure he wouldn't breach her trust. And after all, he had confided in her about his MacArthur Park assignment from Pete Capra, and all the intrigue that went with it.

"Don't worry, Maxi," he said. "I'm Mr. Silent."

* * *

Rosie was already seated when Tom and Maxi arrived at the Sonora Cafe, one of Maxi's favorite restaurants. On La Brea at the corner of Second Street, it was halfway between the downtown jail and McCartney's apartment in West L.A. Rosie was ensconced on an upholstered bench against the wall at a table in the fireplace room, a frosty strawberry margarita in front of him, dipping into a basket of the restaurant's famous crispy cheese toast.

"You know how to live," McCartney said by way of greeting as he held a chair out for Maxi.

"Mmm, I'll have one of those." Maxi nodded toward Rosie's drink.

"So, did you bring them?" McCartney asked him.

"Of course." Rosie patted the canvas duffel on the seat beside him. The raw tapes of his one-on-ones with Councilman Lightner.

"Good man," McCartney said. And he ordered a margarita for Maxi and a Diet Coke.

"Did you guys set up an interview?" Rosie asked them.

"Monday night," McCartney said. "If Maxi can get a crew. It'll either be in the jail, or at his house if he bails."

There it was again, Lightner talking about the mythical knife on tape.

Maxi, Tom, and Rosenberg were settled in McCartney's home office, Rosie leaning against the desk, Maxi sitting in the desk chair, and McCartney running the equipment.

"Could you back it up, Tom; let me see that part again?" Maxi asked. McCartney pushed REWIND, and Maxi took time code notes.

ROSIE: You found her body, but not until you were dressed and almost ready to go to work. How long were you up before you found her?

LIGHTNER: Twenty, thirty minutes. I was about to go downstairs for breakfast, and I went in to say good morning to her first.

ROSIE: Went in—?

LIGHTNER: Went into her room. We have separate bedrooms. *Had* separate bedrooms.

ROSIE: And what did you find?

LIGHTNER: She was lying there on the floor, blood everywhere. Looked like he got her right in the heart. Shot, stabbed, I didn't know then.

ROSIE: Was there a weapon?

LIGHTNER: I didn't see one.

ROSIE: What did you do?

LIGHTNER: I knelt down and listened for a heartbeat, tried to revive her.

ROSIE: How?

LIGHTNER: Mouth-to-mouth. She didn't respond.

ROSIE: Now we know she was stabbed—

LIGHTNER: Yah. And they still haven't found the knife.

"Stop," Maxi said. McCartney pushed the PAUSE button, and she examined Lightner's face frozen on the screen. "So, does he look like he's lying?"

"How the hell can you tell? He's a politician." From McCartney.

"See, I don't think he was lying," Rosie piped up. "About this, I mean. 'Cuz I talked to him several times, and I do think he was lying about other stuff. By now I think I can tell the difference with him."

"Lying about *what* other stuff?" McCartney asked him.

"About the kid. I think he knows something about the kid."

"Roberto," Maxi said, still staring at Lightner's image on the screen.

"Yeah, the kidnapped kid. Here, I'll show you." Rosie got up and walked over to McCartney's playback machine and fast-forwarded the tape to a section where he and Lightner were discussing Roberto Ochoa.

Yessss! There *is* a God, Maxi thought, as Rosie packed up his tapes and made some I-have-to-leave-now noises. "A major Crips council is going down in South Central at midnight," he said. "Corner of 94th and Normandie."

"God, be careful, Rosie!" Maxi said.

"They know me. I'm cool with them." Rosie smiled her way, hefting his duffel bag.

"Thanks, pal." McCartney put an arm around Rosie's shoulders and escorted him to the door.

Maxi stayed back in McCartney's office, still sitting in the big leather chair. Feeling nervous. Sexual tension, she recognized. Sometimes that was even more exciting than sex. This was Saturday night, her night off. Not his—he'd said that he was going to go out to work after their "date" tonight. Would he make moves to leave right away? She heard the front door close, and McCartney came back into the office. He smiled and extended a hand to her. "Come on," he said, "let's go in the other room."

What other room? she screamed silently. *Not the bedroom. I'm not ready for the bedroom!*

He led her into the living room, sat her down on the overstuffed couch, walked around the wide teakwood coffee table, and stood by a club chair opposite her. Was about to sit down, then had a second thought. "Glass of wine?" he asked.

Talk about nerves! She'd overreacted again. As usual. *I am so bad at this man-woman stuff,* she thought. And while he went off to get the drinks, she wondered how that could be, having come from sophisticated parents and a perfectly normal home. She made a mental note to discuss that with a shrink. If she ever had time to see a shrink.

McCartney came back into the room carrying a bottle of California Cabernet, a corkscrew, a wine knife, some napkins, a can of Diet Coke, and two stemmed glasses, and set all of it down on the coffee table. While busying himself with the business of opening and pouring, he said, "So what did we learn, anything?"

"My feeling is that Rosie has the right instincts, Tom. I'm guessing that Lightner knows something about Roberto, and I also think that he didn't kill his wife. Could be all wrong, of course—as you pointed out, the guy is a politician."

"If we could find that kid—"

Maxi cut him off. "Just having a hunch isn't enough to go to Marc Jorgan with this, and the FBI has a team on the kidnapping too."

"I mean us. If we, you and I, could find the boy—"

"What a helluva story it would be," she finished for him. "I know. But this one involves a little boy's life. You and I are not going to risk playing cowboy here."

She meant him, and he knew it. He grinned, handed her the wine, then sat beside her on the couch and clinked his glass of soda to hers. "We're a good team," he said softly, taking a sip.

Then he took the wineglass out of her hand and put both glasses down on the table, and touched her face. Looked at her for a moment. And kissed her.

40

Sunday morning, at the crack of noon. The phone in Jerrold Lightner's tiny bedroom in Chatsworth jangled him awake. Sunlight was seeping in along the edges of the cracked yellow shade covering the window, lighting up strips of dusty air in the room. Lightner looked over at his wife, Elaine—the phone was on her side of the bed. It kept ringing, but she didn't stir. She'd worked till the Roxy closed at two o'clock this morning, then no doubt sat at the bar with some of her colleagues and drank and gossiped and did some coke. She'd crawled into bed beside him sometime around five this morning. As usual. And also as usual, he didn't give a damn. He hauled his tired ass out of bed and shuffled around to her side to pick up the phone.

"Yeah," he rasped.

"Jer? It's James."

"James . . . ?"

"James, your brother." With a laugh.

"Jesus, Jamie, it's been years—"

"Two and a half years. How are you?"

"Fine. Everybody's looking for you. Where are you?"

"When is the memorial for Mom?" Ignoring his brother's question.

"I don't know. The old man's in jail. Did you call him?"

"No." Silence. Then, "Did he kill her, Jerry?"

Jerrold paused. Then, "Yeah. I'm sure he did. Where are you, Jamie?"

"Don't you want to know *how* I am?"

"Yah, sure, how are you?"

"I'm sober."

"Good. That's good, Jamie." He'd heard *that* before.

"This time it's forever."

"Good, Jamie." He'd heard that before too.

"I wish Mom could have known. I just finished a hundred and eighty days at Masterson's in Long Beach. A private clinic. They say the best way to make sure it'll work is to pay for it yourself. I did, and Jerry, I know I've kicked it this time."

"Mom didn't know—?"

"She was so discouraged with me—I wanted to do this on my own. I was going to take a week to get myself settled, then I was going to go see her."

"She's proud of you, Jamie, wherever she is," Jerrold said. Wondering if his brother knew about their mother's will.

"Who's making the arrangements for her memorial?" James asked. Jerrold could hear tears in his voice.

"Um . . . nobody's talked about it yet. Dad is—"

"I know, I know. What about you? I think the two of us should make some plans."

"Dad has a bail hearing tomorrow. He may get out."

"Oh?"

"Give me your number, Jamie—I'll call you tomorrow and let you know what happens at the hearing."

"I'll find out on the news," James said. "I'm sure I can find out about Mom's services on the news too."

"Jesus, bro . . . aren't you even going to let me know where you are?"

"No. Not now."

Jerrold swallowed, and threw it out there. "Do you know about Mother's will, Jamie?"

"Yes. I talked to Jonah. I don't want the money, Jer."

"What?"

"I don't need it. Not all that, anyway. I'll use a little of it, get myself healthy, buy a small house. Jonah is going to set up a trust for me. I want to use the rest of it to do some good."

"Do some— What do you mean, do some good?"

"Medical research, school playgrounds, drug rehab facilities, families who need help—"

"What about me?" his brother interjected.

"You don't need help, Jamie. You make money, Laynie's working, you have a roof over your heads, a car, whatever you need. And you'll still get your quarterlies."

"But . . . I want a house, a better life, too. I want my share. The estate has millions—"

"She didn't leave it to you, Jerry."

Jerrold was stunned. His brother sounded perfectly lucid. Sober. Refusing to tell where he was. And worst of all, talking about giving their mother's millions away. James, the hippie, drugged-out mother's pet. Now a fucking *do-gooder*. Christ, this couldn't be happening. His thoughts buzzed around his head so frantically that he almost didn't hear what his brother was saying now.

". . . and if it isn't too late, I want to get back with Aly. Start a family. We're going to talk . . ."

Fucking heirs. Now he was planning to create fucking heirs.

"Good-bye, Jerry," his brother was saying. "I'll talk to you soon."

"Wait! Jamie! We have to get together, talk about this—" he said into the dead telephone.

His wife turned over and opened her eyes. "Whoozat?" she mumbled.

"Shut up," he said.

41

Sunday afternoon, at Maxi's house in Beverly Glen. Blessed Sunday after her first week on the graveyard. She'd slept most of the day on Saturday, then gone out with Tom McCartney on Saturday night. Tom and Rosie, that is. All of it was . . . interesting. The jail session with Lightner, dinner at the Sonora, Rosenberg's raw tapes, and especially the after-midnight time at Tom's place. When she woke up today (in her own bed, thank you), she couldn't believe she had slept till noon. Ten blissful hours, for which her body and mind were seriously grateful.

Stretching, lounging in bed for a bit, she replayed the scenario at McCartney's apartment the night before, AR, After Rosie, in Technicolor on her mind's screen. Five or six times. Each time bringing on a dreamy smile. No sex, but oh, so close. Then she stopped her mental virtual tape, threw up a wide banner graphic over the cerebral video that read TO BE CONTINUED, and got up to start her day.

She did a run on Mulholland, took Yukon to the dog park, and now she was making an effort to get herself together for tomorrow's start of another year-long work week. Her friend Debra Angelo was going to stop by with her daughter Gia in a while to say hello—they were coming over from a Sunday afternoon birthday party for one of Gia's friends before heading back home to the beach.

Maxi sat at her kitchen table in a white terry cloth robe, her hair doused with a hot oil treatment and wrapped in a towel, and her feet propped up on a gym stool while she gave herself a pedicure. Carla Ochoa was at the sink washing vegetables for a salad.

"I think I'm getting a new job, missus," Carla said, surprising her.

"Oh—the interview you took on Wednesday?"

"Yes. The lady call my friend, said she would like me to work for her." She paused for a beat, then added, "But she doesn't know about Roberto."

This was not good. "Why didn't you tell her, Carla?"

"I couldn't—" she started, and her voice caught.

"You have to. Before you go there. She has to know what's going on with you."

"Sí. I know. I am going to call her and tell her." Carla pulled a folded piece of paper out of the pocket of her shirt. "I have her phone number."

"What's her name?"

Carla studied the paper. "Mrs. Edith Lambert. On Greendale Drive."

"That's close to here," Maxi said. *This is impossible*, is what she thought.

Then she saw that Carla Ochoa knew that too. A tear sprang from the woman's eye as she jammed the crumpled sheet of paper back into her pocket, then turned back to the sink and the lettuce and cucumbers. Mrs. Lambert was not going to be getting a call. And if she did, and if she was made to realize that Carla Ochoa was the woman all over the news whose young son was kidnapped from Councilman Conrad Lightner's mansion up on Beverly Glen, then Carla would not be getting a job, Maxi was sure.

"We'll find Roberto, Carla," she said to her. "And then we'll figure out everything else."

Maxi's tone of kindness seemed to make Carla come even

more unhinged. She turned off the water faucet and held a dish-towel up to her eyes, then sobbed.

"Carla, come over here and sit down. Talk to me," Maxi said.

Carla dried her hands, pulled some tissues out of a box on the counter, and sat herself across from Maxi at the kitchen table. It had been ten days since the woman's two-year-old had vanished from the Lightner house. Other than the three computer photos that had been delivered to this kitchen, no other viable clues or information had surfaced about the Ochoa boy's whereabouts. Raoul Montez had said nothing. Marc Jorgan had complained to Maxi that the case was getting cold. He'd said that Bill McFar-land's team at the Bureau had also come up with nothing. It was as if Roberto Ochoa had disappeared from the country. Maybe he had. Jorgan had not been able to bring himself to say aloud what both of them knew and feared—the more time that went by, the less likely it was that they would find the boy alive.

Maxi brushed bright red lacquer on the last of her toes, then screwed the top back on the bottle of polish. She folded her hands on the table then, and faced Carla Ochoa. The woman looked to-tally defeated. Defeated and depressed, and every day since she'd come here to live her spirits had sunk lower.

"Maybe you should wait until we find Roberto before you take a new job," Maxi said. "It might only make things more difficult if you're working somewhere else."

Carla sniffled, wiped her nose, and nodded.

"You're fine here for now," Maxi went on. "You're safe here." She said a silent prayer that she was right.

"Thank you, missus—"

"Tell me, did you have any boyfriends since you and Mr. Ochoa divorced? Anybody who might want to hurt you?"

"No," the woman answered with a frown. "No boyfriend."

"Was Raoul Montez your boyfriend?"

"*Nunca!*" Never. Carla shook her head fiercely.

"Did he *want* to be your boyfriend, do you think? Did he ever say anything to you like that?"

"Yes. All the time. I tell him no, and I ignore him always. He would come in the kitchen to ask me where was this, where was that. Maybe some soap, a towel, something like that. And . . . and—"

"And try to touch you?"

"*Sí.*" Carla reddened. Not with anger, but with shame.

"Did you tell Mrs. Lightner? Did you complain to her about him?"

"No . . ." More tears. Of course Carla Ochoa wouldn't complain. She didn't want to jeopardize her position in the household—she had a son to feed and house.

Raoul Montez was still in custody at Parker Center, there since Friday morning when Jorgan had picked him up. He wasn't talking, the detective had told her, but they had grounds to hold him because he'd been identified by Mrs. Ochoa delivering the third photo to Maxi's house. They would be transferring him to Men's Central and they would wait him out, Jorgan said. Montez had a story and they wanted to hear it. Meantime, he, Sanchez, and McFarland had been taking turns interrogating him, mostly Remo Sanchez, who spoke to the handyman in Spanish. Montez had so far been intractable. And fearful, Jorgan thought.

"Did Raoul Montez talk to Mrs. Lightner a lot?" Maxi asked.

"She wasn't nice to him."

"What do you mean, Carla?"

"She scream at him. All the time."

"Why?"

"Mrs. Lightner scream at everybody," was the woman's answer to that. "Always screaming. I told this to the police."

"Did she scream at you, too?"

"*Sí.* At everybody. At Mr. Lightner, too."

"Who do you think would kill her?"

"*No se,* missus." She didn't know. Carla was twisting the wad of tissues in her hands.

"Who else had keys to the estate besides you and Mr. and Mrs. Lightner, do you know?"

"Raoul. And Enrique, the gardener. The pool man, Korman. *Sus hijos*, too."

"Their sons?"

The station had done news stories over the years about one of Councilman Lightner's sons being involved in drugs, and the other one caught in some kind of money scandal. Every time one of the sons was in the news, the story would always come around to the other son and his past troubles, as well as to the councilman himself.

"Mr. Jerrold and Mr. James."

"Did they come to the house much?"

"I never see them. Mrs. Lightner say they have their rooms if they want, is very big house. And they have keys to come in, she say."

"Did Mr. and Mrs. Lightner talk about their sons, do you remember?"

"Sometimes. Their both sons make them very sad, I think."

"Do you think Mrs. Lightner screamed at them, too? Maybe on the telephone?"

"Mrs. Lightner screamed at everybody."

Gia, those are absolutely fabulous shoes," Maxi gushed, as Debra Angelo's ten-year-old daughter stood before her, big smile on her beautiful little heart-shaped face, proudly showing off her new pink tie jellies. "The bomb!" Maxi added, doing kid-speak, which made Gia giggle.

Debra and Maxi had, by turns, been married to the same man, their mutual last husband, mega movie star Jack Nathanson, and the two women had become friends during the five years that Maxi was Gia's stepmom. Nathanson was murdered in a searing Hollywood scandal, and both Debra and Maxi had wound up on the DA's short list of suspects. As Debra often put it, out of earshot of Gia, it was lovely that neither of them had had to do it, actually, since one of his mistresses took care of it.

"Do you two want food?" Maxi asked.

"Oh, puh-*lease!* I don't get to have food till about Wednesday. They didn't have salad or something palatable for the adults at this birthday party so I gorged on hot dogs and birthday cake."

"You? Gorge? What does that mean—half a hot dog and two bites of cake?"

"Yes, my carb ration for the month. And I will pay for it to-morrow."

Debra was Italian, gorgeous, of medium height, ultra-thin, with lustrous dark hair, and semi-outrageous, a working actress who was usually wardrobed in sexy size zero slip dresses. At the moment she was playing the second lead in a prime-time television sitcom, and she was fond of lamenting that cameras put ten pounds on you, which was why she never eats them. Little joke.

"Gia, are *you* hungry, honey?" Maxi asked.

"I had two hot dogs, macaroni salad, Milk Duds, birthday cake, and ice cream. And a juice box," the little princess proudly recited.

"And you're a waif," Maxi said. "A mini–Kate Moss. Remember when we could eat like that, Debra?"

"No," she said. And she probably didn't. Debra had been a child star at four.

Yukon sidled up to his old friend Gia, looking for some attention. Gia squatted to his height and wrapped her arms around the furry boy's neck, and Yuke licked her face. A photo op, sending Maxi to pounce on her camera, which she kept loaded and handy in a kitchen drawer. She squeezed off half a dozen shots.

"Darling, do you want to watch a video while Auntie Maxi and Mummy talk?" Debra asked her girl. "Just for a little while— you've got school in the morning."

Maxi settled Gia and Yukon in the family room with *Shrek 2,* pulled from the stash of kid videos that she kept for when Gia came to visit. "Enjoy," she said, giving Gia a kiss on top of her curly head. "Your mom and I are gonna do a little girl talk."

"Gossip," Gia said knowingly. "Can Yuke sit on the couch with me?"

"Absolutely. This is his couch." It was the most comfortable seat in the house, well-worn goosedown covered in soft, ancient leather that couldn't get any more beat up than it already was. Yuke had full dominion on this one, but still, the dear boy always waited to be invited. Gia patted the cushion beside her and he gleefully jumped on board. The two settled in to watch the green guy on the tube.

Maxi joined Debra in the kitchen. Her friend was bustling about, making tea. Carla Ochoa had retired to her room and closed the door. It was a small house, and Carla was a respectful houseguest.

"So, how are you holding up on the shit shift?" Debra asked decorously, setting two steaming mugs on the table.

"Barely. One week down, and I don't think I'll ever feel like I'm fully awake again. Not to mention it is a very strange terrain, and an upside-down life."

The two women kept up with each other—Debra was fully up to speed on Maxi's turned-around life since she'd gone on the graveyard shift.

"So what about the guy?" she asked. True Debra form, cutting right to the guy, be it Maxi's or her own squeeze du jour.

"The guy is . . . intriguing." Meaning Tom McCartney.

"Are you sleeping with him?" Debra, never shy.

"I've known him for a week, Deb."

"Life is short. Besides, you've known him for a few years, you told me."

"Well, yah, I knew him, but I didn't know him."

"When it comes to men, Maxi, you always make distinctions that I don't understand."

"In hindsight, neither of us understands why we both picked Jack." Their mutual ex-husband.

"True. Ancient history. Let's talk about this McCartney guy. A stud?"

"Totally. And interesting, intriguing, thoughtful, fun—"

"Stop. I get it." Debra was reading *sublime* on Maxi's face as she extolled. "So what are you doing about it?"

"Looking forward." Maxi and Debra habitually talked in shorthand, whether by phone, fax, e-mail, or in person, because neither of them ever had time to spare.

"No conflict?" Debra asked. They had often discussed Maxi's on-again, off-again romance with Richard Winningham, continually aborted because the two journalists worked together.

"I don't see one. Tom is an independent stringer."

"Which brings us to . . . what *about* Richard?"

Maxi paused. "You know how much I care about Richard. But I can't hold out hopes forever that we'll ever really get it off the ground."

"You do glow when he's around," Debra observed.

"But he's never around."

"Well, yes, there's a lot to be said for proximity. Just be happy, Maxi."

"And what about you? Any men on your horizon?"

"Since we talked yesterday?"

"Yeah. Knowing you."

"I'm resting."

Debra Angelo was the reigning queen of the Hollywood conquest. But since Jack Nathanson, she'd stopped marrying them. Smart decision, Maxi thought. Though she herself had been married only once, also to Nathanson, she'd stopped marrying them too.

Debra called Gia, who came into the kitchen doing a little dance to "Accidentally in Love" from the Counting Crows' *Shrek 2* soundtrack.

"Excellent taste in music," Maxi complimented her.

"We're going to hit the road, darling," Debra said. It was a forty-minute drive home to the beach.

"What's on your head under that towel, Auntie Maxi?" Gia asked. Maxi and Debra laughed.

"A hot oil treatment," Maxi said. "It makes your hair luxuriant."

"Do I need one?" Gia asked the two women, seriously.

"No, sweetheart." Maxi lowered herself to Gia's level to give her a hug. "Your hair has the natural luster of gorgeous youth."

"When will I need one?"

"Your mom will let you know," Maxi said, smiling.

"You can count on that, darling," Debra confirmed.

Maxi gave Debra a hug, then she and Yukon walked these two people whom they both adored to the door. "We never have enough time," Maxi said.

"But it's quality time," Debra assured her. "We love you, Maxi. Remember, have fun . . . but be careful."

42

Monday night, after the Six O'clock News. Maxi was back at Men's Central Jail in downtown Los Angeles, with producer Wendy Harris and cameraman Jim Jersey. Lightner was denied bail that afternoon—the judge had gaveled him and his defense counsel Martin Hodel out of the courtroom before the attorney could finish his pleading. It was suggested by some in the press that this particular longtime Los Angeles Superior Court judge had witnessed the councilman trampling on too many toes over the years. Pete Capra's politically incorrect take on the finding to his staff in the meeting before the early block was that like everybody else in L.A., the judge just thought the asshole was guilty. In any case, Hodel's plea for bail for the councilman did not carry the day.

Maxi sat opposite the prisoner now at the dented metal table in the same interrogation room where they'd met on Saturday night. Wendy was perched on a folding chair against the back wall, taking notes on her laptop. Jersey had grabbed his establishing shots outside Men's Central on the sticks, and was now going handheld on the interview. Lightner's mood was grim.

"Motherfuckers," he fumed. Then, "You're gonna edit this, right? Don't put any swear words on the air. You got that?"

"We got that," Maxi acknowledged dryly.

"They have the wrong man and they know it. This is nothing but a political rap."

"Political? How so, Councilman?" Maxi, deadpan.

"Everybody knows if I'm elected mayor I'll be coming down hard on the police commission. They've heard me rail a hundred times against all the fucking bleeding-heart liberals who are soft on crime, who let rapists and murderers walk, who are turning our city into . . . Can you bleep out that swear word?"

"It would be easier if you didn't say them, Councilman." Behind Lightner, Maxi could see Wendy trying hard not to giggle.

All of Lightner's political rhetoric would end up cut, swear words or not, the three journalists knew. But it was a tried-and-true technique to start soft, let them rave on, say whatever they wanted to say, then clobber them with hardballs when they were feeling all righteous about themselves and comfortable with the interviewer. You would think politicians would realize by now that in a two-minute piece, journalists will always cut out the crap and cut to the chase, the reason for the interview. In this case, the answer to the question, *Did you kill your wife?* Politicians the world over—it was in their genes, Maxi figured. They had to mount their soapboxes, and they lived in hope that their rant would make air.

She eased into the crimes: the missing boy, and how the councilman had found his wife dead the next morning. Or so he said. Basically covering Rosie's ground. The universal method: ask the same questions a few times over in different ways, see if the answers stay the same. What he said this time was something she hadn't heard before. She asked again who he thought had kidnapped Roberto Ochoa.

"Pros," Lightner said. "Snatched the boy for the ransom, figuring they could unloose some of my wife's millions." Then, as an afterthought, "Which is a fucking joke, trying to get at Gladdy's millions. Another stupid criminal caper." At that, he let out a raspy, guttural chuckle. Evidently cracked himself up with the joke he had made. Then, "Bleep that last part out, y'hear?"

This time Wendy couldn't hold on to it. She broke up, and, hearing her laugh, Lightner laughed some more. Figuring the producer was laughing *with* him. This one was going to take some overtime in the edit room, Maxi lamented silently, rolling her eyes at Wendy over Lightner's shoulder.

"But there was never a ransom note," she said to the man.

"Things probably got too hot for them. Cops swarming, the FBI involved, you people all over it. Kidnapping is a death penalty crime in the state of California if the victim is harmed. Under the Little Lindbergh law. It was made mandatory in 1973. I figure they decided they couldn't risk picking up a money drop now."

Showing off what he knows, Maxi noted silently. Was this a man who actually knew California law off the top, or was it a man who'd looked up the statute when he was contemplating a kidnapping? In an outdated book, by the way—that law had since been revised. Had he been trying to get at some of his wife's millions himself? Maybe it would have worked, knowing Gladys Lightner's abhorrence of scandal, and that it would have come out that the councilman's family had an illegal working in their household. In fact, Mrs. Lightner did manage to dodge that bullet, didn't she? By getting dead. Her murder superseded all the sidebar kidnapping details in the news.

But little Roberto was still out there. Still being held somewhere. Maxi mentally flashed on the distraught face of Carla Ochoa.

"How do you explain Raoul Montez's involvement? He's your employee."

"Obviously they got to him. Cut him in. He's always had access to the house. Those third world people speak the same language."

"Third world people—?"

"You know what I mean." Then realizing his racial slur, "But take that out."

Now Jersey lost it. Maxi heard a little gasp of air coming from behind her, and she turned around to look at him. His shoulders were shaking, and so was the camera. *Great*, she thought—*now I'll have jiggly footage*. Which made *her* laugh then. She'd interviewed her quota of fools in her career, and Lightner was way up there.

"So these professional kidnappers took those pictures, and had Montez deliver them to my house?" she asked.

"That's right. And the pictures tell the story."

"What story, Councilman?"

"Well, the first picture was to show that they had the kid. Symbolic—tied to a chair. The second one, with him crying, was to show that they would hurt him if we didn't take them seriously. And the last one, where he's eating the pasta, was to show that the kid was okay—I think they were getting very nervous by then, which is why they didn't make a ransom demand."

Pasta? That was news to her. And it would be news to Jorgan and McFarland. Big red flag, Maxi registered mentally, but didn't let it show on her face. The third photo had never been shown on the news. Lightner apparently just assumed that it had been because the first two pictures were aired, and behind bars he would not have had access to TV news. No way could he have known what that third photo depicted. Unless he took it. Or he knew the shooter. Pasta? She suppressed the urge to ask Lightner whether it was tomato or meat sauce.

"So, how does the kidnapping connect to the murder of your wife? Or does it?" she asked him.

"Of course it does. I think they came into the house intending to snatch the boy and Gladys intercepted them. And they probably told her if she talked they'd kill her, which is why she refused to call the police that night, never admitted what she saw— she was scared. But they couldn't let an eyewitness stay alive, especially such a prominent eyewitness, so they came back in and murdered her."

He'd been rehearsing that one, Maxi could tell. And it wasn't bad. "And how did they get inside your house to kill your wife?"

"The same way they got in to snatch the boy."

"With help."

"You got it. With help again."

"Raoul Montez."

"I don't know that for sure, but it seems logical. Doesn't it?"

"Who was in the house when Mrs. Lightner was murdered?"

"I don't know for sure. I know that Gladys, myself, and the housekeeper, Mrs. Ochoa, were there overnight. And that you came in the morning. But I don't know what time my wife was killed."

Maxi gave him points for that one. The estimated time of death had not been released.

"And you came into her bedroom in the morning—"

"And I found her like that," he finished. "Murdered."

"You had a lot of blood on your person," Maxi put to him.

In spatters, as well as smears, she thought but didn't say. Spatters could indicate that he was there when it happened. She knew that the LAPD crime lab was all over that physical evidence, his wife's bloodstains on the clothes he was wearing that morning.

"Of course there was blood on me. I tried to revive her. Gave her mouth-to-mouth. It wasn't working. She was obviously dead."

"Mrs. Ochoa and I heard you scream. That was when you found her?"

"Must have been."

"We came right upstairs. Running. We got into the room just seconds after you screamed. Less than a minute. How long *did* you give your wife mouth-to-mouth resuscitation?"

"Not long. I knew she was dead. She had no heartbeat."

"Could you tell how she'd been killed?"

"Not then. Too much blood. But they said she was stabbed."

"Did you see a murder weapon?"

"No. They still haven't found the knife, have they?"

Sticking to his story. On tape. Unless he was a good actor, he wouldn't know that it wasn't a knife. Maxi was actually believing him, but she didn't believe that he was not involved in the kidnapping of Roberto. She concurred with Rosie's call.

Guilty in the kidnapping, not guilty in the murder.

But that couldn't be. The dots had to connect.

43

Monday night, almost nine o'clock. Pete Capra had stayed late in the office to see what Maxi and her crew would bring in. They were working an exclusive jailhouse interview with Conrad Lightner. Wendy Harris had called to say that they should be finished in time to roll back from downtown and get it cut for the Eleven O'clock News. No, Capra had told the producer, he wanted to turn the tape around and have Maxi go live from outside Men's Central—she would lead the Eleven with Lightner. He didn't want to take the chance that they might get hung up on the downtown freeways, in a Music Center concert or at Dodger Stadium traffic. Now he was waiting for Jersey to feed in the tape so he could see what Maxi had managed to get out of the councilman, and bird-dog the editing.

Earlier tonight, the LAPD had picked up a suspect in the murder of the first prostitute near the downtown New Otani Hotel last month. The man was a vagrant who was known to frequent the area, a wino who'd been in scrapes before, had been in and out of prison, and had a long jacket that listed crimes ranging from B&E, battery, and weapons possession, to drug dealing, even indecent exposure. Capra's source at Robbery-Homicide told him that they found the dead woman's wallet with her ID in the guy's overloaded shopping cart. And a pair of her underpants. Sick fuck.

Also from his source, he learned that the LAPD had now dropped the theory of a connection between the murders of the two prostitutes, because the vagrant had an alibi for the morning of the "Marilyn" murder—he'd been in a holding cell at Parker Center for three days on a drunk and disorderly. So, two prostitutes, yes, but two different killers. That didn't surprise Capra, because there were two different MOs. This one was stabbed with a steak knife and found in a Dumpster near the downtown hotel, and the Hollywood hooker was killed in an alley behind her apartment building with an injection of cyanide.

His reporter Christine Williams was also killed with cyanide. If those two murders were committed by his San Francisco serial killer, who were his targets this time around? Not prostitutes, after all. And not people in Capra's world. That had been his biggest fear, but he had no connection whatever to the prostitute who'd been poisoned. In fact, and to the vocal and insistent frustration of some of his staff, he had even downplayed their coverage of the story.

But "Marilyn" and Christine Williams were certainly connected—Christine was doing a story on the prostitute murders the night she was killed.

Capra had seen him again and again, his mystery man, on several of McCartney's tapes. It was almost as if Tom McCartney knew who he was looking for. That wouldn't surprise him. McCartney was thorough and resourceful; he would have come up with six ways from Sunday to sniff the guy out. Including online. The name Peter Capra would be linked to the archived San Francisco "walk-in killer" stories on the Net. That's why he had given the stringer this assignment—because McCartney would get the right shots without Capra having to talk to him about it. He couldn't talk to him about it without talking about it to Maxi Poole, his own reporter.

And he certainly couldn't talk to Maxi about it.

His name blared on a page from the routing room—that meant the Lightner tape was feeding in.

Maxi had tonight's producer of the Eleven, Everett Sims, on her cell phone. Jersey had just fed the raw footage of the Lightner interview back to the station to be edited, and she was giving Sims a rundown of the shots and sound bites she wanted to use.

"And here's the lead, Ev, and it's dynamite," she said, and she gave him the time code on Lightner's comment on the third photo of the Ochoa child.

"Pasta?" Sims asked. "That's new."

"No kidding. We never showed that third picture. We just said that one had been received. Nobody else had it either."

"This is huge. Hang on, Maxi—we've gotta start teasing this right now." Sims put his hand over the mouthpiece to bark an order for a clip of the incoming feed to be lifted, and for one of the eleven o'clock anchors to voice over it for a news tease into prime time. While he was making that happen, Pete Capra picked up the phone from him.

"Maxi—great job."

"Thanks." A little frosty.

"What's it worth, do you think?"

"A good two minutes. I did a bridge explaining that Councilman Lightner could not have seen the third photo because it was never released by the police, or described. And even the police didn't know that what Roberto was eating was pasta."

"Nailed him."

"He nailed himself."

"You burned him down."

"He won't talk to me again, we can count on that."

"He won't talk to any media again, is my guess. Especially when Hodel gets wind of this."

"I need to talk down my roll cue to Everett—is he ready for me?"

"In a second. So, did Lightner kill his wife?"

"I don't think so."

"Why not?"

"Nothing hard. It's my instinct."

"He manipulated you."

Silence on the line. She was stung by the insult. "Pete, I'm exhausted. I want to go home after the Eleven." With an edge.

It was a reasonable request—she'd gone down to Men's Central right from anchoring the Six. She'd been on the clock since a little after three that afternoon without a break. She'd nailed the Lightner interview, which would hold up for the Morning News and beyond.

"No," her boss said. "I want you in the field."

"You're kidding," she said. And she really thought he was.

"Maxi, you efforted the Lightner interview on your own—you weren't assigned to it. That was your choice. On your time."

"You can't mean that. I'm delivering you an incredible lead for the Eleven, it'll go all day tomorrow, and it'll be picked up all over the country."

Capra wasn't moved. "I've told you to stay off this story. Listen to me this time. You're on the graveyard shift now, Maxi."

Silence for a beat. Then she said, "Put Everett back on." Ice.

44

Monday night, eleven-twenty-six, on the sidewalk outside the Men's Central Jail on Bauchet Street in downtown Los Angeles. Close to midnight and January cold. Maxi was shivering. Her lightweight red silk suit with the short flirty skirt and the red high heels had turned out to be a bad idea, but she hadn't expected to be hanging out here to go live on the Eleven. What she *had* expected was to get her interview with Lightner, go back to the station and log in the tapes, go out to dinner with Tom McCartney, then back to the station where it was warm to write and edit the story, go to makeup, and introduce it on the set.

Folding her arms around herself now as she waited for Jersey to pack up the gear, she wasn't sure if she was shivering from the cold or from fury. Both, she decided. There was no way she could top this story tonight—it made sense for her to go home now and get a few hours' sleep, then come in at five and recut it for the Morning News. After the morning show, she was due at the practice range in Glendale for her Tuesday morning target shooting. She was monumentally sleep-deprived, her perennial state since she'd been dumped on the graveyard shift, and the marathon sleep session she'd indulged in over the weekend didn't compensate. If anything, the ten hours' sleep she got on Saturday night only seemed to make her groggy. Thinking about it made her yawn again. And Capra was insisting that she go out in the field now and grub for news. It was insane.

And so was he. Maybe this was the way Corporate got you to quit, so they wouldn't have to pay severance or unemployment benefits. She pulled her phone out of her purse and punched in the number for Tom McCartney's cell. He picked up.

"Yo, Poole." Her name would be displayed on his LED readout. "I caught your lead. Awesome."

"Thanks, Tom. What's going on, anything?"

"I thought you'd be on your way home to dreamland by now." Since she'd had to cancel her dinner plans with him earlier, he knew that she'd worked straight through.

"I thought so too. But the prince of darkness thought different."

"Capra? What's he doing up at this hour?"

"Evidently he felt that he had to micromanage my Lightner piece. He thinks I'm incompetent."

"You made him a hero tonight."

"He hates me."

"Are you hungry?"

"Starving. I have to pick up my car at the station, so I'm riding in with my shooter. We're going to stop for gas at the all-night station on Spring Street, so while Jersey's pumping the truck I thought I'd wolf down one of those ancient sandwiches they keep in the refrigerator case."

"Sounds delicious."

"Mystery meat. They give you a little packet of mustard to disguise the taste."

"Why don't you hold off and meet me at Cantor's after you pick up your car?"

"Okay. If Capra asks I'll pretend I'm investigating delicatessen salami fraud."

"What's that?"

"I don't know, but there'd be great visuals . . . all that food—"

"You're just hungry. See you in a while."

"About an hour, I'm guessing. I'll log in my tapes and head right for Fairfax."

"Then after we feed you, if nothing's shaking we can go for a stroll in the park."

"Sounds like a plan," she said, and they both clicked off.

MacArthur Park again. Well, why not? The park with Mc-Cartney by moonlight. So the sexy little red suit wouldn't be a total waste after all, she thought, and she climbed up into the live truck with Jersey. Smiling.

McCartney was astonished at what Maxi could put away. A pastrami sandwich on rye the size of a football, a large order of curly fries, big side of coleslaw, two giant kosher dills, and Cantor's quart-sized glass of Diet Coke. He sat opposite her in the booth, bemused, while she shoveled it in.

"You didn't used to be able to eat at this hour," he observed.

"This isn't me eating." Chomp chomp. "This is Elvis channeling my body. Would you order me a piece of their New York cheesecake with cherries?" Chomp chomp. "And coffee."

"Where do you put it?"

"Ask Elvis." Chomp chomp.

"Much longer on the graveyard and you'll blow up like Elvis," he deadpanned.

Maxi, ignoring that: "So are we going to the park?"

"Lovely night for it, don't you agree?"

"Think he'll be out there?" Chomp chomp.

"Elvis?"

"No, not Elvis. I *know he'll* be out there. I mean the boss's man."

"He's there a lot."

"Does he have . . . hours? A regular schedule? Habits?"

"Yah, he works the graveyard. Like us."

"Wonder what he does all day."

"Kills people, probably."

"That's not funny."

"Sure it is."

Maxi sighed. "Look at us. We're having dinner at two in the morning and making jokes about murder. This is not a life we're having."

"Well," McCartney offered, "as that great philosopher Frank Sinatra once said, 'Whatever gets you through the night without crying.'" He reached over and picked up the bill.

"I owe you one," Maxi said, dropping her napkin on the table.

"A *big* one." He smirked, scrutinizing her leavings. She stuck her tongue out at him.

Yukon didn't get to come to work with her tonight because Men's Central was not in a pooch-friendly neighborhood and she'd have had to leave him outside in the car. Yes, Yuke could *look* mean when he put his mind to it, but she wasn't about to test him against the baddies who hung near the downtown jail. They decided to leave Maxi's car in the all-night parking lot on the south side of Cantor's Deli and drive down to MacArthur Park in McCartney's Hummer. She felt safe in McCartney's H2—a big, black, mean machine. Nobody was going to hurt you in that thing.

Especially since Tom McCartney came with it.

There he is," McCartney whispered.

He and Maxi were partially hidden in dense foliage about twenty feet to the west of the men's restroom in the park. McCartney gestured to a group of oddly mismatched men, four of them, sitting on dilapidated camp chairs around an upended blue plastic United States Postal Service mail crate on which they were playing cards. Or doing drugs. Or both.

"The one in the black jeans and T-shirt, with the ponytail."

"Jeez," Maxi whispered back. "Do they *live* here?"

"As a matter of fact, a lot of them do. A lot of them sleep in the park."

"That's illegal."

"*Duh!* Every now and then the cops sweep the park, shoo them all out, but not often. They only go somewhere else, sleep in downtown doorways, then the cops have to haul them in for loitering, littering, urinating in public, whatever. They're actually less of a public nuisance sleeping in the park."

"Then they're not all perverts. Some of them are just homeless."

"Right. But it's a safe bet that the ones who hang out here near the men's can are pretty twisted. Don't know what our guy's story is."

McCartney put a finger to his lips then and led the way through the trees to the far side of the quartet for a better vantage point from which to video his target. He set the camera down on a tree stump, aimed upward, and focused the zoom.

"Here, take a look at him," he whispered to Maxi, indicating the eyepiece.

She stooped and peered through the lens. That was him, all right, in living close-up. At least that was the guy whom she, Tom, and Wendy had iso'd on the Nodori tape. The reddish-gray hair, the broad nose, the hooded eyes. And the mole, prominent, high on his right cheek. Serious, looking hard at the hand of cards he was holding. The fourth for bridge in a party for pervs.

Maxi nodded and moved away from the camera. McCartney picked it up, hefted it onto his right shoulder, reaimed, refocused, and rolled tape.

Tom McCartney hoisted his camera up onto the elevated rear platform of his Hummer and snapped two thick bungee cords around it for support. Taking good care of his equipment, Maxi noted. Then he pulled a packet of tape labels and a marker out of his backpack and labeled the two cassettes he'd shot.

"These are so damn good they're gonna get me fired," he said to Maxi.

"Huh?"

"I've got this dude dead center, close up, and in the light," he said, waving the cassettes to dry the ink on the labels. "Capra will know for sure this is his guy, or at least that this is the guy he *thinks* is his guy, the San Francisco serial killer. And if it *is* his guy, he's gonna know for sure that the dude is down here in L.A. now, and that he definitely hangs in MacArthur Park at night. So he'll know pretty much where and when to find him. He's not gonna need me on this caper anymore."

Maxi laughed. "So, you're so good you did yourself out of a job."

"I'm brilliant at that." No expression.

"I've heard."

He slammed the heavy rear door of the Hummer, and he and Maxi went around to the front and climbed inside. They buckled up, and McCartney turned on the ignition.

"Back to your car?" he asked.

"Not yet. I want to take you someplace."

"I can't eat another bite right now, though I'm sure *you* could. I'll wait till tomorrow night for the meal you owe me."

Ignoring that, she said, "We're going to Valencia. Take the Hollywood Freeway north to the San Diego Freeway. Magic Mountain country."

"I can't do the Revolution—I just ate." The Revolution was Magic Mountain's gigantic roller coaster, with a complete 360-degree loop, which hurtled riders upside down.

"Ha-ha-ha. We're going out there to make a house call."

"A house call?" McCartney was looking at her, brow furrowed, not moving the Hummer.

"Well, a trailer call, actually."

"A trailer call. In Valencia." He was getting it, she could see.

"Uh-huh. We can take Fairfax up to the Hollywood Freeway."

"A trailer call out in Valencia to do a break and enter." Still not moving the SUV.

"That's harsh. Not a break and enter. A . . . visit."

"A trailer call in Valencia to *visit* one Raoul Montez."

"That's right." Her piece on the Montez trailer bust had run on Friday night's news.

"He's in jail," McCartney pointed out.

"Exactly."

45

Tuesday morning, ten-twenty. The heavy rain that longtime Channel Six weather reporter Fritz Coleman had forecast on the Eleven last night had broken through the clouds in silver bullets, and was splashing off windshields and creating rushing rivulets on the ten-lane-wide San Diego Freeway. Maxi was driving southbound on her way to Holy Cross Cemetery in Culver City. The downpour was further exacerbating the usually slow-going traffic on that stretch of freeway, almost always clogged in both directions in any weather with travelers going to and from LAX.

Maxi's mood was somber, and she was mind-numbing tired. No sleep at all last night. She'd recut her Lightner interview for the Morning News, intro'd it on the set, then rushed out to Glendale for her scheduled hour of target practice, and now she was back across town on the storm-darkened Westside, still dressed in the red suit and heels—woefully inappropriate for a funeral but it couldn't be helped. This was her sleep time, but services for Christine Williams would be held at eleven o'clock in the Holy Redeemer Chapel, then afterward, interment near the Pietà shrine in the cemetery grotto.

She fervently hoped that she'd be able to get a couple of

hours' sleep before going in to the station to anchor the Six. Thinking about those ten hours just three nights ago that didn't turn out to be nearly enough sleep in the bank. Or maybe sleep was something you couldn't bank, or even catch up on. How long could she keep this up? she wondered. Maybe she would call in sick tonight—a preventive move, before she ran her immune system into the ground and actually *did* get sick.

No. She wouldn't give Capra the satisfaction. And she damn well wasn't going to quit. Focusing on keeping her eyes open while staring through the monotonous back-and-forth *thunk-thunk-thunk-thunk* of the windshield wipers, she poked around in the console CD holder, found her favorite Counting Crows album, popped it in the player, and thought about the night before.

She had navigated while McCartney drove to the trailer park where Raoul Montez lived. He'd parked about fifty feet away, all the while muttering little throwaway phrases like, "I oughta have my head examined." Which continued as he walked around to the back of his H2, opened the rear swing-out door, rummaged around inside, and took out a flashlight, a crowbar, and a box of latex gloves. As the two of them put on gloves, Maxi led McCartney down the path to Montez's trailer.

And they broke into it. Well, *he* broke into it. She stood on the dirt frontage in her impossibly high heels and did lookout duty. And thought, *It's so nice to have a man around the house!* That, as McCartney jimmied open the trailer's back window. Which, conveniently, turned out to be plastic, not glass, so it didn't even break. Nor was there an alarm system, no surprise. McCartney had boosted himself up and climbed inside, then opened up the trailer door and let her in.

The first thing that hit her when she stepped inside was the clotted, rancid air. The next thing that hit her was the fact that the police had already been there, had swept the place. Again, no surprise, though Jorgan hadn't mentioned it, or what they might have found there. Well, Jorgan didn't tell her everything. Fair enough; she didn't tell him everything either.

Her favorite cut on the CD came up, the one that exactly corresponded with her mood this morning, and she reached over and boosted the volume. A cover by the Counting Crows of the Grateful Dead's "Friend of the Devil." The music blared: *Didn't get to sleep last night till the morning came around . . . if I get home before daylight I just might get some sleep tonight.* Yes. Thank you, Jerry Garcia.

Last night she'd flashed back to the rout, remembering that Raoul Montez hadn't had a lot of time to tidy up the place before Jorgan and Sanchez hauled his sorry ass downtown. Not that the man seemed to be a fan of neat in the best of circumstances, she'd observed, following the beam of light that McCartney was moving around the cluttered space. Dirty clothes, grubby rags, rotten food leavings in sour, crusted containers, empty cans and bottles, Spanish-language newspapers and magazines littering every surface, the floor sticky with dirt and grime, tiny sink and galley counter crammed with dirty dishes, and thick black latent fingerprint dust over everything.

She didn't want to *know* what was inside the greasy little refrigerator; she was in danger of losing her pastrami sandwich as it was. But McCartney opened the door and shone the light inside. "It's amazing what people will stash in the fridge," he whispered, then just as suddenly he'd slammed the door shut, the stink inside apparently too much even for him. Thrusting the flashlight into her hand, he mumbled, "I'll be right back," and he bolted out the trailer door and off the rickety steps, presumably to get a shot of fresh air.

Directing the light around the trailer, Maxi surveyed the scene again, slower. In a corner on the floor she saw a small red toolbox. It looked to be the size of the one in the second photo of Roberto. Well, Raoul Montez was a handyman, she thought, of course he'd have a toolbox. And as Marc Jorgan had pointed out, loads of people own a red toolbox. She'd opened the lid, and then the drawers, one by one. Hammers, wrenches, screwdrivers, nails, nuts and bolts. Duct tape. In the first photo, Roberto was shown tethered to a chair with duct tape. Still, that wasn't inculpatory— lots of people had a roll of two-inch gray duct tape thrown in a drawer or a toolbox. She shone the beam on the walls of the trailer, looking for traces of the dour green that showed behind Roberto in the first two photos, but the trailer's walls were a dingy dun color.

She'd heard a thump, then a creak on the floorboards, and her heart had jumped into her throat. Gripping the heavy flashlight like a weapon, she'd wheeled around to face the door at the front end of the trailer. It was Tom McCartney—lugging his video camera.

"No!" she'd gasped. "You can't tape here. That is *so* illegal!"

McCartney couldn't suppress a chuckle. "Like any of this is legal," he'd said.

True enough.

Wasting no time, he'd lifted his camera up onto his shoulder and switched on the headlamp, a three-hundred-watt Ultralight that instantly rendered the small space brighter than daylight.

As he rolled on the mess, Maxi peered at what Raoul Montez used for a bed, brightly lit now. A small, sagging cot, top covers in a heap on the floor around it, exposing a worn, crumpled, and badly stained bottom sheet loosely spread over a thin mattress. Moving in closer, being careful to stay out of McCartney's shot, she picked up the acrid stench of urine mixed with the rest of the repugnant odors.

The rotting sheet had what looked like a pond of yellow on top of the older brownish-tinged grime. Recent, she thought. Somebody wet the bed. Roberto! Terrified, two-year-old Roberto. Then, in the camera's bright light that washed the area she saw two short, bright turquoise threads stuck to the dried urine stain. The vivid turq color against the overall dinginess of the place sparked a memory. On the day that she'd helped Carla Ochoa move up the street to her house, on top of one of the little stacks of Carla's belongings that she'd carried to her truck was a thin wool throw, worn and ragged. It was bright turquoise. Was that Roberto's "blankie"? Was she looking at threads from the blanket his mother said he always hung on to? Threads that might have adhered to the clothes he wore the night he was kidnapped, then stuck to the wet bedsheet?

Tucking the flashlight under her arm, she took a tissue out of a pack in her purse and a pair of eyebrow tweezers out of her makeup bag. Carefully, she picked up the two threads with the tweezers, one at a time, and dropped them onto the tissue, then folded the paper over them several times and slipped the little package into a zippered compartment of her wallet.

Maybe Roberto Ochoa had been there.

Driving east on Slauson Avenue now, she could see the ornate iron gates of Holy Cross Cemetery standing open, their tall twin crosses looming high above them, glistening in the rain. Vehicles were passing through the gates at intervals, a Channel Six live truck and a couple of company vans among them—colleagues, on the job, taking time out to pay their respects. She eased into line and followed the stream up the wet concrete slope toward the chapel.

46

Jerrold Lightner had just come up with what he thought was a brilliant idea. He was an *idea* man after all, wasn't he?

First, he had to find his brother. That shouldn't be so hard. If ancient Jonah Jacobs and his little gang of legal prudes could find the guy, surely he could too. Actually, Jamie had probably called *them*. Figures, when he'd heard about their mother. Well, James had called *him* too, hadn't he? And he'd actually sounded quite civil. Friendly, even. But that was James. Sweet baby James, always. As if they'd ever been friends, Jerrold mused. He'd hated his little brother from the day Con and Gladdy brought the squealing bundle home from the hospital. And from that day on, little Jamie Lightner was king of the house. So much for the concept that the firstborn son was always the favorite. Not in the Lightner house. Of course, his father had never much liked either of them, but his father was a boob. His mother was the one with the money, and she was crazy about her baby.

He'd been able to think of little else since that phone call from Jamie on Sunday. Two days ago. He had immediately called Masterson's Clinic in Long Beach. Said he wanted to get ahold of Mr. Lightner to offer him a job. Like the kid needed a job; he was gonna be worth about thirty million any minute. But the Masterson people didn't know that. Sorry, they were "not at liberty to give out any information on a client," the woman had said. Not even confirmation that one James Parsable Lightner had *been* a fucking client. "Up yours," he'd actually shot through the phone line, which was okay because he'd given her a fictitious name.

Well, now he had a better idea. When guys like Jamie, drunks and druggies, got sober for fifteen minutes, they always went running back to "help" their old friends in the rehab joint, didn't they? With care and counsel, and the usual I-did-it-and-so-can-you kind of shit. First they got Jesus, and then they got the urgent need to "help thy neighbor." Jamie was always a softie sap. Mr. Impressionable. Rehab could change your habits, maybe, but not your personality. And that was a big maybe, by the way. He'd read somewhere that the recidivism rate for rehab was eighty-six percent. He'd tucked that statistic away in the back of his computer brain way back when. Tucked away the fact that the kid had just a fourteen percent chance of kicking the monkey. Bad odds.

He didn't know if Jamie got Jesus, but he wouldn't be surprised. What he *did* know was that Jamie got sober, evidently, and then the kid got the urge to "do some good." Well, big brother knew exactly how to knock that out of him. He would call the Masterson Clinic people back and tell them he was an addict and he needed help; he needed to talk to Mr. Lightner, if he could. Mr. Lightner had been an inspiration to him, and blah, blah, blah. If Jamie was working there, they would tell him when to call back. Then he would show up at the clinic in Long Beach, tell his brother they needed to talk about family stuff, and he'd wait around the place until Jamie was finished do-gooding.

Then he would take him out to a nice restaurant for dinner. And get him drunk. How hard could that be? Nobody ever had a problem getting James Lightner drunk. Or stoned. Or both. It would take Jerrold less than a hundred and eighty minutes to wipe out a hundred and eighty days at Masterson, he figured. Holy Masterson, which Jamie had paid for himself, no doubt with his quarterly stipends, and if that didn't cover the nut they would probably have set him up on a payment schedule. Instill responsibility. Well, little Jamie Lightner would soon be able to buy the place.

Just knock him off the old wagon. Again. And get him back on the road to not giving a damn about doing good, and living only for alcohol and drugs. Killing himself with alcohol and drugs.

Piece of cake.

But he had to get it done before Jamie started pissing their mother's money away.

47

Tuesday afternoon, a little after three-thirty. Maxi was about to make another appearance at Men's Central Jail downtown. This one was unscheduled, and without a camera crew. Not only had she not set up this visit in advance with Sheriff's Headquarters, she hadn't listed it on the station's log either. This trip was not for the news. This one was for Roberto, and it was personal.

She didn't get a nap in after all. She'd amazed herself with a second wind. Or a third, or fourth. On one of Richard's calls from Iraq, he'd told her this was how the troops were living—majorly sleep-deprived. They'd get a couple of hours' downtime in a trench somewhere, then get up and slog on for another twenty hours, he said. Because it wasn't always convenient for them to take a nap.

Not convenient for her either. Funny, how she was acclimating to this schedule, or total lack of any sane schedule, as it was. Her mother had a friend who had been in a concentration camp as a very young child, the daughter of wealthy German Jews. Her earliest memories were not terrible; it was life, with her mama and papa and a lot of other people, people she knew as Uncle Chaim and Aunt Sophia and Auntie Malka, and several youngsters whom she played games with, games they made up. There were no toys, but she had never known what toys were anyway, so she didn't miss them. Over the years after they were liberated, she had listened to her mother's stories about their life in the camp—fascinating stories, basically about adapting. Her mother had adapted, she said, and her father had not. Her father became morose and bitter in the camp and stayed that way for the rest of his life, and he became ill and died in his fifties. Her mother had found a way to set up a makeshift beauty salon in the camp, and she spent her days doing hairstyles and giving cuts to the women and organizing play activities for the children. She would chat, and laugh, and plan for their future with optimism, and she lived a happy and healthy life into her nineties. Her daughter had always felt that life was about adapting, dealing positively and proactively with the hand you're dealt.

That philosophy helped Maxi to adapt to what, after all, was simply a little fatigue today. That philosophy, and Christine Williams's funeral.

During the two hours she'd spent at the chapel and then the cemetery, she'd focused on Christine. Ducking through the rain on entering, she'd met Christine's family at the door, and said somber hellos to news friends. Pete Capra was there; she had acknowledged him with a distancing nod. But mostly, she'd had trouble taking her eyes off the flower-draped casket at the front of the chapel in the middle aisle. So young, so bright, so pretty, so energetic, a hardworking professional, Christine Williams had it all ahead of her. And she was a good person. Now her family was devastated, her friends were hurting, and her colleagues were saddened. And she was gone.

Driving across town from Holy Cross Cemetery to Men's Central Jail now, Maxi really couldn't complain about a little fatigue, which was something she'd be able to reverse with a few good nights' sleep. She called Carla Ochoa at her house, using the calling system they'd set up. She rang once, then hung up to let Carla know that it was her. Then she rang again, and Carla picked up.

She had a question for the woman: What color was Roberto's blanket, the one he kept with him all the time?

"*Verde y azul*," Carla said. Greenish blue. That sounded like turquoise to Maxi.

She popped an OutKast CD into the stereo, the duo with the big reverb, to help her stay awake. Visiting hours at Men's Central were from ten to seven. Because she had not filed a media "green" sheet with Sheriff's Headquarters, she had to wait in what newsies called the "orange crush," the massive daily throng of people waiting to visit the orange-clad inhabitants inside. At any given hour of the day you could count on from eight hundred to twelve hundred visitors to Men's Central, queued up for at least two hours, and usually longer, to get their fifteen minutes with an inmate. Today they were waiting in the rain. Mothers, fathers, sisters, brothers, lovers, bosses, wives holding crying babies, clergy carrying the Good Book, all in slow-moving lines that curved around outside, most of them patiently waiting just for a chance to help someone on the inside in whatever way they thought they could. Because surely not many people would put themselves through this much aggravation to get themselves into a dismal, rat-infested institution because they were planning on having a good time, would they?

Once visitors had made it to the head of the line, they were sent through metal detectors and body screening, then on through the processing procedure, where the watch commander would examine their photo identification. At that point, each person would be subject to random search, seizure, and record checks. Only after they cleared those final hurdles would a call be made to the guard in the inmate's cellblock. The guard would then present the prospective visitor's name to the prisoner, who had the right to either accept or reject the visit.

Maxi knew this drill, of course. She stood in line, getting drenched in the red silk suit and the deadly high heels, and reminding herself again that she had nothing to complain about. Everything in perspective. That one had come from her father.

But she made a mental note that from now on she would keep an umbrella in her car. She had to smile at her plight as she thought about the familiar slogan the station used in ads for its popular weathercaster: "Fritz said it would be like this." Yes, he did, and she hadn't been able to get home to pick up an umbrella or a raincoat.

Raoul Montez accepted her visit. She'd expected that he would, imagined that any visit by a human being from the outside had to be a welcome break in the monotony of prison life. She was processed through to what was called the Visiting Front Area, a huge gray concrete room that accommodated more than a hundred inmates, all secured in cubicles behind thick Lucite screens, with two-way telephones on which they could talk to their visitors on the other side of the barrier for a maximum of fifteen minutes.

Maxi sat on the plastic chair in front of the screen she'd been assigned to, waiting for Raoul Montez to be escorted to the opposite position. Within minutes the prisoner was brought in, dressed in an orange jumpsuit, with his feet loosely chained together and his hands manacled in front of him. He slid into his seat, squinting to get a better look at her, and Maxi could see that he had no idea who she was. Her first thought: This was a guy who evidently didn't watch the news. Then she realized that with her sopping-wet hair and her soaked-through clothes, she hadn't seen any glints of recognition at all in the crowd. That made her grateful for the downpour. Smiling at her "host," she indicated the phone to his right, and Montez moved both chained hands together and picked up the handset.

"H-hello . . ." he said hesitantly into the mouthpiece.

Maxi got right to it. "Mr. Montez, my name is Maxi Poole. I'm a news reporter, but I'm not here to talk to you for the news. I'm here to ask you about Roberto Ochoa. His mother is staying with me. And as you know, she saw you delivering a photo of Roberto to my house on Beverly Glen last Thursday. And she identified you to the authorities . . ."

As she spoke, she watched Montez's expression morph from curiosity to surprise to fear.

"I know that you had the boy in your trailer. I know that, and I have proof."

She didn't mention that she had proof because she and a friend broke into his trailer the night before, which could conceivably land *her* in a cell at the L.A. County Jail for Women. Her proof, concealed within a piece of tissue in her wallet, was not admissible, B&E not being a legal way to obtain evidence, but Montez didn't know any of the particulars. Watching the dismay register on his face now, she felt strongly that she was right, he'd had the boy.

"I haven't told the police yet. But I will," she lied.

He said nothing.

She continued in measured tones. "As I said, I'm not here for the news. I'm here to make sure that Roberto gets back to his mother. I think you know where he is. If you tell me now, and the boy comes home safe, you'll have a good chance of avoiding the death penalty."

"Avoid . . . *qué*—?"

"Kidnapping is a death penalty offense in the state of California. You could go to the gas chamber, Mr. Montez."

Neglecting to mention that actually, the death sentence *used* to be mandatory, but only if the kidnap victim was harmed. Roberto did not look to be harmed in the third photo, where he was all smiles and eating pasta. Furthermore, with the new special circumstance statutes, the death sentence was now mandatory only if the kidnap victim was dead.

"I don't know—"

"Sure you do," she ventured.

Now he was truly uncomfortable. Apparently unsophisticated about his prisoner's rights, what he didn't seem to know was that he could get up and terminate this visit at any time, and that he could tell one of the guards he was being harassed, if he wanted to. Then Maxi couldn't get in here anymore, either as a private person or as a journalist. For her little peccadillo here today, they would make sure that she never again passed muster at Men's Central.

Well worth it if she could pry this guy loose and get him to tell her where Roberto Ochoa was. She felt sure that she was right, that not only did Raoul Montez deliver the photos, he had kidnapped the boy. And he most probably knew where Roberto was. Had she gone through regular police channels, Detective Marcus Jorgan channels, it would all take time. A lot of time, she knew. And she would have to come up with some quasi-convincing story about how she'd come by the turquoise threads. For which even the most inept of public defenders would decimate her in court. And all the while, Roberto would continue to be in jeopardy, pasta or not.

She glanced at her watch. Five minutes to go before they would pull the plug on this rendezvous, and this would probably be her only shot. She doubted that Montez would okay another visit by Ms. Maxi Poole, private citizen.

"The police have combed your trailer," she said slowly and clearly into the phone. "They've found Roberto's fingerprints there, and traces from his clothes, his hair. His urine. They're building a case against you." Writing this script as she went along.

"It was for someone else . . . someone told me to do this."

That didn't surprise her. "Who told you to do this?"

"This man will kill me if I say."

"That's no defense against kidnapping, Mr. Montez. If you want to save your own life, you need to confess, and make a deal with the district attorney. You need to tell them who put you up to it. Or *you* will be the one who goes into *la cámara de gas*." The gas chamber. Though Mexico had abolished the death penalty decades ago, Montez knew that she was talking about *peña de muerte*, which was fully legal in the United States.

Three minutes left. She had his attention now. He was contemplating his options. And perhaps considering that the long, strong arm of American law had pounced upon him in his trailer in the woods and had locked him up in here—what was to prevent it from effecting his demise? She hoped Montez would conclude that he'd be better off if he came clean. But she had to offer him a reason to do so, and time was running out. Either a real or phony reason would do—she was neither law officer nor journalist at this moment, she was just Jane Q. Public visiting a poor sonofabitch in jail.

"I'd like to help you," she said into the phone. Looking at him through the plastic screen with as much sincerity as she could muster. The nation trusted Walter Cronkite; couldn't this dipstick in the slam trust her?

"How you help me?" he asked. Reasonably.

"You tell me where Roberto is, and I'll tell the police that you helped to save him."

Montez sat still, saying nothing, looking perplexed.

"Two minutes, Montez," said a guard who had moved into the cubicle and stood behind him.

"The boy is at my sister's," Montez whispered into the phone.

Bingo. "Where does your sister live?"

"She live at nine hundred and sixty Portal . . ."

"Time's up." From the guard, who rousted Montez out of his chair.

Maxi put down the phone, beamed a sweet smile at the guard, or at Montez, or at both of them, it didn't matter. She stood and quickly left the jail.

48

Tuesday afternoon, five past four. In a logjam of afternoon rush-hour traffic coming out of downtown Los Angeles, made even slower by the steady rain. Five miles an hour, tops, in the teeming four-level interchange, and Maxi had to make it back to Burbank in time to anchor the Six.

The first thing she did when she'd hit the street was speed-dial Marc Jorgan's office at Parker Center. Detective Jorgan was in the field, she was told. She asked the dispatcher to have him call her back on her cell phone ASAP, it was urgent. Then she punched in the number for his cell phone. No answer, so she left a message for an urgent callback there as well.

Her next call was to Pete Capra.

"News," he barked.

"Pete, I'm running late—I'm in gridlock on the Hollywood Freeway. But I'll make it back to the station for the Six."

"You'd *better*." So understanding, her boss.

"Listen, Pete—I just found out where Roberto Ochoa is."

"What the . . . *where?*"

"I can't say on the cell phone, too risky." Good excuse why she wouldn't tell him. She was not going to let him put another reporter on this story.

"The cops told you?"

"No. I'm telling them."

"When are you gonna get here?"

"Looks like forty-five minutes, an hour. Listen, Pete—I'm on this story, okay?"

"Or what?"

"Or I might forget where the boy is."

He hesitated for a beat, then apparently decided not to challenge that. "Did you report this?"

"I have a call in to my LAPD source on the kidnapping. I'm going to insist that I ride along on the pickup."

"Or you might forget where the boy is?"

"Of course not. Roberto's life is at stake, Pete. There happens to be a big difference between a child's life and a story."

He was rankled again—she could hear it in his breathing. Pete Capra wasn't one to mask his feelings. "What do you need?" he grumbled.

"Make sure a crew is available for me. We'll need to get rolling immediately after the Six."

She clicked off. No reason to provoke him further, but she was in the driver's seat on this one, both with Capra and with Marc Jorgan, and the FBI team who would have to be notified as well, since they would come in behind the LAPD on this tip. Jorgan would get a warrant and search the house. And Capra would not mess with her on a story this big. Then after she wrapped this piece tonight, which would probably go live on the Eleven, she was damn well going to go home and go to bed.

Detective Marc Jorgan had been called to Men's Central Jail by Deputy District Attorney Nancy Lowry. A prisoner wanted to talk to him, said her message on his cell phone. He knew that Lowry was on the Raoul Montez case. He also had a message to call Maxi Poole—urgent, she'd said.

He was sitting behind the wheel of his black Ford Crown Victoria, the vehicle of choice with most law enforcement agencies because it was built like a tank and it ran like a rocket. Just not now. Right now it was crawling along with the rest of the L.A. work crowd through the downtown rush-hour crunch. He punched in the number for Maxi Poole's cell.

"Poole," she said.

"Maxi, it's Jorgan."

"Marc—I know where Roberto Ochoa is."

"Ahh." He knew not to ask her where on the cell phone. "And I've just been called to Men's Central by the DA on Montez's case. Is this connected?"

"Sounds like Montez wants to deal. How long will it take you to gear up to make the pickup?"

"I'll touch base with Lowry at the jail, then I'll have to find a judge and swear out a warrant, and notify the FBI team, and get someone from child services on board—in this traffic I'm guessing a couple of hours, maybe a little more."

"Perfect. I want a ride-along. With a crew tailing."

"You got it."

Jorgan didn't know how she'd managed to pull this off and he wasn't about to ask, but he was thrilled. He only hoped that she was right, and they could pick up the boy. And, please God, that the kid was unharmed.

"Give me something concrete to persuade the judge with," he said.

Maxi paused for a beat. "It's a house in East L.A. where Raoul Montez's sister lives. Tell him you'll write in the address later."

"Good enough."

"I'm off the air at six-thirty. Where should I meet you?"

"How about on Bauchet in front of Men's Central? You can park your car in the lot there. I'll be waiting for you at the curb; you know my car."

"Great. Traffic will be lighter then. My crew and I should get there a little before seven. And I'll tell you everything on the way."

Jorgan knew that if something happened that prevented Maxi from getting to the jail on time—and many things could happen—she would call in advance and give him the information he needed. A little boy's life was in danger, and that would be uppermost in Maxi's mind. Knowing that, he was comfortable with their arrangement.

His next call was to Bill McFarland at the FBI. Hoping while punching in the number that the agent was gone for the day, or at dinner with his family but nobody knew where, or at the Laker game where cell reception was bad inside Staples Center. Anyplace where he was unavailable.

No such luck. "McFarland," the man answered.

Without mentioning Maxi Poole, Jorgan told him what was happening.

"Give me the address," McFarland said.

"I don't have it."

"How can you not have it?" McFarland demanded, a don't-fuck-with-me threat in his voice.

"My source hasn't given it to me yet. It's a reporter."

"What assurance do I have that you'll get it?"

"I'll get it. Meantime there's nothing we can do about it but meet and go. The reporter will be with us."

Jorgan was secretly delighted that he really didn't have the address yet to give the agent. If he had it he couldn't lie, he would have to give it over. Then McFarland, with the Bureau's resources, would get there before he could and make the pickup. The agent agreed to the meet at seven in front of Men's Central Jail. And, he said, he would round up someone from child services under FBI auspices.

Jorgan parked at the curb in front of Men's Central. He didn't need to leave his police credentials in the windshield. Every cop knew a cop car.

DA Nancy Lowry was waiting for him just inside the door at Inmate Reception. She was dark-haired, slight, mid-thirties, dressed in a gray business suit and sensible shoes, purse on her shoulder, a briefcase in her hand. Jorgan had worked with Lowry before and he respected her. The two shook hands, and he asked her what was up.

"Raoul Montez," she said.

"I figured that."

"You know as much as I do, Marc, but I'm guessing he wants to cut a deal. We're waiting for his attorney, then we'll go inside and see him."

"Did you call Bill McFarland?" Everybody knew McFarland, and nobody much liked him.

"Nope. Didn't have anything to tell him yet." Giving Jorgan mock innocence.

"Nancy, listen, nobody knows this, it's strictly confidential, but it could influence any deal you make with Montez . . ." Jorgan told her about the possible rescue of the boy. Told her he'd found out about it just minutes ago. He wasn't completely sure that the tip had come from Montez, but it probably had, he said. And he told her he couldn't stay here long, he had to get the pickup in motion.

Lowry was about to ask a question when a short, wiry, bespectacled man with shoeblack hair, in a shiny navy blue suit, burst in the door. He looked around, spotted Lowry and Jorgan, and approached them.

"Montez's lawyer," Lowry said quietly to Jorgan.

She introduced the men, Detective Marc Jorgan and Montez's public defender, Aaron Blige. The three quickly processed through and were taken to an attorneys' room to wait for the prisoner to be brought out to them.

Maxi screeched into her parking spot on the UGN midway, jumped out of her car, slammed the door, and made a run for the artists' entrance while holding her car key remote over her head and punching the LOCK button. Her Corvette beeped back at her.

Upstairs in the newsroom she dashed into her office and

locked the door. Lifting a powder blue suit jacket off a hook on the wall, one of a couple of wardrobe changes she kept in her office for emergencies, she ducked down behind her couch, the only private spot available in her glassed-in office. No time to run to the ladies' room to change.

She took off the damp red jacket and flung it over the back of the couch. Maybe she would burn it later. Seemed like she'd been in it for a month.

Standing up, she looked into her full-length mirror, a cheapie from Target that she'd nailed to the wall, but it did the job. She had to smile at the powder blue jacket clashing with the wrinkled red skirt and the damp red shoes. A fashion felony. But it couldn't be helped—she would change the rest of the way after the show. The fact was, while sitting at the anchor desk she could be naked from the waist down for all anyone would know—the viewers only saw the jacket.

Dropping into her desk chair, she reached down to turn on her computer. While it was booting up she called her home, using the one-ring dialing code that would get Carla Ochoa's attention. The woman picked up, answering tentatively. Maxi told her there was a possibility that they might find Roberto tonight. The boy's mother deserved to know.

"¡Ay Dios mío!" Carla shrieked into the phone.

"Carla, listen to me—I don't know for sure that we'll find him. But I want you to pray hard. Okay?"

"Okay," Carla said, her voice trembling.

Maxi hung up—she had no time. Her computer fired up, she clicked on the several icons in succession that brought up the Six O'clock News rundown. Quickly, she went over each story. The lead was the funeral service for Christine Williams this morning. As Maxi silently read the script, all of her earlier emotions came flooding back. She made herself go on to the next story, a California Coastal Commission scandal, then the next, and the next.

There was a knock on her locked office door. Looking up, she saw Pete Capra through the glass.

"Not now," she mouthed at him, pointing at her watch to indicate that she didn't have time for him.

Capra threw his hands in the air with a look of frustration mixed with annoyance mixed with anger.

Maxi ignored him. *Stew in it!* was the silent message she shot at his retreating back. She had to finish going through the show, make her changes in the computer, run down to makeup to get her face on and her wet, matted hair dried and fluffed up, run across the hall to the set, get seated behind the high-tech desk and turn on the computer there, check her script in hard copy, and anchor the half hour with focus and poise.

Her boss would brook no excuse for missing the countdown to air, she knew. Not even talking to him.

49

Tuesday night, seven-forty. Maxi rode in the passenger seat of Marc Jorgan's Crown Vic; his partner, Remo Sanchez, was in the backseat. Behind them, the FBI team rode in McFarland's car, along with Mrs. Serena Vega, a caseworker from the Los Angeles County Department of Children and Family Services. Then an LAPD backup team, six uniformed officers rolling in a marked police van. A Channel Six live truck brought up the rear.

Bill McFarland had been furious with the caravan arrangement, but Maxi would not give him the address for Montez's sister before they set out. "Look, young lady, if we lose you—" he'd started. With a polite smile, she'd interrupted. "My name is Maxi Poole, Agent McFarland, and you'll just have to keep up." With that, she'd climbed into the front seat of Jorgan's car and pulled the door closed. Looking back at McFarland, Detective Jorgan had given him a little what-can-I-do? shrug. Then he got into his car with Maxi and Sanchez and they drove off.

That's when Maxi gave Jorgan the address of Montez's sister in East L.A., along with her name, Mrs. Olimpia Torres.

"But you already knew that, right?" From Maxi, with a mischievous smile. She knew Roberto's location was the first thing Jorgan would have demanded from Raoul Montez in the jail.

"Gee, I guess I forgot to give it to McFarland just now."

"Understandable—you're in a rush," Maxi allowed. Still smiling.

East Los Angeles, just across the Los Angeles River from Men's Central Jail, had been home to the Gabrielino Indians for more than two thousand years. By the onset of World War II, East L.A. had become a nearly exclusively Latino community, populated mostly by Mexican workers who had arrived to man the machines in L.A.'s burgeoning war industries. The area's urban society rapidly expanded, and although the face of Los Angeles and its surrounding communities had changed considerably over decades since then, East Los Angeles had maintained that basic character.

Portal Street, north of Marengo near Hazard Park, was a narrow, curving slip road on which were houses that could be described as less than humble, most having once been painted in colorful pastels that had now worn and weathered to dusty shades of gray, indistinguishable in the gathering dusk. Nine-sixty was one of the smallest, most run-down houses on the street, one of the dreariest among the drear. The four-vehicle procession pulled to a stop a block beyond it on the opposite side of the street.

Rodger Harbaugh, Maxi's shooter, was first out. He'd hauled his camera from the back of the van and had it up on his shoulder and switched on before any of the others opened the doors of their vehicles. Harbaugh rarely missed a shot, and now he was shooting video of the rest of the raid team getting out of their cars. Always confident with Harbaugh on the case, Maxi knew she'd have the whole story on tape, from beginning to end. Whatever this story would turn out to be.

The players merged on the street: the FBI men, the child services woman, the uniforms, and Jorgan, Sanchez, and Maxi in the top *and* bottom of the powder blue suit now, with flat shoes in case she had to run. It would be interesting, Maxi thought, to see who would emerge as alpha dog here. McFarland had the rank, but her money was on Jorgan, since the FBI agent still had no clue which house they were targeting.

Jorgan and Sanchez led, and Maxi walked with Harbaugh, who handed her a wireless microphone. McFarland and troupe looked tentative. Actually, McFarland looked cranky. He probably was, Maxi knew, which was too bad because she might have to get a sound bite from him later. Usually she made an effort to ease any ruffled feathers among her prospective on-camera subjects, the better to get maximum cooperation out of them. Tonight, though, her focus was on getting little Roberto Ochoa out of this house, unhurt. If he was in there.

January darkness had almost completely claimed the day. As they neared the house, Jorgan pointed to it with his left hand to tip those behind him, and with his right he unholstered his standard LAPD-issue Beretta nine. Maxi knew that the detective had another, bigger weapon strapped to his ankle. Behind him, McFarland and his partner, Hugh Brown, also drew their guns.

The LAPD officers quickly fanned out and took up positions surrounding the house. Jorgan and Sanchez walked across the front-yard stubble to the near side, the Feds loped to the other side, Maxi stayed with Harbaugh out front, keeping both teams within camera range, and Serena Vega hovered behind the cameraman. The four front men edged along opposite sides of the house, casing the windows.

After a couple of minutes, Jorgan raised an arm and beckoned to Maxi. She moved forward and stood beside him; Harbaugh followed her, rolling tape. Jorgan made room for Maxi to look through one of the dusty windows.

What they saw was a small living room, with a round wooden dining table and six chairs at the far end. There were no adults in the room. Three small children, six or seven years old and under, sat on the floor playing with Legos. Two more youngsters sat at the table, working intently in what looked to be coloring books. The younger of those two was Roberto Ochoa, recognizable from the photos of the two-year-old that had been delivered to his mother.

Maxi looked silently at Jorgan and both of them nodded, confirming that it was indeed Roberto Ochoa. Standing aside then, she gave Harbaugh room to get shots of the interior, while Jorgan signaled to Sanchez to go around and cover the back of the house. The lead detective made his way to the front door then, with Maxi and Harbaugh right behind.

Jorgan rang the doorbell. Maxi stood close to him, microphone in hand. Harbaugh rolled tape.

"*¿Quién ahí, por favor?*" came a woman's fractured voice from behind the closed door.

"*Policía,*" Jorgan said, badge wallet in one hand, gun by his side in the other. "Open the door."

The door opened to the extent that a rusty metal chain allowed, about three inches, behind which could be seen a pair of tired, frightened brown eyes.

"*¿Sí? ¿Qué es, por favor?*" What is it? the woman was asking.

"Open the door," Jorgan said again, then he said it in Spanish, holding his LAPD shield up to the opening so the woman could see it.

Hearing the raised voices, the two FBI agents came running around to the front of the house. McFarland bounded up the three steps onto the small landing at the slightly ajar front door, gun held in two hands out in front of him, and muscled Jorgan and Maxi out of the way.

"*Open this fucking door or I'll shoot it down,*" he shouted.

Out of range of Harbaugh's shot, Jorgan looked at Maxi and rolled his eyes. "Bill," he said, "there are children inside—"

"I know that," McFarland snapped, still holding his gun on point.

The woman shrieked and bolted from the doorway, disappearing inside the house. McFarland's face flamed to an angry red. He lowered the gun, raised a foot, and gave a mighty kick, yanking the security chain out of splintered wood and ripping the door half off its hinges, then he pushed his way inside. At this, the woman screamed louder, children started crying, and an aging golden retriever appeared in the doorway, skittered around them, and waddled down onto the sidewalk.

A boy of about five came running out of the ruined door toward the street, waving his arms and crying. Intercepting him with a deft move, the child services woman pinned him to her while he yelled, "¡Oro! ¡Gold-ee!" Beating small fists against Mrs. Vega, the youngster sobbed and continued to shout after the dog, whose yellow tail could be seen disappearing briskly now, down the block and around the corner.

Jorgan and Maxi went inside, followed by three of the police officers and Harbaugh, still rolling. Behind them, Mrs. Vega propelled the still struggling youngster back into the house, then made an unsuccessful attempt to close the broken front door. Giving up, she picked up the boy, coaxed his head onto her shoulder, and asked, "¿Es Oro macho o embra?" Is Goldie a boy or a girl?

"Una chica . . ." between sobs. A girl.

"Pues, ella volverá, usted verá." Well, she'll come home, you'll see. Patting his curly head.

Jorgan quickly checked out each of the few rooms in the house, emerging from the last of them with an all-clear signal to the others. The rest of the LAPD team remained outside, while Sanchez came hustling in through the front entrance and joined Jorgan. What they found was the woman and children all huddled together in the living room. No one else in the little house. There seemed to Maxi to be no threat here.

A fine mess, she thought. Thank you, Mr. Big Deal Federal Agent. She'd have laughed if it weren't for Roberto, crying and clutching the woman's leg now. And four other sobbing children, and one runaway family dog.

Maxi eased down until her face was level with the Ochoa boy. "Roberto," she said.

The toddler, three fingers in his mouth, nose running, tears streaming down his cheeks, looked over at her with big wet eyes.

Maxi nodded to Serena Vega. Gently putting the older boy down, Mrs. Vega went over and made moves to pry Roberto from his grip on the woman of the house, presumably Mrs. Torres.

As Maxi moved to the three of them, Harbaugh zoomed in on a close-up. Microphone to her lips, she said, "Mrs. Torres, whose children are these?"

"*No hablo inglés.*" No English.

Maxi repeated her question in Spanish. Four of them were hers, the woman said, and indicating Roberto, "*Pero este pequeño es un amigo.*" But this boy is a friend.

"*¿Por qué está aquí Roberto Ochoa?*" Why is Roberto Ochoa here?

"My brother . . . he bring," the woman said, trembling now. Roberto still crying, still trying to cling to her as Mrs. Vega murmured to him in Spanish that she was going to take him home to his mother.

"Raoul Montez?"

"*Sí, mi hermano.*"

"*¿Por qué?*"

"*Mi hermano me pidió que cuidara por Roberto por unos días. Para su amigo.*"

"Her brother asked her to take care of Roberto for a few days, for his friend," Maxi translated for the viewers. Then she asked, "*¿No vio las noticias? ¿Un niño de dos años que fue raptado deun hogar donde su hermano trabaja?*" Didn't you see the news? That a two-year-old boy was kidnapped from a home where your brother works?

"*Yo no sé donde trabaja mi hermano.*"

"She doesn't know where her brother works," from Maxi, then she tried again. Told Mrs. Torres that the story had been on the news almost every day now.

"*Yo no miro a las noticias,*" the woman answered with a shrug, one hand still comforting Roberto.

"She doesn't watch the news," Maxi repeated for the camera. Then, "*Gracias,*" to Mrs. Torres, and she stepped out of frame.

All of her instincts told her that this woman was telling the truth. She had four children, five in her care now; she didn't have time to watch the news, not even in Spanish. Glancing around the small living room, Maxi saw that there wasn't even a television set. No way to keep this brood occupied with cartoons even, let alone watch the news.

Harbaugh kept rolling while Mrs. Vega told Mrs. Torres, in Spanish, that they were going to bring Roberto to his mother. Then she picked the boy up, the youngster still hanging on to Mrs. Torres's hand, which told Maxi that the woman had been good to him, had treated him well. The other four children were hovering close to her.

Maxi was relieved. They were done here, without a struggle. McFarland and his partner were out the door first, then Mrs. Vega carrying Roberto, who'd calmed down now and was asking for his mama.

Jorgan's Spanish was limited. He asked Maxi to tell Mrs. Torres that someone from the police department would be coming here within the hour to fix her door.

"Alguien del departamento de policía vendrá aquí en menos de una hora para arreglar su puerta, Sra. Torres," Maxi said.

The woman gave her a grateful look, and Maxi couldn't help herself—she went over to her, holding the microphone down at her side, and gave her a hug.

Harbaugh got it all on tape.

Before she was off the front steps of Mrs. Torres's house, Maxi had her cell phone out and on speed-dial to the station. She asked for the Eleven O'clock producer, gave him highlights of what she had on tape, and estimated that she would need about two and a half minutes for her intro, the cut piece, and her stand-up tag. She would be going live on the Eleven from this location. Her next call was to Carla Ochoa at her house, using their code, to let her know that her boy was found and he was safe.

As she approached the Channel Six live truck, snapping her phone shut, Bill McFarland intercepted her. "I don't want to be part of your story," he said.

Looking up, she spotted Jorgan standing a few feet away, smiling at that. Because they both knew that what McFarland was really saying was he didn't want to be shown on the evening news kicking down Mrs. Torres's door as if this were a crack house instead of the sorely run-down home of a woman living below the poverty line with a clutch of children.

"But you *are* part of my story," she said sweetly.

McFarland reddened but didn't respond. Turning, he walked stolidly over to his BMW, got in, and with his partner at the wheel and Mrs. Vega in the backseat holding Roberto on her lap, off they went.

Jorgan joined Maxi, and together they watched the swirl of dust that was kicked up by McFarland's car. Then they laughed. At McFarland, yes, but with relief too. For the two of them, this was a case and a story that had ended well, and in both their professions that was rare. Roberto Ochoa was alive and well and going home to his mother.

"Seems the man doesn't want to be part of your story," Jorgan deadpanned.

"That's right. Let me just make a note of that."

"Maybe you should check with Capra and find out when Agent McFarland became your new boss."

"Hey, maybe that wouldn't be a bad thing. Do you think McFarland would take me off the graveyard shift?"

"McFarland needs to take his blood pressure off the ceiling," Jorgan said. "Have you ever seen that shade of red before?"

"On shoes," she said, flashing back to the outfit she'd had on earlier. "But not on a face. Hey, Marc—we did good, huh?"

"The best. So how the hell did you get Montez to admit that he took Roberto Ochoa, and tell you where he was?"

"I told him he was gonna get the gas chamber if he didn't."

"Good one. Even though it's a lie."

"A lie? Gee, what do I know? I must have been absent the day they taught California death penalty."

Jorgan smiled. "Whatever you said to Montez, you nicely inspired the gentleman to have his lawyer make a plea bargain with Nancy Lowry. We had a very productive chat for a fast ten minutes. On tape. Quite congenial."

"Excellent. What did he give up?"

"Not for broadcast?"

"Not for broadcast." When Jorgan looked skeptical she added, "Honest."

"Well, the whole plan sounds as wacky as one of Lightner's speeches to the city council, but here's the yarn Montez spun: Lightner paid him twenty-five thousand bucks to kill his wife and snatch Roberto. Montez was supposed to make it look like it was a kidnap for ransom by a team of pros for Gladys Lightner's money, but that Mrs. Lightner walked in on them so they murdered her."

"Whoa! So Montez killed Gladys Lightner?"

"Montez says no. Says he went into the house at around six o'clock the night of the kidnapping when he knew Lightner would still be at work, and he found the lady in the kitchen. Mrs. Lightner asked him what he needed, and since everything he ever needed was in the garage, tools and such, he asked her for a bottle of water. He says she got crazy-furious like she does—did—and screamed at him that there was plenty of water in the refrigerator in the garage, as he damn well knew, so he could just get the hell out of her kitchen with his nasty germs."

"Yup, that was Gladdy all right, all skin and bones and rattlesnake temper. So why didn't he kill her?"

"He says the housekeeper was in the kitchen with her, polishing the stainless steel. Then he added—which just might save his dumb neck, plea bargain or no—that he realized he couldn't kill her anyway, because he couldn't kill anybody."

"The time of death was sometime the next morning. Think Montez came back into the house early Friday to finish the job?"

"I don't. Unless he's a really good actor, and I doubt that. I don't think he's a really good anything."

"Not even a really good handyman?"

"Not even a really good kidnapper. He says while the two women were in the kitchen, he picked up Roberto in his mother's bedroom where the little guy usually played, and he told the boy he was taking him for ice cream. Roberto knew Montez and he liked ice cream, so off they sailed, unnoticed, right out the front door. But instead of going for ice cream, Montez took the kid out to his mangy trailer, kept him there overnight, and staged those horrible pictures the next day. By that time Roberto was terrified of course, and kicking and screaming."

"So what *was* the genius kidnap plan?"

"To stash Roberto here," Jorgan said, indicating Mrs. Torres's house behind them. "Tell his sister that his friend needed her to take care of the boy for a few days. Then Montez was going to bring Roberto back to the Lightner house, say he found him in the front yard, that somebody must have dropped him off there. Since the boy would be returned unharmed, because these mythical kidnappers were supposedly feeling too much heat, the kidnap case would go away and Lightner would be a rich widower. He was going to pay Montez another twenty-five thousand when it was over."

"And Mrs. Torres had no idea what her brother was up to."

"No. That's why we didn't arrest her. Even McFarland got that much. If we need her later we know where she is—she's not going anywhere."

"What was the purpose of the photos?"

"The first one was supposed to make it look like these big-time kidnappers had the boy, and the second was to make it look like they wanted money or they'd hurt him." An echo of what Councilman Lightner had told Maxi on tape.

"But they never sent a ransom note."

"No, because they had no intention of asking for ransom.

Lightner just wanted his wife dead, Montez said. And he probably figured that a phony ransom note would leave tracks."

"Like the JonBenet Ramsey case."

"Right. Montez said Lightner knew that you would put the pictures on the air. He counted on that."

"And I did."

"I told you not to."

"Don't go there. Actually, with the third one I listened to you."

"Thank you. By keeping that one off the air we were able to trap Lightner into spilling that Roberto was eating pasta, which he couldn't have known unless—"

"Excuse me, Detective—what's this *we* shit?" Big grin.

"Don't you ever worry that you could slip with a four-letter word on the air?"

"No."

"Why is that?"

"Because I'm on the air."

Jorgan rolled his eyes. "Where was I? Oh—that third photo was supposed to show that the kid was fine after all, and the next step would be to return him."

"I see that he took that third picture right here, at the dining room table. Where were the first two taken? Not in his trailer—"

"Montez has a son who lives in a room in East L.A. He says his son is in San Diego on a construction job, so he used his place to take the pictures. We're bringing this kid back for questioning, but I'm guessing he doesn't know anything."

"Does the son have a computer?"

"No. Montez went to a drugstore self-service kiosk and made the prints himself. That eliminated the chance that some one-hour photo person might connect the pictures to the kidnapped boy on the news and drop a dime."

"Meantime," Maxi said, "Gladys Lightner somehow got dead. If not Montez, who?"

"We're thinking the usual suspect."

"The husband. Lightner. Montez burned him."

"Burned him down. Thanks to you."

"How do you think Montez will come out of it?"

"He'll do time. Five to ten. But not life."

"And the DA will get Councilman Lightner, the big fish."

"Oh yeah, Lightner will do a *lot* of time."

Maxi gave him five. "Good work," she said.

"Back atcha. Am I driving you to your car?"

"No. I'm going live from here on the Eleven."

One of the LAPD officers walked over to Jorgan and asked if he could clear his team to leave. "Yes," the detective said. "We're finished here—good job." He and Maxi watched the officers scramble into their van and take off, then the two congratulated each other again and said good-bye.

As Maxi turned back toward the Channel Six truck she saw something moving in her peripheral vision. Something yellow. *Goldie!* Calmly sashaying down the sidewalk on the opposite side of the street.

"*Goldie!*" she called.

Goldie ignored her and kept walking.

"Maybe she speaks Spanish," Jorgan said.

They both started toward the dog, slowly so they wouldn't scare her into a run, and at the same time Sanchez got out of Jorgan's car, which was still parked across the street, and he started moving toward the dog from there. As the three converged, Maxi called, "¡Oro! ¡Aquí, Oro!"

Goldie stopped. She peered from Maxi to Jorgan to Sanchez and back again with a look that said, Who-are-you-people-and-how-do-you-know-my-name? Goldie thinking this in Spanish, Maxi guessed. Reaching the dog, she knelt on the sidewalk, took hold of her collar with one hand and ruffled her fur with the other, making gentle talking noises. Goldie sniffed. Smelled Yukon on her clothes, Maxi was sure. While petting her, she flashed a guilty thought to her Yukon, who probably figured she'd abandoned him by now. Yuke would be thinking this in English, of course.

Jorgan and Sanchez helped her lead the golden dog to Mrs. Torres's front door. Goldie eyed the splintered door suspiciously as they went inside, and she gave Maxi a now-what's-happened-here? frown, clearly annoyed. Until all four kids bounded into the small foyer and pounced on her at once, jabbering in English and Spanish. Mrs. Torres was right behind them, big smile on her face.

"Gracias," she said. Then she added, "Ya extrañamos a Roberto." We miss Roberto already.

More hugs all around, then Jorgan and Sanchez left. Maxi climbed into the Channel Six truck and booted up the computer to write her story. After their live shot, on his way back to the station Harbaugh would drop her off at the parking structure at Men's Central Jail to pick up her car. Then she planned to go right home, and go right to bed.

Well, she was planning to go home, hug Carla Ochoa, who would soon be reunited with her son, and then go right to bed. For about ten hours again. She was so due.

And to hell with Pete Capra.

50

Tuesday night, quarter to ten, at The Gardens on Glendon. The Westside restaurant was a star magnet. Mario Van Peebles was hosting a table of friends, Bob Newhart and his wife were enjoying a quiet dinner in a back booth, Keanu Reeves was head-to-head with some beauty in the far corner, and stunning supermodel Tyra Banks had just walked in, drawing every pair of eyes in the place. The food was always fabulous. Jerrold Lightner was doing a job on a huge New York steak and home fries, and across the table from him, his brother was having baked whitefish and spinach.

And no damn booze.

Unbelievable. Jerrold had started with a Manhattan on the rocks, then he had another. His brother nursed a Perrier. Then Jerrold ordered a beautiful bottle of chilled Cristal. "We need to celebrate," he'd said. "Your success, our reunion . . . and let's drink a toast to Mom." The champagne cooled in a silver ice bucket beside their table now. And so far, Jerrold had consumed most of it himself.

None at all for Jamie.

When Jerrold had called the Masterson Clinic this morning, impersonating an addict needing help, they'd put him right through to James. It was too easy. Turns out he was right, his brother was working there after all. Every day.

Jerrold topped up his champagne flute. "C'mon, Jame, a few sips of this bubbly isn't going to hurt you," he urged. "At two hundred bills a bottle, we can't waste it."

"Of course a few sips would hurt me, Jerry—that's the lesson I've learned."

Jerrold swirled his frosty flute, watching the bubbles dance for a bit, then he brought the glass to his mouth. Slowly. And drank. All the while keeping his eyes on Jamie's eyes, and he saw the longing there. His brother could not hold out forever. He never did before. Yes, this was definitely gonna happen.

"I've been thinking about Mom," James said.

"Yeah, she really loved you." Jerrold, romancing his champagne glass.

"I mean I've been thinking about a fitting memorial for her."

"Sure, bro. We'll have a big wingding. Half the city will come. We'll do it at the Church of the Good Shepherd. Sinatra's funeral was there. Then a big reception at the house—"

"No," James interrupted. "Not under these circumstances."

Meaning the warm and cozy family circumstance that their father killed their mother, Jerrold knew his brother was saying. "Have you gone down to see Dad?"

"No."

"Me neither. He can rot in hell."

"Let me tell you what I would like for Mom," James said.

Oh, do tell me what you'd like for Mom, Jerrold wanted to mock, but he held his tongue. And took another swig of champagne.

"I'd like to charter a boat and take her about halfway out to the Channel Islands. She loved Catalina, and—"

"Take her out . . . ?"

"Have her cremated, and take her ashes out there," James explained, "and bury her at sea. It's what she wanted."

"How do you know that? Was that in the will too?" The will he never even fucking saw.

"No . . . she told me. Several times."

How the hell could their mother have even *found* James, let alone have talked to him about what she wanted done with her mortal remains when she shuffled off? Jerrold had thought *he* was the smart one, always being there for every damn boring family event he was summoned to attend. *Ordered* to attend. And driving his mother to Costco and rolling a cart the size of a Volkswagen around the warehouse while she shopped. Constantly taking her to doctor appointments for this and that, and waiting till she was done to drive her home again. Running her cars in for maintenance, then picking them up. She loved her cars, she just didn't like to drive them. She liked to be driven. Four times over the last few years he'd schlepped her in for plastic surgery. Eyes, neck, breasts, and *arms*, for God's sake. And he never did anything right. He'd had to sit and listen to her complain that he drove too fast, he drove too slow, he talked too much, he wasn't talking at all. Whatever.

But not James. Never James.

Evidently James did everything right. Just by staying away. Dumb like a fox. *Drink the damn champagne, little brother, before I grab you by the neck and pour it down your gullet.*

"She always told me she wanted to be cremated, and her ashes scattered in the Pacific," he was saying now.

Jesus. "They haven't even released her body," Jerrold said.

"We're in no hurry. I just want to know if that's all right with you. I'll make all the arrangements."

"Sure. It's fine with me." Like he gave a damn.

"Good. It's settled then."

"Dessert?" Jerrold asked.

"Not for me. I need to get going. I have to go to work tomorrow."

"At the clinic?"

"Yes. It feels really good. And I'm taking Aly to dinner tomorrow night. We have a lot to talk about."

"Great," Jerrold said.

The bottle of Cristal was three-quarters empty. So what did he get out of tonight? Nothing. If you didn't count the fucking check, and the prospect of a big hangover in the morning.

51

Just turned Wednesday, half past midnight, at the end of what had seemed like the longest two days of her life. Home, finally. Maxi zapped her garage door up and pulled the car inside. Yukon heard her 'Vette coming in and skittered across the Saltillo tiles on the kitchen floor; she could hear him panting and pawing on the other side of the door. Good, her dog remembered who she was. He was all over her the second she opened the door. Laughing, she dropped her tote on the floor along with the wrinkled, weary red suit and hugged him, then did their usual little dance with him for a minute. Oops, two shoes and two paws dancing right over the red suit. Not a problem, it couldn't get any more limp or dirty. Maybe the dry cleaner could revive it. Or not.

Tired as she was, Maxi was feeling great. That's what a huge story always did for her, but tonight's lead had the even bigger bonus of seeing little Roberto Ochoa safe and well and coming home. She gave Yukon a proper curtsy for their dance, then walked over to the kitchen table where Carla was up out of her chair and waiting for *her* hug. The woman had been crying, Maxi could see, and now she was laughing. And why not? What a night *she* must have been having since she'd heard the news about Roberto a few hours ago.

"I make tea for you," Carla said, and she headed for the stove while Maxi caught her breath.

Would tea keep her awake tonight? Not a chance, she knew—fireworks in her bed wouldn't keep her awake.

Hmm. Fireworks in her bed. Now, *there* was a concept. She was getting that old feeling, that it was just a matter of time. Fireworks in her bed with Tom McCartney. That thought gave her a little jolt, in all the interesting places. She dropped into a chair at the table, Yukon at her feet, and accepted the fragrant mug of tea that Carla handed her.

"Sit down, Carla, and let me tell you all about it," she said to the woman.

And Carla sat, ignored her tea, and started weeping all over again. Like sun shining through a rain shower, she was weeping big tears with a smile on her face. Maxi told her about finding Roberto with the police, about Mrs. Torres and how well she'd cared for him, about the other four children in the little house, and Roberto coloring pictures, and how excited he was that he was going to see his mama. Carla couldn't get enough of it. Like a child at bedtime, she wanted to hear every part of it again and again.

Roberto had been taken to Children's Hospital on Sunset, just for overnight observation, Maxi quickly pointed out. He would be coming home tomorrow. She wrote down Serena Vega's name and phone number, and made sure that Carla understood exactly what would happen and when. Because she planned to be asleep when the little guy arrived. Carla didn't need her for the homecoming. She only needed her son.

When they'd exhausted all the news about Roberto and completely covered all the plans for the mother-son reunion, Maxi had other news on her mind. Who killed Gladys Lightner? Jorgan didn't think Montez did it. Rosie didn't think Lightner did it. Professional kidnappers didn't do it; that scenario was a hoax.

She took a sip of her tea, which had cooled down perfectly. "Carla," she began, "you and I were there on the morning Mr.

Lightner found his wife dead. The morning I came for you to help you move to my house. Tell me everything you remember from the minute you woke up that morning."

Carla looked pained. "I got up, I packed my things, then you came, missus . . ."

"Do you remember any unusual sounds? Voices? Did you hear Mr. Lightner get up? Turn on the shower? What about the dog? The little dog was there that morning. What's its name?"

"Janie. *Sí*, I fed Janie."

"Where's Janie now, do you know?"

Carla shrugged. *"No sé donde está."* She didn't know.

Good Lord, Maxi thought, was anybody taking care of Janie? Conrad Lightner was arrested on Wednesday, six days ago. She remembered that because it was the same day they'd found Christine's body on Mulholland Drive. The arrest of City Councilman Lightner on a murder charge, which normally would have been the lead, had been dropped to the second lead behind the Christine Williams murder story.

Six days ago. Since then, Lightner had been in jail, Montez was in jail, Carla was staying with her, and Gladys Lightner was dead. Perhaps nobody was living in the Beverly Glen villa now. The police and the FBI had access to the house. Would any of them, intent on doing their jobs, even notice the little dog? Had Lightner, with his own survival uppermost on his mind, thought to arrange for someone to take care of the dog? Who was feeding Janie?

She made a mental note to find out.

"Do you remember if Janie acted odd that morning?" she asked Carla. "Did the dog do anything unusual? Maybe she heard something—"

"I don't remember."

"Did you notice anything out of place in the house? Anything strange—?"

"No."

"In the kitchen? In Mrs. Lightner's bedroom? I know we didn't stay in that room very long, but think about it, Carla. You cleaned Mrs. Lightner's bedroom suite every day, didn't you?"

Carla closed her eyes. "Yes . . ."

"Was anything different that morning that you can remember?"

"I didn't clean that morning."

"I understand that. But you *know* that room. Was anything in the wrong place? Think hard."

"No . . ."

Maxi could see that Carla was uncomfortable with the questions. Understandable, she knew—the woman had to be reliving the horror of discovering Mrs. Lightner stabbed to death, and the terrible fear she'd had that Roberto might be harmed too. But it was over now; her little boy was safe and coming home tomorrow.

"I was so frightened, because she—" Carla started.

Maxi jumped in, tried to console her. "I know, I know," she soothed.

Carla suddenly started crying uncontrollably, was wracked with huge sobs as if her heart was breaking. Maxi got up from the table, walked around to the other side, knelt, and put her arms around the woman's shoulders. "Shh, shh, shh," she comforted gently. "I know how awful it's been. But Roberto is coming home now. *Todo estará bien.*" Everything's going to be all right.

Maxi held on until Carla's tears subsided and she quieted. Getting to her feet then, she said, "I have to go to bed now before I fall over. And you need to go to sleep too, Carla, so you'll be full of energy when they bring Roberto in the morning."

She hugged Mrs. Ochoa again, and watched as the woman went into the little guest room off the kitchen. Then, picking up her tote bag and the sorry red suit, she rallied Yukon to follow her—not that it took much rallying—and headed up to her bedroom. Fishing her cell phone out of her tote as she climbed the stairs, she dialed Marc Jorgan's home number. He answered.

"Marc, it's Maxi. Were you sleeping?"

"I never sleep."

She didn't challenge that. Who slept these days? "Listen, Marc . . . I need to get into the Lightner house. Is right now out of the question?"

Jorgan actually laughed.

"Okay, first thing in the morning then."

"It's a crime scene, Maxi."

"I know that, but the Lightners had a dog, and I just need to make sure that she's not locked up in that empty house, and hungry. Did any of the crime lab techs say anything about a dog being there?"

"Not that I heard."

"See, she's just a tiny thing. She could be hiding somewhere. They do that when they're frightened."

"I don't know if we've got anyone scheduled in there tomorrow." Then, softening, "Okay, I'll take you in myself, Maxi. I owe you that, for Montez. What time do you want to meet there?"

"When's the earliest you can do it?"

"Eight o'clock. I'll be in front of the house. If you oversleep, I'll come up the street and bang on your door."

"I won't oversleep. And Marc?"

"Uh-oh—I know that tone of voice."

She laughed. He was right. "Did you find the murder weapon?"

"You know we're not disclosing that, Maxi."

"I know." That never stopped her from trying. "But you *did* tell me that it wasn't a knife, right?"

"The wound was not consistent with any knife blade we know about."

As soon as he'd said that, she knew he regretted it. What he'd said meant that they had not found the murder weapon after all, they had just characterized the weapon by the wound. And he knew that she'd picked up on it.

"That it wasn't a knife was classified information," he said, taking a shot at damage control.

"I didn't tell anybody," Maxi lied. But she knew that she could trust Tom McCartney.

"You know what I mean." Meaning the fact that they hadn't found a weapon had not been released.

"Don't worry, Marc," she said. "I promise I won't use that, and it's absolutely confidential."

This time she meant it.

52

One wound.

Jorgan had said *the wound* was not consistent with any knife blade they knew about. Maxi kept thinking about that phrase. Only one wound. Singular. Unusual with stabbings. So it had to have been one *fatal* wound.

She remembered the scene. She remembered the body. And she remembered the wound. Blood emanating from the left side of the chest area. It had probably been caused by one thrust to the heart. Electromechanical dissociation, the autopsy would say: persistence of electrical activity in the heart without associated mechanical contraction; cardiac rupture. Medical examiner–speak for stabbed in the heart.

It was Wednesday morning, five to eight. She was standing in front of the locked gates of the Lightner manse waiting for Marc Jorgan to arrive. Exhausted as she was last night, still she'd slept fitfully, wracked by frustrating dreams of searching in vain for Janie. And of Janie stuck in a dark closet, Janie locked in a dresser drawer, and one flash dream of the pup dressed in a white satin gown with flowers in her hair and lying, paws crossed over her tiny chest, in a doll-sized casket. Good Lord, she really needed to see a shrink. Shaking off the still vivid images, she threw her head back and took in a deep breath.

There had been no calls or e-mails from Pete Capra this morning, no bitching about her going home after the Eleven last night instead of out in the field. The Morning News led with the kidnap recovery story that she'd filed the night before, so the Channel Six graveyard ghouls, she and Harbaugh, were well and majorly represented on the program. She figured even *Capra* knew when his shit wouldn't fly, as they say in the army. Somebody's army.

Looking up at the imposing, desert-colored sandstone walls of the Lightner estate, she wondered if Janie was still somewhere inside, alone. If she found the dog she would take her home, at least until she could figure out where the poor baby belonged. Carla Ochoa knew Janie well, and Maxi was sure that Roberto would love having the little doggie around—after he had spent some frightening time in Montez's fetid trailer, and more than a week in a house with strangers, then was brought this morning to another home he didn't know, Janie would be a welcome element of familiarity for the two-year-old. When Maxi had left this morning, Roberto was sitting on the kitchen floor cautiously eyeing Yukon, who was twice his size.

And Yukon would adore having Janie in the house. Yuke loved sleepovers, and he played the perfect host. One of his favorite guests was Mac, Fritz Coleman's loving chocolate lab. Fritz had left Mac with her when his seventy-something mom got married in Florida and he flew east to walk her down the aisle. Mackie and Yukon had the best old time together, eating, sleeping, chasing bugs, playing games, doing guy talk—they were inseparable. And Maxi was thrilled that Mac hadn't eaten her loveseats like he'd chewed up Fritz's couch one time. But that was back when Mackie was just a kid. Last year. When Fritz took Mac home, Yukon was inconsolable. Maxi brought him hot fudge sundaes every night for a week, his favorite special treat, just to help him get through his separation blues.

Then there was that gorgeous, fiery, redheaded girl, reporter June Grayson's young Irish setter Annie Laurie, who'd stayed with them for four days while June's house was being fumigated. Yukon was totally besotted with Annie. It was pathetic to watch her virile, hundred-pound hunk of a dog totally losing it around the girl. He would fawn over her, show off for her, bring her presents—his chew bones, Maxi's slippers. He would even stand aside and let her eat his dinner. Yukon was in love. Then she left him. He actually cried. And Maxi had suspicions that he was writing to Dear Abby.

When Marc Jorgan's Crown Vic pulled up to the curb she was smiling, feeling better now, thinking how she most definitely was a dog person. Yesterday she'd helped rescue Goldie, and today she was going to make sure Janie was okay.

Jorgan had keys to the Lightner estate and let them in. Their footsteps echoed hollowly in the thirty-foot-high marble foyer. Dust motes hung in the broad sunlight streaks that shot through the leaded glass windows, and stacks of mail were piled up on the giltwood side table against the wall, probably brought inside from the overflowing mailbox and skimmed through by police personnel who had been coming and going since the murder. Towering indoor trees and plants were beginning to look peaked.

"Sure feels empty, doesn't it?" Maxi said, looking around.

"The Lightners had two sons. I guess they'll be the ones who'll have to deal with this fortress."

"You don't think Lightner will be coming back?"

"Not a chance."

"They sold O.J.'s mansion and tore it to the ground," she said.

"Couldn't happen to a nicer guy," Jorgan responded dryly. The LAPD was still smarting over the O.J. Simpson double murder debacle.

Maxi called out to Janie as they moved from the foyer through the downstairs rooms. She poked her head into every possible doggie hiding place—under overstuffed chairs, behind sofas, on lower bookshelves, even in waste cans.

"She's small, weighs only five or six pounds," Maxi explained to Jorgan. "If she's here I'm sure she's traumatized, and she'll be hiding someplace."

"How long can she go without food?" he asked.

"Longer than you'd think. These pups are survivors."

"Even that small—?"

"Yes," Maxi said. Then added, "But if she's here we'd better find her today."

They were in the councilman's darkened den, heavy with leather furniture and double-thick, tasseled silk drapery. Maxi took in the feel of the room with a sweep of her eyes. Big-screen TV in a corner. A carved mahogany antique desk topped with a traditional leather-cornered desk blotter and matching leather and gilt accessories. Lightner surrounded himself with style, or more probably his wife had done the decorating. Telephone and fax machine over to the side but no computer. Pen set, paper clip container. Small gold-colored clock, a crystal award from the Cancer Foundation, a glass globe paperweight that produced snow on a miniature Hollywood sign—cute. Fancy gold papier-mâché trash can with no trash in it under the desk, beside a carton containing some dusty work files that looked long untouched. The councilman didn't do much work at home, if any. More likely his den was his retreat.

But no Janie.

They went down the hall into the stainless steel kitchen. Again, no Janie.

The second floor yielded the same results—no little Lhasa Apso came when Maxi called. They examined several rooms and hallways and, finally, the master bedroom suite. Jorgan took down the yellow crime-scene tape that was doubled across the doorway and entered first, and Maxi followed.

It was pretty much the same as she remembered it from when she'd last been there, on the day that the body of Gladys Lightner was sprawled on the floor. The curtains were drawn, the bed unmade, and there were bloodstains on the ivory-colored carpeting.

The air had a metallic smell, and a heavy layer of charcoal fingerprint dust covered every surface, including the built-in marble countertops on the wet bar and in the luxurious bath, the antique armoire holding the TV set, the two nineteenth-century Regency nightstands, and the glass coffee table, end tables, and delicate Chippendale fruitwood writing desk in the sitting area. This was the last room on their search for Mrs. Lightner's pet, with no results.

"Should we give up on the dog?" Jorgan asked.

"Guess so. Somebody in the family must have come for her. I just wanted to be sure."

Maxi didn't even want to *think* about the possibility that police coming and going might have left doors open, allowing Janie to run out onto heavily trafficked Beverly Glen Boulevard. She and Jorgan had done everything they could.

"Thanks for doing this, Marc," she said.

"No problem. Let's get out of here."

They were hustling back through the foyer and heading for the front door when Maxi suddenly stopped midstride and put a hand on Jorgan's arm.

"Wait a sec," she said. "Did we see the maid's room?"

"I have no clue. In a medieval castle like this, which one would be the maid's room?"

"It's where Carla Ochoa stayed. Off the kitchen, she said. Wait here while I go check again, okay?"

Jorgan nodded and sat on the bench in the foyer while Maxi doubled back through the house. Carla was the one who'd fed Janie; the little dog might be hanging out in her old room. In the twenty or so rooms they'd cased, Maxi couldn't remember seeing anything that had resembled a maid's room.

She went back into the steel and granite kitchen and scanned the periphery. There was a door leading to a long, narrow butler's pantry, double glass doors to the dining room, plus doors to a small sitting room, a bathroom, and a service porch, and at the far end, another door that led into a laundry room. No maid's room off the kitchen that she could see.

She walked into the laundry room again and looked around. It was tiled in white and big enough to house a family. Around an L behind three side-by-side sets of washers and dryers there was a narrow hallway, and at the very end of that hall there was a closed door. They'd completely missed that door the first time around.

Opening it now, she looked inside, then went inside. Yes, it was definitely the maid's room. But there was no dog. She opened another closed door, this one into an adjacent bathroom, and there was Janie, lying lifelessly on a rug on the floor. Someone on the crime-scene team must have shut her in there for safekeeping and forgotten to release her. Maxi scooped her up and listened for breathing, and a heartbeat. She was alive, but barely. Totally limp. Quickly, she carried the pup back out into the kitchen, rummaged through cupboards with her free hand, and came up with a bowl. She filled it with water at the sink and set it down on the floor, then held Janie's face down to the bowl, stroking her, talking to her, getting her nose wet, trying to make her drink. Janie opened her eyes a little, but not her mouth.

Still cradling her in one arm, Maxi pulled open drawers until she found a teaspoon, then carefully spoon-fed water into Janie's small mouth. The pup swallowed. And had some more. And after six or seven spoonfuls, Janie dipped her mouth into the water bowl and drank, until Maxi thought she was never going to stop.

Jorgan wandered into the kitchen. "I wondered what happened to you," he said. Then, seeing Janie in Maxi's arms, "Is she okay?"

"I think so. But we weren't a minute too soon. Would you look around and see if you can find her something to eat, Marc?"

He found the half-full bag of kibble under the sink, took down another bowl, filled it, and set it down next to the water, and Janie went to town on it. When the dog food was gone, she licked the bowl.

"Should we give her some more?" Jorgan asked.

"No—her stomach will be shrunk from fasting and dehydration, and with this itty-bitty gal it's probably the size of a walnut by now. If she eats too much right away she'll get sick. Let's get her out of here."

Which was a prospect that seemed to appeal to Janie—she actually wagged her little tail.

"You're taking the dog home?" Jorgan asked with a frown, as he pulled the front door locked behind them. "Yukon will eat her for breakfast."

"No he won't. He'll baby her. I know my boy. Anyway, I'm taking her to the vet first to make sure she's okay."

"You and I have a regular dog rescue operation going," Jorgan observed. "We could make side money doing this."

"You know," Maxi said, giving Janie a little smooch on her furry head, "that's actually something I would love to do. Someday when I have time."

They said their good-byes. Jorgan got into his car and headed downtown, and Maxi walked up the street to get her truck, carrying Janie. "Hey, girl," she said, "we're going to the doctor, then I'm taking you home to Carla and Roberto."

Wednesday afternoon, close to three o'clock. Maxi had left early for the station. For the first time in days she wasn't dragging, and she wanted to check on something before prepping for the Six O'clock News: the raw tape that Jersey had shot inside Mrs. Lightner's bedroom on the morning the woman was found murdered almost two weeks ago. She wanted to see if anything in that bedroom looked different between the morning of the murder when Jersey had shot the tape and this morning, when she and Jorgan had examined the suite looking for Janie.

She'd managed to get an editor—not an easy feat this close to deadline for the early block, but after her major breaker on last night's kidnap story she was the queen of the heap in the newsroom. Every reporter knew enough to take advantage of that rare position of superiority, because it never lasted long. Tomorrow, or the next day, someone else would break a newer, bigger, better story and knock you off your exalted but ephemeral perch. So she'd come in this afternoon and asked for an editor to recut her Roberto recovery story, still the day's lead, and an extra half hour to view some raw footage. The extra half hour is what she wouldn't have gotten if she were just the lowly graveyard-shift schlub today.

Before going into the edit bay she corraled a news manager to unlock the dead file for her, and she logged out the tape slugged "Lightner Crime Scene," dated January tenth, the day that Gladys Lightner was found dead.

Ray Springer was her editor. "Nice get," he said by way of greeting when she walked into his edit room. Referring to her Roberto story.

"Thanks, Ray. Before we recut the kidnap recovery, I need to view this tape. It's raw footage," she explained, handing him the crime-scene cassette.

"Fast forward or real time?"

"Speed through it, and I'll tell you if we need to stop."

Springer popped the tape into the playback machine and pressed FAST FORWARD. Maxi watched closely as the images flew by: establishing shots of the Lightner house exterior, close-ups of the iron gates and the security system, the grand staircase leading up to the second floor, the double-door entrance to the murder bedroom crisscrossed with yellow crime-scene tape, the interior of the room, crime lab personnel working, video of Mrs. Lightner's body, close-ups on her face, her hands, her bloody wound. The bloodstains on the carpet. Some shots of Janie slinking around furniture legs. Then Jersey's methodical inventory of the room, covering every square inch of it. The bed, the dressers, the antique burl walnut armoire with a television set, DVD player, and VCR inside, an ivory silk-covered chaise longue with matching pillows, a seating area with a couch and two wingback chairs, the glass-topped coffee table between the grouping, the low fireplace, the fruitwood writing desk and chair—everything was essentially the same as she and Jorgan had seen it earlier today.

Then she saw something that they hadn't seen. Something that was definitely *not* there this morning, or she would have noticed it.

"Stop," Maxi said.

Springer paused the tape.

"Roll it back, Ray, and show me everything we shot on top of that desk."

Springer rolled back to the beginning of the footage of the antique desktop, then played the tape forward in real time. Maxi watched a slow pan over the surface of the desk, followed by a series of close-ups of each item on top of the desk. It was all there. Thank you, Jersey.

A close-up shot came up of a beechwood box lined with taupe-colored felt, displaying a bronze magnifying glass with the multicolored seal of Los Angeles County on the handle. Next to the magnifier in its display case was an empty slot in the distinctive shape of a wide-bladed letter opener. So this would have been a boxed set containing a souvenir magnifying glass and letter opener.

What she'd learned about Gladys Lightner, and what she'd observed to be the results of the woman's meticulous sense of order and decor, told her that this perfectionist would not have left a box with just half of the beautiful bronze set displayed on her fastidiously arranged writing desk. And Maxi was sure that the half-empty wooden case had not been on top of that desk this morning.

So where was the letter opener?

Jorgan had confided to Maxi that what had killed Gladys Lightner was some kind of blade, but not a knife. She and Carla Ochoa had gone into Mrs. Lightner's bedroom before the police had arrived on the morning of the murder—could she have missed seeing that box with the magnifier in it and the empty slot for a letter opener on top of the desk?

Of course. In those frantic few minutes when she had come upon Gladys Lightner's body and her husband standing over it dripping blood, then made the 911 call, she couldn't get herself and Carla out of there fast enough. Later, while Jersey was taping the crime scene, she was downstairs eavesdropping on the detectives' questioning of Lightner and taking notes.

But there was the box, on tape.

She knew now that the police had not found the murder weapon. The medical examiner would have determined at the scene that Mrs. Lightner had been stabbed to death, so police personnel would have been looking for a knife, a blade of some kind. Finding none, they would have gathered that suspicious double-slotted box containing only the magnifying glass and booked it into evidence.

53

Late Wednesday afternoon, twenty to six, in Tom McCartney's kitchen. He had just woken up, his night's sleep beginning in late morning, and his morning beginning now, in late afternoon. McCartney did little in his life the normal way, and nothing at all the easy way. He had lunch after the network stations' Eleven O'clock News signed off, usually a sandwich in his SUV, and he had what passed for dinner at four or five in the morning, usually at Cantor's all-night deli. Right now it was time for breakfast.

He opened his fridge and took out two eggs, a fresh Roma tomato, a tub of nonfat cottage cheese, and a breakfast steak. McCartney was a low-carb, high-protein, raw fruit and veggie kind of guy, and like every other routine in his life, he was fairly strict about that one. Okay, he'd been known to have the occasional pint of Häagen-Dazs. Coffee was his flavor, and now and then chocolate. He loved rum raisin best, maybe because it had booze in it, but there were times in the past when he'd found himself chasing it with a pint of vodka.

He dropped a dollop of olive oil and the steak into a sauté pan, then washed the tomato and chopped it on his cutting board. He pulled a plate down from one of the cabinets, dropped a scoop of the cottage cheese onto it, picked up the cutting board and swept the tomato pieces on top of that, and added a little more oil and some balsamic vinegar. Then he flipped the steak over. Taking another pan and adding more olive oil, he cracked the eggs into it and scrambled them with a dinner fork. He liked his scrambled eggs soft and his steak rare. The two dishes were ready at the same time, and he served up both onto the plate. He had already done his coffee ritual. He poured himself a mug of French roast, fished a napkin and silverware out of a couple of drawers, carried all of it over to the kitchen counter, and dropped onto a stool. Picking up the salt and pepper shakers on the granite countertop, he shook a little on everything, and there was breakfast. In exactly six minutes.

The television remote control was also kept on the counter. He zapped it at the flat-screen TV on the kitchen wall, and the theme music came up for the Channel Six news at six. A close-up of Maxi Poole filled the screen. This was McCartney's favorite show on television these days, ever since he had come to know its anchorwoman.

She was wearing a short black jacket over an ivory-colored silk shirt, with a string of creamy pearls at her throat and a tiny diamond pendant that hung just below them. Small diamond earrings, hair and makeup perfect, personality pleasing, as always. But she had so much more. She projected a warmth, a glow that came at you right through the screen, and that was something a television personality couldn't buy, couldn't fake, and couldn't slather on with a makeup sponge. You either had it or you didn't, and Maxi Poole had way more of it than her fair share.

She was reporting a helluva lead, one she had broken herself last night, the recovery of the kidnapped toddler Roberto Ochoa. The story was well shot, well written, and well delivered. No question, Maxi Poole was as good as he was, and he honestly didn't know of another newscaster in the L.A. market he was able to say that about.

That thought made him laugh out loud. Okay, so modesty wasn't his long suit. It was fair to say that he knew what he was and he knew what he wasn't. He wasn't well-rounded; his life was work, work, and work. He wasn't diplomatic or compromising, like you had to be when you worked for the networks. He wasn't motivated by money, he wasn't sober all the time, and he didn't play by the accepted rules of journalism.

Also, unlike most heterosexual men, his lifestyle, his actions, his heart, and his soul were never, ever ruled by women.

Or one woman.

Until now? Maybe until now. That concept perplexed him. Could he really have fallen for the woman who was live on his television screen? Is that what this feeling was about? If so, this was a first for him, and he had no idea what to do with it. Or whether he should do anything at all.

Yet on some level he sensed that he had to deal with it because he was becoming obsessed with the woman, thinking about her all the time, which wasn't good. It was no secret that his personal Achilles' heel was his obsessive personality, so he had to be cautious about the things he became obsessed with. Like vodka, Vicodin, and Maxi Poole—none of the three were good for him. The two Vs much too often proved as much, and the woman represented something he couldn't have. Not in this lifetime. McCartney was a realist, and all of the thousand or so reasons why he couldn't have Maxi Poole in his life were patently obvious to him.

Rigorous morning training sessions had given her some late-night street cred, but as tough as she appeared to be, it was still unseemly to him that she prowled the L.A. night scene like he did. He knew what was out there. He could handle it. Truth be told, he actually thrived on it. He couldn't imagine working in the corporate media world again. Could never deal with the constraints that were handed out with established press credentials. He was born to be his own boss, and now he was. But in his view, Maxi Poole was still a fragile flower and she needed protection. Pete Capra was making a big mistake leaving her out there in the nightside mire. McCartney had done everything he could do, showing her the terrain, talking down the players, introducing her to kickboxing and handling a gun, but sometimes, in what stringers called the weird hours, even that level of self-protection was not enough.

Especially now that he had figured out what Mr. Channel Six News, Peter Capra, was up to. He'd done some deep research on Capra, he'd shot tape in the park for him, he'd probed into the San Francisco "walk-in killer" case from every angle, learned everything there was to know about the suspect, and now he was certain that he knew the score. And he knew that Capra had known that he would fit the pieces of the puzzle together, and that was the reason the Channel Six boss had put him on the case. Capra had asked him to protect Maxi. "Watch her back," he'd said. It was only later that McCartney had realized Capra's full implication, the reason why the man had charged him with protecting Maxi on the graveyard.

And the reason why Capra wouldn't spell it all out, to him or to anybody, was simple: His plan to use Maxi to get at this creep was unethical, dangerous, and could ruin him. Could get him ostracized in the news business, not to mention royally sued, which would likely cause him to lose everything, including the career he loved. But he sensed that Capra had to go forward with his plan because he was obsessed by this case, and obsession was something that McCartney could relate to. The man with the mole on his face had haunted Pete Capra for thirteen years. The "walk-in killer" was the one who got away, and now that the prime suspect had stumbled back into Capra's orbit, he was damned if he was going to let that happen again.

And he was using Maxi Poole to get to him. McCartney had learned that the killer only murdered blondes. Beautiful blondes. Though neither Capra nor McCartney knew his name, they both knew where to find him now. But it was up to Pete Capra and the police to bring him down. McCartney wasn't interested in justice. What he was interested in was protecting Maxi Poole. What he hadn't yet decided was whether he could best accomplish that by letting her know how her boss was using her, or by keeping her in the dark about it.

He would do anything for her. He broke into that loser's trailer for her. This no doubt helped her crack tonight's lead story. Yes, he got the scene at the trailer all on tape. He couldn't sell it, it was illegal entry, but he would definitely be able to incorporate shots into future pieces—with L.A. city councilman Conrad Lightner up on murder charges, the related kidnap story had a major place with the tabloid shows and publications. Their money was good, too—in fact, it was usually much better than the elite media's money. This kind of thing showed up in the tabs all the time. And who was gonna sue him? Raoul Montez? He thought not. The man was in jail, and more than likely he would be going down for a long time.

That kind of tactic was another reason why McCartney could only work for himself. If he reported for a network, or a station, or CNN or MSNBC or the magazine shows, they would never let him use those illegal shots. They would never have let him shoot them in the first place. Fact was, they would not allow him to do *half* the stuff he did to nail his big "gets."

Another potentially big "get," he'd gone to see the dead hooker's partner, Monroe, this morning after making the station rounds with his Chinatown shooting story. A consummate businesswoman, she had already recruited a new prostitute to team up with her; the new girl was working out of the M&M apartment and calling herself Marilyn. And Monroe had readily agreed to go ahead with the interview as scheduled tomorrow night. McCartney had never really doubted that she would keep their tape date. She'd seen the news. She knew that Councilman Conrad Lightner would never be knocking on her back door again and laying money on her dresser, but Tom McCartney had promised her plenty of money for the interview. She still insisted on doing the shoot in disguise—no need to risk raising the ire of the Hollywood Division cops, who pretty much left the M&M establishment alone. If she went high-profile, like Heidi Fleiss did, she would be inviting a raid on her place of business.

Thinking about the Marilyn and Monroe angles made him smile again. No way would he have broken those stories if he worked for a legitimate news outlet—with his renegade news-gathering style he could only work alone. He was the lone wolf of the nightside, its recognized leader and king, and he wouldn't have it any other way.

Maxi Poole was as legitimate as you get. So what the hell was he thinking, falling in love with her? If that was what this was. How would he even know? That particular blind emotion had never reared its complex head in Tom McCartney's universe. And he would never, *could* never change his life now.

He couldn't help wondering, though, if she might change her life for him. He knew that she was feeling the intense chemistry between them; it was too hot for either of them to deny. And they worked well together. They were a strong team. Physical attraction, a compatible work ethic, they both made money, and they both got the joke. The cosmic joke.

Would Maxi Poole ever think about stepping into *his* world?

54

Wednesday night, seven-thirty-five. After the Six, Maxi had come home on her dinner break to see how mother and son were doing, and to change clothes. Working this shift complicated her wardrobe choices, since she was on camera from nighttime into morning. After being stuck for days in the wrinkled red suit, she'd decided to change after her nightly anchor shift whenever she could so that she'd be wearing something different on the Morning News the next day. She got out of the black jacket and pants, and into a pale pink wool suit and matching heels.

Roberto, exhausted after this big reunion day, was asleep in the guest room. Carla Ochoa, in a loose-fitting blue smock, was in the kitchen fussing over Janie, who was standing in dog-show pose on a kitchen countertop, loving the attention. Carla launched into an avalanche of news the minute Maxi came in through the garage door.

"Missus Maxi, I have a new job today," she said. Maxi had not been able to steer her out of the habit of addressing her as "missus." "At a children's school. My friend spoke for me. A very, very good job!" she bustled on, brushing the pup's long, silky hair back from her eyes. "And I'm going to take the test for citizen of this country. I start to study my books now."

Maxi had made a trip to the district office of the CIS in down-town Los Angeles and brought home the requisite books on American history and government for her, along with the forms she would need to fill out to apply for citizenship, but until now Carla hadn't been able to focus on the task.

"Mr. George Washington, now I know all about him, and—"

"Wait, wait!" Maxi stopped her, laughing. "First tell me about the new job."

"In the cafeteria. Dishing out food for the kids. I will love doing that. My friend does that. Helping the little children."

"Sounds wonderful. What school?"

"It's called Woodrow Wilson."

"Ahh—Woodrow Wilson Elementary. Out in the Valley—"

"Yes, the San Fernando Valley. In the city of Sherman Oaks. I signed a paper that I promise to take my citizenship test, so now I must study hard."

"So, do you know who Woodrow Wilson was?" Maxi, smiling.

"No. Not yet. But I have to learn it, *sí?*"

"Yes. Especially if you're going to work there. Our twenty-eighth president, the architect of the League of Nations."

"A great man," Carla enthused.

"Right, he was a great man." She was thrilled for Carla.

"And," the woman went on, "we will move with my friend. Roberto and me. A very nice apartment and we will share the ex-penses."

"This is a good friend?"

"Alma is my very good friend. *Hace tres años somos amigas.*"

"That's wonderful, Carla. Now, tell me all about Roberto's first day home today."

Carla was beaming. Roberto was strong and healthy, she said. He'd been well cared for, just as Maxi had assured her. And he was very happy to be here. Who was this Gold-ee? Carla wanted to know. Roberto didn't say many words yet, especially in English, but he'd been saying "Gold-ee" all day.

Maxi told her about the golden retriever in East L.A., and

about the other children at the house, Mrs. Torres's children. Carla first got quiet, then she laughed, and then she inexplicably broke into copious tears just as she had last night, looking nervous and uncomfortable again. Realizing that the woman had lost her son and now he was back, Maxi could understand why she would be on an emotional seesaw, and that it would be a while before she would level off.

"Who will take care of Roberto while you're at work?" she asked gently.

That sent Carla swinging back up on the seesaw. "I will take Roberto with me," she said, and her pretty face lit up, though still wet with tears. "To the daycare center at the school. There will be children for him to play with. Roberto has been a lonely boy, only with me all the time. Now he will have friends."

"Did Roberto get to know Yukon today?"

"Oh yes. Roberto calls him Gold-ee."

Maxi laughed. Roberto probably got to know Yukon better than Yuke got to know the little boy during their first day together. And then there was Janie, assuming her place as the pampered princess of the house. She looked down at her own big baby, who rested his chin against her ankles underneath the table now. Hiding out, Maxi figured, taking a break from the strange people and happenings all day in his heretofore well-ordered castle where he previously had been king.

"Hey, big guy, is your new name Goldie?" Maxi purred. Yukon looked up at her peevishly—he was not amused.

Carla laughed. "Poor big Yukon," she said.

"Poor boy," Maxi echoed, bending down to rub the Alaskan's beautiful gray-and-white coat. "We'll go to the dog park on Saturday, I promise, Yuke. And we'll take Janie too, okay?"

Carla took a pair of trimming shears out of the pocket of her smock and started carefully trimming the long hair falling in front of Janie's eyes.

"With so much hair, she can't see. I always cut it. Every week," she said.

Carla laughed some more. Maxi hadn't seen her this happy, or happy at all, really, since the day they'd met. The day Roberto was kidnapped. She watched as Carla carefully snipped the hair around Janie's dark, deepset eyes, then around her feathered ears. Janie, looking like a tiny version of an Old English sheepdog, seemed entirely content in her new environs.

"Would you like to take Janie with you to your new apartment, Carla?" Maxi asked.

Carla thought for a minute, probably reflecting on the fact that Janie no longer had people to care for her. Then the tears flowed again.

"Roberto loves her very much," she said. "Janie used to sleep in our room with him. I'll ask Alma if we can bring her. I think she will love Janie too."

Carla smiled down at the pup and gave her a sweet series of pats. Then she went to work clipping the hair along the bottom of Janie's long double coat that cascaded to the stone countertop. This was a dog who could mop your floors if you didn't keep up the regular hairdressing sessions. Unlike Yukon, Janie was definitely high-maintenance, but Maxi could see that Carla was enjoying it, even in her fragile up-and-down mood.

As she watched the woman cut and snip, it occurred to her that she had never seen that pair of sleek, gold-toned trimming shears in her house before. "Where did you get those scissors?" she asked Carla, curious. The woman was certainly adept with them.

Carla paused for a beat, looking at the shears in her hand. "I had them from Mrs. Lightner's house. For cutting Janie's hair."

"But you didn't know that Janie would be coming here to live," Maxi said. "Why did you take her scissors with you?"

"I kept the scissors in the drawer in my room. When I pour everything in the bag to move here, I didn't pay attention," she said with what Maxi sensed was a defensive tone, continuing with the doggie haircut.

*　　*　　*

Doing seventy on the 405 southbound, Maxi was on her way to the Santa Monica Airport. The night assignment editor had called her cell phone—a private plane had crashed on landing about a half hour ago, and there was an unconfirmed report that popular British rock star Reggie Morris was on board.

She had no trouble finding the scene. The plane had come down in a field north of the airport, and the area was already daytime bright with portable floodlights illuminating the wreckage and the fire trucks, ambulances, police cars, and various personnel milling around the crash scene. Showing her press pass to officers who had secured the area, she was allowed to go through the barriers. By the time her crew arrived she had talked to enough people to piece the story together, and had tapped the top airport official, who was standing by now waiting for their interview.

Jersey was her cameraman, and he quickly shot B-roll on the cataclysmic scene in the field. Next, they taped Maxi's stand-up in front of the downed plane, which was still smoking:

"Heavy metal rocker Reggie Morris has been rushed to Saint John's hospital on Twenty-second Street here in Santa Monica after his MU-2 high-wing turboprop crashed near the Santa Monica Municipal Airport tonight. Santa Monica fire captain Jim Danes told me that the private jet had apparently hit power lines over this field in the twenty-eight hundred block of Ocean Park Boulevard. Authorities say the pilot may have died in the crash—we haven't confirmed that, and we don't have the man's identity yet."

At that point she picked up her notes and read the track she'd written that would be run over corresponding pictures of the scene in editing, leaving space for a sound bite with a witness who worked at the airport explaining how he'd first heard a loud bang, then the sky north of the airport lit up with the blaze. She ended her track with a notice that all roads surrounding the crash area had been closed to traffic, and the public was being kept out of the area.

Next, she did a short Q&A with the Santa Monica Airport

manager, Scott Wylie, who said the jet went down at 10:24 P.M., and he was alerted at home. The flight plan that had been filed indicated that the plane was inbound from London when it crashed. Airport response was immediate, he said, followed by the arrival of municipal emergency vehicles. The plane, a popular and reliable private turboprop, was registered with a UK-based aviation company.

Maxi did her stand-up, giving out a local phone number, to be Chyroned on screen, that friends and family of those involved could call for more information, and a recap of what was known about Reggie Morris's condition, which wasn't much. Her next stop would be at Saint John's a few blocks away to see what she could learn.

As she approached her Corvette in the darkened parking lot, she saw what looked like Tom McCartney's big black Hummer parked next to it. Drawing closer, she saw McCartney himself leaning against it, arms folded, smiling.

"Hi—did you get it?" he asked her.

"Yes. Did you?"

"I got it, and I didn't see Seven or Nine here, so maybe I'll have a couple of customers. Are you going over to the hospital?"

"Yes. You?"

"Yup. I hope Morris will be okay. He's a young guy. He did a lot of pop radio music with his band for a few years, but he recently went solo and just came out with a CD that's a screamer, serious rock 'n' roll. He was probably coming to this country to promote it."

"You're a fan?"

"I'm a rock 'n' roll fan, remember?"

"Let's go see how he is."

Maxi got into her car and McCartney got into his. They rolled out of the airport, followed by Jersey in the Channel Six live truck. After learning at Saint John's that Morris was pretty badly injured but would survive, they each shot their stories, and

Jersey left for the station with Maxi's tapes, which would be cut into an all-inclusive package for the Eleven.

"Coffee?" McCartney asked when they were out in the parking lot getting ready to leave.

"I can't, Tom. I need to make a pit stop at my house."

"Problem?"

Maxi figured he could read that on her face. She had never been good at hiding her feelings. Back when Pete Capra and she were on friendly footing, he'd once told her that was a big reason for her success in communicating with viewers. She was sincere, and she wore her emotions on her face.

"Kind of," she said.

"Wanna talk about it?"

She did want to talk about it, she realized, and she trusted McCartney. It also helped that the two of them didn't technically compete on the graveyard—she reported for Channel Six, and he was an independent operator who sold his stories to stations that didn't have crews out covering them.

"Step into my office," he said, opening the front passenger door of his H2 with a flourish.

She climbed inside, and he walked around the front of the SUV and got in behind the wheel.

"Okay," he said, "the doctor is in."

She told him about Carla and the scissors, and that the woman had been acting erratically since the morning of the murder. And she reminded him that Jorgan had characterized the murder weapon in the Gladys Lightner case as "not a knife."

"Look, I'm sure I'm completely overreacting," she said, "but what do *you* think?"

"I think it's probably just as she says, but you should nab the scissors and turn them over to the LAPD. The crime lab people will take them apart and analyze every tiny thread of every tiny screw, and if there's any blood on them that's invisible to the eye, they'll find it. It never all washes away. If they don't find anything, then there's your answer, and at least you'll be satisfied that you checked it out."

"I know you're right. That's why I'm going home now—to look for the scissors and give them to the detective on the case."

"Marc Jorgan."

"Yes, Marc."

"Good plan."

They sat in silence for a minute, and Maxi could feel the heat of his body. The sexual tension between them was palpable. She looked over at him at the same moment he turned to look at her. They both smiled, and he reached out and put his arms around her. Drew her close, and kissed her gently. Pulling away, they stayed close, looked into each other's eyes, then kissed again. As the kiss deepened, she felt a raging surge down to the tips of her toes. And in other places too.

"Uhh," he said when they finally separated, "why don't you come to my place after your shift."

"I have target practice in the morning. Remember?"

"Skip target practice tomorrow," he whispered.

"Tom . . . I'm not ready for that. But . . . I'm not saying I won't be." She grinned, and heard herself adding, "Pretty soon, I think."

"Well, how about dinner Saturday night?"

"Another date?"

"Yes. Our second date."

"But without Rosie?"

"*Definitely* without Rosie."

They kissed again. "You're on," she finally managed. "Now I'm going to go, before I completely weaken and change my mind about . . . uhh . . . breakfast at your place."

"If you do, call me."

He winked, and she opened the door and let herself out of his Hummer. Not an easy trick in high heels, she realized, as she slid the two feet down to the ground. With a little wave at him, she scrambled into her own car and turned on the ignition. Before she could pull out, he materialized at the driver's side window of her car.

She pushed the DOWN button to lower the window. He reached inside and took her face in his hands, then squatted down and kissed her again. Staying in that position, he said, "Look, Maxi, there's something I have to tell you."

"What?"

"I've thought about this a lot, and I've tried not to let my personal feelings about you get tangled up with business. But that's not possible anymore. Not when it involves your safety."

"What are you talking about?"

"Your boss. Pete Capra is using you. He didn't put you out on this shift to punish you, or because he thinks you're not cutting it on dayside."

Her look was one big question mark. "Why, then?"

"He put you on the graveyard because he's using you as bait. His 'walk-in killer' only killed blondes. Beautiful blond women. And Capra wants you to lure him out."

"To lure him out and . . . *what?*" None of this made sense to her.

"Now that he's found this murder suspect again after all these years, and he knows where he hangs out, he wants the guy to make a move on you so he can turn the cops onto him and get him arrested. Attempted murder would get the man put away for a while, and it would be enough to get the San Francisco cold case reopened. They would still have physical evidence in the unsolved murders up there—now it would be a matter of DNA testing, which they didn't have back then, and they'd have a good chance of putting the guy away for good."

"Pete Capra wouldn't be that cold-blooded . . ."

"Pete Capra is a journalist. And he has a heavy personal hook into this case. The 'walk-in killer' story drove him and his family out of San Francisco, disrupted his whole life. Capra wants this chance to do what he failed to do back then. He wants to finish it."

"And he would put my life at risk for a damn story?"

"Maxi, that's the reason he put *me* on the case. Why do you think I insisted that you take kickboxing lessons and buy a gun? Do you remember telling me the county wouldn't give you a permit to carry a concealed weapon unless you could prove that you were in grave danger? And I said that you *were* in grave danger."

"You knew then?"

"I was guessing then."

"But Capra knew?"

"Of course he knew. He took a calculated risk. And before you even came out on this shift, he asked me to protect you."

55

Thursday, in the weird hours, after two in the morning. Maxi pulled up to the curb on the Alvarado Street side of MacArthur Park.

After leaving Saint John's hospital in Santa Monica, she had stopped at home. Switching on the lights in the kitchen, she'd found that Carla and Roberto were asleep in the guest room. No surprise at that hour. And there on the kitchen counter where Janie got her haircut earlier were the gold-toned cutting shears. The sight of them had made her smile. She should be writing novels, she'd mused, with her overactive imagination. Carla Ochoa hardly fit the profile of a hardened killer.

But her mind flashed back to the morning when she'd picked up Carla and her belongings at the Lightner manse. And to her surprise at how extremely agitated Carla was, even before the two of them had come upon the body of Gladys Lightner with her husband standing over it dripping blood. Conrad Lightner was in custody now, charged with the murder of his wife. But Lightner said he didn't do it. No surprise, of course, but the councilman had remarked more than once that the police had never found the knife. And there was no knife.

Marc Jorgan had told Maxi only that the murder weapon was

not a knife, and she'd figured out that even the police didn't know for sure what it was, that they only had the wound it left to guess by. And the gift box with the magnifying glass and the outline of a letter opener from Mrs. Lightner's bedroom. But at this point, only one person knew for sure what blade had killed Gladys Lightner: the killer. Did Lightner actually know what the murder weapon was? Was he just trying to put everyone off track by suggesting that he assumed it was a knife? Probably. The case against him depended on that.

Carla Ochoa, murderess? She didn't think so. Still, she'd opened one of the drawers and taken out a Ziploc baggie, then ripped a paper towel off the wooden towel holder on the counter and carefully bagged the scissors without disturbing Carla's fingerprints on them. Then silently scoffed at herself again, and her sense of the dramatic. She had definitely read too many murder mysteries. Or covered too many crime stories. The idea that this pair of scissors could be the Lightner murder weapon was ludicrous. And if it were, Carla would never have carelessly left it lying around out here in Maxi's kitchen. Would she? For that matter, she certainly wouldn't have been using it to give a dog a haircut. She would have tossed the shears into a Dumpster somewhere. If she were a stone killer.

Placing the baggie in an inside pocket of her shoulder tote, she'd switched off the kitchen lights, gone out the garage door, and gotten back into her car. It was too early to go in to the station to recut her plane crash story for the Morning News—she had to wait for the dayside editors to get in at four.

Besides, she was fuming. And disappointed, and hurt, and horrified. If what McCartney said was true, if Capra was actually using her to get his San Francisco killer suspect to make a murderous move on her, then she was damn well going to find this guy before he found her. And if he threatened her, get him arrested. Get him put away. Get herself off this damn shift. And never speak to Pete Capra again. She'd decided to come out here and scout the park again, see if Capra's man was here tonight, or at least find out more about him—it was still early enough for the perverts to be out.

The shadowy park with its dense foliage looked eerie, and she didn't have the protective presence of Tom McCartney with her this time. He had called it right—after he'd turned in that conclusive footage of the mystery man, Capra didn't need him to shoot any more tape in the park. McCartney had decided to go home and edit his plane crash tape on his own equipment. He would sell the finished piece instead of the raw, he'd told Maxi. Usually he didn't cut his own stories, but he too had a few hours to kill tonight before the stations' morning execs came in to work and he could do business with them.

Looking down the broad avenue into the park, she was suddenly grateful for her new martial arts skills, much as she had resisted the whole idea at first. Thank you, Zeke Fairstein. And thank you, Tom McCartney—her two-part self-protection regimen had been his idea. She patted her purse, somewhat comforted that her little Glock 19 was inside, and loaded, and she knew how to use it. Okay, onward.

Getting out of the car, tote on her shoulder, she zapped the remote to lock her Corvette, threw the keys into her bag, and set off down the road into the park. Ambient light filtered through the trees from neighborhood streetlights, suffused with a pink wash from the huge neon sign atop the Westlake Theater on Alvarado Street, once a grand L.A. movie palace, reduced now to a swapmeet venue where trinkets and toys, dishes and books, discarded electronic equipment and cheap clothes were hawked.

Kickboxing training and her gun notwithstanding, Maxi shivered with unease. The dilapidated and notoriously violent MacArthur Park, infamous for gang shootouts and dumped bodies, littered with used condoms and hypodermic needles, was an L.A. landmark that most people avoided after dark, residents and tourists alike. The park had a 10:30 P.M. curfew, but those for whom that curfew was created ignored it, and the ranks of the thinly stretched Los Angeles Police Department were too busy trying to keep up with night crime in the rest of the city to enforce it.

McCartney had printed out a picture of Capra's mystery man for her, the clearest shot he had, taken from a close-up freeze frame of him during the card game on that final shoot in the park, his perfect video. She'd been showing the hard copy photo to stringers on the overnight, stringers who weren't likely to cross paths with Pete Capra. The "odd couple" had thought they recognized the man. They'd told Maxi he looked like one of the lowlifes they'd seen while shooting a drug rout on Seventh Street a few weeks ago. That sounded credible; Seventh Street bordered MacArthur Park on the south.

As she neared the restroom area she found a few of the usual breed of scuzz and scum loitering, slouching about, doing whatever they went there to do. For an uncertain minute, she asked herself what the hell *she* was doing there. Was this what her boss wanted? Was he really so self-absorbed by some deranged killer out of his past that he would actually risk his reporter's life to get him? Or to get the story?

She thought about Christine Williams and shuddered. That's when the full realization hit. She decided that she'd pushed her luck far enough. This level of jeopardy was not in her job description. Tomorrow she would confront Capra, tell him she knew what he was up to, and refuse to work the graveyard another night. Let him fire her. She would sue him, sue the company, she would win with what she knew, and Capra's irrational, obsessive behavior would be aired all over the news. And damn the consequences. If this cliquish business would no longer have her because of some perceived "disloyalty" to her boss, she could always teach journalism. And open her dog rescue business.

But since she was here now . . .

She shook her head in disbelief at her own obstreperous mind-set, but there it was. This was her. She'd come out here to do something, and she was going to give it a shot. She realized how she must look to these disparate night crawlers in her fitted pink Azzedine Alaia suit and matching high heels. It had crossed her mind when she was at home to change into jeans, a jacket, and running shoes, and to shove her hair up under a baseball cap before she left for the park, but she would be going live on the set on the Morning News in a couple of hours with her plane crash story so she needed to look professional or people would call, e-mail, write cards and letters, complain about the way she had "presented herself." Judging by a goodly chunk of her viewer correspondence, she sometimes wondered if a lot of the audience even heard what she said, or if they just passed judgment on her clothes and her hairdo.

Singling out the least dangerous-looking creeps from the sparse bunch in the vicinity of the restrooms, as if she could tell which ones were violent as well as sick, she excused herself politely, showed each one the picture of Capra's man, and asked if they knew him. In the pink suit and the Jimmy Choo heels. And black pantyhose. Damn Capra. She belonged on the graveyard shift like Queen Victoria belonged at a whorehouse.

"Yah," one guy was saying, looking at the photo she held out to him—a burly black man with a bushy beard, alcohol on his breath, in khakis and a dirty T-shirt, who actually hadn't guffawed at her, or drooled on her. "The guy hangs here."

"Have you seen him tonight?"

"Don't think so."

"What's his story, do you know?"

"No clue. I don't know if the dude is gay or straight, I don't think he's a junkie, I don't know *what* the hell he is. Nuts, I guess. Do you want to have sex, girlie?"

Girlie? "Do you know his name?"

"Nah. I don't know nobody's name. Don't wanna know."

"Well, does he—"

"Hey ya, there he is. Ain't that him?" Pointing at someone behind her.

Maxi turned around and saw a man coming out of the men's room. Oh! My! God! Yes, that looked like him, in black jeans and a short-sleeved T-shirt, with a red-tinged gray ponytail. In the glow of the dingy light spilling out of the restroom she could even see the mole on his cheek.

"No, that's not him," she said to her new friend, and she walked hurriedly off in the opposite direction.

And watched the mystery man. Then followed him at a distance, giving him a wide berth. He led her out of the park onto Lake Street, north to Third Street, then left past sprawling Saint Vincent Medical Center to a shabby, four-story yellow brick building that looked like it might have once been a hotel but was now converted to a rooming house. On closer inspection, a flophouse. Dirty, peeling paint and broken windows, ominous and seamy, a crash pad for losers.

The man opened the front door and disappeared inside.

Maxi stood on the sidewalk for a moment on the corner of Third and Rampart. Now she knew where he lived. Maybe. Probably. She would come back with a crew in the morning when it was light. No, not possible—what was she supposed to call this story when she made her crew request? Pete Capra's boogeyman? She had not one thing to hang the story on, and it would open up a can of worms in the newsroom.

McCartney. She could come back with Tom McCartney in the daytime and let him video the place. And go inside and smoke the guy out. Or stake out the building till the mole-man came back out the door. Let McCartney have the story—he deserved it, and it would serve Pete Capra right. Most important, it would get this crazo off her case.

But McCartney didn't do daytime. What she had to do, in her confrontation with Capra tomorrow, was to tell him she knew all about the man he was after, and she knew where he lived. Give him the information and let him do what he wanted with it.

She decided to take a quick look inside. She had no intention of confronting the man, but right now she knew he was in there, and she knew he was awake. By seeing light under a door, or hearing movement inside, maybe she could suss out which unit, or apartment, or room he was in, which would be next to impossible to do in the morning.

She had her gun, didn't she? Well, she wasn't about to *use* her gun, she was terrified at the prospect of shooting an actual human being, but she had her cell if she needed to call for help. Taking the phone out of her bag, she punched in 911. The NO SERVICE prompt did not come on, so the phone was good to go. She left the three numbers up, locked them in, and dropped the cell phone into her jacket pocket. If she got in a bind, all she had to do was put her hand in her pocket, feel for the prominent square SEND button, and push it. The LAPD's Rampart Division was right around the corner.

Tentatively, she started walking toward the building. She thought she heard a muffled noise behind her, rubber-soled footsteps, but before she could turn to look something smashed into her from behind—tackling her, pinning her with a bare, hairy arm around her waist and another arm around her neck. The right hand held a knife, and on the left arm, tightening under her chin, she could see a tattoo, a green-and-red snake wound around a thick, blue-black anchor. The tattoo in the composite drawing of the suspected "walk-in killer."

It *was* him. The man Capra was after, the man whom she'd followed out of the park tonight. How did he get behind her when she'd watched him go inside the building? He'd have had to go through the building and out a back door, then come around the block and approach her from behind. So he *knew* she'd been following him all along. He had consciously led her here.

She struggled to free her arms. She needed to put a hand in her pocket, feel for her cell phone, and press SEND. It would take two seconds. The 911 system would pinpoint exactly where she was. Help from the Rampart station would get here in minutes.

"Move," the man said, and he urged her forward.

Her legs were Jell-O—she willed them to perform, but at the same time she couldn't let him take her into that building. Just two seconds, please. Meantime, talk to him.

"How did you know I was following you?"

He actually laughed. "You mean in those little click-click-clicky-lady pink high heels? Gee," sarcastically, "how would I know?" A cultured voice. Educated.

"I didn't make any noise—" She was pathetic, she knew. And terrified.

"You're on a surveillance and you're dressed like that? Some sleuth you are."

"I'm not a sleuth. I'm a journalist. And I'm not on a surveillance, I'm on a story."

"I know what you are. You're Capra's girl. Walk."

He shoved her forward. *Please, give me just two seconds,* she silently begged again. To Whoever was listening. Her assailant kept her pinned tightly until they reached the door to the building.

"What do you mean, I'm Capra's girl?" Her voice wobbling.

He let up on his grip around her waist to push the door open, freeing her arms momentarily. The break that she'd prayed for. She thrust her hand into her pocket, got it around her cell phone, and felt for the protruding SEND button on the front. But before her finger could connect with the button he let go of the door, ripped her hand out of her pocket, and wrenched the phone away from her.

"Well, what have we here, missy?" he cooed, looking down at the 911 readout. He pressed the OFF button, then he hurled the cell phone across the street. Her heart plummeted as she watched it skitter over the pavement and bounce up against the opposite curb. Then he kicked the door open and shoved her inside.

She stepped into a tiny, musty, low-ceilinged vestibule. There were no mailboxes, no tenant roster, no elevator. Yellow patterned linoleum floor worn down to the brown backing in heavy-traffic areas, and littered with old newspapers and menus from a local Chinese take-out restaurant. He pushed her toward a dark, narrow staircase to the left, and nudged her up the stairs.

"Where are you taking me?" she managed.

"Be quiet," he said, almost in a whisper. Then, "We're going to have a little chat about our mutual friend."

"Who?"

"Quiet, I said."

He pushed her up three flights of creaky wooden steps, then down a hall covered with ancient, stained brown carpeting to a door on the right side marked with a K. Holding the knife to her throat with his left hand now, with his right he took an old-fashioned metal key out of the back pocket of his jeans and inserted it into the keyhole, opened the door, and pushed her inside. And closed the door behind them.

But he didn't lock it. And Maxi could see that the mechanism was too old to be the kind that would lock automatically when the door closed. Pushing her down onto a soiled, threadbare, barrel-back chair in a corner of the squalid room, he hovered over her, holding the knife menacingly a few inches from her chest. He wasn't a big man, about five foot eight and slight, but she was at a disadvantage sunk low into the chair. She focused on high alert for a chance to get him off guard and smash him with a kick, then run like hell out of the unlocked door.

"So, Maxi Poole, did Peter Capra send you to follow me?"

"No. How do you know Pete Capra? And how do you know me?" Keep him talking.

He slapped her across the face with his free hand. "Don't tell me no," he said. "Do you think I'm stupid?"

She winced. "Of course not. My boss assigned me to this shift and I'm just trying to do my job. Trying to cover news stories."

"And I'm some kind of news story? Why is that?"

She had no answer. She certainly wasn't going to tell him she knew he was a suspect in a string of serial killings up north.

"Answer me, Maxi Poole," he said, and he struck her again, this time so hard it brought tears to her eyes.

Her heart was racing in her chest, she couldn't swallow, and her head was throbbing with fear. She had to think, keep the dialogue going until she found a way to strike and run. She could do it, she just needed an opening.

"The LAPD has announced a new program to crack down on crime in MacArthur Park," she improvised, trying to stabilize her voice to mask her terror. Trying to talk like this was just some everyday news interview, discussing the public interest of the citizens of Los Angeles.

"They're putting on police bicycle patrols, they're installing surveillance cameras to zoom in on drug dealing, they're putting new emphasis on enforcing the curfew, and they're involving the community in cleanup efforts in the park. That's the story I'm working on," she lied.

"At three in the morning." With an ugly smirk.

"Well, this is my shift. I work the graveyard. I report for the Morning News."

Was he buying this? What did he want from her? *He only kills blondes*, McCartney had told her.

"Let's talk about Mr. Capra," he said, brandishing the knife.

"You mean P-*Pete* Capra?"

"Stop fucking with me. You're making me nervous. What did he tell you about me?"

"Nothing." That was the truth. "I don't know who you are." A lie.

He slapped her again, this time with the back of his hand, and a bulky university ring he was wearing scraped across her cheek. She could see his face contorting in anger.

"I'm telling you the truth. Pete Capra never mentioned you to me. He just assigned me to this . . . story. In the park."

"I've seen you out there before." Holding the knife within an inch of her throat now, his eyes fierce. "With your cameraman."

He thought McCartney was her cameraman. "Yes. Working on the story. About cracking down on night crime in MacArthur Park."

"Listen, you little bitch, don't tell me about your stories. You were following me, and I know you weren't going to ask me to help clean up the fucking park. Now I want to talk about Peter Capra," he said, and she felt a sharp sting as the blade slit the skin under her chin. She was aware of her own warm blood trickling down the front of her neck.

"What? What about him?" she pleaded, seeing that he was losing control, trying to wipe away the blood from her face and neck with the back of her hand. "He's my boss—"

The door burst open then and a figure hurtled inside and pounced on the man. Tom McCartney! The two struggled, and Maxi watched in horror as McCartney took a deep knife slash across the upper part of his chest. He clutched at the wound and tried to beat off the attacker with his other hand, but he was shoved to the floor, and the man poised himself to stab again.

Maxi couldn't move from the chair. The two men scuffling blocked her way, and she was half paralyzed with fright. As the man from the park started to bear down with his knife again, McCartney quickly reached inside one of his socks and pulled something out. His gun? She knew he owned a gun—did he have it with him? She couldn't see what he held in his hand until he jabbed it into the other man's thigh, then pulled it out.

A needle!

The man dropped his knife, reared back and howled, then crumpled to the floor. His chest bleeding heavily, McCartney crouched over, holding firm to the dripping needle in his hand.

Maxi leaped out of the chair and helped McCartney into it, smearing his blood on her hands and clothes. "Give me your phone," she said to him. "I'll call for help."

"No," he rasped. "We have to get out of here."

Was McCartney in shock? Blood drenched the front of his shirt now. The other man was writhing on the floor.

"Tom, I need to call the police. Rampart Division is two minutes away from here. They'll send an ambulance—"

McCartney was trying to get to his feet. "We have to leave," he said. "Help me, Maxi. My car's out front. You'll drive."

"Drive . . . ?" The other man was still now, his eyes bulging, his face contorted in pain. "Tom, what's going on? What did you do to him?"

It had all happened in less than a minute. Maxi tried to grasp the situation. The assailant seemed to be dead or dying. A needle! McCartney had jabbed him with a needle. He'd had a syringe hidden under his pant leg.

"I killed him. For you, Maxi. He was going to kill you."

"You killed him with . . . ?"

"Yes, cyanide. I followed you. I saw you in the park, and I—"

"*Why?* Why would you follow me?"

"To protect you, Maxi. I told you, my job is to protect you."

Maxi felt as if she were somewhere in the twilight zone. None of this was making sense. Tom McCartney wasn't making sense. Maybe she'd passed out, and this was a dream. She looked down at her hands, sticky with blood. Her own blood and Tom's.

Then, in a flash, she got it. Got the whole, horrendous picture.

"*You! You* killed Christine Williams."

"Of course I did. She was going to take your anchor job away from you. I picked up her location on the scanner and went to the hotel, invited her for a drink when she finished her shoot . . ." He seemed to weaken then, and fell back in the chair.

"And . . . that prostitute? The one who was murdered with cyanide?"

"Yes, Marilyn. Lightner was a regular. I knew the cops would look at him for her murder . . . good sidebar . . ." His breaths were coming in shallow gasps now. ". . . doing my interview with her partner tonight . . . gonna break it tomorrow . . ."

Maxi's head was spinning. With his life's blood draining from a massive stab wound, the man was crowing about a story. McCartney had shot an exclusive on the Hollywood prostitute murder. He had told her he'd picked up the alert on the police radio in his car after he'd left Cantor's that morning, and that he got to the victim's apartment within minutes. He'd sold the story to Pete Capra, and to just about every other news outlet in town. She remembered something he'd said back then that she'd thought was odd, that Conrad Lightner was evil and useless, and so was the hooker, and they both deserved to die. She'd been tempted to comment at the time that a journalist's job was to report, not to judge, but didn't.

My God, she thought now, he's insane. All the drugs, all those years . . . had they affected his brain? Or was he always mentally ill? The cowboy of the nightside . . .

She felt as if she was going to pass out. She couldn't let herself. "Tom, give me your phone," she tried, "we have to get you to a hospital."

"I'm not going to a hospital. We'll take care of each other," he breathed. "We're a team, Maxi . . . I love you . . . I'll protect you . . ."

He reached up haltingly from the chair, extending both arms as if he wanted to embrace her. His jacket parted and she saw his cell phone clipped to the waist of his jeans. She moved in closer and went for the phone. With a sudden burst of energy he grabbed her wrist, and with his other hand he reached down to his ankles and came up with another syringe. Maxi's eyes widened in horror as she struggled to break from his grip. ". . . have to kill you now . . ." he was mumbling.

She remembered the scissors in her tote bag, which was still on her shoulder. Plunging her free hand inside, she came up with . . . the Glock. The gun that this man had painstakingly picked out for her, and put her into lessons to learn to use. She flipped the safety off with one hand. He had chosen this particular weapon because it was so easy to use. In case she was ever at risk for her life.

McCartney was lifting the syringe. She was at risk for her life. Squeezing her eyes in a squint, she aimed the gun square at Tom McCartney and pulled the trigger. Tears streaming down her face.

A gurgling sound erupted from his lips. She opened her eyes, and saw what she had done to his forehead. She looked over at the other man on the floor. He wasn't moving. Trying to keep herself from throwing up, she reached down and unclipped the cell phone from McCartney's waistband. Switched it on, and punched in 911.

More calmly than she thought she was capable of, she told the dispatcher her name, where she was, and that there were two men in the room. Dead, she thought. Then she did throw up. And let out big, uncontrollable sobs. Her entire body started to shake. She could hear the dispatcher's insistent voice droning out of the cell phone in her hand, urging her to stay on the line. That's when she passed out.

Someone was talking to her. A familiar voice. Telling her to hurry up, she was late, the show was about to start. But she couldn't find the script. Then when she did find it, it was written in some foreign language that she didn't know.

"Maxi, wake up . . ."

Her boss was shaking her gently. She tried to explain to him that she couldn't do the show because she couldn't read the script, but when she opened her mouth to talk no sound came out. She opened her eyes.

It was her boss. Pete Capra was standing over her.

"Come on, Maxi—you're okay. Wake up—"

She looked past Capra. Oh God, she was still in that room. This wasn't a dream. "What—?" she started.

"You passed out. But you're going to be okay," Capra said. "Can you stand up?"

She was sitting on the floor at Tom McCartney's feet—he was still in the chair, gunshot wound to his head, blood draining from the slash across his chest. Hypodermic needle in his hand.

It hadn't been a dream.

"Oh God—Tom," she cried.

"He's dead, Maxi."

"How could this be? That man . . ."

"He's dead too."

There were tears in Capra's eyes. Then she saw that there was someone else in the room, standing in the doorway. Cameraman Rodger Harbaugh. Looking at her with concern in his eyes.

"You brought . . . a *crew?*" she stammered at Capra.

"Can you get up, Maxi?"

He helped her get to her feet, tried to steady her.

"I can't . . . "

"The police have been in and out. They've called for the Robbery-Homicide detectives, and now they're downstairs securing the scene. We're going on the air live, Maxi," he said, glancing over at Rodger Harbaugh.

Harbaugh just looked at Capra as if he thought the man was mad.

"Pete, for God's sake, I can't," she squeaked. She was shaking.

"Well, either you have to, or I have to, because we're breaking in live with this story. And I haven't done this in years."

She started to cry. "What's *wrong* with you? Why are you *doing* this to me?"

"Because . . . because you have to get right back up on the horse, Maxi. This is for your own good."

"You have no heart—"

"Yes, I do. And it's broken."

He pointed to the dead man lying on the floor. The mystery man with the mole on his cheek, whom they'd all been after.

"That man," Capra said, with a catch in his voice. "He's my brother."

56

Friday afternoon, quarter past three. Jerrold Lightner had waited in the lineup outside Men's Central Jail for more than two hours, and now he sat in the plastic chair he'd been directed to on the unconfined side of the Lucite shield in his designated cubicle, waiting for his father to be brought in.

He and Lightner senior were soul mates of a sort now, both of them having heeled to Gladys Parsable Lightner's every noxious and demanding whim for most of their lives, only to be shit out of luck when it came time for the payout. In his new world of last resorts, Jerrold, the idea man, had had a thought. Maybe by teaming up with his father, by working together, they could salvage something out of this pigscrew. After all, how hard could it be to get the better of little Jamie Lightner, perennial loser-boy?

Jerrold was shocked when a guard brought the prisoner in, heavy-jowled, stubbly beard, unwholesome dark pouches under his eyes, fleshy body in a faded orange jumpsuit and worn sandals, bound in manacles, totally stripped of any dignity he had ever possessed. In this odd context, from a few feet away, this man he knew as his father looked like a stranger. It surprised Jerrold that the sight of the man in this state of degradation did not make him feel good after all, it just depressed him.

"Fifteen minutes," the guard said, handing Conrad Lightner into the chair on the other side of the scruffy plastic barrier.

His father picked up the phone. "What do you need, boy?"

"I wanted to see you, Dad. How are you doing?"

"Is that supposed to be a joke?" Lightner looked down at himself as if to say, check it out, see for yourself.

Jerrold saw that small talk and pleasantries were not going to accomplish anything here. "She left all the money to James."

"Tell me something I don't know."

"Dad . . . we have to do something about it."

"Like what? And how's your latest business venture going, by the way? With the drugs."

"Prescription drugs. Totally legal—"

"Sure. Drugs from Canada, right? So how's it going?" Dripping sarcasm.

"It's going fine, Dad—"

"Oh, good. So now you have another completely legal idea to circumvent your brother, the courts, and the wrath of your mother from the grave to get some money for the two of us, huh?"

"Dad—"

"Dad, what? I'm only 'Dad' when you want something. What do you want? As you can see, I'm not in a position to give you fucking anything. Not that I would even if I could. Where were you when they hauled my ass in here? I don't remember you coming around offering to help."

"What could I do . . . ?"

Lightner's sallow face reddened with anger. "What could you do? Maybe you could have been there for me for moral support, show the fucking press that you were a son who believed in me, stood by me, even if it was a crock."

Navigating what was looking to be a turbulent road, Jerrold Lightner switched gears. "Have you spoken to Jamie?"

"Screw Jamie. Screw both of you."

This was not going well. A dose of reality had not mellowed the old man. Jerrold resisted saying that he didn't come around sooner because he knew he'd be in for a ration of abuse like this. And that furthermore, his father was right, he didn't give a rat's ass about him or his public image because the feeling was mutual, had been for all of both their lives. But looking at him now, unhealthy, bitter, and most of all powerless, he realized that this trip had been a waste, that there wasn't a damn thing his father could do even if he'd wanted to help get them cut in on his mother's millions. The man was completely impotent.

Before Jerrold stood up to leave, he was struck by an impulse. He leaned in close to the transparent shield, holding the phone receiver close to his chin, and stage-whispered into the mouthpiece, "Did you kill her?"

His father's cynical response didn't surprise him. "I thought *you* killed her," he said, and he laughed.

A guard materialized behind the senior Lightner and checked a timer mounted on the wall above the prisoner's head. "Ten minutes," he said, loud enough for Jerrold to hear over the divider.

"We won't need it," Lightner growled, and he lurched his heavy bulk out of the chair and turned his back on his son.

As Jerrold watched the guard lead his father off without a backward look, he seemed unable to move, until another guard on his side of the booth came over with a woman in tow, presumably the next inmate visitor whose turn it was to sit in the chair that Jerrold Lightner now occupied. Without a word he rose and headed for the exit doors, his shoulders slouched, his demeanor resigned. He had failed with his father, he had failed with his brother, he'd failed with the lawyers, and in the end there was nothing at all that he could do about the money that had for so long seemed to be his prime reason for living. Like his father in the end, he was completely impotent too.

On his way past the incoming crowds of dispirited-looking jail visitors, and for just a fraction of a minute, Jerrold had an uncharacteristic insight into the possible meaning of his situation. He thought about the kind of person his father was, and he thought about the kind of person he was himself. Cut from the same cloth, people had said. Finally, he got it. Then he thought about his brother. Weak-willed, unmotivated, drugged out from the time he was a teenager, having spent mostly useless time on this earth, at least until now. But his brother James, to his knowledge, had never directed a mean, abased, corrupt, or selfish thought or deed toward anyone. Jamie had never willfully hurt another person in his life except himself.

Maybe, Jerrold Lightner thought as he pushed his way out of the thick metal doors of Men's Central Jail, maybe there was something to that damn karma thing after all.

57

Sunday, late afternoon, at Maxi's house in Beverly Glen. Maxi and Wendy were curled up on opposite loveseats in the living room, both of them lounging in sweats, sipping twelve-year-old red wine. A pricey California Cabernet out of a case sent over from The Wine Merchant in Beverly Hills, along with a lavish basket of goodies, all courtesy of Pete Capra. For which Maxi had not thanked him. She had nothing to say to him, and her silence over the past three days had let him know that.

"Well," Maxi quipped, "at least I'm off the graveyard shift."

Wendy was not amused. "You could have ended up off the planet," she said.

Maxi sighed. "But I wasn't hurt, just superficial cuts and bruises." She stroked the sensitive area under her chin where the knife had pierced. Then, wistfully, "If you don't count my psychological wounds. This ended . . . horribly."

"Pete's brother, for one thing," Wendy acknowledged. "Pete told me the whole story. Did he tell you?"

"I'm not talking to Pete, remember?"

"Well, Pete's older brother was evidently some kind of genius at Berkeley up in the Bay Area—that's where Pete's from, as you know. Pete had never met this half brother, who'd lived with his father after his parents divorced, before Pete was born. His mother remarried, and she never saw that son again. And she rarely talked about that son. The fact is, there was something very wrong with him."

"He was mentally ill?"

"Yes, but an idiot savant, if that's the term. Brilliant in his field, chemistry, but a loner and an oddball. Something like Ted Kaczynski."

"If Pete knew he had a half brother, why wouldn't he look him up? That doesn't sound like Pete."

"He didn't even know the brother's name. But he was a television news reporter covering the San Francisco cyanide killings, and he saw the suspect once, briefly. He says it shocked him—this man looked so much like himself."

"He *did* look like Pete," Maxi said. "I couldn't figure out why he looked so familiar to me from the first time I saw him on tape. I thought I'd seen him before. But I hadn't. I was seeing Pete in him. Even more than looking like Pete, he had his gestures. And he pursed his lips the same way Pete does."

"Capra was very visible on the news in San Francisco at the time. When he started suspecting his own brother in the serial killer case, which had the whole Bay Area terrified, he began to get the feeling that this brother was aware of him, and was dogging him, even 'performing' for him."

"Old newspaper stories said all of a sudden the killings stopped. They figured the so-called walk-in killer must be dead."

"Turns out he wasn't dead, he was in a hospital for the criminally insane," Wendy said. "He'd been arrested, but not for the cyanide murders. It was for stalking a woman. He was certified mentally ill at that time, and institutionalized for years, but Pete never knew that. Pete also never knew if the man he saw that day really was his brother. He thought he would never know for sure, and that case haunted him ever since."

"Pete told you all this?"

"On Friday night after work. He seemed relieved to talk about it. And Maxi, he's very upset about what happened to you. He knows it's his fault. He wants to talk to you."

Maxi wasn't moved. "What happened with the brother?" she asked, changing the subject.

"He was finally released from the institution. Again, the doctors there had no idea he was a murderer; they just knew that he had been mentally ill, and he was pronounced cured. The brother set out to find Pete. That wasn't hard, because information on Peter Capra is all over the Internet. Remember, this brother is a very smart man."

"So he came down here."

"Yes, to his brother's city again, this time Los Angeles. The guess is that he had always needed to show Pete, his important television journalist brother, that he was important too."

"Then it wasn't just coincidence that Pete stumbled on the man again."

"Yes and no. His brother needed to connect. If he hadn't been caught on tape during the Nodori bust, Pete feels sure that he would have eventually hooked up with him."

"And Pete became convinced that his own deranged brother was the Southern California serial killer."

"Sure. He looked like the man, and we had murders using cyanide. Remember, his brother was a chemist. And he seemed to be killing blond women again. First the prostitute, then Christine Williams, one of Pete's own reporters."

"So Pete tried to back us off the first cyanide murder story."

"That's what he told me. He was devastated, sensing that his brother wanted to hurt him, and do it by hurting people around him."

"But he shoved me right out there in harm's way—"

"Pete admitted to me that he put you on the graveyard shift to smoke his brother out, but he trusted Tom McCartney to watch out for you."

Maxi looked pained. "But his brother wasn't the killer after all. It was Tom."

"McCartney doing copycat murders. He'd researched the 'walk-in killer' case, as you know, and he meant to make it look as if the San Francisco suspect was down here in Los Angeles and killing with cyanide again."

"Where would Tom get cyanide?"

"Turns out it's easy to get," Wendy said. "They sell it for pesticides, to clean jewelry, in lots of household applications. Evidently McCartney made up a simple, injectable solution."

This was all a nightmare for Maxi. She'd liked Tom McCartney. She'd trusted him. She was falling for him. Her heart and soul felt as if they'd been ripped inside out and beaten raw. She was hurting bad, and Wendy could see it.

"You know, Max," she said, "thinking back, we were always amazed at some of the stories McCartney brought in. So many times he seemed to hear about them first, get there in an instant, and shoot angles that nobody else was even aware of."

"You're saying he probably staged them."

"Hindsight is twenty-twenty. But remember the PriceCo fire, and McCartney's arson suspect?"

"Of course. I was the one who cut it. They compared it to the Richard Jewell case, the Olympics bombing suspect who was exonerated—McCartney's suspect was cleared four days later."

"Right. Well, Pete told me last night that now they think Tom McCartney set the PriceCo fire."

Maxi was quiet. She patted the cushion next to her, which was Yukon's cue that he was allowed up there. A rare indulgence. He immediately hopped up on the loveseat and snuggled down beside her, and Maxi stroked his fur. She needed to bond with her dog. She needed to heal. She needed more wine.

Reaching over to the coffee table, she picked up the bottle and topped up both their glasses. This was the first chance she and Wendy'd had to go over everything. Maxi had spent most of Friday at Cedars being checked out and getting her cuts and abrasions treated, and she'd spent most of yesterday at home sleeping.

"You've got to cut Pete some slack," Wendy was saying now.

"He's been through his own personal hell, and he never meant to hurt you. He told me the hardest thing he did was force you to go on the air with the story—"

"Maybe that's the one thing he did right. Shoving a microphone in my hand and telling me I was on live probably saved me months of therapy before I could work again. If ever."

"You're going to win the Peabody," Wendy said thoughtfully. The George Foster Peabody Award represented the country's most prestigious recognition for distinguished achievement in broadcasting.

"I cried on the air."

"Doesn't matter. You reported the story. An incredible story, and it's been picked up all over the country."

"Pete should win the award, for producing. He got me up, held me up, and made me do it. Harbaugh was appalled, but he kept rolling."

"You'll both get the Peabody, you'll see."

"Not important, Wen. What's important is Pete became my therapist on the spot."

"So talk to him."

"He's been calling once an hour since Thursday morning. I'm not taking Capra's calls," she said, sipping Capra's Cabernet.

"He's sorry, Maxi. You need to forgive him. He's the one who's needed a therapist all those years—"

"Hah. No kidding. Nobody in the known world needs a shrink more than Pete does."

Wendy laughed. "So return the favor, give him a little counseling."

"Like he'd listen."

"Trust me, he has definitely learned a big lesson. Talk to him."

"I'll think about it."

She had a lot to think about. Carla and Roberto had moved out this morning and moved in with her friend Alma. She would be starting her new job on Monday. The shocker—Carla actually *was* the person who'd killed Gladys Lightner. But not with the scissors. When Marc Jorgan had come to the hospital to see Maxi on Friday, she'd told him about the scissors. She'd reached for her purse on the bedside table and fished them out, still encased in the plastic baggie. LAPD techs did some rush testing on them and found no traces of blood in the seams. "False alarm," Jorgan had said when he called her last night with the results.

"But," he'd said, "they *did* find the letter opener."

When Maxi had told him first about the scissors, then about the letter opener box with no letter opener in it, and that her silly suspicions about Carla Ochoa were backed up only by the woman's state of extreme stress on the morning Mrs. Lightner was found dead and her erratic emotional behavior ever since then, it had started Jorgan thinking. Because in fact they *did* have the letter opener box in evidence, and it *was* the blade they were looking for, but no one had ever suspected Mrs. Ochoa. Jorgan called for another search of the Lightner house, but this time the target was not the master bedroom suite, the crime scene, but the maid's room and kitchen area where the housekeeper had spent most of her time.

The police found the letter opener lodged behind one of the three washing machines in the laundry room. They processed it in the crime lab and lifted Gladys Lightner's blood and a good set of latent prints. Since they couldn't find Mrs. Ochoa's prints on record in any of their databases, they sent a technician back up to the Lightner estate and dusted for prints in the maid's room, the laundry room, the kitchen, the housekeeper's areas. After the Lightners' prints were excluded, the predominant prints that were left matched the prints on the letter opener. Carla Ochoa's.

Jorgan and Sanchez took her in for questioning. They held her for most of the day Friday and into the night, while her friend Alma took care of Roberto. Carla broke down during questioning and told the detectives that on the morning she was leaving the Lightner house to move to Maxi Poole's, she went upstairs to ask Mrs. Lightner for the pay she was owed. Gladys Lightner, in a fit of one of her famous rages, screamed that Carla and her stupid son had caused her family all this trouble, and she flew at Carla in a fury. Startled, Carla backed up, and when Gladys Lightner kept coming she stumbled into the desk behind her and reached around to brace herself, and her hand lighted on the letter opener and closed around it. Mrs. Lightner was just about upon her, and instinctively Carla thrust her hands up in front of her in a defensive move. The woman literally fell onto the letter opener, and she immediately went down without even a scream, Carla said.

Terrified by what had happened, Carla flew downstairs and stashed the letter opener in the laundry room, as Maxi was ringing the doorbell. Carla told the detectives that she could not tell anyone about it because she feared she would be deported and lose her son, and she'd broken into more sobs.

The detectives believed her, and when they brought the facts to the DA's office she was charged with involuntary manslaughter because of the accidental nature of the killing, and released on her own recognizance. The educated guess was that she would be looking at a period of probation with no jail time. For Carla's part, she was just enormously relieved to finally have it all out in the open.

As to why Conrad Lightner had blood all over him in his wife's bedroom that morning, on his hands, his clothes, and his shoes, in spatters, he really *had* been surprised to walk in and find the woman dead. He'd thought Montez had blown it, but then must have come back in to do the deed. And he really did get down and give the woman mouth-to-mouth resuscitation, because he needed to be able to say that he'd done that. Her blood transferred onto him, and there was so much of it that it spattered. Lightner didn't kill his wife, but he would be tried for conspiracy to kidnap and conspiracy to commit murder on the testimony of Raoul Montez. If convicted, the sentence would be twenty-five to life, twice.

"Lightner put it all in motion to get rid of his wife and get his hands on her money," Wendy said to Maxi. "Pure greed."

"It's interesting that the younger son inherited all of his

mother's fortune," Maxi said. "We did so many stories on him, every time he was busted for drugs. And on the other son too—Jerrold, the con man. He got shut out of the money. Strange family."

"Dysfunctional to the max. But there was a story on the wires yesterday saying the first thing James Lightner is going to do with his inheritance is open a free drug rehabilitation clinic, and have medical doctors, psychiatrists, nurses, and other staffers pitch in pro bono to help recovering addicts."

"Well, at least some good has come out of this—"

"Oh, and there's more good news," Wendy said, trying to cheer Maxi up. "Guess who Capra hired yesterday?"

"*Please*. No guessing. My head aches."

"Rosie. Harvey Rosenberg. He's our new cameraman."

Maxi smiled. Rosie deserved it. He was going to be fun to have around. And she knew that he would work harder than anyone in the shop. That was Rosie.

Her mood brightened a little. She was about to pour more wine when the phone rang. Thinking it was Pete Capra again and maybe it was time she talked to him, she reached over to the end table, picked up, and said hello. And beamed when she heard the voice at the far-off other end. Richard Winningham, calling from Fallujah.

"Richard! It is so good to hear you. How's Iraq?"

"Scenic. You know."

"And how are *you?*"

"I'm fine. I understand it's peaceful here compared to where you are."

"Um . . . It's been . . . eventful."

"I heard."

"You heard? How?" Hoping that he hadn't heard everything.

"Half a dozen people from the station e-mailed me, including Capra."

"Oh." Richard was not sounding warm and fuzzy about the whole thing.

"By the way, Capra says he's sorry for putting you in the middle of it."

Good, Maxi thought. Maybe Richard was going to skip the part about her almost falling into bed with a lunatic killer who happened to be extremely attractive, and about whom she still felt oppressively sad. Or maybe Richard didn't know about that part. Though she doubted that, the Channel Six grapevine being alive and hearty, and the Channel Six newsies being tops in the communication field. She couldn't assume that Richard didn't know most of the sorry details by now about what went on between herself and Tom McCartney.

She responded with, "Why doesn't Capra tell me himself that he's sorry?"

"He says you won't talk to him."

"That's true."

"You should forgive him."

"Excuse me, Richard, but when did you become his spokesman?"

"When Capra said if I can get you to forgive him he'll let me come home."

Richard was only half kidding, Maxi knew, and having him come home would be medicine she sorely needed now. "Oh, please, come home, Richard," she said. "I'll forgive Pete. I'll even go down to the commissary when I go back to work tomorrow and buy him his favorite roast beef on sourdough with mayo."

"Wait a second—from what I heard, I think *he* owes *you* a sandwich."

"Oh, no. Capra owes me dinner at Spago, an upgrade on the obsolete computer equipment in my office, and an extra week's vacation during which I will sleep the entire time."

"Sounds right."

"Richard. Seriously. When are you coming home?"

"Seriously, Friday."

"*This* Friday?"

"Yup. Have you been true to me?"

Loaded question. Reading the subtext, she guessed he was asking her if she'd slept with Tom McCartney after all, as was rampantly rumored in the newsroom. Not that it was his business. She and Richard had had sex once. It was wonderful, but it was once, when he was home over the last Christmas holidays. Had she been true to him? Technically, yes.

"Yes," she said.

"Good. Stay true till Friday."

"Easy. I'll pick you up at the airport."

"I'm coming in at ten in the morning. What if you're on a story?"

"I'll make sure I'm not on a story. That'll be another thing Capra owes me."

"How long do you think you can hold this over Pete's head?"

"Couple of months at least. Don't you think?"

"Oh yeah. I'll tell him that was one of your conditions in the negotiation."

Everything in the television news business was a negotiation, Maxi thought, even a reconciliation.

"Okay, I'll pick you up right from my kickboxing class. By the time you get through customs—"

"Kickboxing . . . ?"

"Yes. And I carry a gun now."

"Oh boy. This is gonna be a challenge."

"You'll be up to it," she said with a laugh. "You're coming from a war zone."

Acknowledgments

MAXI POOLE AND I WANT TO THANK SOME VERY IMPORTANT FRIENDS OF OURS WHO HELPED GET GRAVEYARD SHIFT "BANGED OUT AND ON THE AIR," AS THE HARDWORKING FOLKS IN THE SWEATY NEWSROOM AT FICTIONAL CHANNEL SIX NEWS WOULD SAY:

Thanks to dynamic NBC-4 News executive producer **Wendy Harris**, the soul of the newsroom and my longtime friend, who plays herself in all my books.

And to my former news director **Tom Capra**, who would jump on the desk in the newsroom and point and scream, "*You—get a vest on and scout the riot area! You—get downtown and smoke out the mayor!*" (and who would get severely cranky every time he gave up smoking); and my former managing editor **Pete Noyes**, who was known to punch out a reporter for burying the lead (before they put you in jail for that). Together these two inspired my character, Maxi Poole's boss, Pete Capra. Thanks, guys, and don't get mad.

I'm indebted to **Dr. Paul Khasigian** of the California Poison Control System, Fresno/Madera Division, for teaching me how to poison people; to a very helpful officer at the **U.S. Department of Citizenship and Immigration Services** who needs to remain anonymous, but you know who you are; to **Detective Sergeant Richard Longshore** of the Los Angeles County Sheriff's Homicide Bureau for letting me enroll in his LASD-LAPD "murder" school for rookie detectives; to **Dr. Rick Gold** at Cedars, medical adviser to me, Maxi, and all the doctors in my books, and to his hardworking nurse, **Jeannine See**.

I owe Maxi Poole's very life to my late editor and friend **Sara Ann Freed**, and to her successor, Mysterious Press editor **Kristen Weber**, who guided Maxi's continued life and adventures in *Graveyard Shift*.

My special thanks to the irrepressible **Susan Richman**, the patrician of New York public relations; and **Kim Dower** of "Kim from L.A.," Susan's counterpart in La-La Land.

And to the wonderful Warner Books family: Time Warner Book Group President **Maureen Egen**, the mother of us all; publisher **Jamie Rabb**, the first to read Maxi Poole and run with her; production editor **Penina Sacks**, who went to the mat with me on the minutiae of grammatical correctness (she won); and to my astute and exacting copy editor **Roland Ottewell**, who dazzled me with his canny input.

Love and gratitude to my literary agent, **Robin Rue**, and her fabulous assistant, **Emily Sylvan**, who have championed my Maxi since her inception.

A zillion hugs to America's reigning queen of the mystery genre, author **Sue Grafton**, for her invaluable mentoring and generous support.

My thanks to KLOS disc jockey **Jim Ladd**, L.A.'s most popular rock 'n' roll DJ, who programmed the music in *Graveyard Shift*.

To my good pals NBC-4 weathercaster **Fritz Coleman** and his dog **Mac**, who play themselves in *Graveyard Shift*.

To **Roberto Inigo**, assignment editor at the Spanish language network Telemundo, for help with the Spanish translation in *Graveyard Shift*.

To **Bart Cannistra** of NBC Technical Operations, my longtime friend and ever-patient computer guru.

To my super-readers: **L.A. Deputy District Attorney Edward Nison** for keeping me honest about legal procedure; brilliant comedy writer **Gail Parent**, my partner on the TV show *Kelly & Gail*, who loves brainstorming plot twists over a bottle of wine; and gorgeous **Gale Hayman**, co-founder of Giorgio, Beverly Hills, Maxi's arbiter of taste and fashion.

To **NBC Electronic Field Supervisor Carl Schumacher**, who updates me on the latest broadcast technology; **NBC West Coast Bureau Chief Heather Allen**, who heads up the *Today* show in Los Angeles; NBC cameraman **Rodger Harbaugh**, who plays himself in my books; NBC-4 reporter and business editor **Doug Kriegel**, who also plays himself; inspirational pro bono attorney **Scott Wylie**; and television news reporter **John Marshall**.

I am indebted to **Terry Beebe, Sharon Kelly**, and the gang at the NBC Credit Union for letting me monopolize their copy machine; actor/screenwriter **Bob Factor** for helping me out of deadline jams; **Jim Alvarez**, head of NBC Wardrobe, for suitably dressing Maxi; and **Patti Hansen**, head of NBC Travel, for keeping Maxi and me flying between the palm trees of Los Angeles and the publishing canyons of New York.

My eternal gratitude to **Shawn Kendrick** of Borders Books and Music, who walks behind me with a wheelbarrow full of my books at outlandish events (on the Santa Monica Pier during an afternoon cloudburst; on the pitcher's mound at Dodger Stadium during seventh-inning stretch) and manages to hang on to both his aplomb and his cash box; and to restaurateur **Ron Salisbury**, who throws me book parties at his legendary El Cholos, and feeds me besides.

Special thanks to **Dr. David Walker** of the Los Angeles Church of Religious Science, who teaches calming metaphysics to Maxi and me; to my CRS practitioner, dazzling actress-comedienne **JoAnne Worley**, who kicks my butt when necessary; and to the inimitable **Vera Brown**, skin-care specialist to me, Maxi, and half of Hollywood's glamorous movie stars.

And finally, my profound adoration goes out to Maxi Poole's spiritual family, my fascinating sister **Ellie Poole**, and the whole **Poole** clan. And always and forever, eternal love and gratitude to my sturdy bookends, **Alice Scafard**, my incredible mom, and **Kelly Lansford**, my princess daughter.

IF YOU LIKED *GRAVEYARD SHIFT*, AND YOU'D LIKE TO SPEAK TO ME OR MAXI (WE'RE VERY CLOSE), VISIT OUR WEB SITE—WWW.KELLY-LANGE.COM. BOTH OF US WOULD LOVE YOUR COMMENTS AND INPUT FOR OUR ONGOING "MAXI POOLE" SERIES. (IF YOU DIDN'T LIKE *GRAVEYARD SHIFT*, IN THE WORDS OF THAT GREAT NEWSWOMAN ROSANNE ROSANNA-DANA, "NEVER MIND.")